THE
HOSTAGES

A Novel

By David A. DeWitt

PUBLICATIONS

P.O. Box 88095
Grand Rapids, Michigan 49518-0095

relationalconcepts.org

*This book is dedicated to my nine grand-
children: Andrew, Caleb, Emily, James,
Jacob, Isaiah, Sam, Eli, and Anna.*

This book was written by David A. DeWitt (B.S.
Michigan State University; Th.M., D.Min. Dallas
Theological Seminary). Dave is an Equipper and
Discipler in Relational Concepts' School of Disci-
pleship. He is married to Ellen and has three mar-
ried daughters and nine grandchildren.

Prologue

The pain was unbearable. Sandra screamed as the contractions came again. Only one minute apart now. *She should call Larry. No. Never! Not Larry. 911. She needed to call 911.* Alone in a dingy hotel room, which had been her home for the last three months, she was determined to have this baby on her own. *She didn't need anybody. She didn't want anybody.* But then, she didn't have anybody. Even if she'd wanted help, there was no one to whom to go. No one to call. But now, with the pain intensifying, she was scared. *911. She'd call 911.*

But as she reached for the phone, the contractions relaxed, and she lay back on the bed, drenched in sweat. Alone.

She wanted her mother. But that was impossible. She had left her Chicago home eight years ago, at the age of 15. *Her Baptist, God-fearing, church-loving parents had driven her away. She just wanted freedom, freedom to experiment with drugs. And sex. With both boys and girls. And the shoplifting, even the drugstore robbery, was because her parents wouldn't give her freedom. They wanted her to be a Baptist. She hated Baptists. She hated Christians. Sanctimonious hypocrites, all of them. More lectures, more restrictions, more screaming, more rules. Rules. Rules. Rules. She couldn't take it anymore.*

So she left.

In order to be certain her parents could not find her, she moved several times before she found regular "employment" in Detroit with a pimp named Larry. She had the looks for it, and she knew it. She used it to make money the oldest and easiest way a pretty girl on her own could. Larry had recognized her potential, so he introduced her to regular clients who paid well. She no longer had to hit the streets.

Larry also introduced her to drugs. First, just marijuana, then cocaine and meth. But then she got pregnant. She didn't know how. *She was careful, practiced safe sex, took the pill. Well, I guess it doesn't always work.* She had no idea about the father of her baby. There were several possibilities. She could *have DNA testing and force some guy to pay. But that would end her career and give someone else rights over her baby. And she wanted the baby. Maybe she could start over. They could be a family.*

The pain started again. More severe this time. *The phone. 911.* No. It was too late. The baby was coming. She screamed and pushed and pushed and pushed harder. She was torn and bleeding. She knew she was bleeding before she saw the blood.

Between her legs lay a baby girl. Sandra was weak but managed to hold the infant upright and clear her mouth. Immediately, the infant began to cry. She knew she had to tie off and cut the umbilical cord. She had planned for that. It was finally over. She had a daughter. Sandra lay back with the infant against her chest as the placenta was delivered. She was bleeding more. She was in pain. The drugs. Larry had given her cocaine, but she had refused to take it during the pregnancy. Coming off her addiction had nearly killed her, but she would not have an addicted baby. *But now. Now it was over. Now she needed the help.* She struggled to reach the drawer. Her fingers could just barely reach the bottle.

Yes! She had it. *Just one. Maybe more than one. She needed it.* Finally, the euphoria began as the pain ceased. Sandra lay back on her bed. Her eyes rolled up in her head. Her body gasped for one last breath as she died in a pool of blood and sweat.

It was Larry who discovered her body the next morning. Somehow, the baby was still alive. She was taken to the hospital where she began her childhood as a ward of the State of Michigan. A piece of paper was found in Sandra's room with various names on it. The girl's name that was circled was Abigail Edna.

PART I
THE ATHEIST

The following events take place between May 11 and May 27

Chapter 1

Wednesday, May 11
Washington, D.C.

United States Senator Roger Benedict was pleased, excited, sometimes ecstatic. The project was proceeding beyond his expectations. Within a few months, he would have accomplished what the entire liberal element of both houses of Congress, and their weak-willed president, had failed to do after years of trying. He stopped, in the middle of returning his emails, to once again admire the headlines on the newspapers scattered across his desk. The *New York Times* said:

> POLLS SHOW EIGHTY PERCENT DEMAND
> CONGRESSIONAL INVESTIGATION OF
> ALL DRUG COMPANIES

The *Washington Post* announced:

> CONGRESS TO HOLD HEARING
> ON BAD DRUGS

Of course, the liberal elements have always wanted more government control of the drug companies. But only those to the far left, such as Senator Benedict, would dare dream of the government actually taking over those drug companies. And with the new surge of conservatism into the Congress, that was not going to happen any time soon. But Benedict's plan would skirt all that.

Roger Benedict had been a U.S. Senator for 15 years. He was in the middle of his third term and was known as a firm, persuasive, but distinguished liberal "progressive." At 58, he had sharp features, with dark eyes and a thick crop of snow-white hair, which sat atop a 6-foot 2-inch frame. Married with two married daughters, he was respected, even by most conservatives who opposed his views. But what he did publically was only a thin veneer on the surface of Senator Benedict.

Benedict was not trying to get rich. He was not trying to gain public fame or popularity. And that's what made his plan so perfect. True, he was using his influence and the government's money, but he was not taking it for himself. Following the money would never lead anyone to Benedict. For him, it was ideological. He might even end up being a political martyr to the cause. But it would be worth it.

Together with two members of the House of Representatives, he had a plan that would go further than any debate on the floor of the House or Senate. With his plan (well, the plan of all three of them, but it was his baby), the government would actually sell the drugs. The government would directly control everyone with a prescription for anything. And it wouldn't need to get past the RINO Republicans, the Tea Party, or even the Democrats. The people were now, or soon would be, demanding it. It was beautiful!

The senator had just returned to his emails when the cell phone jingled in his briefcase. This was not his regular phone. Only one source had this cell number, and in all cases it demanded an immediate answer. His smile flattened, and a small crease began to form between his eyebrows. This would not be good news. This phone was never good news. He flipped open the top of the old-style phone.

"What's up?"

"We've got a problem."

"I assumed that. What's up?"

"There's a problem with the drugs. The mixture is wrong. Four people have died, two from Nexium, one from Lipitor, and one from Vicodin. The press hasn't made the connection yet, but they are for sure ours."

"DIED! THAT'S ... How could that happen!"

"I told you. The mixture was wrong."

"You were supposed to make people sick, just sick enough to get people to distrust the pharmaceutical companies. Sick, not dead! That could ruin everything. Sick people invite investigations into drug companies. Dead people invite investigations into how they died. It pushes the public demands in the wrong direction. They have to distrust the drug companies, not go looking for murderers."

"Yeah, well, the good news is we can probably control it, if we act fast."

"Talk to me."

"If we get our pills off the market immediatcly, then the deaths will likely be attributed to natural causes. So far, there have just been three old people and a young child."

"Can we do that efficiently?"

"Yes, I have some pretty good people in place who can probably make that happen. But you understand, that will mean all our stuff will be off the shelves, and the drugs will be good again. The drug companies will say their pills are good, they will test good, and they will be back in business."

"That would slow down our momentum. Get the bad stuff off the market ASAP, but we also need the right formula so we can get our drugs back on the market right away. How'd we get it wrong?"

"I hate to say this, senator, but our guys at the lab just guessed. I know that sounds absurd, but it seemed simple. They claimed that the safe amounts of the poison could be found on the Internet. I guess they got it wrong."

Senator Benedict was fuming. But he knew it would do no good to exercise his temper. The priority was to solve the problem—fast. "All right. You...we made a mistake. Now the point is to fix it."

"Yeah, well, I do the dirty work. I don't figure out solutions. That's your job, senator."

"All right. I'm on it."

Chapter 2

Monday, May 16
Ann Arbor, Michigan

"Mom! They've only been gone, what, four days? They're on a two-week trip. They're probably fishing and forgot to turn their phones on." Cassandra Lynn McMurray walked, cradling her phone between her ear and her left shoulder, while juggling a briefcase, a six-inch sub, and switching a Coke from one hand to the other.

"But, Cassy, it's not like them." Her mother's panicky voice coming from the device on her shoulder sounded almost convincing, this time. "They said they would call every day, and they haven't called yesterday or today. I can't get an answer on either of their phones. I know there is good service up there. I had no trouble getting them the first two days. They might have gotten lost in the woods or eaten by bears. They could be laying bleeding to death, somewhere."

"Mom, they're not laying somewhere bleeding to death. They are both healthy adult men, capable of taking care of themselves. They just don't want to be bothered by females for two weeks."

"But they said they'd call."

"And they will."

"But..."

"Okay, okay. If you don't get them by this evening, I'll call the flying service that took them in and see if they can check on them."

"I think you should call them now. I mean, well, I guess I could do it myself, but you know how flustered I get. I'll just start to cry, and they'll think I'm some crazy old lady."

"I'm on my way to class right now, my last class, my absolutely final last, last, last class. The one I've been looking forward to attending for the last eight years. Then I'm finally finished. Well, I won't get my Ph.D. until I complete my dissertation, but that should be done this fall. Anyway, I need to get to this class. I need to turn in two essays and my field work analysis, because the professor won't let us e-mail them in. He wants them delivered personally in a hard copy. Tell you what. After class, I'll call and see what I can find out, okay?"

"Thank you, dear. I know I'm a worry wart, but it's been two days and..."

"Yeah, Mom, I know. I'll check on it in about two hours. Okay?"

"Oh, thank you, Dear."

"I'm walking into class now. Gotta' go. Love-you-Mom, bye."

"I'm sure they are just fine," Cassy actually said out loud as she took her seat in the final class of her doctoral program. By the end of the fall, she'd be a real geologist. She had already applied for a job with the USGS (the United States Geological Survey) and had received several letters indicating their interest. She figured her chances were pretty good. So far, her life was one of being a professional student, and she was itching for a real job in "the real world."

And a real life.

Cassy didn't have any significant hobbies, she wasn't into sports, and she had no serious boyfriends. Her social life was centered in her family and their Assembly of God Church, which was one reason she had no serious boyfriends. She had no lack for dates. But the guys from her church were lazy, geeky, boring, or spiritually immature (or all of the above). And the U of M guys she'd dated were liberal, irresponsible, immoral, or focused on sex (or all of the above). Not that she wasn't interested in a romantic relationship, but the Bible forbids premarital fornication, and that limited most of her dating. And it was the Bible and her personal faith in Christ that kept her a virgin.

Chapter 3

There was one significant exception to her conservative co-coon. Cassy had a longtime friend named Abigail Edna Davidson. Cassy had known her since eighth grade. Abby had always been a strawberry blond, freckled-faced, ball of energy. When they were teenagers, she would drag Cassy along as she terrorized their neighborhood, their school, and the Assembly of God Church to which Cassy made her go. Boys swarmed around Abby like flies. She loved to flirt with them enough to antagonize them to frustration. It was a wonder she didn't get raped.

Although Abby never liked church much, it brought God into the discussion, and three days before her 15th birthday, Cassy was able to pray with her friend to receive Jesus Christ as her personal God and Savior.

When Cassy led Abby to receive Christ, it not only saved Abby's soul, it saved her virginity. It did not, however, change the personality of either girl. Cassy got Abby to read the Bible. Abby got Cassy to help sell Exlax chocolate bars to a gang of bully-types at school. Cassy got Abby to go to her Assembly of God Church once in awhile. Abby got Cassy into detention for releasing a skunk under the opponent's bleachers during a homecoming football game. Although Cassy was disappointed that Abby had no interest in attending her church, Cassy was actually (secretly) thankful that her friend's Christianity had not made her into a conservative.

Abby's background was very different from Cassy's. Abby was an orphan. All she knew about her mother was that she was found dead of a drug overdose, and Abby had been lifted from her dead mother's body. Growing up as a ward of the state, Abby lived in orphanages and temporary foster care, first in Detroit, then in Ann Arbor. But all of her foster parents found her hard to handle. As she began to develop into a teen-ager and her boney frame began to take on shape, her craziness scared off two sets of foster parents who were afraid of being liable for a pregnant girl. A third couple agreed to take her in, but they couldn't wait for her to graduate from high school and move out. So, except for Cassy, Abby was pretty much on her own.

It was on the day of her graduation from high school (which probably wouldn't have happened without Cassy constantly threating her with bodily harm if she didn't study) that Abby's life changed forever. The graduation itself went as usual—cap and gown, diploma, hugs, throwing caps in the air. But then, during the time of refreshments in the high school gym, a lady approached her.

"Excuse me, miss. Are you Abby?"

"That would be me," Abby said to the voice behind her, before she turned and saw she was speaking to an elderly woman leaning on a cane. "Can I help you, ma'am?"

"Are you Abigail Edna Davidson?"

"That's what it says on my diploma."

"Could you tell me the name of your mother?"

"My mother? Ha! I never knew my mother. They told me she died of a drug overdose right after I was born."

"But was your mother's name 'Sandra'?"

Abby stared at the old lady for a few uncomfortable seconds. Finally, Abby said, "Yeeees, how did you know that?"

"It is uncanny how much you look like your mother. I thought I was looking at Sandra. And your middle name is Edna. You are Abigail Edna Davidson. Is that correct?"

"And you are…?"

"Edna Davidson. Amazing, after all that time and rebellion and hatred, your mother chose to give you my name. I'm your grandmother."

Chapter 4

Edna Davidson had never stopped looking for her daughter, ever since she ran away from their home in Chicago's southwest side, but with no success. In the interim, a couple from Ann Arbor moved to Chicago and joined Edna's Baptist Church. To keep up with things back home, the couple continued to get the Ann Arbor News and to monitor their old high school's web site. While checking the names of the new graduates, they noticed the name *Abigail Edna Davidson*. Knowing Edna had been looking for her daughter, they thought the names *Edna* and *Davidson* might be more than coincidental. With that, the research had begun, ending with the meeting at Abby's graduation.

After that, Abby visited her grandmother on a regular basis. They got along famously, and three months later, Abby moved in with her grandmother. Grandma Edna lived in a small row house in Chicago's southwest side—just above, just at, and sometimes just below, the poverty level. She had one other child besides Abby's mother, a son who had died in a car accident ten years earlier. Her husband died the year before she located Abby, so Edna had been living alone, and just barely got by. She lived off a small pension and a house cleaning business she had established after her husband's death. But, by the time she found Abby, Grandma Edna's arthritis was flaring up enough to limit her house cleaning. So Abby found a part-time job at a small restaurant in the Chicago business district at the corner of a major intersection, appropriately and uncreatively named "The Corner Grill." The owner, Joe Gorki, hired her on a temporary basis, but Abby was hardworking, attractive, efficient, and friendly. The customers loved her. She joked and flirted and gave nicknames to the regulars. Soon, she became everybody's favorite waitress, and Joe took her on full-time.

Joe, both the owner and the cook, was 53, bald, and overweight, but friendly, energetic, and honest. He demanded an hour's work for an hour's pay, but he was not a tyrant. As long as he wasn't shorthanded during the breakfast and lunch hours, he let his waitresses determine their own schedules, swap with each other, and even take time off when they needed it. Joe's wife, Alice, also did some cooking and waited tables when need be. Besides Abby, there were two other waitresses—Sally Mansfield, a 32-year-old single mother, and Anita Garcia, the 24-year-old daughter of a Mexican immigrant.

For two years, Abby took courses at a community college, but when her grandmother's arthritis got worse, they needed more money for medication, so Abby dropped out of college to put in more hours as a fulltime waitress at The Corner Grill. Grandma Edna, now 81, was often confined to a wheelchair.

Living with her Baptist grandmother did not make Abby into a conservative—or a Baptist. When she realized Abby was truly a believer in Jesus Christ and sincerely interested in the Bible, Grandma Edna became amused with Abby's craziness and often joined in the fun. Although they were now separated by a couple of hundred miles, Abby and Cassy kept close contact, texting daily with approximately monthly visits.

Chapter 5

Monday, May 16
Ann Arbor, Michigan

Unlike Abby, Cassy was definitely a conservative. She was 26 years old, and had basically not lived outside of the lifestyle she had inherited—her family, her church, and her studies. She had more-or-less followed her father into the academic world.

Dr. William Benjamin McMurray was a tenured professor at the University of Michigan. This fishing trip to the Canadian wilderness was his 65th birthday present from his son, Cassy's 21-year-old brother, Michael.

Michael was rather irresponsible. Well, actually, he was a slob. He could be a poster boy for what the book of Proverbs calls *a sluggard*. He partied his way through college, after partying his way through high school, until he'd flunked out. Now he lived at home, while dabbling in dead-end jobs. Currently, he was working at the best job he'd had since high school, a waiter at the Wilmington Country Club. Cassy and her mother hoped this fishing vacation would be a character-building trip, or something. Cassy told herself that, although her brother was generally lazy and irresponsible, he was an able-bodied man with enough common sense not to get lost in the woods.

Probably.

She was sure they were fine. They probably just got involved in their fishing. They probably just forgot to turn on their phones.

Probably.

But the more she tried to convince herself, the less successful she became. She realized she didn't even know where they were. She knew they flew into Winnipeg, Manitoba, but had no idea where they went from there.

The minute class was over, she began punching in her father's number. The phone went to voicemail. Then she tried her brother's number, with the same results. Next, she sent a text to each of them.

Nothing.

She began scrolling through her phone "Notes" until she found where she recorded the name of the company her brother had used to schedule the trip—THE DONAVAN FLYING SERVICE. She went to Google 411 to locate the number, and let the mechanical voice connect her.

"Donavan Flying Service, this is Fran," an elderly female voice answered.

"Yes, um, is Mr. Donavan there?"

"I'm sorry, Mr. Donavan is flying a group into a campsite today. He should be back before dark. Can I help you? Or can I have him call you?"

"Well, I guess so. My name is Cassandra McMurray. My father and brother, William and Michael McMurray, used your flying service to go on a fishing trip. My mother has not been able to contact them for two days, and she's worried. I was wondering if there is some way to check on them."

"The only way would be for one of our pilots to fly in there. We also leave each party with one of our cell phones. It is only for emergencies. It stays off to preserve the battery unless the party needs to call for early pick up. They have not tried to use that phone. Let's see, yes, I see the schedule here. William and Michael McMurray. They are not scheduled to be picked up for ten days yet. We often have relatives concerned when they can't reach their loved ones. Things are almost always fine, but I will have Mr. Donavan call you when he returns."

"Thank you. I would appreciate that." Cassy gave the lady her number and tapped her phone off. But she was not comforted by the call.

Chapter 6
Monday, May 16
Winnipeg, Manitoba

Jack Randolph Donavan was an atheist. He was not what he considered a pseudo-atheist. False atheists were people who say things like, "A good loving God would not allow cancer, earthquakes, tsunamis, and the like." According to Jack, those people believed in a God they didn't like. They were just God-haters. If there was an all-powerful God, how do they know what He would do as a loving act? And how could anybody but a sovereign God know what was all-loving, anyway?

No, Jack considered himself a true atheist, one who believed there was nothing but the natural world. Jack was an anti-supernaturalist. He figured "atheism" was a bad label anyway. You can't define a position by what its followers do **not** believe. And the only thing true atheists **do** believe is that there is the natural, material universe. Jack saw no evidence for the supernatural, so he had no use for any religion of any kind.

But that did not mean he was uninterested in people. Quite the contrary. He figured that because he did not waste time or energy chasing an imaginary God, he could concentrate on helping real flesh-and-blood people. He didn't know how he or the universe got here, but it was here, and that was that. Why not just help others and make the best of it?

Jack's business owned three airplanes: a Cessna 180, a DeHavilland Beaver, and a DeHavilland Otter. All of them were amphibious, meaning they had floats with retractable wheels, so they could land on water or on hard surfaces. Today, he was flying the Beaver.

It was nearly dark when Jack arrived back home at the James Armstrong Richardson International (YWG) Airport in Winnipeg, near the southern border of Manitoba, Canada. It took him another hour to clean out, refuel, and hangar the Beaver, so it was nearly 7:00 P.M. when he entered his office, located off the back end of the hangar. He used the restroom and opened a beer before he sat at his desk and saw Fran's note. He dug his phone out of his pocket and sent a text to Fran: "Call me WRT note. No hurry."

Within two minutes, she called. He said, "Hey, Fran, sorry to bother you at home."

"No problem, Jack."

"You think this Ms. McMurray note is something I should deal with tonight?"

"Yeah, I'd say so. She was calm but seemed quite concerned."

"No contact in two days, huh. Have there been any reports of unusual activity in the parks?"

"Not that I've heard."

"Any unusual bear activity, rabid wolves, anything like that?"

"No."

"And they haven't attempted to use our cell phone?"

"No."

"Did you check with the Mounties to see if anyone found a couple of guys wandering around the woods?"

"I did. Nothing."

"Well, that's probably what it is, nothing. But I'd better follow up on it. Thanks, Fran."

"Good night, Jack. See you in the morning."

Jack clicked off, then dialed the number on Fran's note.

"Hello."

"Hello. This is Jack Donavan returning your call."

The deep voice was clear and mature sounding, but not terribly old, about 30, she guessed. Then she wondered how tall, how ... *oh cut it out, how ridiculous,* she scolded herself. And all that in the split second before she said, "Oh, yes, thank you for calling. It's probably nothing, but my mother has not been able to reach my father or brother for two days, and she's getting panicky. Well, you know how mothers are. Anyway, I thought I would see what you think. Is that common, or should someone check on them?"

"Well, it's not uncommon, but it is a reason for concern. There has been no unusual activity in the area, and the Mounted Police haven't had any reports. It's probably nothing, but we should check on it. I'll get in the air early in the morning and

16

fly up there. They are about a 2-hour flight east of here, but the phone service is usually good. I'll call you as soon as I learn something. Okay?"

"Oh, thank you, Mr. Donavan. My mother and I would really appreciate that."

"Talk to you tomorrow." Jack tapped off the phone, and while continuing to stare at it, he thought, *hmmm, lovely voice, maybe mid-twenties.*

As Jack left the airport, his mind turned toward home, a hot meal, and the pretty girl who would be waiting for him. Winnipeg was a city of some 700,000 people. The downtown area offered a lot of culture, shopping malls, and historical sites. But Jack preferred the open spaces, and he wanted to live fairly close to the airport. So when he moved there five years ago, he bought a small, white-shingled, two-story house on the Red River, a fifteen-minute drive from the airport.

The side of the house that faced the road was plain, with a bank of wooden steps leading up to a single door. But the back of the house opened to a grassy area dotted with pine and spruce trees for about 300 feet before it touched the bank of the Red River. Running along the whole back side of the house was a screened-in porch, where one could sit and watch various birds, deer, moose, and an occasional elk stroll through. Bears, too, once in a while, but they were usually not a problem, as long as you didn't leave your garbage out near the house. The summers in Winnipeg are as hot as the winters are cold, so with the long daylight hours, the back porch was one of Jack's favorite places, especially after he'd screened it in to keep out the black flies.

As Jack entered the front door, he was greeted by an ugly mass of fur named Ralph, with only a wet nose and an even wetter tongue sticking out to identify his forward end. Jack stuck his hand out to be generously licked. "Hi, Ralph. WHERE'S THAT PRETTY LADY YOU ARE SUPPOSE TO TAKE CARE OF?" he said, loud enough for her to hear.

He knew she, and his mother, were in the kitchen because he could hear his mother rattling on about something going on at her church. As he entered the kitchen, his mother interrupted her monologue to greet her son. Then she continued both the church story and the final touches on a venison roast. But Jack received a flying hug from the most significant person in his life—his six-year-old daughter, Jenny Sue.

Chapter 7

Tuesday, May 17
Ann Arbor, Michigan

Cassy jumped when her phone made a marimba sound in her jeans pocket at 11:35 A.M. The morning had been nerve-racking at best. After trying to keep her mother calm at breakfast, she had to overhear the thirteen phone conversations her mother made, asking for prayer. She tried to block it out by answering some e-mails and doing some cleaning. Truth was, she was nearly as antsy as her mother.

Around 9:00, she called Abby, who suggested Cassy's father and brother were finally able to get away from their religious relatives, that they were drinking, smoking pot, and partying with some wild women they'd run into. It was all silly, but it helped—some. Cassy kept checking her watch. She kept telling herself the uneasiness was all about her father's and brother's welfare. It was certainly not that deep, intriguing voice she had talked to yesterday. But, then, why did she keep thinking about that voice? *How absurd,* she said to herself somewhere around 11:00. But the tension only got worse until the phone rang in her pocket at 11:35.

"Hello, this is Cassy."

"Ms. McMurray, this is Jack Donavan."

"Yes."

"I am at the campsite where we dropped your father and brother. There is no one here. The place has been torn up. But there is no sign of a human struggle, no blood, or torn pieces of clothing. I'd say it was trashed after they left. Bears, probably. There are bear tracks around the outside, and the door was open. My initial guess is they went hiking too far into the woods. That's not unusual, and we almost always find them pretty fast. This part of Canada is not as deeply wooded as some. They may have wandered outside of cell coverage and gotten lost. Do you know if they had a GPS with them?"

"No, I really don't know much about what they took with them. Can't you call the police or park service or something?"

19

"We've already notified the Mounties and the park service. But the fact is, they get lots of calls like this, and they won't do much for the first couple of days. That's because most people just show back up on their own. I'll make some circles and have another look from the air, but I don't have enough fuel to do much more today. I'll have to come back with some extra fuel. I will call you, same time tomorrow."

"No. Wait. I mean, I want to come out there."

"There's really no need. Let me put a couple of hours into it first."

"But you can't do that until tomorrow, right?"

"That's correct."

"So if you can't get back out there until tomorrow, I could fly into Winnipeg tonight or early tomorrow and go with you. If you are searching, an extra pair of eyes can't hurt, and it will help calm my mother. And, well, just sitting here waiting is awfully difficult."

"Yes, I can imagine. If you want to come, there is a flight arriving in Winnipeg from Chicago at 9:50 P.M. If you can get to Chicago, you can probably get a seat on it. It's rarely full."

"Thank you. I'll try to do that. Goodbye, and thank you so much, Mr. Donavan."

"No problem."

Cassy rushed to her computer and began looking at airline schedules. Within 10 minutes she had booked a flight from DTW (Detroit Metro), which just barely gave her time to get dressed, pack a few things, and drive to Detroit in time to catch the flight to ORD (Chicago O'Hare) to make the connection to YWG (Winnipeg, Manitoba).

Then, before saying anything to her mother, she jumped in the shower and washed and dried her hair. She took the time to put on a bit of make up and curl her hair. Then she got out a suitcase.

The explanation to her mother had to be made while she was packing. She repeated everything Mr. Donavan had said at least three times in response to her mother's questions. A lot of it went something like, "I don't know, Mom. That's all he said."

But she also had her own questions. *How long would she be gone?* She didn't know. *Two days, maybe three? What to wear?* She was really uncertain about that. She took two casual jeans-based outfits, a windbreaker, and a pair of tennis shoes. She stuffed in some underwear and socks, packed her toilet kit and make-up case, grabbed a jacket, hugged and kissed her mother, and flew out the door.

Chapter 8

Tuesday, May 17
South Central, Manitoba

Jack Donavan took off and circled the campsite at low altitude. Then he went up to 1500 feet AGL (above ground level), but he saw nothing unusual—no sign of people, no pieces of clothing, camping gear, or trash. And his fuel was running low. So he headed back, back to put a face with the voice on the phone named Cassandra McMurray.

By 3:00 P.M., Jack was in his office behind his hangar at YWG. He would do no more flying today. There was a day's computer work to catch up on and some scheduling only he could approve. There were three agencies in the States, ones in Chicago, Detroit, and LA, which advertised for him. Plus, they had brochures with all the major travel agencies and a web site with photos and a three-minute video. Most of the bookings were routine and handled by Fran. But at least once a week, during the summer months, they would receive some requests unusual enough that Jack had to follow up on them.

The Donavan Flying Service had four employees: Jack Donavan, Frances DeVry, Matthew Riley, and Audrey Moses.

Fran wouldn't weigh 120 pounds if you covered her in tar, but she was efficient, tough, and considered the office her kingdom. She told Jack as much when she became his administrative assistant five years ago. That was just ten days after Jack began the business. She was now 68-years-old. Her husband was in a nursing home with advanced Alzheimer's disease. Her two sons were married and living in the States. The oldest one, who lived in Duluth, invited her to move his father down there and come live with them. But she would have nothing to do there. Here, she was busy and needed.

Jack had one other pilot. An old veteran bush pilot named Matthew Riley. Matt was 66 now, but with no thoughts of retirement. He was short and a bit overweight. His face was round and red, surrounded by a crop of white hair and a beard that came down to the second button on his plaid shirts. He looked like a short Santa Claus and was almost as jolly.

Audrey Moses was a 19-year-old black girl who began working there two years ago. At first, she just cleaned up and did whatever Fran needed. But recently she started taking flying lessons. She soloed in the Cessna 180 two weeks ago, on her 19th birthday, and was now working on her private license. She was still basically a gofer for Fran, but she just knew she'd be a pilot some day.

Jack drove around the airport to the public terminal at 9:00. Cassy had called, saying she was on the Chicago flight. He told her he would meet her just outside of security. She tried to probe him about his appearance, so she could recognize him. But all he said was, "I'll be the only guy wearing a blue flight jacket with the name DONAVAN FLYING SERVICE on the front."

Now he waited. Her flight had landed, and it was the only one this late, so it was just a matter of picking her out of the people who walked down the sloping exit ramp. First came an overweight man in a crumpled business suit, then a teenager oblivious to everything but whatever was coming through the earphones plugged into his ears. Then came an elderly lady, followed by a middle-aged guy in jeans. Then came … *wow*.

He actually mouthed it under his breath. Guys will tend to pick out the pretty girls in a crowd, but this one had Jack in a trance. He guessed she was about five-foot-eight, a bit on the thin side, a fine-featured nose and mouth, with big brown eyes, and silky dark hair that danced in loose curls below her shoulders. He couldn't stop staring at her, so he was a bit embarrassed when her eyes caught his. She smiled, walked up to him, stuck out her hand, and said: "Hi, you must be Mr. Donavan. I'm Cassandra McMurray."

Chapter 9

On the flight from Detroit to Chicago, Cassy thought about getting to Chicago in time to catch the flight to Winnipeg. She only had 45 minutes between flights. If this flight was late, she could be in trouble. She made it, barely.

On the flight from Chicago to Winnipeg, Cassy thought about her father and her brother. Were they lost in the woods? Had they been attacked by bears? Were they out of food? How long could people last in the Canadian wilderness by themselves? How hard would it be to spot them from the air? From the AIR? For the first time, it occurred to her she had never been in a small plane, let alone one that landed on lakes.

But when the flight attendant said they would be landing in 10 minutes, Cassy's thoughts turned to what she did not know about Mr. Jack Donavan. *He's probably short and fat with a big nose and no teeth, and he probably smokes,* she thought. *Well, I guess you can't be too fat and fly an airplane, and he didn't sound...short. That's stupid, how can you sound short? Maybe he's....* The screech of the tires on the runway interrupted her thoughts. But now she was getting really nervous. She looked down at the tissue her fingers had shredded. Maybe this trip was a dumb idea. *What did she know about searching from the air with a short, fat, ugly smoker with no teeth?* After a brief taxi, the doors were opened, and she wrestled her backpack-type carry-on from the overhead rack. Then she stood awkwardly in the aisle until the line began moving out the jet way.

After clearing Canadian customs, she walked down a hall until she saw a cluster of people waiting to greet arriving passengers. There were no short, fat guys with a blue flight jacket. Then she caught the eye of a dark-haired man who was a whole head taller than the elderly lady standing in front of him. She guessed he was about six foot. He had bright blue eyes and dark hair, which curled just a bit over the collar of his... Then the lady in front of him ran to greet a grandson, and Cassy noticed that hair curled just a bit over the collar of a blue flight jacket displaying the words DONAVAN FLYING SERVICE on the front. Not only was he not fat and toothless, he was lean, tall, with rather muscular shoulders, and disarmingly handsome.

On the way out of the terminal, they spoke casually about her flights, where the bags were picked up, tomorrow's flying weather, and where Jack was parked. They walked to the parking ramp. He put her bags in the back of his SUV, and they headed out of the airport.

"Nice," Cassy observed, "A new Cadillac Escalade. Leather seats. And they are getting warm. Your business must be doing well."

"We do all right. The economy has slowed us down a bit, but we are still all booked up for the tourist season."

"I didn't have time to make a reservation for a hotel tonight. Could you recommend something?"

"I've already booked you in a hotel near the airport. It's just south of here, near our hangar. The manager is a friend of mine."

"Oh, thank you."

"I thought about putting you up in my mother's guest room. Her house is about five minutes from mine. But she'd keep you up all night drilling you with questions and warning you about what a pagan I am."

"That sounds more interesting than a hotel."

"Interesting, yes. Restful, no. My mother is the unofficial gossip leader in her Catholic church. I don't know, maybe she is actually the official gossip leader. I think she's the Minister of Gossip. They call it a 'prayer chain.' And I don't want you to be their next 'prayer request'."

"Oh, I don't know. Maybe I could use the prayer. Why does she think you are a pagan?"

"Because I'm an atheist."

"I see. And are you a pagan atheist?"

"Maybe. Do you like atheists, Ms. McMurray?"

"I didn't care much about the ones I knew at U of M, but I'm open to being convinced that you're a non-pagan atheist."

Jack smiled, "You a church-goer, Ms. McMurray?"

"I'm a Bible-believing Christian, and yes, I go to church. And could you please stop calling me Ms. McMurray. My name is Cassandra, my friends call me Cassy."

"Cassandra, I like that. Greek, isn't it?"

"Why, yes, most people don't know that. I'm named after my Greek grandmother. But I prefer Cassy."

"I prefer Cassandra. And I'm Jack. Mr. Donavan was my step-father, and he's been dead for ten years."

"I'm sorry, was your step-father a good man?"

"He was a decent guy. He was my mother's second husband. He adopted me when I was a baby and gave me his last name. Anyway, just call me Jack."

"So that would be 'Atheist Jack'. Right?"

He looked over at her for a few long seconds then grinned and said, "Yeah, I guess."

He checked her in and carried her bags to her room. As he put them on the dresser, she asked: "When do we leave in the morning?"

"Actually, there is no need to leave super early. They're calling for lots of fog. I'll pick you up at 8:00. Have a good rest, Cassandra." As he closed the door, he smiled when he heard her say, "Good night, Atheist Jack."

Chapter 10

Wednesday, May 18
Winnipeg, Manitoba

Cassy set her alarm early enough to give herself some extra time to get ready. She had to repack for the day. She also spent a little extra time with her make-up, her hair, and deciding what to wear.

At 7:15, there was a knock at the door. "Yes, who is it?"

"Room service."

"I'm sorry, I didn't order room service."

"Yes, ma'am. It was ordered for you by Mr. Donavan." With that, she opened the door, and a waiter brought in a large tray with multiple covered dishes and drinks. She opened her purse and took out her wallet. "Oh, no, ma'am. It's all been covered. You enjoy your breakfast now." And with that, he closed the door and left.

It wasn't until she moved the tray onto the bed that she realized there was also a long white box on the tray. The top lifted off to reveal a single long-stem yellow rose, surrounded by some green ferns and tiny white flowers. A single note said: "Have a nice breakfast," and it was signed, "Atheist Jack."

At 7:50, Cassy, with her backpack and yellow rose in one hand, rolling her larger bag with the other, went to check out.

"I'm Cassandra McMurray. I am checking out of room 105."

"Ah, yes, Ms. McMurray. Did you rest well?"

"Yes, thank you."

"My name is Alex Russo. I am the manager here. Jack Donavan is a good friend. We are so happy to have you with us."

"How nice of you to say so. I may need the room another night. I'm not sure how long I am staying."

"You can have the room as long as you like, but Jack called a few minutes ago and told me to have you take all your bags with you."

"All right. Mr. Donavan is meeting me any minute, so I'd better check out now."

"Yes, ma'am. It's all taken care of."

"No, I haven't paid for…"

"It's all been taken care of, Ms. McMurray. You just run along and have a nice day."

"And the room service?"

"All taken care of."

"Well, thank you again."

As she carried and rolled her bags through the front entrance, she could see the black Escalade coming up the drive. Jack got out and put her bags in the back.

"You look really nice this morning, Cassandra." Then he noticed the flower in her right hand. "I see you had breakfast. How was it?"

"Terrific, but I couldn't eat half of it. And thanks for the rose, Atheist Jack."

They made the short trip to the Donavan hangar, with its adjacent office space. Jack introduced Cassy to Frances DeVry, Matthew Riley, and Audrey Moses. After handshakes and greetings, Matt excused himself to get the Otter ready to take in a group of five. Jack asked Cassy to wait in the office, while he loaded the Beaver. Then he, too, disappeared into the hangar.

"Nice flower," Audrey noticed, nodding her head in the direction of the yellow rose in Cassy's hand.

"Yes. Mr. Donavan left it on my breakfast tray this morning."

"Really? Jack bought you a flower? Wow, I've known Jack to buy lots of folks breakfast, but I've never seen him buy anybody a flower. He must be sweeeeet on you."

"Audrey, you're embarrassing our guest," Fran interrupted.

"Well, you must admit it's true, Miss Fran. Have you ever known Jack to buy anybody a flower?"

"Audrey, you need to take that bank deposit into town now. And don't forget to get us some more copy toner, and stop by the post office box."

"I'm off. Real nice to meet you, Ms. McMurray. I sure hope you find your daddy and brother real soon."

"Thank you, Audrey. Nice to meet you, too." After the door closed, Cassy said, "She's a cutie. Black pigtails and a smile that's a mile wide. How long has she been working here?"

"A little over two years," Fran reported. "She's from Chicago. That South Chicago Black accent makes her sound naïve, but that girl is sharp as broken glass, and sometimes just as refined. She just turned 19. Jack found her living on the streets about two years ago."

"She was homeless at 17?"

"She was a street prostitute at 17. Never did know her parents. Her mother was probably a prostitute, too. She came up here with a boyfriend who dumped her. Some pimp picked her up and made money off of her, until Jack saw her throwing up on a street corner downtown."

"Really?"

"As she tells it, Jack tried to help her, the pimp confronted him, then Jack beat the crap out of the pimp. Jack put her up in his mother's guest room, where she lived for almost a year. Then he got her an apartment of her own. Jack made her finish high school and gave her a job here, helping me mostly. She's been taking lessons in the Cessna 180. She thinks she's going to be a pilot. I'm not so sure about that, but she is a gem. Of course, she thinks Jack is king of the world. She calls him her 'atheist savior'."

"I can imagine. And how did Matt come to work here?"

"That's another interesting story. Matt's been a bush pilot most of his life. But he's no businessman. Jack met him in a bar, drinking down his financial worries. He was about to lose his business and his airplane. Jack bought both and hired him to fly his own plane. That DeHavilland Otter out in the hangar is Matt's old plane."

"Sounds like Jack saved him, too."

"And me, too. I mean, I didn't have any financial disasters to contend with, but I needed to be useful. My husband has Alzheimer's. We could go live with our son in Duluth and tread water until we die. But Jack gave me a job, a real job, with lots of responsibility. It keeps me active, involved, and, well, alive. And now he's going to help you."

"Yeah, ...and he's an atheist."

29

"Yes. Does that bother you, Ms. McMurray?"

"Of course, it does. Atheists go to hell."

Fran smiled as she said, "This is going to be one real interesting flight."

Chapter 11

[The drawing is a DCH-2 de Havilland Beaver]
Wednesday, May 18
Winnipeg, Manitoba

"For a small plane, this thing is big," Cassy observed from her position in the co-pilot seat, as Jack loaded the last of their supplies. "I'm a long ways up in the air, and we haven't started the engine yet."

"She's a great old bird," Jack began, as he mounted the pilot's seat and strapped himself in. It's called a DCH-2 Beaver, originally built by DeHavilland here in Canada in 1948. It weighs 3000 pounds, and it will haul another 2000 pounds. It can carry six passengers, but I took the back seats out so I could put in extra fuel. It only cruises at 145 miles-per-hour, but it'll carry about anything you can put inside. It will go 455 miles on one fueling, so this should give us plenty. Are you all strapped in? Headset on?"

"Yes, I think so."

Jack went through a paper checklist on a small clipboard, then set it beside the seat, opened the window, and yelled "CLEAR." When Cassy jumped, he said, "Oh, sorry. I should have told you, that's standard procedure before starting an airplane on a public ramp." Then he pumped the primer twice and turned the ignition switch fully to the right. The big three-bladed propeller turned slowly two complete revolutions before one jug fired, then another joined in. Soon the Pratt & Whitney 450 horsepower radial engine was running...loud, and rough.

"How come it sounds like it's going to quit?" Cassy asked with a concerned frown.

"Oh, that's just the nature of radial engines. When we get leveled out at altitude, mixture leaned, prop, throttle, and manifold pressure adjusted, she'll purr like a kitten—well, maybe a lion, but anyway, that's normal for a radial."

"Will it always be this loud?"

"Oh, I forgot to tell you. That headset you are wearing has a noise-canceling device. Just push that button on the cord until the little green light comes on."

She pushed it. Immediately the loud engine noise went to a quiet background hum. "Wow, that's fantastic. How does it do that?"

"Yeah, it's great, isn't it? I don't know exactly. Somehow it recognizes the sound frequency and produces an alternate frequency that cancels out most of the noise."

"Now it's like we're just talking in a living room with a hum in the background." Cassy was relieved. She had a lot to talk about.

Jack taxied the Beaver to the end of the runway. He talked with clearance delivery, then ground control, then the tower, and finally departure control. Cassy didn't understand most of what was said, except, somewhere along the way, she heard, "Cleared for take off," and later "contact departure" all mixed with a bunch of numbers.

She watched as their big little plane roared down the runway, lifted off the ground, and within seconds disappeared in the fog. Jack had to file an IFR (instrument flight rules) flight plan because of the fog, but he planned to change to VFR (visual flight rules) after about a half hour into the trip. Within a minute, they broke through the fog into clear sunshine. The white blanket below was already breaking up, and the air above was clear.

"We have about two hours until we get to the lake, right?" Cassy inquired.

"Yup. GPS says 1 hour and 58 minutes."

Jack opened a box alongside his seat and hauled out a thermos bottle and some paper cups. "Coffee?"

"Yes, that would be nice."

"There's cream and sugar and some apple scones in here, too. It's not Starbucks or Seattle's Best, but I like it. I get it from a coffee shop near the airport, and it's pretty darn good."

Cassy sipped her coffee. It seemed to make the cockpit homier, more relational somehow. "So, you up for some conversation, or are you too busy?"

"Sure, we'll be at cruise altitude in about two minutes, then we just set the autopilot and monitor everything until we get there. You know what they say about flying—hours of boredom followed by a few minutes of sheer panic."

Cassy looked concerned again. "Just kidding about the panic. Anyway, I'd love to talk, as long as it's not trivial nonsense. I prefer things that set everybody off, like religion and politics."

"I'm not very interested in politics, but I'd like to ask you more about your atheism."

"Figured you would. And that's fine, as long as I get to ask as many questions as you do."

"Oh, sure." Since he seemed to be in a talkative mood, Cassy wanted to sneak in a couple of other questions. "First, I'd like to ask you about my father and brother. I know you don't have any new information, but I'm starting to be as worried as my mother. Do you have any theories or anything? What are the chances of finding them in the woods? Could they have been killed by bears or wolves or drowned, or lost?"

"There's no point in speculating and then worrying about our speculations. I can't tell you what you want to hear Cassandra. But it is very unlikely they were killed by animals or drowned. It is likely they wandered too far off and got lost, but if that's the case, we should be able to find them. I suggest we talk about something which will take your mind off your family members until we have some solid information."

"I guess. Well, okay, umm, you didn't actually agree to personal questions, but it would help me if I knew more about you, personally."

"Okay, Cassandra, what would you like to know, personally."

"Are you married?"

Chapter 12

Wednesday, May 18
South Eastern Manitoba

"No, I'm not married." Cassy didn't know why that made her feel relieved, but it triggered her to ask, "Have you ever been married?"

"No. I got close once. But we decided against it."

Cassy's relief grew into a surprisingly good mood. But just as she figured she had pushed the personal angle as far as she dared, he asked, "And you?"

"Me, what?"

"Married?"

"Oh, no. I'm, I've been a professional student. Geology. I will finally get my Ph.D. this fall. I dated some very strange guys and a few rather nice guys, but never got close to marriage." Since he did not respond to that, she branched over into the theological discussion he'd agreed to. "How long have you been an atheist, Jack?"

"I grew up in my mother's Roman Catholic church, but I couldn't see the sense of it. It seemed to me like a lot of hocus pocus and mystical nonsense. So when I was in high school, I quit going to church. My stepfather never cared much if I went. My mother threw a fit, of course. Actually, she's still throwing it. Don't misunderstand, my mother and I get along fine, except when it comes to religion."

"Jack, tell me the number one reason you consider yourself an atheist."

"Simple, I believe there is nothing out there but the natural/material universe. I see no evidence for anything supernatural or mystical or whatever. Nobody has ever been able to show me any miracles or any evidence for anything but the natural world."

"But you don't know everything, so God could exist outside of what you know. So doesn't that make you an agnostic?"

"No, that's a silly argument. Agnosticism is illogical because it says 'Truth cannot be known.' But if that is true, then the statement 'Truth cannot be known' cannot be known. Agnosticism is, by its own definition, self-defeating. Nobody knows everything, but we can know some things. The question is, what's the most reasonable conclusion we can come to, given what we know? Whatever exists outside of what we know is irrelevant because there is no evidence for it."

"And you think there is evidence for the natural world, but not God?"

"The natural universe exists. We are here. We live. We die. That's it. Good stuff happens. Bad stuff happens. That's just the way it is. Morality is to promote the good stuff and help people with their bad stuff. No need wasting time thinking about some imaginary God."

"Are you saying a good God would not allow the bad stuff?"

"Oh, no, those people are just mad at God for all the evil in the world. They are actually focused on God. They are basically God-haters. I just focus on people and the real world, the one we really live in."

"Have you ever read the Bible, Jack?"

"Wait a minute. It's my turn to ask a question."

"Oh, sorry, go ahead."

"Do you believe God answers your prayers?"

"Yes."

"Do you have any verifiable evidence for that?"

"I see God working in my life. I pray, and then look for what God will do in my life."

"But that could be just a mental game you play with yourself. I could pray to this coffee cup and define the circumstances which follow as answers to prayer."

"It's not the same thing."

"Sure, it is. People believe in a lucky T- shirt, a lucky coin, a lucky rabbit's foot. All religions all over the world believe in idols, gods, fairies, and patron saints. And they all give them answers through circumstances. Now Cassandra, if you are not going to honestly deal with reality, then there is no need for us having this discussion."

"Okay. All right. I'll admit there is no way for me to prove my circumstances come from God."

"So you admit there is nothing whatsoever in the circumstances of your life which in any way gives you objective proof for the existence of God."

"You are right. I will agree to that. But now, it's my turn. Have you ever read the Bible, Jack?"

" Four times."

"Really! I'm impressed. What did you think?"

"Y'know, here's the problem with the Bible. It's a great book and all, but none of that stuff happens in the real world."

"What stuff?"

"God talking to people, parting the Red Sea, water from rocks, manna from nowhere, the sun standing still in the sky, healing, resurrections from the dead, ascensions into heaven. In the real world, there is nothing like that. Since the Bible-world does not match the real world, I can only conclude that the Bible-world is not real. It's just a bunch of religious stories—interesting stories—but just stories."

"In your reading of the Bible, do you ever remember it saying that these miracles were something everybody was supposed to experience in everyday life all through history?"

"I don't recall it saying that, no."

"Do you get the impression that the Bible is saying these events are regular, every day events, or unusual events?"

"Unusual, I guess."

"Well, if the miracles in the Bible are rare events, which only a few people in all of history experienced, why would you expect to be one of those people? Why would you be surprised that you haven't seen any miracles, if only a few people saw them?"

"Well, Christians sure believe in miracles today."

"You are changing the subject. I'm asking about the Bible, not Christians. Now Jack, if you are not going to honestly deal with reality, then there is no need us having this discussion."

Jack couldn't help but smile. "Okay, I don't remember the Bible saying miracles would occur regularly."

"So, then, there is absolutely no inconsistency between the Bible and what you observe today, is that correct?'

"In a sense, I suppose that's true."

"So, then, the God described in the Bible and the events of the Bible could very well be real. There is no evidence whatsoever to prove they are not real. Is that right, Atheist Jack?"

"You're something, y'know that? I think I'm going to like you, Cassandra."

Chapter 13

[The picture is the cockpit of a DCH-2]
Wednesday, May 18
South Eastern Manitoba

"I think I'm going to like you, too, Atheist Jack, but that's not going to get you out of answering the question. Isn't it true that the God of the Bible may very well exist? Your 'I don't see any miracles' excuse for disbelieving in God is not valid. Right?"

"I suppose, but..."

"No, no. Not 'I-suppose-but.' There is no 'but'! Your objection was that you couldn't observe anything supernatural today. We have established that that's not inconsistent with the supernatural miracles listed in the Bible, so the God of the Bible might very well exist. Right?"

"All right. The fact that I can't see any miracles does not prove they did not happen in the past." Jack raised his hand to waylay her interruption. Then continued, "Therefore, the existence of God is possible. But that's a long way from proving God exists."

"We'll get to that, but first let me ask you..."

"No, it's my turn again."

"Oh, yeah, sorry."

"Cassandra, do you believe in miracles, I mean, today?"

"You're really hung up on this miracles thing, aren't you, Jack?"

"Never mind my hang-ups, just answer the question."

"Well, there is an old song which goes: *I've seen a lily push its way up through the stubborn sod, I believe in miracles, for I believe in God.* There are some pretty fantastic wonders of nature, the living cell, the existence of life a mile below the surface of the ocean, the birth of a baby. It seems appropriate to call them miracles."

"Not so, Cassandra! Those are all observable things in the natural world. If everything is a miracle, then nothing is a miracle. To call them miracles, and then to call supernatural events 'miracles' is to define the word 'miracle' two different ways

38

and use one definition to prove the other. You can't do that. Your miracles are natural events. The question is, do you believe in supernatural events today?"

"Well, um, okay, I guess you're right, Jack. My description of miracles today is natural, not supernatural."

"So, then, Cassandra, we have established that not only can you not prove God answers your prayers, but you have no objectively verifiable evidence for any miracles done by God today. Is that right?"

"All right. That's true. Now it's my turn."

"You want some more coffee first?"

"Oh, yeah, sure, thanks."

They flew on in silence for a few minutes while Jack got the thermos out and poured them both some coffee. He put some cream in hers, because that's how she took the first cup, then he offered her a scone. It wasn't until her second bite into the scone that she glanced over and noticed that he was looking at her. "What?" She said it like he'd noticed a stain on her blouse.

"I want to make an observation from the natural world."

"Okay. What?"

"You're beautiful." He also looked at her mouth and wondered what it would be like to put his on it. But he didn't mention that.

She turned beet red. Swallowed. Then she opened her mouth, but Jack continued, "No, please don't respond to that, just eat your scone and hit me with your next question. It's your turn."

She finished her entire scone, drank some coffee and sat for a moment looking out the window at the Canadian wilderness far below. The nicest, best looking, most interesting man she had ever met just told her she was beautiful. And he was an atheist. Well, she would just have to fix that.

When she finally turned back toward Jack, she realized he was still looking at her. He smiled and said, "We don't have to continue this discussion, if you don't want to."

"No, no, I do want to, I enjoy it, and it helps keep me from worrying about my father and brother. So, you admit that the

God described in the Bible could exist, then what keeps you from believing He does exist?"

"Facts, evidence, proof. See, I don't like this whole believe/faith thing. Faith proves there is a Santa Claus, an Easter Bunny, a tooth fairy, and God. I don't need an imaginary friend. I need real things, not imaginary things."

"But Jack, you have to start somewhere. You have to believe in something and then build on that."

"So I should just believe in Jesus and the Bible?"

"Well, yeah. Doesn't your belief in anti-supernaturalism begin with the assumption, 'there is nothing but the natural universe'?"

"No, it begins with rational conclusions about observable evidence. If your Bible is true because you believe it, then so is the Muslim Koran, the Hindu Gita, and the Book of Mormon. If belief creates truth, then contradictions are true, and there is no way to distinguish between sense and nonsense. In that case, anything can be true. Come on, Cassandra, that's ridiculous."

"Okay, you're right. Faith must be based on something."

"Yeah, on a reasonable assessment of objectively verifiable evidence."

"So, you admit that you also operate by faith, it's just faith based on evidence. Is that right?"

"Well, I guess, if you want to call that faith."

"You have faith this airplane will get us safely to the lake and back, right?"

"How is that like faith in God?"

"Both are based on objective, verifiable evidence."

"Wait a minute, Cassandra, are you telling me your faith in God is based on objective verifiable evidence?"

"Absolutely!"

"Then you admit that you were wrong about faith being the starting point."

"Okay, Jack. I'll admit I was wrong about that. Faith should be, as you say, based on real evidence. But you have to admit that you also operate by faith."

"I believe you are beautiful, does that count?"

Chapter 14

Wednesday, May 18
South Central, Manitoba

By the time they reached the lake, a layer of cumulus clouds had formed beneath them. It was a little bumpy as they descended through the overcast. Jack commented on how pretty the clouds were, but Cassy was too concerned about her father and brother to notice. The landing was smooth. The pontoons skimmed the water gently before they settled in and supported the full weight of the plane.

They taxied for almost five minutes before Cassy saw the cabin. It was built out of logs, with a porch in front and a stone chimney on the left side as you faced it from the lake. It seemed simple and basic, but it was not dilapidated, and it did not appear to be very old. It was small but not tiny. Cassy suspected it was big enough for three or four rooms. Outside of the front door was a path, which stretched over the approximately 30 yards between the lake and the cabin. The path led to a long dock that reached out into the lake where it teed at the end, making two places to tie down. Jack shut down the engine at just the right distance so that they glided slowly until the left pontoon gently bumped the dock.

"Let's just look around the cabin first," Jack suggested. "I'd like you to see it. I haven't changed anything. Maybe you will see something I missed. You might recognize something which belonged to your father or brother we can use as a clue."

Cassy agreed. Besides, she wanted to have a look inside the cabin, just out of curiosity. She had no idea about finding a clue, but she wanted to see the last place she knew her father and brother had stayed.

The cabin walls, windows, ceiling, and appliances were clean. It was as well-built on the inside as the outside. But the place was a mess. Food, clothing, furniture, and blankets were strewed all over the place. The table was on its side, and the cupboards were open, their contents spread everywhere.

"Oh, my," Cassy exclaimed. "What do you think happened here?"

41

"As I said on the phone, it looks like bears. There are numerous bear tracks outside. But it seems they came in when no one was here. I see no sign of human struggle. Have a look around."

"I don't know where to start."

"First, you should see what you can identify as belonging to your father or brother. Then we'll take to the air and see if we can spot them."

There were two bedrooms and a bathroom in between them. The bathroom was small, with only a shower, a toilet, and a wash basin. There was a larger combined kitchen-dining area. One had to leave the bedroom and enter this area to access the bathroom. Cassy found quite a bit of their clothes, toilet articles, and a few books she recognized. She even found her dad's iPad. But no wallets or cell phones. "I'll try calling their cell numbers," Cassy suggested.

"Okay, but you've been doing that, and it just goes to the recording, right?"

"Yeah, but if their phones were here, they would ring and we could find them."

"Oh, yeah, good point."

Cassy dialed her father's number, then her brother's. Silence. Then Jack dialed the number of the phone their company sent along with everybody, just to cover all the bases. Again, silence. Cassy uprighted an overturned small wooden chair, sat down hard, and said, "Well, I guess we haven't learned anything."

"That's not quite true. We have learned that wherever they went, they left most of their clothes and personal articles, which makes sense if they went hiking or just walked over to go fishing on another lake. But why would they take all three phones with them? Our company phone was tucked away in the emergency supplies case we sent along. The case is here on the counter, and the supplies are here, but the phone is gone. I doubt the bears ate the phone. Why would your father and brother take out that phone and bring it along if they were already carrying two others?"

"Yeah, and leave all of them turned off. What do you make of that?"

"Too soon to make guesses. Let's have a look from the air."

Jack refueled the DHC-2 from the cans he brought along. Then they took to the air. They began near the cabin with small circles. Next, they widened the circles little-by-little, until they were beyond any reasonable walking distance from the cabin. They also circled low over several nearby lakes to see if there was any sign of life.

The Donavan Flying Service owned another cabin on a lake five miles east. When Jack flew over it, he noticed the campers were at home, so he landed to ask them if they had seen anyone. But everything came up empty. So did their fuel, so they were forced to head back to the cabin.

It was late in the day when they got back. Cassy looked depressed and said nothing on the way (a short flight of about 7 minutes air time from the other lake). When they got out and began walking up the dock, Jack suggested, "Let's have another look around. That's where we found some information, and that's the last place we know where they were." Cassy nodded, but without much enthusiasm. "You look inside again, and I'll look outside." She walked in without saying anything. Jack began to walk around the outside of the cabin, looking for something unusual, or different, anything out of the ordinary.

Cassy re-examined every room. Each room left her more depressed than the last. While she was sifting through the trash in the kitchen, she heard Jack say, "SUFFERIN' SUCCO-TASH!"

"What is it?" Cassy spoke while running out the door.

"I don't know actually. It's what Sylvester used to say on Looney Tunes. Daffy Duck said it, too, sometimes. I always liked it, so I use it from time to time."

"No, I mean, what did you find?"

"Tracks."

"Tracks? We already found the tracks—bear tracks—the yard is full of them, that's how we know the bears hit the place."

"Come over here a minute." She came and stood next to him. He was pointing at the ground. "What do you see here?"

"A bear track."

43

"Now look at this one next to it. Does it look to you to be the same as the other one, or different? Look close."

Cassy bent over, then she got down on her knees to study the paw marks in both tracks. Then she stood up and said, "Sorry, Jack, but they look just the same to me."

"Exactly, they are exactly the same. And now I ask you, my beautiful Cassandra, have you ever heard of a bear who hopped all over the place on one left foot?"

Chapter 15

Wednesday, May 18
South Central, Manitoba

"The tracks are fake!" Cassy announced her conclusion mainly to herself. Then she turned, faced Jack, and repeated her conclusion, with her nose only inches from his. Then, looking back at the tracks, she continued, "Which means someone made it look like bears did this. Which means bears didn't do this. Which means someone wanted us to believe bears did this. Which means someone else was here. Which means someone—OH MY WORD. Jack, someone kidnapped them!"

"Sure looks that way."

"But why? Why would anyone want to do that? We don't have anything. We barely get by on my father's salary. My brother is a borderline bum. We have no property, money, jewelry, rich relatives, nothing."

"What does your father teach?"

"Chemistry, Pharmacology, some pre-med courses."

"Wait, did you say Pharmacology, as in training pharmacists to work in drugstores?"

"Yes, he's just been promoted to the head of the Pharmacology Department. Why?"

"And has he published any articles?"

"All professors publish articles. Haven't you heard 'Publish or perish!'?"

"And have any of those articles had anything to do with, oh, say, the safety of prescription drugs, or the way to pollute them?"

"Well, he recently did an article on the way to test certain drugs. I can't remember which ones."

"Like maybe Nexium and Lipitor?"

"I don't know, yeah, maybe. Why?"

"Cassandra, have you heard the news lately? The number one issue with all the talking heads is the pollution of prescription drugs, and whether it will lead to a government takeover of the drug companies."

"Yes, but… Oh, for heaven's sake. You don't think my father would be involved in anything like that? Absolutely not. He is an honorable man. He would never…"

"Not willingly. But what if he was kidnapped for his services? I suggest that your father **does** indeed have something worth being kidnapped for."

"Oh…my…word." Cassy felt dizzy. She looked up at Jack and held his arm to steady herself. "They kidnapped him to work for them. You are saying my father was taken to be forced to pollute the drugs."

"I'm just saying…Well, it certainly fits."

Suddenly Cassy felt better. "That means they are alive. And the kidnappers have to keep them alive because they need them. Even my nearly useless brother must be alive. They are probably holding him to force my father to work for them. Wow, Jack we've got a lead. But we don't know where it leads."

"Yeah, well, it won't lead anywhere tonight. We're stuck here until tomorrow morning." Before she could respond, Jack took out his iPhone, tapped his radar App, and showed it to her. "There is Winnipeg, and we are here. See that red line between here and there? There is a nasty line of thunderstorms heading our way. It already passed over Winnipeg, and it will get here sometime tonight. No way I'm flying through that."

"You didn't arrange that so we would have to spend the night together in the same cabin, did you, Jack?"

"No, I was thinking probably you'd arranged it. You're the one with a God, not me. I'm strictly a chance guy. So what about it? Did you arrange for us to spend the night together, Cassandra?"

"Cute, Jack. Real cute. I guess I stepped into that one. But I'm still going to whip you theologically."

"I can hardly wait."

Chapter 16

Wednesday evening, May 18
South Central, Manitoba

They spent the next hour getting things organized for the evening. Fearing the wind might blow it over during the night, Jack tied down and anchored every corner of the Beaver. Fortunately, they had installed tie-down poles beneath the surface of the water in addition to the ones on the dock. That way, a plane could be tied down from every angle—each wing, the pontoons and the tail. It took a while, but eventually Jack got it all secured. Then he took in the supplies they had unloaded.

Meanwhile, Cassy cleaned up the cabin. She swept the floors, made the beds (in the two separate bedrooms), and set up the table and chairs. Then she began sorting out what food they had.

Jack started the cabin's generator, which gave them lights and enough electricity to recharge their phones, but for cooking, they would have to use the wood stove. There was already some dry wood on the porch, but Jack gathered some more and lit a fire.

Cassy found a large frying pan and began heating up some cans of stew she'd found in the cupboard. She boiled water for tea, figuring they should save the coffee for morning. Then she dished up the stew on two paper plates, laid out some plastic silverware, put out some crackers she'd found, and poured the tea. She even set out some candy bars for dessert. But when they sat down to eat, she said, "Wait a minute, Jack, we have to pray first." Before he could respond to that, she reached out and grabbed the baseball cap he had on, pulled it off his head, and put it on her own.

"What are you doing?"

"I have to have my head covered when we pray, and you have to have your head uncovered."

"Oh."

"Now, I'm sure you won't pray, so I will, but I want you to fold your hands and bow your head."

"Oh, for Pete's sa..."

47

"DO IT!"

"Okay, okay, but let it be known I'm doing it under protest."

"Whatever... 'Dear God, thank you for this food and the safe trip we had coming here and flying today. Thank you so much for the clue we found and for letting me meet Atheist Jack. But God, we don't have any idea where dad and Michael are, so please give us some idea about where to look. And please use your Holy Spirit to convict Jack to believe in You and to receive Jesus Christ as his personal Savior. In Jesus' name, amen.'"

Jack just stared at her a few minutes, then he said, "You prayed for me to become a Christian?"

"Hey, when you pray, you can ask for want you want. When I'm doing the praying, I'll ask for what I want."

"Can I have my cap back now?"

"No." She took it off and tossed it on the couch. "It's uncouth to wear a hat at the table. You look better without it any way." Then she abruptly changed the subject by adding, "We have the whole evening together, Jack. We can't learn any more about dad and Michael tonight, so I suggest we return to our discussion about God, so I can whip you theologically, as I promised."

"Fine with me. You had the silly idea that unexplained natural events were miracles."

"No, I agreed that you were right about that. But you had the silly idea that you didn't operate by faith."

"No, I said I operate by reasonable objective evidence, not hocus pocus. I'm like the Sunday school kid who was asked to define faith. He said, 'Faith is the ability to believe what you know ain't so.'"

"Well, that might be your idea of faith, but it is not the faith described in the Bible. Biblical faith is a decision to trust the evidence."

"But it's not real, objective, verifiable evidence."

"Yes, it is," Cassandra responded with a mouth full of stew.

"What! Are you kidding? What evidence do we have that Moses heard God speaking to him from a burning bush?"

"Ten real plagues ending with the real death of the first-born Egyptians, a real pillar of fire by night and a real pillar of cloud by day, and a real Red Sea that really opened and really closed, killing the whole Egyptian army."

Jack didn't respond to that right away. He sat quietly for a while. As they finished their stew and crackers, Cassy changed the subject back to their situation, and they both joked about their meal.

But when they began to clean up, they returned to the discussion about whether belief in evidence was indeed biblical faith. Cassy had her hands in soapy water, cleaning the pan, while Jack stood to her right repackaging the crackers they hadn't eaten. He continued, "You know, that's really stupid. Nobody in the real world parts the sea."

Cassy turned to him and pushed a soapy finger hard into his chest saying, "You are the one being stupid. You refuse to..." Then their eyes met, and suddenly the conversation stopped. They looked deeply into each other's eyes. They both felt a twinge of desire that was surprising, elemental, physical. Cassy's mind clouded over, and she couldn't speak. Jack wanted to reach out to her. His gaze moved from her eyes to her mouth, then back to her eyes again. They began to lean toward each other. That scared both of them so bad, it broke the spell.

Chapter 17

One week earlier
Thursday, May 12
Near Carlsbad, New Mexico

"Michael, are you awake?"

"I've been awake for hours. You've been out for a long time, Dad. I kept looking over at you to make sure you were still breathing. Not that I could do anything about it. We're tied up with zip-type tie wraps so tight, we can't move."

"How long do you think it's been since we were abducted?"

"Hard to say. I remember waking up a few times. I think they woke us up just enough to feed us, then knocked us out again."

"Yeah, I seem to vaguely remember eating something."

"Well, I guess that's a good sign. At least we know they want to keep us alive, for now."

"I wonder where we are."

"I don't know, dad. We are obviously in a closed room with no windows, but I have no clue where the room is. As I said, I've been awake for hours, and I haven't heard any outside noise, no cars, or any street noise, or even people talking."

At that point, the door opened, and two men came in. One was carrying an automatic rifle the McMurrays couldn't identify. The other one cut the tie wraps from their wrists and ankles. "Get up, gentlemen," he said. "It may take you a few minutes to steady yourselves and get your legs back. Take your time and get the circulation moving. When you think you can stand, follow me."

Michael was up almost immediately, then he helped his father, who took several minutes to get to his feet, steadying himself on his son. Finally, arm-in-arm, they hobbled out, following the man who was speaking to them. The one with the gun walked closely behind. They were led out of the dark room into a bright hall past several closed doors. Then the hall turned left, and after a few more yards, they came to another closed door on the right side of the hall. The lead man knocked on the door, then without waiting for a response, opened it and escorted the McMurrays inside.

This room was well-furnished. But nothing fancy. The floors were painted concrete, with a gray throw rug in the center. To the left, there was a small square conference table with six chairs around it and a few additional chairs by the walls. At the back of the room, facing the door, stood a metal desk. Behind the desk sat a stocky man with virtually no neck, a short flattop haircut, and gray eyes that seemed to match the decor of the room. His body was not fat or flabby. The muscles in his arms filled out his open-necked short-sleeved white shirt, and the ones in his jaw moved as he talked. "Dr. William McMurray and son Michael, we are glad to have you with us. Have a seat."

"Why are we here? What do you want? We don't have anything worth kidnapping us for," Michael protested.

"All in good time. Just have a seat, and we will talk about it. Sit over there at the table. Can I get you some coffee?"

"NO," Michael spat in disgust.

"Actually, that sounds good. I'd like a cup," his father said. "Just black."

"Coming right up." The no-neck man poured a cup from a Mr. Coffee sitting behind him, then he brought the mug to Professor McMurray and joined them at the table. "You can simply call me Mr. Max," he announced. "I trust your trip over was comfortable." As Michael opened his mouth, Max raised his hand and continued, "Oh, I know. It is a bit nerve-racking to be kidnapped, that's to be expected, but I assume my boys handled you well. I don't see any bruises or scratches."

"Give me a break," Michael interrupted. "You actually think we should feel comfortable about being kidnapped? What are we doing here anyway? And where the heck are we?"

"Your location will have to be off the table for now, but your reason for being here is about to be revealed. In a moment, a man in a white coat, who we call 'Rabbi,' will come through that door. We call him that because he always wears one of those little Jewish caps on his head. Actually, I don't even think he's Jewish. Anyway, call him 'Rabbi.' He's in charge of our lab. Dr. McMurray, you will work for him."

51

"Doing what?"

"Whatever he tells you to do."

"And what are you going to do with me?" Michael wanted to know. "I don't know how to do anything."

"Yes, I know. You are ignorant, lazy, and stupid. But you have one important function here—to make sure your father keeps on doing what we ask him to do. If he does, you'll have no problems. If not, we'll take you out, shoot you in the head, and kidnap your sister Cassandra to keep him motivated. Meanwhile, you'll be kept in a comfortable room. But understand—you are a prisoner in that room. You will be held there until your father completes his work for us. If you try to escape, or your father does not cooperate, you will be killed. Clear?"

Neither of them said anything. At that moment, the door opened, and the one they called "Rabbi" came in and escorted Dr. William McMurray out of the room. Michael was then taken out and turned to his left down the hall. After about 20 yards, the hall made a turn to the right. They passed the room where they were tied up, then about five yards further, a door was unlocked on the left, and he was put into his quarters/cell. It looked quite nice, actually. It had two beds, a table with two hard-back chairs, and a refrigerator in one corner. A door in the back was open, revealing a bathroom. There was also a TV and a stack of books.

"You will be comfortable here as long as your father cooperates," the guard reported. "He will sleep here with you in the evenings and take his meals with you here. Other than that, you will be totally isolated."

Chapter 18

Wednesday, May 18
South Central, Manitoba

"I...I...I should get back to washing the pan."

"Yes, right, of course, and I should get back to putting away the crackers."

"Yeah, you should...you should do that." Jack finished putting away the crackers before she finished with the pan, although he took enough time that you'd think he was performing surgery. Then he went back to finish clearing off the table. They said nothing for a couple of minutes. Then Cassy, still washing the pan, asked, "Jack, can I ask you another personal question?"

Relieved that she broke the silence, and the tension, he said, "Sure."

"You said you were never married, but you didn't say anything about... Are there any special women in your life, I mean, besides you mother?"

"Yes, there is. One very special lady."

"Oh." Cassy felt her stomach turn, her heart stop, and her mouth get dry all at once. "And are you...do you...love her?"

"Absolutely. She's the love of my life!"

"Oh, I see." Now the pan in front of her, which couldn't get any cleaner if it had been boiled in acid, began to get blurry. She blinked at the tears and swallowed something large in her throat.

"Would you like to see a picture of her?" Jack offered.

"Um, well, no. That's all right. I was just wond...."

At that point, she felt his presence behind her. He reached his cell phone around in front of her face with a picture on it. She blinked, looked, blinked again, then her eyes widened. As she focused on the picture, his voice behind her head announced, "She's my six-year-old daughter, Jenny Sue."

"Daughter? Daughter! You have a daughter? You love your daughter!" Then she turned to face him and repeated, "You have a daughter?" She wanted to wrap her arms around his neck and kiss him. But she didn't.

"The love of my life."

"But you said that you were not married, never married. How…, oh, I'm sorry, now I've really gone beyond my personal question limit."

"No, it's okay. I want you to know. Her mother was a very attractive woman. We had a few dates, then one evening it got heated and went too far. Six weeks later, she told me she was pregnant. It was clear to both of us that we were not in love with each other, but we had one huge disagreement. I wanted the baby and she didn't. She wanted an abortion, but I talked her into carrying to full-term and signing the baby over to me. I paid all her expenses and gave her a significant check for her inconvenience. I haven't seen her since Jenny was born."

"Her mother doesn't want to see her own child?"

"I don't think she ever saw her. The baby was immediately put in the nursery, and I was given full exclusive rights as Jenny's only parent. The next day I went to see her mother in the hospital. I kissed her on the cheek, handed her a check, and never saw her again."

"And you raised Jenny, all by yourself?"

"Well, not exactly. I was in the Air Force at the time, flying transports back and forth to Afghanistan. Since it was back and forth, I got to see her a lot, but my mother raised her mostly the first few years. Five years ago, when it came time to re-up, I resigned my commission and went home to raise my daughter. My mother is still a big part of her life, of course. Now that Jenny is in school, I usually bring her in. Mom picks her up in the afternoon and stays with her at my house until we finish supper. We could live together, but it seems to work better for my mother to have her own separate house, and her own separate gossip chain based on her very Roman Catholic life. So you see, it's this God thing that's keeping our family apart." Jack smiled and winked at her.

"I'm not even going to bite on that one." Cassy dried her hands and the pan. Then she took Jack's hand and led him to the cabin's only couch, where she sat facing him with her legs folded under her. "Since you brought it up, let me get back to the point I was making when I was…interrupted. You said, when we were talking about Moses, that nobody in the real

54

world parts the sea. But how do you know that somebody in the real world, in 1500 B.C., didn't part the sea? What if you really experienced the burning bush, the plagues of Egypt or the parting of the Red Sea in the real world, Jack?"

"I'd go see a shrink."

"But then you would be denying the evidence and imposing the faith of your atheistic religion upon the real world. So you really don't believe in what you claim—observations from the real world. Because of your faith in anti-supernaturalism, you would ignore the real evidence and conclude you need to see a shrink."

"But..."

"Shut up, Jack. I'm still preaching, and I'm getting angry."

"Wooooh. She's getting rough."

"That's right!" But they both were hiding a grin. "Are you telling me that all the thousands of Egyptians who experienced the plagues should go see a shrink, and the thousands of Israelites who watched the Red Sea part and walked across on dry land should go see a shrink? It was such a generally verifiable event, even Rahab knew about it up in Jericho years later. Should she go see a shrink? And tell me, Jack, what about when the Egyptian army drowned in the Red Sea? All the people to whom they did not come home, wives, mothers, fathers, brothers, sisters—they should all go see a shrink, too, is that right, Jack?"

Chapter 19

Wednesday, May 18
South Central, Manitoba

"Yeah, but Cassandra, how do we know those stories in the Bible actually happened?"

"Tell me, Jack, how do we know Socrates drank poison hemlock? How do we know Plato wrote "The Republic"? How do we know Alexander the Great conquered Persia? How do we know Augustus Caesar defeated Anthony and Cleopatra? Because we have reasonably reliable evidence, so we believe the evidence."

"But your evidence is all in the Bible."

"Actually, that's not true, extra biblical writings and archeology support the Bible. But what's wrong with the evidence in the Bible? All our evidence about lots of things come from only one source. We get evidence from Caesar's Gallic Wars, Thucydides' History of the Peloponnesian War, Josephus' Antiquities of the Jews. And many times those are our only source for certain information. And the Bible is 66 books which have no conflicting messages."

"But those other books don't record miracles. They record life like we see it every day, without the supernatural. There are also religion books from the past that record the miracles of the gods of the Babylonians, Persians, Greeks, and Romans. But reasonable people don't believe any of it is real."

"But, Jack, look at the nature of that religious literature. It is based on faith without evidence. Zeus and Aphrodite sitting on Mount Olympus zapping Hercules, come on, Jack, that's just silly. There is no evidence for any of that. That's faith contrary to the evidence. And you're right, religious people around the world have always thought that way, but not the authors of the Bible. They never wrote hocus pocus nonsense. The Bible is not written like religious literature that wants you to put faith in non-evidential fairy tales. The Bible is written exactly like those historical books I just mentioned. For example, most reasonable people believe Abraham, Moses, David, Jesus, and the apostles were real historical people."

"How does somebody as pretty as you get to be that smart?"

"It's not about being smart. You don't get a Ph.D. in geology at the University of Michigan and hold to biblical Christianity without having to think through and defend your faith."

"That, I can believe."

"But can you believe in God?"

"No, Cassandra, I'd have to believe in the inerrancy of the Bible."

"Not necessarily. You believe in Socrates, Caesar, and Alexander the Great without believing in the inerrancy of the texts that tell us about them. Now don't get me wrong, I believe every word of the Bible is true without any errors whatsoever. But that is not necessary for you to believe that its basic message is true. What if the Bible is only as true as the writings of Socrates, Plato, and Aristotle? Is it really reasonable to say that Matthew, Mark, Luke, and John were all wrong? If you just give the gospels the credibility you would any serious historical manuscript about anything, you cannot deny that they are reporting the life, death, and resurrection of Jesus of Nazareth as a publically verifiable event. Even Josephus said Jesus rose from the dead—and he wasn't a Christian."

"The revelation of the Koran to Mohammed is also a publically believed event."

"But not a publically **verifiable** event. Nobody else actually saw the angel who supposedly revealed the Koran to Mohammed. The same number of people witnessed the angel Gabriel revealing the Koran to Mohammed as witnessed the tooth fairy putting money under their pillow. But hundreds of people witnessed Jesus' teaching, His miracles, and His appearances after He rose from the dead. It's not just one guy who said so. There are multiple witnesses, an empty tomb, and the apostles whose lives were changed dramatically. For example, Matthew and Mark wrote their gospels in the 50s. Then Luke, in the late 50s or early 60s. Luke said he researched the whole thing again and recorded what he found. And there was no contradiction between what Luke found and what Matthew and Mark wrote in the 50s."

"Wait, I've got a question."

"No, you wait, Jack, I'm not done ranting and raving yet."

"Oooookay."

"You have no reasonable grounds for denying the truth of the general message of the Bible. You just refuse to accept it because you refuse to believe the evidence for the supernatural. You opt for your anti-supernaturalism over reasonable evidence."

"Can I ask my question now?"

"No! Well, okay. What!?!"

"Why do you care?"

"Care what?"

"Whether or not I believe in God. Why do you care so much? You are not just making an argument, you are making an appeal. You don't just want to make some points, you really want me to believe. Why?"

"Because, Jack, atheists go to hell. I don't want you to go to hell."

"Oh." They sat in silence a few minutes. Jack was staring at the floor. Then he looked up and said, "You know, my mother always wanted me to become a Catholic. I have an aunt, my step-father's sister, who wants me to be a Presbyterian. I have had several friends ask me to go to their church. But never once has anyone told me I was going to hell, well, not in a theological context anyway. And nobody ever told me they did not want me to go there."

They sat in silence for a few more minutes. Finally, Cassy got up the nerve to say, "You need to accept Christ as your Savior, Jack."

"It's getting late," he said. He looked at the floor again as Cassy sat silently. Then he looked at her and said, "One thing you said puzzles me. You said Josephus wrote that Jesus rose from the dead?"

"Yes, in two of his works."

"So, then, why wasn't he a Christian?"

"I don't know. He was probably as stubborn and pig head-ed as you are."

Jack laughed a little, then he said, "No, I mean, if he believed Jesus rose from the dead and still wasn't a Christian, what makes a person a Christian?"

58

"You have to make a personal decision to receive Christ. John 1:12 says: *But as many as **received** Him, to them He gave the right to become children of God, even to those who believe in His name.* You have to make a decision to receive Him. Like, pray and ask Him into your life or something. Are you ready to do that, Jack?"

"No. But I see what you mean."

Chapter 20

They began to secure the cabin for the night. Jack went outside to shut down the generator. It stayed light so late in the summer, that even with the power off, there was still a bit of light coming in the windows. Cassy called her mother to update her on the day. She had called her twice already since she arrived in Canada, but this time she could give her the good news/bad news that her father and brother were probably kidnapped but also probably still alive and not lost in the Canadian wilderness or eaten by bears.

While she was still talking on the phone, Cassy fished a flashlight out of her backpack to keep by her bed. She pulled the curtain back of the small window in her room and watched Jack as he disappeared around a corner outside of the cabin. She looked down at her phone to hit "end call." As she turned to leave the room, she nearly collided with Jack in the doorway. They apologized simultaneously and then bumped into one another two more times as they clumsily jockeyed for positions to pass one another.

"Is this room going to work for you tonight?" asked Jack.

"Yeah, sure," Cassy quickly responded, with obvious nervousness in her voice.

"Don't worry," Jack reassured her. "Everything is going to be fine." Cassy wasn't sure whether he was talking about her dad and brother, or whether he was talking about the two of them spending the night together alone in a cabin in the Canadian wilderness.

"Oh, yeah, I'm sure it will," Cassy responded, still not knowing what exactly she was responding to.

After Jack had stowed his gear in his room, he met her in the kitchen/dining room. Jack sat down at the table across from Cassy. After a few seconds of silence with Jack starring at her, Cassy became nervous. "What?" she said, with a combination of worry and frustration in her voice.

"You seem unsettled," Jack responded.

"Well, yeah, wouldn't you be if your family was missing?"

"Of course, I would," said Jack, "but you seem unsettled about me." Cassy suspected Jack had never been nervous about anything in his life. While she found his confidence attractive, there was a part of it that worried her.

"Well, okay, since you mention it, I am nervous. Spending the night alone with a man I just met is a little scary. Wouldn't you be nervous, Jack, if you were me?"

"Don't worry," Jack responded, "I'm not going to jump you."

Shocked at his choice of words, Cassy said, "Okay..., I guess that makes me feel a little bit better."

"Only a little bit better?" Jack asked, with genuine concern.

"Yeah, well, call me old-fashioned, but I was planning on the first time I spent the night alone with a man, it would be with my husband."

"Are you hitting on me?" Jack asked.

"No! What!"

"Well, are you proposing to me?"

"What? No!"

"Oh, good. I don't like fast women. Call me old-fashioned," Jack said, "but I like to be the leader of any relationship I'm in."

Cassy laughed and then wondered if she had just gotten herself into a relationship. Jack stood up and offered Cassy his hand. She took it and stood up from the table. Jack gently moved some of Cassy's hair off her shoulder to her back. Letting go of her hand, he looked her in her eyes and said, "Good night, Cassandra." He smiled, then turned and went into his room. As he closed the door, he could hear her say, "Good night, Atheist Jack."

Chapter 21

Wednesday, May 18
South Central, Manitoba

Cassy was in bed 15 minutes later. She read a book for another 20 minutes, then turned off her flashlight and stared at the dark ceiling, wide awake. She could hear Jack snoring steadily in his room. Then she heard the first rumble of thunder. Then another. And another. It was still in the distance but getting closer. She pushed the button on the side of her watch. It lit up, displaying a bright green 10:17. *It's late. What time is it in Chicago? Oh what the heck.* She dug out her cell phone and called Abby.

A scratchy voice squeaked out a "Hello."

"Abby?"

"CASSY, where have you been? It's been months. What are you doing?"

"Abby, it's been two days."

"Whatever. So did you find your father and your useless-as-a-turd brother?"

Cassy proceeded to explain how they found much of their belongings but no cell phones. She talked about how she and Jack were flying most of the day, finding nothing, then how Jack noticed the fake bear tracks and concluded her father and brother had been kidnapped, but were undoubtedly still alive.

"So they are probably okay, then, at least for now."

"Yeah, probably. Jack thinks so."

"Ya'know, I'm hearing Jack, Jack, Jack. I'm not hearing Mr. Donavan. Sounds to me like something's going on there."

"Abby, your imagination always borderlines insanity."

"So tell me what he looks like."

"Well, actually, I can do better than that. When he was busy, I sort of secretly took a few pictures of him with my phone."

"Well, send them along girl! Like now."

Cassy sent them over to Abby's phone.

"CASSY, he's gorgeous. And you thought he was some short fat guy with no teeth. So what's happened, have you fallen in love?"

"Abby, you are a genuine nut case."

"Hmm, I didn't hear a denial there, not that I would have believed it. So have you kissed yet?"

"Ummm, well…"

"YOU HAVE! You kissed him! Oh my word, I was like just kidding, but you really have. So how was it? Tell me. Tell me. Tell me."

"No Abby, we have not kissed. But…"

"But?"

Well, we were talking and washing dishes and sort of arguing, and then our eyes met, and everything just stopped, and, well, I can't really explain it. It was just…actually, it was sort of…absolutely wonderful."

"You **are** in love."

"Abby, you are psychotic, you know that? Besides, there is a big problem."

"He's married."

"No, he's not married, he's never been married, but he does have a 6-year-old daughter."

"Well, that's okay. You just end up with a bigger family. The Bible only says you can't marry him if he's divorced. A daughter is no problem as long as he was never married. Right?"

"Right. No. Abby, it's not about that. We were just sort of attracted to each other for a strange moment. It will probably never happen again."

"Wanna bet?"

"There is a bigger issue with him."

"Other women? A girlfriend? Not to worry, they can't possibly hold a candle to you, girl. You're a knock out."

"Abby, would you stop with that. You are a sexual pervert. You find romance everywhere."

"True. And true. But that does not mean I'm wrong here. You are head-over-heels for this guy. So what's the bigger problem?"

"He's an atheist."

"Oh. Oh, no. That **is** a problem. The Bible says you can't be unequally yoked with an unbeliever, doesn't it? Cassy, you've got to get on that."

"That's what we were arguing about when he…we…"

"Cassy, you have to get him saved, so you two can get married."

"Will you cut that out!?! I need to get him saved so he'll go to heaven instead of hell."

"Oh, yeah. That, too."

Chapter 22

Thursday, May 19
South Central, Manitoba

Cassy woke up to the smell of bacon and coffee. She could hear Jack shuffling around in the kitchen area. She checked her watch. 8:37. Apparently, after she finally got off the phone with Abby, she fell sound asleep, even though the storm was raging at the time.

The bathroom in the cabin was located between the bedrooms, but it only had one door, and you had to leave the bedrooms to get to it. She gathered her bathroom things and stuffed her clothes for the day under her arms and peeked out the bedroom door. Jack was standing with his back to her, facing the woodstove, frying bacon. Without turning around, he said. "Good morning, Cassandra. The eggs come from a box, but the bacon is real, and so is the coffee. I can make some toast, too. There is no butter, but I found some little jam packets in the cupboard. So hurry up and do your bathroom thing before this gets cold."

"Good morning, Atheist Jack. Smells good." She rounded the corner into the bathroom and did her best to hurry through her chores. She wrestled into the only clothes she had with her, did her makeup, and brushed her hair. It hung a bit longer now that the curl was mostly gone. She decided it wasn't too bad, so she emerged from the bathroom, ready for the day. Jack's back was still to her, so she dumped her stuff off in her room and came quickly back to the kitchen area. Then he turned to look at her.

"You look terrific!"

"Thanks. I slept good, once I got to sleep."

"My snoring keep you awake? My mother and daughter plague me to no end about my snoring."

"No. I was just wound up, I guess. I can't stop thinking about my father. What are they making him do? Are they torturing him? What are they doing to my brother? So I called my friend Abby. She's kind of a motor mouth, but she calms me down."

65

"Sounds like my mother, except for the calming part."

"Wow, eggs, bacon, coffee—it looks great, Jack."

"Yeah, well, eat up. It's getting cold." When they sat down, he handed her his cap. "I'm sure you want to pray again, so you need your head covered, right?"

"Yes. Thanks." She put it lightly on top her head. Then she prayed, "Dear God, thank you for this food and thank you for this trip and what we have learned, and please show us some way to locate dad and Michael because we don't know where to go from here to find them. And thank you for Jack and please help him become a believer so he won't go to hell. In Jesus' name, amen."

She took off his cap and laid it on the table. He reached for it and she slapped his hand. "No caps at the table."

"What, there's some biblical law about that, too?"

"Nope. That's a Cassy law. But you darn well better keep it."

Jack immediately drew back his hand, looking at where she had slapped it. Then he smiled and began eating. "The plane weathered the night real well," he said through a mouth full of box eggs. "It will take us about an hour to load her up and secure the cabin. Then it's two hours back to Winnipeg. The weather looks good this morning. It should be a nice flight. When we get back, we'll figure out what to do next, I mean about finding your family."

"What can we do, Jack? It seems to me we are at a dead end. We have no clue as to where they were taken, or how to find them. Yesterday, I felt better because we know pretty sure they are still alive. But today, I'm feeling a bit down again because there is nowhere to go from here."

"Not exactly. We know that it's likely they were kidnapped to work on the bad drugs. That means the government will be making this a priority. I have some friends at the FBI who owe me some favors. I flew some ops for them on some drug dealing across the border. I also have a friend there who was in the Air Force with me. I'll lean on him to see what he can do."

"I thought the FBI was strictly for the States, isn't this CIA jurisdiction?"

"Actually, the FBI has a much wider range of responsibilities than the CIA. In addition to addressing some domestic intelligence issues, the FBI also has offices abroad to coordinate information collection. The Canadian offices of the FBI alert the U.S. offices to potential threats and areas of interest. Then the FBI determines if action should to be taken to ensure domestic security. When I alert them of what we know, they will have to look into it, especially with the current drug threat. Cassandra, I want to help you with this. I'm not going to lie to you and say 'I'm sure we'll find them and everything will be fine.' There is no way to be sure of that. But I have some assets. I have airplanes and contacts. I can help."

"I appreciate it, Jack, but I can't afford that. Even with the breaks I get because of my father, I have about $80,000 in college debt. I haven't secured a job yet, and we have very little cash. I maxed out my credit card just to buy a ticket up here. I just can't do that."

"Cassandra, I don't want your money. I don't need your money. I want to use mine to help you. Trust me, I have plenty. I won't bore you with the details but I inherited a bunch of money. I bought the planes and started this business without making a dent in it. Trust me, Cassandra, I do not need your money. Please, let me help."

"I don't know what to say. I have no one else to turn to. I appreciate it so much. But why? Why would you want to help me? We have no idea how dangerous this could be. I know you like to help people. You have significantly helped all the people who work for you, but this is different. These are criminals. If they kidnap people, they will likely also kill people. Why would you…?"

He laid his hand on hers. "Stop asking me 'Why?' It's not just that I like to help people. I want to help **you**. Maybe some day we can talk more about my motives. But, for now, just let me help."

Chapter 23

The same day, Thursday, May 19
South Central, Manitoba

As Jack predicted, it took them nearly an hour to police the cabin and load the airplane, but they were finally ready for take off. Since Cassy's side of the plane was up against the dock, Jack handed her a small paddle and said: "Push us off a bit. We'll need to just drift out a little before we start the engine."

"I can't quite reach it. I'll have to unbuckle and step out on the pontoon."

"Okay, just be careful you don't fall in, that water is a lot colder than it looks."

"Okay, I think I can reach it now. There." As the airplane began to slowly drift out, she stared into the water. "Boy, this water sure is clear, isn't it? You can see the bottom, even though it drops off real fast here."

"Yeah, well, get back in here. I don't want to have to fish you out of the lake."

"Jack, WAIT. I see something."

"What?"

"I don't know. It looks like a wallet or a book or a purse. We're drifting away from it now. I think we should go back and have a look at it. Maybe it's something the kidnappers dropped."

"Lots of tourists use this cabin. It could have been there a while."

"I don't think so. It looked like it was laying right on top of the weeds."

"Okay, we'll have a look." With only their small paddle, it took a while to work their way back toward the dock. Jack straddled the pontoon, sitting on it like it was a big clumsy canoe, and inched their way back through the water. "See anything yet?"

"No...not yet...wait, there it is on your left. See it?"

"Yeah, wow, that's past the drop off. It's really down there. There's no way we can fish that out with a net. Let me guess, you want me to dive in and bring it up, right?"

"Pleeeeese. You'd be my hero."

Jack just gave her a sideways look. He took off his shirt and his shoes then dove into the cold clear lake. He was down, what seemed to Cassy, an awfully long time, even though she could see him clearly. When he finally broke the surface, he yelled "SUFFERIN' SUCCOTASH! It's cold down there." He handed the wet hunk of leather to her as she was helping him back up on the pontoon. "It's a wallet, all right. And it seems to have been recently lost. You were right about it sitting right on top of some weeds, and there is no sediment from the lake on it. Let's go back to the cabin. I want to change into a dry pair of jeans. We can look at it there.

Ten minutes later, Cassy and Jack, with dry clothes, were sitting at the kitchen table where Cassy had the contents of the wallet spread out and drying. Cassy began to report on their find. "Well, there are four different credit cards with four different names on them. There is $357 in cash and several folded up papers that look like receipts or something. No name card, no driver's license or other primary identification. That's about it. I guess it's not much."

"We'll have those credit cards checked out. What are the receipts for and where are they from?"

"Looks like construction products. A huge order of concrete, metal studs, wood paneling, light fixtures, and some other building materials. These receipts are all from one company, Johnson Building Supplies in Carlsbad, New Mexico."

"So if this wallet belonged to one of our kidnappers, they would seem to have a project going on near Carlsbad, New Mexico. And if our kidnappers were connected to the drug poisonings, then it would make sense that they would be building a place to hide out and do their work. And what better place than the desert areas of New Mexico."

"Wow, Jack. We have a significant clue. We know where to look."

"It doesn't exactly pinpoint their location. Those deserts are a vast wilderness. But if one of those credit cards reveals a purchase in the vicinity of Carlsbad, New Mexico, I'd say you're right. At least we have a place to start."

69

Chapter 24

The same day, Thursday, May 19
Near Carlsbad, New Mexico

After a week in his well-furnished, but secluded, prison room, Michael McMurray was getting impatient. The first few days were not so bad. He spent most of the time watching TV. His father was allowed to join him for meals, three times a day, and they both slept there. They were sure the room was bugged with both video and audio surveillance, so they were not able to communicate much about anything significant. But now, Michael was getting sick of all this and willing to take some chances. So during the evening meal, he left the television on quite loud and sat close enough to his father to carry on what he figured was an undetectable conversation.

"How long do you think we'll be here, dad?"

"Not sure. Until they get what they need from me, I guess."

"What are you doing for them?"

"Rewriting drug formulas for almost every pill on the market. Somehow, they plan to introduce these bad prescription meds into drugstores all across America. That will completely destroy the drug companies because nobody will be able to trust their prescriptions. When people get sick everywhere for taking prescription drugs, there will be a public outcry for the government to take over the distribution of all prescription drugs."

"Wow, so these **are** the guys behind what we've been hearing about in the news."

"That's what it looks like."

"But I thought they were already doing that, why do they need you?"

"It seems they had no professional pharmacists. They were just guessing at the amount of poison to put in the drugs. Apparently, some people died. And that's not the press they wanted. Dead people inspire criminal investigations. I am forced to poison the drugs, but at least I am making them so they won't kill anybody."

"Yeah, I heard on the news that some people had died, but nobody is sure it was from bad drugs."

"I guess they want to make sure it doesn't happen again, then those deaths will be considered 'natural causes.'"

"What will they do when they are done with you, dad? They'll probably kill both of us, don't you think? I mean, we can identify these guys, so they can't let us go."

"I don't know, but we should be thinking about ways to get out of here alive."

"Like what?"

"I have no idea."

"I did something that might help."

"You did? What did you do?"

"While we were still in the cabin at the lake, I picked the pocket of one of our kidnappers."

"What? Where did you learn to do that?"

"One of my suite mates in college taught me. He was not a thief or anything, he just did it as a gag at parties."

"I wondered what you learned at college. So what did you find when you picked his pocket?"

"A wallet."

"What did you do with it?"

"I dropped it in the lake when they were putting us on the airplane."

"Dropped it in the lake! Why on earth would you do that?"

"As a clue for somebody to find. If I left it in the cabin or on the dock, our kidnappers would see it. So I dropped it in the water. I figure after we are gone for a while, the authorities will come looking for us. Surely, they will get around to dragging the lake, looking for our bodies, if nothing else. They should find this easily, since it's near the dock. It's a long shot. I'm not sure there is anything in the wallet that can trace us, and it may be too late when they find it. Anyway, I figure it was worth a shot."

Chapter 25

The same day, Thursday, May 19
South Central, Manitoba

It was 11:30 before Jack and Cassy finally took off and pointed their aircraft back toward Winnipeg. Jack chose a cruising altitude of 8,500 feet. They were VFR (visual flight rules) westbound, so they needed to be at an even thousand plus 500-foot altitude. Jack climbed up to 8,500 (instead of 4,500 or 6,500) because it put them on top of a broken cumulus layer that was forming. Since it was usually bumpiest under the clouds, this would give them a smooth ride. Cassy looked out the window during the departure and climb. When they leveled off, she turned and looked at Jack. His hair, still slightly damp, was messed and curling a bit at the bottom. His lean muscular frame and sharp features were distracting. She thought he was the most gorgeous thing she had ever seen. Then he noticed her looking at him, and said, "Wanna fight?"

She was shocked. "About what?"

"God."

"Oh. Yes. Um, actually, I had a question for you. We prayed two times for God to give us a clue to help us find my family, and when it seemed like we were at a dead end, we found the wallet. Wouldn't you have to say that was an answer to our prayer?"

"Nope. It was just luck. Somehow somebody lost the wallet, and we found it. That's all there is to it. Luck happens all the time, and it leads religious people to mystical belief. People wear their lucky shirt to the football game because when they wore it before their team won. Then they wore it again, and their team won again. When they wear it, their team wins more than it loses, so they think wearing the shirt helps the team win in some unknown mystical way. Your belief that this is an answer to prayer is nothing more than that."

"I will admit that this does not **prove** God answered our prayers, but it's pretty good **evidence**. In a football game, somebody is going to win anyway. The odds may not be exactly 50/50, although most matchups allow a pretty good chance that either team would win. But spotting a wallet at the bottom of the lake, that's hardly 50/50."

"But it's not beyond reasonable doubt, the criteria for conviction in criminal law."

"Okay. But it is evidence, and the preponderance of the evidence grants conviction in a civil case. So maybe it's not conclusive, but it is real evidence. I mean, it really did happen."

"Lots of unexplained things happen. Everybody with some wacko idea claims their theory is the explanation, aliens from another planet, magic beads, lucky charms, in ancient times it was idols, today it's an invisible God."

"You know those aren't the same, Jack. There is credible evidence for God."

They flew along in silence a few minutes. Then Cassy asked, "We've talked about a lot of issues, Jack. Tell me what keeps you from receiving Christ. Just what's the **real** issue for you."

"I told you, proof for the existence of God."

"That's impossible and unfair, and you know it. Most of what you believe is not based on proof."

"So how about undeniable evidence."

"But you will just deny it according to your atheist presuppositions. If it is supernatural, you'll say it is deniable. How about the preponderance of the evidence, as in civil law?"

"How about beyond reasonable doubt, like in criminal law?"

"Okay, Jack. You've got a deal. If I show you, in the course of our discussion, that the existence of God is demonstrated to be true beyond reasonable doubt, you will believe in God **and** accept Christ as you personal Savior, right?"

Jack chuckled, "You should have been a lawyer instead of a geologist, Cassandra."

"When you are a Christian and become a geologist, you get to be both. Now answer my question, Atheist Jack."

"Well, all right. I'll take that challenge, if you can prove to me..."

"No. Not 'prove' to you. That stacks the deck in your favor. Proof is subjective. You could simply say that I haven't proved it to you yet. I'm talking about evidence which is beyond reasonable doubt, not what you think is proof."

Jack thought a minute. "All right. I'll agree to that. But take this 'answer-to-prayer' thing. It depends on a belief in God in the first place. If there **is** a God, then finding the wallet would be good evidence of answered prayer. But that's only true if there is a God who could answer prayer. Finding the wallet itself is not evidence for God. So if God exists and you say faith in the existence of God is based on evidence, then where is the evidence?"

"Good question. The evidence for God is in three places— the natural universe, your inner conscience, and the Bible." She counted them out on her fingers.

"Then let's start with the natural universe," Jack suggested. "You've just graduated with a Ph.D. in geology."

"Well, I still have to finish my dissertation."

"Whatever. Anyway, surely you have had to deal with evolution all the way through. I'd like your summary of it. You don't have to go into details. Actually, I am no fan of evolution myself. It has lots of statistical difficulties with it. But I'd like to hear what you think."

"It's not just a theory with difficulties, it's not a viable theory at all. A scientific theory needs verifiable evidence, something I can observe, and you can also observe by checking my results. There is no evidence for evolution at all. Zilch, zero, nata, nothing. All the so-called 'evidence,'" she made air quotes with her fingers, "is either for microevolution or it already assumes the theory to be true. Microevolution is just adaptation. To use microevolution as proof for macroevolution is the same as the mistake you pointed out with miracles. It's like using wonders of nature to prove supernatural events. Adaptation is not evidence of evolution. There is no observation of any creature becoming a different kind of creature. And that's true in living creatures and the fossil record."

"What about Darwin's survival of the fittest?"

"There is no evidence that survival of the fittest creates new creatures either. Like, where are all the supposed pre-human cave people, Nebraska man, Neanderthal man, and so forth? If they were more able to survive than the apes, why didn't they survive? We still have apes. Also, things go from order to chaos, not the other way around. And life never generates itself from non-life. You already mentioned the statistical absurdity of... Why are you smiling?"

Jack reached over and pushed back some hair that had worked its way over one of her eyes. Then he tangled his fingers in it and said, "I'm sorry. You are just so darn pretty when you are arguing."

Chapter 26

The same day, Thursday, May 19
YWG Airport, Winnipeg, Manitoba

It was nearly 2:00 P.M. when they landed. After the taxi and shut down, Jack attached a small tractor to the pontoons, now supported by wheels, to pull the Beaver inside. Both Audrey and Fran came into the hangar to see if they found anything. Jack had called Fran about their need to stay the night, but she knew nothing about the phony bear tracks or the wallet.

Cassy noticed, with an annoyance that she couldn't explain, when Audrey gave Jack a prolonged hug. Jack reviewed what they'd found. "Obviously, you are going to turn the wallet over to the authorities," Fran commented, as all four of them walked toward the office. "But which one? The Mounties? CIA? FBI? Canadian Central Authority?"

"Do you remember Billy Montgomery?"

"Y-e-a-h," Fran strung out the word thoughtfully. "Wasn't he your friend from the Air Force? Yes, I remember now, he came here to visit once when we first got started."

"That's him. Well, he's been with the FBI for five years. I've helped them out on some drug ops."

"Yes, yes, I remember that. You flew their people into some remote locations west of here."

"So I was thinking he owes me a favor or two. I'm going to have a talk with him about all this."

"Oh, by the way, your mother called and wondered if I could pick up Jenny from school at 3:00. She has some meeting at her church. So I'll be out of the office for an hour or so."

"We'll get her," Jack volunteered. "I'd like Cassandra to meet her."

"Should I get a room for Ms. McMurray?"

"No, I'm going to have her stay with my mother tonight."

"Oh," Fran said. She looked at Jack a few seconds then, smothering a grin, she said, "You're sure you want to do that?"

"What?" Cassy interrupted the conversation she had not been invited into.

"Well," Jack put his arm around Cassy and looked at her as he answered Fran, "she's been a bad girl and needs to be punished."

"OOOOOkay," Fran said and returned to her desk.

"What?" Cassy repeated. "Come on, now, that's not fair. What are you two talking about?"

Fran looked at Cassy. "It's just that she'll talk your ear off, dear."

"Both your ears, your nose, your mouth, and whatever other metaphor you can throw in," Jack corrected.

"Mrs. Donavan is a wonderful lady," Audrey injected. "Why if it wasn't for her, I'd still be on the streets I reckon', well, her and Jack, of course."

"Now, Audrey, you know we all love my mother, but you have to admit she has a mouth like a machine gun."

"Well," Audrey began to giggle, "maybe something like that."

"Cassandra," Jack changed the subject, "if you will step into my office, we will see if we can get the ball rolling on this wallet."

Jack called the cell number of Billy Montgomery. He left the phone on speaker so Cassy could hear the conversation. He explained what they'd found and his theories. Montgomery immediately tied it into the drug scandal and arranged for an agent to pick up the wallet the next day. When Jack hung up the phone, he carefully took everything out of the wallet.

"What are you doing that for?" Cassy wanted to know.

"I'm going to photocopy everything in here, just in case."

"In case of what? I thought you trusted Mr. Montgomery."

"Oh, I do. It's the system I don't trust. Something is rotten here, Cassandra."

"What do you mean?"

"Things just don't add up. This kidnapping is not the work of some two-bit hood or a group of thieves, even sophisticated thieves. There is somebody high up in the ranks pulling some strings here. This is a huge operation. It requires a ton of money. But it doesn't seem as though it makes any money because the government ends up distributing the drugs. And why do they need your father? I'm just saying, something smells, and I intend to find out what's causing it."

"Wow, you're right. Jack, I...I wouldn't know...I just can't thank you enough for doing all this. I would have no one to turn to."

Jack put both arms around her. She returned the hug and they held each other for a few minutes. Then he ignored the tears starting to form in her eyes and made a copy of everything in the wallet, plus he took pictures of everything and every inch of the wallet with his iPhone. Then he locked the wallet in his office safe. "Now we need to go get Jenny." Cassy's face turned white. Jack noticed the sudden change and asked, "Are you all right? What's the problem? Don't you feel well?"

"Jack, it's like meeting your parents or something. She's your...family. What if she doesn't like me? I don't know how to act around children. I don't even have any nieces or nephews. I've been with university people for years. I don't even remember when I was a kid. I've taken her father away from her for two days. She's going to hate me."

"Jenny will love you. She's really outgoing. She takes after her grandmother, I'm afraid. Here's my plan. We'll all fix a big dinner together. We'll decide on something when we pick her up, then go buy all the food, go home and have a picnic out on my back porch. We might even see some deer or a moose walking down by the river."

Chapter 27

The same day, Thursday, May 19
Winnipeg, Manitoba

They decided on a fish fry, with steamed vegetables, fried rice, homemade biscuits, and baked Alaska for dessert, just because it was fun and complicated. They even made their own tartar sauce. At first, Cassy was shy, almost hiding behind Jack for protection. But Jenny talked non-stop and asked Cassy tons of questions. After dinner, she showed Cassy her dolls. Then she got Cassy to read her a few chapters from a new book. By the time the evening was drawing to a close, Cassy was having so much fun with Jenny that she almost forgot about Jack being there. Then he walked in and spoiled the fun.

"Come on, girls. It's time to break up the party. Cassy, my mother will be by to pick you up any minute, and Jenny, you need to get your PJs on and get in bed." After some complaining, they both complied.

Jenny said good night to Cassy in the middle of a big hug, then she looked seriously at her father and said, "She's really sweet, daddy. And pretty, too."

"Yes, I know, Dear."

"Are you going to marry her?"

"Yes, Dear, but not tonight. Now get in bed. I'll be there to tuck you in in a minute."

Jenny reluctantly shuffled down the hall and into her bedroom. When Jack turned around, Cassy's mouth was wide open. He reached up and put his finger on the bottom of her chin and gently pushed her mouth closed.

"Flies. We have lots of flies this time of year. It's dangerous to hold your mouth open like that."

"She opened it again, but before she could speak, the doorbell rang and the door opened simultaneously. Enter, five-foot-two, gray hair, rather chunky, Mrs. Josephine Donavan, Jack's mother. "Yooo hooo, I'm here."

"Saved by the bell," Jack smiled.

"You are one lucky…"

"Lucky? I'm the one who believes in luck, remember?"

"Jack, you can't just tell your daughter…"

"Whew. What a day. Meetings, meetings, meetings. Well, you must be Cassandra. I'm Josephine Donavan, please call me Jo. I am so glad to meet you. It is such a shame about your father and brother. We have been praying for you. Sorry you had to hang around with this pagan son of mine. He's an atheist, you know. Where is my precious little Jenny Sue?"

"She's already in bed, Mom. You can't see her tonight," Jack winked at Cassy as he spoke.

"You see what I have to put up with! My own child thinks he can keep his only mother from seeing her only granddaughter." She kept talking as she walked down the hall toward Jenny's room. "A reprobate son, that's what I've got. The thought of a son keeping his mother from kissing her granddaughter goodnight. It's just preposterous." Then she rounded the door and walked into Jenny's room. "Oh, Jenny, baby, how are you? Oh, it's been so long since I've seen you."

"Oh, Grandma, I've missed you so much."

"My baby, it's been ages, you've grown so much."

"Grandma, you've been gone so long."

"You are all grown up now."

All of this came in loud and clear down the hall where Jack and Cassy were standing. Cassy looked at Jack with a confused frown. "Just how long has it been since they have seen each other?"

Jack looked at his watch. "Oh, about five and a half hours." With that, Cassy broke into a laugh. Moments later, Jack's mother returned down the hall. Jack said to Cassy, "You better get going. My mother will talk half the night, so if you plan to get any sleep at all, you'd better let her get started early."

"You see, you see what I have to put up with? That boy is a troll looking for a bridge to live under. I swear I will wear my knees out praying that boy out of purgatory. Come, Dear, we have so much to discuss." She took Cassy by the arm and headed for the door. "I've made a fresh batch of cinnamon rolls and a pot of tea. I'll fill you in on everything. We'll have a great evening." Cassy turned and looked back at Jack as his mother, still talking, pulled her toward the door. Cassy waved by raising her free hand and wiggling her fingers. Jack made a

80

kissing pucker with his lips, as his mother continued, "Now, when Jack was only eight years old, he skipped out on church. We didn't know it and figured he was with some friends. Well, when we got home…"

Click. The outside door closed and they were gone.

Jack moved over to the window and shook his head as he watched his mother holding on to Cassy's arm with one hand and gesturing wildly with the other, her mouth moving like the wings of a humming bird. Cassy was just looking at her and nodding her head. *I love that old woman,* Jack thought. *I'm afraid I'm also in love with the young one.*

Chapter 28

Friday, May 20
Near Carlsbad, New Mexico

Only a few miles north of the Carlsbad Cavern National Park, in a bunker southwest of the city of Carlsbad, New Mexico, corrupted drugs, which appeared to be the same as many of the most common medical prescriptions, were being produced. Now, with the help of Professor William McMurray, they would be tainted just enough to make people sick and afraid to use the prescriptions they needed. The hope of Senator Roger Benedict was that this would lead to a massive government takeover. Like in many socialist and communist societies, the government would actually own the drug companies.

At 10:30 in the morning, Ronny Blaine knocked on the door of Mr. Max's office and slowly slithered in with his head down.

"Good grief, what's the matter with you?" Max began when he looked up at the sullen looking 23-year-old.

"I lost my wallet," Ronny said, almost in a whisper. "I swear I don't know where it could be. I know I had it when we got the McMurrays from the cabin, but now it's missing. I have searched everywhere. I've been looking for days, hoping it just got lost in my stuff somewhere. I swear it was in my pants' pocket, and we flew directly from the cabin in Manitoba to here, with only a fuel stop in Rapid City."

"Was there anything in it that can lead to us?"

"I don't think so. We paid for all the materials with cash. We almost ran out of gas once, and I had to use my credit card. Also, there may have been some receipts for some of the building material we bought in Carlsbad. We had to keep them because they wouldn't exchange anything without a receipt. A couple of them may have still been in the wallet. But even so, that could only place me in Carlsbad, not out here in these desert hills."

"You should have said something earlier, but I'm glad you told me. I'll check and see if anybody found a wallet."

Chapter 29

Friday–Monday, May 20-23
Ann Arbor, Michigan

The next days were hard for Cassy. When she got up in the morning, everything was fine. Jack's mother had breakfast on and continued her non-stop, rather one-sided, conversation, but she was actually fun to listen to. Cassy learned about Jack's childhood, his military service, and his having a child. Although Cassy noticed that she said nothing about Jack's biological father, her first husband, or Jenny's mother. She also told Cassy that Jack was the most generous person she knew. Jack sponsored every homeless girl her Catholic church's prostitute ministry suggested. They talked and sipped coffee until almost 10:00.

Then Cassy remembered she had forgotten to turn on her cell phone. Immediately, it displayed a voice mail and a text message from Jack, both saying that he could not take her to the airport to catch her 2:25 P.M. flight home. Jack called later that morning to say Matt Riley was sick, and there was a group he was scheduled to pick up. So Jack had to make the trip. They said goodbye over the phone, but it wasn't the departure she had envisioned. She went to lunch with Josephine, Fran, and Audrey. The conversation was lively and she learned a lot more about the prostitute problem in Winnipeg, the deterioration of Fran's husband, and Matt's love life after his wife died, now twelve years ago. Then the three ladies took Cassy to the airport. She had a smooth trip home. But no more word from Jack that day.

Or the next day.

Or the day after that.

She told herself to simply not think about him. She would work on her dissertation. She was also worried about her father and brother. There was no reason to think about Jack Donavan. So she would simply think about other things. She would just erase him from her mind. She would refuse to think about him.

She thought about him all of the time.

Matt was sick, so he was probably busy taking Matt's trips plus his own. But he had a cell phone, for heaven's sake. How hard would it be to make a quick call? But maybe she was making too much of their relationship. There was just a physical attraction any man and woman might have for each other. She was being ridiculous. Maybe the whole thing was to help keep her mind off of her father and brother. And the statement to his daughter about marrying her, well, that was clearly a jest. Like telling her that the tooth fairy would put money under her pillow or something. It was just a quick answer to a little girl's fantasy. Nothing serious.

But.

By the morning of the third day, Cassy was bouncing between panic and depression. That irritated her more than the fact that Jack hadn't called. Why did it bother her so much? Why couldn't she just let it go? They had a good time together. She enjoyed meeting his staff and family and that was that. So why wasn't that, that?

She shared her frustrations with Abby. Abby told Cassy to call Jack and chew him out for not calling. "Men don't get the subtle stuff," Abby said. "They are social introverts, make that perverts, romantic morons. I once dated a guy whose definition of communicating was that he looked at my shoes instead of his own shoes when he was talking. Okay, so that's an oldie. But it's a fact, girl. Jack is madly in love with you, but, like most men, he's romantically challenged."

Abby babbled on without Cassy inserting her usual corrections and reality checks. But Cassy still couldn't bring herself to call Jack. Maybe it was her upbringing. Maybe it was her conservatism. Maybe she was afraid of what he would say. Anyway, it just wasn't done. Besides, she didn't want to sound like she was chasing him like some love-crazed teenager. After all, she was just real interested, or something. She didn't love him. Did she? This thought added terror to her misery, dragging her down into a full-blown depression.

She moped through her morning bathroom chores and dragged herself down the stairs for breakfast. Her mother was also very worried. About William and Michael, of course, but now she was also worried about Cassy. She noticed Cassy's somber mood and questioned her about it. Cassy said it was concern about Michael and her dad. But her mother sensed something else and got her to talk in vague terms about Jack. After Cassy choked down a few mouthfuls of cereal, her mother handed her a list and asked her to go the store for groceries. After kissing her on the cheek, Cassy took the list and headed for the store, only a couple of miles away.

In less than an hour, she returned with a large paper bag full of food. She pushed the front door open with one hand, while shifting the rather heavy bag to the other. As she entered she called to her mother with no answer. She turned to her right and headed toward the kitchen, when she heard a deep male voice say, "Hello, Cassandra."

Cassy swung around so fast that a loaf of bread flew off the top of the bag. Atheist Jack Donavan sat, draped like a rag doll, on the living room recliner, sipping a cup of coffee. Then he smiled, put down the coffee, got to his feet, and extended his arms out toward her. Cassy dropped the bag on the floor and flew into his arms.

They held each other tightly without speaking for a few minutes. Then Cassy pushed herself back and slugged him in the chest. "Why didn't you call me? Three days. What, did your phone break?" She slugged him again. "You can't just... You should have called me about...something." She tried to slug him a third time, but he caught her fist in his hand.

He lowered his head and brushed his lips lightly over hers. Then, while holding her fist in his right hand he tangled the fingers of his left hand in her hair and pulled her mouth toward his. He nibbled at her lower lip before pressing his mouth firmly on hers. As the kiss deepened, Cassy's hand wiggled free, her arms wrapped around his neck, and the world went away.

Chapter 30

They held each other a while in silence. Then Jack said: "I hope there weren't any eggs in that bag."

"Yeah, well, there **were** two dozen of them. And, by the way, where is my mother?"

"Next door."

"What's she doing next door?"

"Talking, I suspect."

"No. I mean, why did she go next door?"

"Because I asked her to. Well, actually, I asked her if she could give us about a half hour alone. And she suggested bringing some of her fresh apple cobbler to someone named Millie next door."

"You talked to my mother?"

"What, you think I just broke in and planted myself in your living room? We talked about 20 minutes. Sweet lady, your mother, not at all like mine."

"Now, Jack, I spent a whole evening and morning with your mother, and she is a wonderful person."

"True. Best mother and grandmother in the world, but I wouldn't call her 'sweet.'"

"But, well, okay, maybe that's not the best word to describe her."

Jack started laughing. "Told you."

"Jack, you should have called me. I mean, I know you've been busy with Matt being sick and all, but…"

"Oh, he's fine. Some 24-hour bug. Now he's flying my trips as well as his. I spent the whole day yesterday in Washington, DC."

"Washington! Why were you in Washington?"

"Let's put away what's left of those groceries you abused while I tell you about it."

They picked up the groceries (finding only 4 broken eggs), put them in their places, and settled in at the kitchen table with a piece of apple cobbler and a cup of coffee.

"Day before yesterday, I called Billy Montgomery and asked him for an update on the McMurray kidnapping case. He said he hadn't heard anything. I asked if they found anything helpful in the wallet. He said he'd check into it. About a half hour later, he called back and said there was no wallet."

"WHAT!"

"Yeah, that's sort of what I said, except with more descriptive words. I said I was coming down there to get to the bottom of this. Billy discouraged that, of course, but I showed up yesterday about 10:00 A.M. and spent the whole day interviewing everybody they'd let Billy and me talk to."

"So did you find the wallet?"

"No. It vanished. I traced it from the guy I gave it to, to the guy in security he gave it to, to the guy in the evidence lock up facility who put it in a secure compartment in a vault. He said he knew he put it in there, and indeed his records showed that he did, but he had no idea why it was not there. Then we went through the list of everyone who withdrew evidence from his vault for any reason during the time that wallet was there. Since nobody checked out the wallet, I figure somebody who checked out something else must have somehow stolen the wallet. Billy and I made him think about everyone who came in. He claimed he was with all of them until they left and signed out their evidence."

"Who can check out that stuff anyway?"

"There are only a few people who have access to FBI evidence—mostly the FBI agents, also some lawyers, and members of both houses of congress, if it's about a congressional investigation."

"Congress?"

"Yeah, well, here is what's interesting. After we pushed this guard for maybe an hour, and Billy suggested he undergo hypnosis, he remembered one instance where he left his inquirer for maybe three minutes. He got a phone call requesting the filing number for a piece of evidence. Of course, that meant he had to go look up the number on his computer."

"So who was the inquirer he left alone in the vault?"

"United States Senator Roger Benedict."

Chapter 31

Monday, May 23
Ann Arbor, Michigan

"Why on earth would a U.S. Senator be interested in our wallet?"

"I don't know, Cassandra. But that is not our priority right now. We need to find out where the information in that wallet leads to."

"But we don't have…Oh, yes, we do, don't we?"

"Exactly. I made a copy and/or photo of every inch of that wallet and of everything in it. While I was still in D.C., I talked Billy into running the credit cards. We only came up with one relevant location, but it might be significant. It's a filling station between Carlsbad, New Mexico and the National Park southwest of town. Plus, I have the receipts from the building supply house in Carlsbad. So I have somewhere to start. I will fly there tomorrow and start asking questions. Maybe I can find somebody who can give me an identity of who bought the material or where they took it."

"Wait a minute. Did I hear you say 'I'? What's this 'I' stuff? I'm going with you, big guy. It's '**WE** are going to Carlsbad, New Mexico', not 'I'. Got it!"

"Cassandra, what I am planning is not safe, and probably not even legal. Just let me do this. I am flying the airlines back to Winnipeg tonight. I'm having the Cessna 180 converted back to conventional landing gear as we speak. Tomorrow, I will fly it to New Mexico. That will allow me to do some aerial surveillance. But if I find them, it could get real dangerous, real fast."

"There you go with that 'I' illusion again. What, you don't hear well, or is it a brain problem? I'm going with you, Jack. It's my family out there, and I want to know what's happening."

"I'll call you and keep you updated."

"OH YEAH. We **know** how efficient you are at that. So I'm supposed to sit here all day wondering what you are doing and waiting for you to call. Fat chance!"

At that point, Cassandra's mother returned and was encouraged to join Jack and Cassy at the kitchen table. Cassy talked about her surprise at seeing Jack, and about dropping the groceries. They all had a chuckle over it. Jack smiled at Cassy and wiggled his eyebrows when she clearly skipped the details about their greeting. Cassy glared back at him and continued, reviewing the whole story about Jack's day in D.C., with Jack adding details, some he'd forgotten to tell Cassy earlier. Then, when she got to the part about the evidence pointing to Carlsbad, she said, "So Jack and I are leaving today for Winnipeg, and tomorrow we're flying his Cessna to Carlsbad."

"Oh, dear. Do you have to go with him?" Mrs. McMurray said, looking at Cassy.

"Absolutely. I tried to talk Jack into going by himself, but he insists that this is a two-person job, and he needs me along. Isn't that right, Jack?" Cassy glared at him while waiting for a response.

Jack put his head in his hands. Then he began to chuckle before he said, "Now, Mrs. McMurray…"

"Janice. My name is Janice. Please call me Janice."

"Janice. I'm sure you didn't raise you daughter to lie. And everything she has said up to that last statement was true. She left out a few details, but her report was true. However…"

"Okay, okay," Cassy broke in. "Maybe it wasn't exactly like that. He was a little less insistent than that."

"Uh, uh, hum," Jack cleared his throat very loudly.

"Okay, so maybe it was more like an invitation."

"Uh, uh, hum," Jack cleared his throat even more loudly.

"Okay, so, actually, he wants me to stay here and suffer anxiety, despair, depression, and have a nervous breakdown, wondering what he is doing. Well, I've been doing that, and that's over. OKAY!?!"

Chapter 32

Monday, May 23
Ann Arbor, Michigan

For a second time, Cassy hurriedly packed for a trip to Winnipeg, and beyond. She took a quick shower, since she had been too depressed to take one that morning. She dried and put some curl in her hair and began to pack. Having no idea how long she would be gone, she put in a few more changes of clothes this time. She added her make-up, and headed down the stairs.

Meanwhile, Jack returned some phone calls, then got out his computer and made a reservation for her on the airlines. He managed to change his seat so they could sit together on the two-seat side of the aisle on both flights.

Cassy's mother, Janice, drove them to the DTW (Detroit Metro) airport. Most of the time, Jack was on the phone—to his mother, to Jenny, to Matt, to Fran, and to several names Cassy didn't recognize. During the flight from DTW to ORD, they talked about the trip ahead. Tonight, Cassy would again have the "experience" of staying with Jack's mother. In the morning, she and Jack would fly the Cessna 180 toward Carlsbad, New Mexico. But Jack said that they would do it in two legs, with a stop overnight at the home of a friend of his in North Platte, Nebraska. The next day, they would fly into Carlsbad, rent a car, and begin checking to see if they could find any leads, using the gas credit card slip and the building supplies' receipts. They also had pictures of Cassy's brother and father to show around, to see if anybody had seen them. After that, they would fly the 180 over the area to look for any new construction south out of Carlsbad, in the direction of the gas receipt, or in the direction of any other clue they might pick up. Jack also indicated that he might see about renting an ultralight type aircraft and fly over the area to get a closer, slower view. Cassy only wanted to make sure it would have two seats in it.

They had a three-hour layover in Chicago before they caught the late flight to Winnipeg, the same flight Cassy took a week earlier. Cassy thought about trying to see Abby, who was just across town. But, of course, there was no time for it, so she just called to give her an update. Then they found a noisy, but nice, restaurant and had supper. After they ordered, Jack looked Cassy in the eyes, and with a pensive tone said, "Cassy, I need to ask you something."

"That's a scary look, Jack. What?"

"Have you ever used a gun?"

"What!?!"

"A gun, specifically, a semiautomatic handgun. Have you ever used one?"

"No. Why would I use a handgun?"

"I'm going to explain, and then I am going to give you another opportunity to not go on this trip."

"What! You…"

"Now don't bite my head off. Just listen a minute."

"No." She folded her arms, then said, "Well, okay. What?"

"Somebody is going to get killed."

"Killed?! How do you know that?"

"Just shut up and listen a minute."

"Okay, okay."

"These kidnappers are forcing your father to tamper with drugs. They are probably holding your brother hostage to make sure your father keeps working. When they are finished with your father, they're not going to let them walk. Your father and brother know who the kidnappers are, what they are doing, and where they are doing it. There's no way they can let them live. If we catch up with them, they will have to kill us, too."

"Oh my! Why can't we just locate them, notify the authorities, and let the cops pick them up?"

"That would certainly be 'Plan A.' But the likelihood of that happening is small. First of all, the authorities are ignoring this case. Somebody high up in the government is pulling some funny strings. That's why I, correction **we**, are going down there. And second, if we get close enough to identify them, most likely we will also be too close to walk away. That means we will be in a fight for our lives. We may very well be faced with killing or being killed or watching your father and brother killed. If you are going on this, I need to know you can shoot and kill somebody if it means saving someone else—someone like yourself, or your family members, or me."

"Oh dear! I had no idea. I thought you just didn't want me with you."

"Cassandra, I will always want you with me. But, on this, I need to know if you can shoot and kill somebody. Look, it's no problem for you to change your mind. If you can't tell me that you are sure you can kill somebody to save somebody, then you can stay with my mother and Jenny as long as you want, or return home whenever you want."

Chapter 33

Monday, May 23
Chicago

"No, Jack, I'm going. I've never shot a gun, but if I need to shoot somebody to save you or my family, I can do that."

"Not just shoot, shoot to kill. If you have a shot at someone trying to kill you, or one of us, and you try to just shoot them in the leg or something, you'll end up dead. You have to aim at the center mass of their body and shoot without hesitation."

"Wow! Um, well, okay. I can do that. But Jack, I don't have a gun or any idea how to shoot one."

"That's why we are stopping in North Platte, Nebraska. I have a friend there, another Air Force buddy. He has a farm and a shooting range out back. I've already called him and arranged it."

"But I don't have a gun."

"I do. Actually, I have nine of them."

"You have NINE GUNS, like, hand guns?"

"Yes. Canada is down on guns, but I have a special dispensation due to my occasional border work with the FBI. And in America, I have a concealed pistol permit, good in most states."

"How did a Canadian get an American pistol permit?"

"I'm not a Canadian, I'm an American."

"You're kidding. I thought you were born in Canada."

"Nope. I was born in Chicago, where my mother met my biological father when she was going to Northwestern University. They married, had me, and divorced a year after I was born. My biological father is an American and my mother is Canadian. But I was born in Chicago, so I carry an American passport. After the divorce, my mother and I moved to Canada, and she married Carl Donavan, who adopted me and gave me his last name. We've lived in Canada ever since. After my stepfather died, my mother moved back to Winnipeg, her home town. But I always maintained my American citizenship." Jack reached into his carryon bag and handed her his American passport. She opened it and began to giggle. "What?"

93

"Your picture, it hardly looks like you. Your hair is all combed back and you are clean-shaven with a dress shirt, a tie, and a sport jacket. You really clean up good, Atheist Jack."

Two hours later, they were on their flight to Winnipeg. During takeoff, Cassy watched the lights of the Chicago skyline from her window seat until they faded into the distance. As they reached altitude, she could feel Jack's hand on top of hers. In a few minutes, their fingers were tangled together. Cassy leaned away from the window and put her head on Jack's shoulder and wrapped the fingers of her other hand around his arm. She felt Jack kiss the top of her head. What a different flight than a week ago. She still didn't know where her father and brother were, but now she had some clues. And the man with the airplane had become her protector. She couldn't prove it, of course, but she believed God had sent him to help her. God had sent an atheist to help her. And maybe he would be much more. She wanted him to be…but, as an atheist, they couldn't…she wouldn't let her thoughts go there. She couldn't keep her thoughts from going there. She knew he cared about her but…suddenly, she picked up her head, so suddenly that it bumped his mouth. As he massaged his lips together, she said, "Oh, sorry. Jack, you have to promise me something."

"I take it this is a 'you-don't-get-to-hear-what-it-is-first' kind of promise."

"Jack, I want you to promise me that you won't leave me."

"Cassandra, I will never leave you."

"Jack, you are not being serious. I mean, on this trip."

"Oh, yeah, that, too."

"Jack, I mean it. I don't want to be afraid to go to a restroom or a store and come out finding you have left me behind because you think it's too dangerous for me, or you are protecting me, or something. I believe you keep your word, so just tell me you won't leave me anywhere, Jack."

"I won't leave you anywhere, Cassandra."

She laid her head back on his shoulder and went to sleep.

Chapter 34

Monday, May 23
Winnipeg, Manitoba

Cassy didn't wake up until the wheels touched down in Winnipeg. She slept so hard, it took her a few minutes to remember where she was. They gathered their bags and wrestled them into Jack's Escalade. As they approached his house, he turned out the lights and then the engine, letting the SUV coast to a quiet stop. Cassy looked puzzled. "What are you doing?"

"Trying to sneak up on them."

"Who? Why?"

"Mama and Jenny play games until all hours. When I'm not around, they play poker. They think they are hiding it from me."

"They, like, play for money?"

"Oh, yeah. But I don't think the pot gets much over a dollar. Now just quietly open your door and don't slam it shut. We'll come back for our things in a minute. First, let's see if we can catch them at it."

They approached the house like a couple of thieves, then Jack quietly turned the lock with his key and burst into the house. Surprised, the card sharks tried to quickly hide their game. "Gotcha. What kind of a grandmother leads her own flesh-and-blood into debauchery?"

"What kind of a son sneaks up on people? Of all the nerve. You stay away for days and then come sneaking in just to trick us." His mother kept talking, but Jenny jumped up and into her father's arms, then his mother followed with a big three-way hug. Then, for the first time, Jenny noticed Cassy.

"Oh, there's Cassy." Jenny ran to her and pulled her in for a four-way hug.

Jack got their bags out of the Escalade and put Cassy's into his mother's Lincoln Navigator. When he came back, his mother was alone in the kitchen. "Where are Jenny and Cassandra?"

"Jenny pulled Cassy into the bedroom. Said she had some 'secret' to tell her."

After closing the door, Jenny made Cassy sit on the bed next to her. Then she said in a half whisper, "Cassy, I want you to be my mother." Cassy was sure her mouth dropped open this time. Jenny continued, "I've never had a mother, and it's not just that I want a mother. I mean, I suppose I do, but not just any mother. So I thought about it a lot and I decided that I want you to be my mother. It's just between you and me. You can tell daddy later if you like, but don't tell grandma. She'll blab it all over town."

"Jenny, I..."

"Here," Jenny handed her a Kleenex. "You're crying."

"No. Well, maybe a little. It's just that no one has ever wanted me to be a...their...mother. Jenny I'd love to be, I... I'd be honored...but it doesn't just work that way. It's..."

"Complicated, I know, all adults say everything is complicated. And I know how it works. You have to marry daddy. But I've never seen him look at anybody like he looks at you. So I figure maybe there is a chance...well, anyway, I just wanted you to know what I want. You have to work out the stuff that's 'complicated.'"

They hugged a long time. Cassy needed another Kleenex. Then they emerged from the bedroom. "What was that all about?" Jack inquired.

"It's a secret, just between Cassy and me," Jenny answered. Jack looked at Cassy, who just did the zipper sign across her lips.

Chapter 35

Monday–Tuesday, May 23-24
In route to North Platte, Nebraska

Josephine Donavan was unusually sedate during the evening. Jack briefly told her the nature of the trip, while Jenny was proposing daughterhood to Cassy. Josephine was taken back by the potential hazards of what they were doing. Even though Jack had not mentioned the guns, she knew he would be carrying one, and that meant it could get dangerous.

Josephine and Cassy talked for only a half hour before they went to bed. The next morning, they drove back over to have breakfast with Jack and Jenny. The conversation, like the wind that morning, was light and variable. But the danger of the trip hung like a cloud over the table. At 8:00, Jack and Cassy hugged and kissed Jenny and Josephine and left for the airport. Forty-five minutes later, they had their gear packed into the Cessna and were ready for take off.

"This is really different," Cassy observed. "It leans way back."

"Yes, it has a small tail wheel instead of a large nose wheel. It's called conventional landing gear. It's harder to take off and land than the nose-wheel configuration, but it gives you more options for landing in tricky places, and it's more efficient in the air. The tail will be up within seconds after I give it full power."

Sure enough, it was. They lifted off smoothly, but once again, the ground soon disappeared, replaced by a window full of white nothingness. Cassy looked concerned, but Jack assured her they would be "on top" soon. In about five minutes, they broke through into bright sunlight and slowly began to put distance between themselves and the white blanket of clouds below. "There is a front moving through under us between here and North Platte," Jack reported. "There are no thunderstorms in it, just lots of rain. But we will probably have those clouds under us the whole way. The autopilot will take us there, and we can see the ground terrain on the GPS screen."

"You up for another discussion about God?" Cassy asked through her noise-canceling headset.

"Sure, why not? The only thing is, we will be headed south into American air space on an instrument flight plan, so we will hear chatter on our headsets from controllers and other aircraft. They will also be talking to us from time-to-time."

"They can't, like, hear me, can they?"

"Not unless you push that red push-to-talk button on the yoke there in front of you." With that, Cassy jerked her hands back, as if the button would bite her. "It's okay," Jack chuckled, "nobody else will hear you. Go ahead. Where were we?"

"All right," Cassy began, giving the little red button a wary look. "Well, I said there are three ways to know about God: nature, our conscience, and the Bible. We were talking about nature, and you agreed that evolution is without evidence. So doesn't that mean the designs we see in nature require the existence of a Designer?"

"It's true that design assumes a designer, but there is no way to prove that the intricacies we see in nature are a design. You front load the question in your favor when you assume that what we see are designs."

Chapter 36

Cassy had to think about that a while. She poured herself a cup of coffee from a thermos they filled on the way to the airport, put some cream in it, and sipped. Then she pushed at her hair and asked, "So what are they? Where did intricacies we see in nature come from?"

"I don't know. But just because I don't know, does not mean a Creator God designed them. I once read a book by a guy named Denton. He pretty thoroughly disproved evolution, but he rejected creation because he said it was religious. He simply concluded that he did not know how nature got to be what it is. That's kind of where I am. Once you know there is a God, you can conclude He designed everything, but you can't prove design from intricacy. So you have to admit that your 'design requires a Designer' proof is no good because you can't know the natural world is a design."

"Okay. I can see that, she said. But symmetry in the right and left sides of most living things, the DNA code, cell repro- duction, things like that all look like designs."

"It could be that's just the way nature is. Just because it is full of awesome details does not mean some Designer designed those details. Maybe nature formed those details all by itself. All we know is, what's there is there. We don't know how it got there or that it was designed to be that way."

"You're right, Jack. I can't prove that the wonders of nature are a design, but there is a problem with your answer that na- ture did this all by itself. In nature, everything we see has a cause, right? Cause and effect says if it exists, something caused it, would you agree?"

"That's true, I guess. But where are you going with that?"

"I'll show you, then I will let you go back and reconsider, all right? I'm trying to make a point, I'm not trying to trap you."

"All right, Cassandra. In that case, I will admit it seems like every effect has a cause."

"Also, every effect has a cause equal to or greater than itself. In other words, if we have a bird nest, then there exists a bird more complex than the nest. If we have a computer, then there is a human more complex than the computer. Actually, there are only a few examples where the cause has the same complexity as the effect, and that's because it's part of the same process, like reproduction of offspring."

"I see where this is going. The universe needs a complex cause. But how does that get me to God being that cause?"

"Well, Jack, the cause of the universe must also be personal and moral, not an 'it' but a 'He'."

"Why?"

"Because **we** are personal and moral, and we have a sense of justice, purpose, and destiny. So a cause must exist who is at least personal and moral, with a sense of justice, purpose, and destiny. And it is reasonable to call such a cause 'God'."

"Cause and effect is what we see inside the natural universe. Couldn't the origin of nature be different from what we observe inside of nature, Cassandra?"

"Yes, of course. Since nature does not create, we are forced to look outside of it for a cause. But you are the one insisting we look inside of nature. Your anti-supernaturalism is based on observations inside the natural world, not outside of it. 'Cause and effect' is universally true within the natural world. But 'cause and effect' demands at least a personal, moral cause with a sense of justice who is at least as complex as everything we see in nature. Look, it comes down to this, Jack. Either you have to give up on your assumption that the supernatural does not exist because you can't observe it, or you have to give up on reason as the basis for knowledge."

"Okay, but it's not just that I can't observe the supernatural, neither can you, neither can anybody in a scientific sense of a repeatable observation."

"Well, that's true by definition. If it were generally observable, then it would be natural not supernatural."

"True, Cassandra, but it still leaves us with no way to demonstrate that the supernatural is real."

"But either it is, or we give up on reason as a way to determine reality. And remember, the Bible does give us reports by people who said they did observe the supernatural in a real generally observable way, not as something repeatable but as something historically real. And these were intelligent, rational people, not religious kooks."

"Why can't we just say we don't know how to answer all the questions?"

"Because, Jack, there are tons of things we do know, the complexity of the living cell, the presence of moral evil, the existence of a vast universe that cannot create or develop the more complex from the less complex, and so on. It's intellectually dishonest to stick our head in the sand and just say we don't know how those things got here. We know they are here, and either they came about from a supernatural God or we have to abandon reason."

"That's a good point, Cassandra. You can be proud of yourself."

"Proud!?! PROUD! This is not about pride. This is about keeping you from going to hell, you BLOCKHEAD."

Chapter 37
Tuesday, May 24
In route to North Platte, Nebraska

Neither spoke for a few minutes. They listened to the chatter on the radio. The controller called them and Jack answered, changing to the next frequency. Cassy looked out the window, but she saw nothing. She knew there were tears in her eyes when she turned back toward Jack, but she was too angry to care. "Jack, I can't talk you into believing in God. I have made the mistake that nearly all women make—thinking they can change a man. I know that unless the Spirit of God makes things clear for you, there is no way my arguments will matter. I have just been hoping and praying that God might somehow use me as a messenger, or an instrument, in bringing you to Christ. But God has to convict you, and you have to believe. I can't do that."

"Don't give up on me, Cassandra. Give me a chance to consider what you've said. I can't believe what my mind rejects."

"That's true, Jack. But that's not all there is to it. It's not just about what your mind can accept. All your helpful charitable work is getting in the way. It makes you think you are a good guy. Well, you're not. You are a filthy rotten sinner who falls short of the holiness of God, just like the rest of us. I don't know all what you do that's sinful, but everybody is a sinner, and you're no exception. Your good works will not get rid of your sin. And if you can't see yourself as a sinner in the hands of a God to be feared because He will judge your sin, well, then forget it. You are a sinner, Jesus died on the cross to pay for your sins. So you need to pray to receive Him as your God and Savior. But you'll never receive Christ's payment for your sins if you don't think you are a sinner. And as the Apostle Peter said, *...there is salvation in no one else; for there is no other name under heaven that has been given among men by which we must be saved.* Everybody thinks you are a good guy. Well, you're not. You are an atheist who rejects your Creator and His Word and His Son's payment for your sin. And you are going to hell for it. And I don't want you to go to hell. So don't make this some sort of game where I should be 'proud' of making a few points."

Jack said nothing. He glanced over the instruments a few minutes. Then he answered Chicago center's new directive to change the radio to the next in-route frequency. He just looked down into his lap a while. Then he looked out the window a while.

Cassy was panicky now. She was afraid she had pushed him away. Lost him. The only man she had ever felt this way about, the only man she ever had thoughts about spending the rest of her life with, the most handsome, honest, caring man she had ever met. And she had just called him a "Blockhead" and a sinner who was going to hell.

Chapter 38
Tuesday, May 24
In route to North Platte, Nebraska

"Cassandra, I want to tell you something I did about a year ago."

"What's this? Some sort of confession?"

"No, no, this was an experiment. About a year ago, I decided to create my own religion."

"Interesting! How'd that go, Jack?"

"I didn't want anyone else in my religion, it was just for me. And it had no eternal destiny or God. But it did have a moral code. I wrote down 10 commandments I thought I should live by. I honestly thought through how I wanted to live, morally speaking, and wrote out commandments I believed I should live by."

"You going to tell me what they were?"

"No."

"Oh."

"The point is," Jack continued, "I decided to create my own religion, with nobody but myself telling me what to put down as commandments. And to my surprise, I was not able to keep those commandments. Then I started to fake it, which means I was a hypocrite. I was not keeping the commandments that I preached. And I was the only one I was preaching to."

"Let's see if I have this right. You made up your own religion, converted yourself to it, couldn't keep it, backslid from it, began to fake it, and became a hypocrite about it. And you were the only one in it. That's amazing!"

"There's something more amazing, Cassandra. Where did I get the idea for those moral commandments? Where did I get a conscience? Why do I know about a moral standard that I cannot keep? Animals aren't like that. They keep all their standards just fine. Maybe I got them from God, and maybe I got them from nature, but either way, I know I'm a sinner, Cassandra. Even if there is no God, I am full of evil thoughts and deeds against people. And if there is a God, then I have committed grievous thoughts and deeds against Him. The difference is, if there is a God, then I need to repent to Him. So the discussion about God's existence is not just academic for me."

"I'm sorry, Jack, I didn't know that. But let me pursue one point. You said that your moral standard could have come from nature or God. But if it came from nature, then the less complex produced the more complex, and that's contrary to all observations in the natural world. Right?"

"That seems to be true. But you are asking me to accept the existence of the supernatural, and I can't find any evidence for the supernatural."

"But I am not asking you to accept the mystical, or hocus pocus, or magical nonsense. What we call supernatural would be natural for God. You're ability to fly an airplane, use a computer, a GPS, or read a book, for that matter, would be supernatural to a dog. The supernatural is natural for a higher being."

"It is still different because the natural world can be observed. God and miracles cannot," Jack declared.

"It seems to me, anyway, we are forced beyond the natural world. The natural world does not create, yet it exists with a lot of pretty complex stuff going on. Since it does not create, it could not create itself. So it had to come from somewhere outside of itself."

"Couldn't the universe itself be eternal?"

"The laws of thermodynamics prove that the natural world could not be eternal because it is gradually slowing down, getting cold, and dying. It's deteriorating, not creating. As I'm sure you know, Jack, the first law says the amount of energy in the universe is constant. The second law says energy is becoming increasingly useless. So if you back up in time, you eventually come to a place where the amount of useful energy is greater than the total amount of energy, and that's impossible. You can't have more than there is. So there is no possibility that the universe existed forever."

"What's your take on the 'Big Bang Theory,' Cassandra?"

"With the 'Big Bang Theory' you have the problem of where the stuff came from that went 'bang' and how impersonal stuff became personal and moral all by itself. What you end up doing is believing really unreasonable things just to avoid

105

believing in a personal, moral Creator. The answer is simple, Jack. *In the beginning God created the heavens and the earth."*

Chapter 39

Tuesday, May 24
North Platte, Nebraska

The rain clouds underneath them thinned out a bit. They made one fuel, food, and potty stop enroute. When they finally arrived in North Platte, it was 6:20 P.M. Jack's friend, a man named John Styles, picked them up, gave them a tour of his farm, then introduced them to his wife Susan and their two sons, Billy age 5 and Joshua age 7. John took them to the gun range and invited them to shoot whenever they liked. But, by the time they had supper, it was getting late, so Jack and Cassy decided to just take a late evening walk, watch the sun set, and go shooting in the morning.

They found a large, lonely tree on a hill, where they could sit and watch the light drain from the western sky. Their conversation had been casual—observations about the farm mostly, the animals, the fields, the trees, the large turtle they saw in a creek. But now they sat silently, facing west, with their backs up against a large oak tree. The fingers of Jack's right hand and Cassy's left hand found each other and got tangled together again.

"'Blockhead,' huh?"

Cassy giggled a little. "Okay, well, maybe that was a bit much."

"Isn't that what Lucy calls Charlie Brown?"

" I think so."

"So, does that mean I'm a Charlie Brown, or that you're a Lucy?"

"I guess I have been sort of a Lucy, haven't I?"

"Actually, Cassandra, you are the first person I have ever known who did not accept me for who I am."

"Your mother seems to want to change you."

"Not really. She'd like me to be a good Catholic boy, but other than that, she's not trying to change me. She loves to complain about me, but, in the end, she accepts me for who I am. She certainly never told me I was a sinner going to hell. And nobody I know would separate from me because of what I

107

believe. But I get the distinct impression you would. I care about you, Cassandra. I want to be with you. I think you feel the same, but I believe you will leave if I don't change my beliefs. That's something new for me."

"Everything you just said is true. I've never met a man before you that I even thought about spending the rest of my life with. And with you, I can't stop thinking about it. But I can't do that with anyone but a Christian, and not a Catholic or a Pentecostal or a Baptist or something. He has to be someone who has actually, personally received Jesus Christ as his Savior. But I really didn't want to tell you that. You just somehow figured it out by yourself."

"Why didn't you want to tell me?"

"Because, Jack, you have to come to believe in God and receive Christ because you believe it, not because of me. I didn't want to tell you because I was afraid you'd just say you believed so we could be together."

"Hopefully, you have come to know me well enough to realize I would never do that. One thing I try to be is honest."

"Was that one of your religion's commandments?"

"Yes."

"Did you keep that one?"

"Not always. But I know I should, and that makes me a sinner. Anyway, you have my word on this, Cassandra. I will honestly consider the truth of what you have said."

"No, you need to consider the truth of the Bible. What I say is irrelevant."

"Yeah, I know—the truth of the Bible. My point is, as much as I want to be with you, I will not tell you I believe it if I don't. That much I promise you."

As they walked back to the farmhouse, Cassy's head did not leave his shoulder, his arm did not leave her waist, and they said nothing. Cassy didn't know if they would find her family. She didn't know if Jack would ever become a believer. She didn't know if they would be together. She didn't even know if she would ever see him again after this search was over. But one thing she knew for sure. Without any doubt, without any hesitation, without any qualifications, she had fallen head over heals in love with the atheist named Jack Donavan.

Chapter 40

Wednesday, May 25
North Platte, Nebraska

Breakfast was lively, traditional, and early at the Styles' farm. Cassy slept in the downstairs guest room. Jack had taken one of the boys' rooms upstairs. But everybody had to be up and ready for breakfast at 7:00. Pancakes, eggs, sausage with biscuits and gravy were inhaled by the boys and enjoyed by all. After breakfast, Cassy joined in cleaning up the kitchen, and Jack helped John load a wagon with hay bales. Then Jack got out a satchel with his guns and ammunition, collected a plastic bag full of cans and walked with Cassy to the shooting range.

"I carry a Sig .45 caliber semi-automatic," Jack said, beginning his gun lecture even as they walked. "But I think the best gun for you is a 9 millimeter. The 9 mil I have is also a Sig."

"What's a Sig?"

"Sig Sauer. It's the name of the company that makes the gun."

"Oh."

"I also have a Smith and Wesson .357 magnum revolver with a five-inch barrel. It's a bit bigger and heaver, but it will also shoot a .38, which I think would work for you. The advantage to the revolver is that it is safer and easier to operate. But in a confrontation, the semi-autos are quicker, easier to reload if you have a loaded clip, and usually easier to carry. I do have a light Smith .38 revolver, which is a great carry gun, but it beats up your wrist to shoot it. It's great if you are carrying a gun for emergency protection and you never plan to actually use it. But if you shoot it much, the recoil will bang up your wrist pretty bad."

"So you are saying that is not good for me?"

"That's right, because I think you will actually have to use it. At least we have to prepare for that. I think you should carry the 9 millimeter Sig, but I want you to also feel comfortable with the Smith and Wesson revolver."

The shooting range was wedged between three small man-made hills, one on either side and one at the end. They took the cans out of the bag and set them up in a row at the base of the downrange hill. Then Jack explained the basic rules for using a handgun. "First of all, never point a gun in a dangerous direction. Don't point it at someone else or at yourself. Don't point it at, say, your leg or your foot. A gun should never be pointed at anything you do not intend to shoot. A good stance is to hold a gun about 30 degrees up from the ground. Always hold a gun low and come up on your target. Don't hold it high. You are more vulnerable when you hold your gun high, and you are blocking your own vision. You have more control coming up on your target. And there are documented cases of people who have accidentally shot themselves in the head by holding a loaded gun up under their chin."

"Oh, my!"

"Second rule," Jack continued. "Never put your finger on the trigger of a gun until you are ready to shoot. Since you are righthanded, hold the gun in your right hand with your point finger up alongside of the barrel. Only bring it down to the trigger when you are ready to fire. Be sure you keep both hands below the slide because on a semi-auto, the slide comes flying back as it ejects the shell, and it will cut your hand, sure as the world, if it's sticking up in the way. Then wrap your left hand around, in front of, and a bit below your right. When you shoot, do a slight push-pull action. Push with your right hand and pull with your left. That will keep the gun from jerking up with the recoil and make your shot more accurate. The third rule is to never load a gun until it is ready for use. But 'use' does not necessarily mean ready to shoot. If you are carrying a gun for protection, that gun is in use. And when we begin looking for kidnappers, we will be carrying loaded guns."

It was all a bit overwhelming for Cassy, but after a little work, she was handling the 9-millimeter correctly. Then she actually had to shoot it. Jack handed her some earmuffs and safety glasses. "We won't have the advantage of this ear and eye protection in actual combat situations, of course, but if somebody is shooting at you, you'll have bigger problems to deal with. Today, we need to wear these because I want you to shoot long enough to feel comfortable with the gun."

Jack fired his .45 first to demonstrate the correct stance and let her hear the muffled blast and see the recoil. "On a Sig, once the loaded clip is in, pull the slide back and release it. Don't ease it forward or you will confuse the loading mechanism. Just let it fly forward on its own. The spring is designed to enter a bullet into the barrel."

"What's this little lever do?"

"That releases the trigger and the hammer so that it will shoot like a revolver. You can then either cock the hammer or you have a long pull on the trigger. But what you have to keep in mind on this Sig is that after the first pull, all the rest of them are short pulls with a rapid-fire sequence. In other words, after the first shot, you have a hair trigger, bang, bang, bang, bang."

Cassy went through the loading process and shot. "Wow, that really kicks."

"I watched the gun snap up on you. Add a little more push-pull pressure, and it will cure that. And remember, since you fired once, you now have a hair trigger. She shot again. Even though she was warned, it surprised her that the gun fired by just touching the trigger. She emptied the clip without hitting any cans. The next clip she hit a can. But it wasn't the one she was aiming at. "My guess is you hit the can to the left of the one you aimed at."

"Yes, how'd you know that?"

"Most right-hand shooters pull a gun to the left. You don't even realize you are doing it, but as you squeeze the trigger, you tend to pull the gun ever so slightly to the left. Look, it's not important that you become real accurate. The point is to be able to handle the gun, be familiar with it, know how to load a clip, slide a clip into the chamber, and discharge it in the direction you want without shooting yourself, or me. You should be able to use it without it surprising you."

Cassy hung in there and kept trying until she could go through the whole process of loading, shooting, and reloading. She was even able to hit the can she was aiming at about every other shot. Jack made her shoot the .357 Smith and Wesson revolver, too, just so she would be familiar with a revolver.

"Sometimes in a firefight, you might end up using your ene-my's gun," he said, "and it might be a revolver."

Chapter 41

Wednesday, May 25
Between North Platte, Nebraska
and Carlsbad, New Mexico

By late morning, Jack and Cassy were on their way. The Styles asked them to stay for lunch, but Jack wanted to be sure they made it to Carlsbad before nightfall, so they left around 11:00. The rain had all passed and the sky was clear. They could see for miles. The Cessna seemed to climb eagerly into the clear air to 6,500 feet, their VFR cruising altitude to Carlsbad.

When they were back on autopilot, Jack reached over and put his hand on top of Cassy's. Their fingers tangled together once again. "You want to talk about it?" he said.

"About what?"

"You know, God and stuff?"

"Well, actually, I do have one more question for you, but I don't want to be a Lucy."

Jack chuckled a bit. "Ask me. You're no Lucy."

"Here is a multiple-choice quiz.

A. You don't believe in God.
B. You think God may exist by the preponderance of the evidence, as in a civil case. Or
C. You think God exists beyond reasonable doubt, as in a criminal case."

"Well, it's not D. God exists beyond any doubt."

"Well, of course not. Don't be silly, Jack. No one can say that, this side of heaven. For reasons all His own, God has chosen to remain invisible. The author of Hebrews says *without faith it is impossible to please Him.* Certainty is the culmination of faith, not the beginning of it. So don't set up an unreasonable standard. Now what about my options?"

"I would have to say you have moved me from A. to at least B. The preponderance of the evidence would indicate that the existence of God is certainly possible. But even if God does exist, that does not lead to the eternality of the human soul. And it's the eternality of the soul about which you, and every religion on earth, are concerned."

"We have discussed the existence of God from nature and our conscience. The third evidence is the reliability of the Bible. And that's where we find the eternality of the soul. Just read the Bible, Jack. It does not read like religious literature. And Christianity is not like any other religion. The Koran, the Gita, the sayings of Confucius and Buddha, they are all just somebody's ideas. One guy claiming he had a revelation from God or an angel or the universe or something. You have to accept them by blind faith. On the other hand, the Bible is written by 40 authors over 1600 years. It is full of real historically and archeologically verifiable people, places, and events. Take, for example, the writings of the physician Luke. His books, the gospel of Luke and the book of Acts, are full of people, places, and events. They are vulnerable books in that they could be easily disproven. Yet not one detail in Luke or Acts can be demonstrated to be in error. Also, the message of the Bible is completely different than any world religion. It says: *by grace you have been saved through faith; and that not of yourselves, it is the gift of God; not as a result of works, that no one should boast.* No other religion says the Son of God took on humanity and died for their sins. Religions all have a works system to offset your sins, like balancing your good deeds against your sins on a scale. The Bible says you have to get rid of your sins, not just offset them with good deeds. Oh, dear, I'm sorry. I'm preaching. I'm sounding like Lucy again."

Jack smiled. "No, Cassandra, you're just interested in me. I understand that. But it's up to me now. The last two nights I read the Gospels of Matthew and Mark again. Tonight, I'll read more. I'll continue through the New Testament. I told you I read the Bible four times, but it's been years ago. I'm reading the New Testament again. I appreciate your help and concern. But it's up to me now. From now on, we'll have to concentrate on finding your father and brother."

"Yes, I know, I … know." She looked in his eyes and realized she was being dismissed. She wanted to do more, make more arguments, answer more questions, be part of his thoughts. But that was over. He had heard her and was politely dismissing her. He wanted to think about it himself, and that meant Cassy had to leave it up to God to convict him, and Jack to believe.

She leaned over, put her hand on the back of his neck, then brushed his hair lightly with her fingers. He looked at her and their eyes became intimate with each other like they did that night in the cabin. But then it was like they both knew that their love could not proceed. There was an impassable barrier. God stood between them. They just held hands and said nothing until they began the approach to the Cavern City Airport in Carlsbad, New Mexico.

Chapter 42

Wednesday, May 25
Carlsbad, New Mexico

Jack taxied to the local FBO (fixed base operator) at the Carlsbad Cavern City Airport and arranged for the Cessna to be hangared. Then they went to the public terminal and rented a 4-wheel drive Ford Expedition. It was too late for exploring, so they got two rooms in a nice hotel. They unpacked their bags, and Jack made reservations at a restaurant for dinner.

As they were driving to the restaurant, Cassy's cell phone rang. She looked at it and said, "I need to get this. It's my friend Abby. She's called three times since we left North Platte."

"Sure, go ahead."

"Is there anything she shouldn't know?"

"Probably a good idea not to mention the guns. Otherwise, no problem."

"Okay." So Cassy pushed 'Answer'. "Hi, Abby."

"Where you been, girl? I've been calling you for days."

"Actually, it's been three hours."

"Whatever. Where are you? What's happening?"

"We just arrived in Carlsbad, rented a car, and got a hotel."

"Are you in the same room?"

"No."

"The same suite?"

"Abby!"

"Well?"

"No."

"He's right there next to you, isn't he?"

"Yes. We're on the way to a restaurant for dinner."

"Look at him for me. Is he as gorgeous as his picture?"

"Abby, will you stop!"

"Well?"

"Okay, yes."

"Let me talk to him."

"No. Are you crazy? There's no way."

"Why? Don't you trust me?"

116

"No. I certainly do not."

"Cassy, he's practically family. I'm your best friend and he's your best guy. Actually, I'm your only friend and he's your only guy. So, just let me say 'Hi.'"

"No."

"Come on. I need to meet this guy. You'll have to introduce me sooner or later."

"I'll take later."

"Let me at least meet him, just to say 'Hello.'"

"Oh…all right, but don't say anything crude."

Cassy turned to Jack and said, "My friend Abby would like to say hello, but I need to warn you she's not from this planet. She is the only actual evidence we have for life from outer space, WAY OUT IN OUTER SPACE." Then she passed the phone to Jack.

While steering with his left hand, he took the phone with his right. "Hello, this is Jack."

"Well, hi there, handsome. Cassy says you are as gorgeous as this picture she sent me of you."

"She sent you a picture of me?"

Jack looked over at Cassy, who grimaced and sheepishly said, "Sorry, she wanted to know what you looked like."

"Ooopsee," Abby continued, "She didn't tell you that, I guess. Anyway, thanks for talking. I just wanted to say that you've got the best girl in the whole world there. I'm serious, Jack. Nobody would believe there is anybody as sweet and sincere and honest and smart and beautiful as her left in the world."

"I'll go along with that."

"Good. Now, what do you say we have some fun?"

"What did you have in mind?"

[Then the following conversation took place. And, of course, Cassy could only hear Jack's side of it.]

Abby: "Okay, Jack. Say, 'Really, how often does she do that?'"

Jack: "Really, how often does she do that?"

Cassy: "Do what? What did she say I do?"

117

Abby: "Say, 'With all the guys she dates?'"

Jack: "With all the guys she dates?"

Cassy: "What!?! What did she tell you? Give me that phone!"

Cassy reached for the phone, but Jack, grinning from ear to ear, switched it to his left hand and put it up to his left ear. When he did, he could hear Abby laughing so hard she could hardly talk. But she managed to continue.

Abby: "Now say: 'She wears what to bed?'"

Jack: "She wears what to bed?"

Cassy: "What! Jack Donavan, you give me that phone right now."

Abby: [Now laughing hysterically] "Say, 'Every night?'"

Jack: "Every night?"

Cassy: "Jack, you give me that..."

Then Cassy unbuckled her seatbelt and crawled over top of his head reaching and wrestling with him, struggling, even blocking his view of the road, until she got her hands on "... that phone." Then she put it to her ear and said, "Bye, Abby." But all she heard was laughing. Then she clicked off the phone, looked at Jack and demanded— "What did she tell you, Jack?"

Jack just smiled and did the zipper sign across his lips.

Chapter 43

Wednesday–Thursday, May 25-26
Near Carlsbad Caverns, New Mexico

That evening they watched an old movie on TV. Most of the time, Cassy had her head on Jack's shoulder or he had his arm around her, or both. They joked about some of the movie lines and ate popcorn. They kissed only briefly before Cassy went to bed. Jack stayed up until he read the entire gospel of Luke.

The next morning, they went out for breakfast. Then they began the arduous task of driving up and down the National Parks Highway. They showed the pictures of William and Michael McMurray to every establishment along the road. They stopped at the gas station that issued the only credit card receipt they had, but no one recognized the McMurrays. They were hoping for some response—someone who would recognize them, someone who would get nervous when they showed their pictures, maybe even follow them, or do anything that looked suspicious.

Nothing.

Next, they began showing the picture on the same highway heading northeast between the airport and Carlsbad. This was harder and even more discouraging because there were more public establishments, but no one knew anything about the McMurrays. At 1:00 P.M. they stopped for lunch. "This just isn't working, Jack," Cassy's voice was full of defeat.

"You're right. After lunch, we'll play our other card. We'll go look up the building supply address that's on the receipts from the wallet."

"That sounds like a long shot, too."

"Yeah, I know." Jack took Cassy's hand and kissed it lightly. "Since we know they bought gas between the airport and the National Park, they had to be in that area. I was hoping someone would recognize them, or give us some clue, anything that would lead us one step further. The next thing is to try the building supply place."

After lunch, they put the address into the Expedition's GPS, which led them to a location just outside Carlsbad called

Johnson's Lumber and Building Supplies. They went to the customer service desk. A lady in her thirties said, "Can I help you folks?"

"I hope so," Jack answered. "We have this copy of a receipt from an order purchased here a month ago. Can you tell from this order who helped this customer?"

"Well, let's see. Yes, here is the code for the salesman, #4592. That's George Mendez. He's out back. I'll call him." In a few minutes, a young, thin man in his mid-twenties, wearing glasses, with a pencil stuck behind his right ear, appeared at the desk.

"I'm George. What can I do for you?"

"George, we really need your help. My name is Jack Donavan, and this is Cassandra McMurray. This might sound a little crazy, but we suspect her father and brother have been kidnapped and taken somewhere between here and the National Park. We have reason to believe their kidnappers bought these supplies here. We are really hoping you can help us locate them."

"You guys cops, private investigators, or what?"

"No, no. For some reason, the cops are dragging their feet on this. As I said, she is a relative, and I'm just a friend helping her out. We are really desperate for any help you can give us."

George Mendez checked his computer. "Well, they gave us several big orders, but they never said where they were taking them."

"And you didn't deliver any of the supplies?"

"No. They picked them all up themselves. It took them several trips, too. They only had a four-wheel-drive pick-up truck."

"Do you have a copy of the complete invoice listing everything they bought?"

"Let's see, I have a total here. It must have been quite an order. It came to $82,294.49."

"We should have the complete order in the computer… Yeah, here it is. Hmmm, that's interesting."

"What?"

"Well, there's lots of concrete, metal studs, flooring material, material for inside walls, drywall, paneling, carpeting, even wiring, heating, air conditioning, and lighting fixtures."

"What's so interesting about that?"

"Well, nothing, except there are no external materials. There's nothing for outside walls or roofing. There's no timbers, plywood, felt, or shingles. It seems they were rebuilding a huge basement. Of course, they could have gotten the roofing supplies somewhere else, but I doubt it. We are basically the only dealer in the area. I'd say they were remodeling something which already has a roof and walls around it."

"Thanks, George, that's very helpful. Do you remember the names of any of them? They would probably use fake names on the orders, but they may have called each other by their real names. Do you remember anything like that?"

"Umm…I'm not sure, but one guy was obviously the boss. He looked like a drill sergeant from the Marines. A chunky guy, all muscle, no neck. Had a short haircut, like a flat top. I think one guy called him Mitt, or Max, or Mack, or something like that."

Jack thanked him for his help, and they left the store. On their way out, Cassy seemed to be even more depressed. "If they were building a basement somewhere, we could look forever and not find them. It could be any of these warehouses along the National Parks Highway or on all those roads leading off into the hills. There is no way we can check out all that."

"They're not building or remodeling a basement."

"Why? How do you know?"

"No basement requires that much concrete."

"So what are they doing?"

"It's a cave. They remodeled the inside of a cave. The area North of Carlsbad Caverns National Park has to be full of small, unattractive caves the National Park is not interested in. Our kidnappers have remodeled the inside of one of those caves and are using it for their prescription drug scam. I'm sure your father and brother are in that cave."

Chapter 44

"Let's go flying," Jack suggested. "Let's get the Cessna out and take pictures of the whole area north of Carlsbad Caverns and west of the National Parks Highway. There has to be caves in there that the National Park is not interested in because they are too small or ugly for tourists, yet perfect for our prescription drug terrorists."

"Actually, there are over 100 caves within the park, and they are some of the longest in the world. Remember, Jack, I'm almost a geologist. You are in my world now."

"Good, talk to me."

"Well, the caves are currently being formed by sulfuric acid mixing itself with surface water. The rock here is mostly limestone and the caves are formed when surface water flows down through cracks in the limestone and slowly enlarges the passageways. So these caves are usually very wet and have streams, rivers, and sometimes lakes or waterfalls in them. But what most evolutionists can't explain is that the caves are full of ocean fossils, like from salt-water creatures. How did salt-water fossils get to New Mexico? Of course, they say that happened millions of years ago, but the fossils are stone, so there is no way to carbon date them. Carbon dating only accurately goes back a few thousand years anyway, so their dates are based strictly on their blind faith theory of evolution. It makes more sense to say it happened during the flood at the time of Noah. A global deluge would force tons of water through the limestone, carve out the majority of the caves in short order, leaving the sea creatures behind to be fossilized into the rock. The rest of their structure was probably carved out slowly over the next, maybe, two thousand years. Once the water subsided, the slow processes we now observe would begin to form the features we see on the cave surfaces."

"So it would be easy to set up a laboratory in one of these caves with running water for bathing and toilets. Could you drink the water?"

"Yeah, you'd probably want to filter it a bit, but that's pretty easy to do these days."

"Seems to me they found the perfect place to set up a secret lab. Let's go have a look."

So they went to the airport and got the Cessna 180 out of the hangar. Jack topped off the tanks, and they began to fly. They covered the area at 1000 feet AGL (above ground level), like they were spraying blueberries. They flew from east to west, starting on the south side of the large triangle of land that extended north from the National Park. Then they turned around and flew back east, then back west again over and over until they had crisscrossed the whole area. All the while, Cassy took pictures on her iPhone, logging every inch of the terrain.

It was about two hours before they returned the 180 to the hangar and got some supper. Then they synced all the pictures to Jack's computer and began studying. "What are we looking for exactly?" Cassy wondered.

"Anything unusual. Maybe a trail that deadends into a mountain, maybe the side of a rock that looks fake or manmade or camouflaged, maybe a suspicious trail, or some vehicle in a strange place."

They looked for almost an hour, with their heads close together staring at the screen. At one point, Cassy kissed him on the cheek. Jack turned and their eyes held for a long time. Then he lifted a wave of hair that had fallen across her eye and laid it on her back. But he didn't let go. He grabbed a larger handful of it and pulled her lips to his.

She slipped her arms around his neck and leaned into him. Reality faded. Then it disappeared altogether. When their lips finally separated, Cassy said, "Could you, like, maybe, just remind me where we are. And...while you're at it, what's my name again?"

Jack chuckled a little. She laid her head on his shoulder. After a few minutes, he said, "Cassandra."

"Hmm?"

"Cassandra. Your name is Cassandra."

"Oh, yeah, that was it. Thanks."

It was another 15 minutes before they recovered and were able to start looking at photos again.

For another two hours they studied the pictures of the terrain. The whole place looked like it could be honeycombed with small caves. But they located five places that merited a closer look. One was a two-track trail that seemed to end abruptly. One was a strange, artificial looking cliff, and three of them were trails that ended into the side of a hill. Then they circled those places on an aviation sectional chart.

"How are we going to get in there, Jack? That place is full of rocks the size of Chevys and sharp ravines we couldn't possibly drive across. We couldn't even get a 4-wheel drive SUV in there. And the Cessna goes too fast to get a closer look at any of it."

"Remember my other idea? I think we should go exploring in an ultralight aircraft."

"Where are you going to find one of those?"

"I checked Trade-A-Plane on-line. They are the biggest movers of aircraft. There is a two-place Quicksilver ultralight for sale at a small airport very near the National Park. It's just south of a town called Whites City."

The next morning, Jack called the owner of the Quicksilver and arranged to meet him at 9:00 on the airfield. He told Cassy to wear her jeans and a long-sleeve shirt, even though the temperature was slated to be over 90 by mid-day. They got breakfast on the way and headed down to the small airport near Whites City. The owner was in his 70s. With wrinkled skin, a deep tan, and slits for eyes, he looked like he grew up in the desert. He took them to an old hangar and peeled a dusty clear plastic cover off of a pretty nice looking two-place Quicksilver.

"$8,000, not a penny less," the owner mandated.

"Actually, I just need it for a few hours. I am a bush pilot from Winnipeg, and I have some time in a Quicksilver. I was wondering if I could rent it for a few hours," Jack requested.

"Oh, that could probably be arranged. $100 an hour."

"That's a bit much for an ultralight, but okay, I'll do that."

"You also have to leave a security deposit."

"Okay, how much is that?"

"$8,000."

Chapter 45

He wouldn't take a check. So Jack and Cassy had to drive back into Carlsbad and withdraw the cash, using Jack's MasterCard. Then they drove back to the small sod strip and paid the $8,000 "Security Deposit."

Jack gave the Quicksilver a thorough pre-flight inspection, filled it with gas, and made three takeoffs and landings by himself. Cassy did not like the idea of staying on the ground and watching as he made the landings without her. But Jack explained that this Quicksilver aircraft was not strictly speaking an ultralight. "Legal" ultralights do not require a pilot's license to fly them. But legal ultralights can carry no passengers and have restricted weight, fuel, and engine capacity, all of which were exceeded by this Quicksilver. This was actually a two-place light sport aircraft, which was registered with an "N" number on the tail, and it required a pilot with a license to fly it. As with any registered aircraft, a pilot has to make at least three full-stop landings every 90 days in order to legally carry passengers. So Jack was making his three landings, while Cassy watched from the ground.

She trusted him now without hesitation, but she still felt better when he taxied the small aircraft back to the hangar after his third landing. He shut down the engine and topped off the fuel tank. Then he took Cassy back to the car and said, "Load your gun, put it in the holster, and clip it to your belt. Then put another loaded clip in your pocket."

"Do you really think that's necessary? I mean, we're just going for a ride in a really small airplane, right?"

"We are looking for bad guys, and if we find them, they won't like it. It's like looking for a wasp's nest. It's only dangerous if you find it. And we are trying to find it. And if we do, it could get nasty. So load that gun and strap it on. Got it?"

"Okay, okay, I got it."

They loaded themselves, their guns, and their map, into the small cabin of the Quicksilver. Cassy climbed in behind Jack, put on her shoulder harness and her headset, then zipped up the clear plastic door. It was snug but not uncomfortable. The engine started with a high-pitched sound very different from the Cessna or the Beaver. As they taxied out, Jack went over a checklist and made sure Cassy was ready and strapped in. They lifted off in less than 100 feet and quickly gained altitude. But Jack leveled off at only 300 feet AGL.

"You doing all right back there?" Jack inquired.

"Yeah, I guess. This thing is really slow, and loud."

"It's supposed to be slow. That's the whole point, and remember, we have the same headsets from the Cessna, so if you haven't pushed your noise canceling button, do that."

"Oh, yeah, I forgot…oh, that's better."

"Now get out your map and tell me where those spots are."

"Well, let's see. Aaa…first head about 10 degrees east of north. That should take us over the place where the two-track trail ended abruptly. It's not far past the National Park, so you should be on it real soon. There. I think that's it on your right. See it?"

"Oh, yes. There it is. Well, it looks like somebody loaded some stuff from wheeled vehicles to horses or mules or something. But whatever, there is no one here now and no place nearby where they could be holed up. Let's move on."

"All right. The next site is due west of here, maybe three miles. It's that flat looking rock we thought might be manmade." They flew for a few minutes, then Cassy continued her directions. "It should be just ahead now. Do you see any flat rock surfaces? Oh, I think I see it just ahead and to the right. See it?"

"Yes, I see it. But it looks pretty natural to me. You have it just off your right now. What do you think?"

"Yeah, that's just a rock. Okay. The next one is north about five miles. If you follow that valley on your right, it should take you to it." They flew north for maybe five minutes. "There it is, Jack. See where it looks like a trail ends right into that hill or mountain, or whatever it is?"

"I'll circle down and get in closer. That really looks suspicious."

"Whoa! What was that! JACK, I'M COVERED WITH GASOLINE."

"SOMEBODY SHOT A HOLE IN THE TANK!"

Chapter 46

Friday, May 27
Near Carlsbad Caverns, New Mexico

"Are you all right? Did you get hit?"

"No, I'm okay. I'm just covered with gasoline."

"Yeah, the gage says the tank is almost empty. We have to land."

"Land! Jack, there is nothing but rocks, rocks, and bigger rocks down there, unless you count that ravine over there, which would tear us up for sure."

"I'll try to find some flatter spot, but…" Just then a shotgun blast splattered the fabric on the tail and a rifle bullet penetrated the instrument panel. "Sorry, we're going in now. Make sure your harness is tight and grab hold of the frame."

Jack slowed the Quicksilver to near stall speed and touched the ground under 30 miles an hour. The small aircraft skidded across the rough terrain for about 20 yards, then it hit a rock too big to negotiate, and flipped over forward, the tail burying itself in the dust, leaving Jack and Cassy hanging upside down from their belts.

"You okay?"

"I think so."

"Release your belt and get out. We need to get to cover— like, right now." Cassy bumped her head when the harness was released, but she managed to keep her wits about her and unzip the door. As her arm reached outside the upside-down cockpit, Jack grabbed it and unceremoniously pulled her from the plane.

"We'll head for that big rock over there, the one that's about eight feet high." They scrambled and stumbled as they ran hand-in-hand, but they made it behind the rock. Just then another shot hit the Quicksilver, causing what was left of it to explode in a ball of fire. "Well," Jack said as they both panted to catch their breath, "I'd say we found them."

"Now that's what I'd call having a firm grasp of the obvious."

"Get your gun out and slide a bullet in the barrel, we are going to have to shoot our way out of this." Bullets began to ricochet off their rock. Jack, his .45 Sig in hand, kept peeking out to find a target, but they were pretty well dug in. What bothered him the most was, the direction of the shelling was changing. Slowly, the snipers were spreading out and surrounding them. "They are trying to get all the way around us so we have no cover. I'm going over to that rock over there behind us. That way I can cover you from an eastern attack and you can cover me if they come from the west. Remember, if you get a shot, don't try to wound them. Center mass. Shoot center mass, got it?" Cassy nodded nervously.

Jack ran quickly to the rock behind them. That drew fire from a sniper on the north. Jack hugged the south side of his rock and noticed a dark spot, which he guessed was a gunman's shoulder. He took his time, steadied the .45 on the rock, and fired. There was a sudden scream and a rifle came flying out from behind the rock and landed in the dirt between them. Cassy gave him a thumbs-up from her rock about 10 yards away.

But the shelling continued. And it continued to change direction. Slowly, cautiously, the snipers were surrounding them. Jack was facing east now toward Cassy, and she was facing west toward Jack. Every so often they could see a brief movement as the shooters changed rocks, but the target was gone before they could get a shot.

Then one of them made a mistake. While trying to move to a position further behind Jack, one of the snipers stumbled and fell into the open. Cassy had a clear view of him. She took time to aim at his chest and fired. Then again. And again. The first two missed but the third 9 millimeter hollow point hit the man in the neck and blew a hole behind his head that sprayed blood in every direction. He grabbed his neck and tried to stand, but he only made two steps before his knees buckled and he fell face forward in the dirt.

That brought a firestorm of shelling from all directions. A man appeared behind Cassy's rock, coming quickly forward. Jack had no time to aim. He simply raised his gun and pulled the trigger. His shot went left of target and the man opened fire. Two bullets hit the rock beside Jack and the third one went through his arm, knocking him to the ground. Seeing this,

129

Cassy stepped into the open and fired at the sniper. This surprised him. Before he could get his gun trained on her, she emptied her clip at him. Most missed, but two shots hit him in the chest. The man fell backwards. As Cassy reached in her pocket for the other clip, she felt the touch of hot steel pressing against her cheek. A male voice said, "Drop it, honey." She let the gun fall to the ground and immediately looked over at Jack.

"How bad is it?" she asked, as Jack was being pulled to his feet with a gun jammed into his ribs. "It's okay. The bullet went through my arm."

"He's bleeding, you moron," Cassy addressed the man dragging Jack away. "He needs that..." then a sharp pain in the back of her head rendered her unconscious.

A few minutes later, a small trackhoe emerged from the painted door opening to the cave. Within fifteen minutes, the machine had dug a hole, scraped the remains of the ultralight into the shallow grave, and smoothed over the surface. Then it lifted several rocks over the site and returned to the cave, leaving no trace of the crash.

Chapter 47

Friday, May 27
Near Carlsbad Caverns, New Mexico

Cassy woke up with a splitting headache, laying on a couch, looking up at her brother. She groaned, rubbed a growing bump on the back of her head, then gradually opened her eyes. "Michael!" She reached up and hugged his head with both arms.

"Hi, Sis. You've been out for half an hour. How do you feel?"

"My head feels like it was hit with a sledge hammer. Other than that, I seem to be all right. Where am I? What is this place? Where is Dad? Is he okay? And Jack, where is Jack?"

"Slow down, Sis. You've had quite a blow on your head. You are in the room Dad and I have lived in for about two weeks now. Dad is still healthy. And I don't know anyone named Jack."

"Yes, you do. He's the man who flew you to your cabin in Manitoba, Canada."

"Mr. Donavan? What's he doing here?"

"It's a long story, but first, are you sure Dad is all right?"

"He was when they came for him this morning. They let him eat breakfast here, then they take him to work in the drug lab. They bring him back for lunch and in the evening. We eat and sleep here. Then in the morning, they take him back to the lab again. That's been going on for two weeks."

"What is this room? Like a furnished prison cell?"

"That's exactly what it is. I'm in here all day and night except for two hours a day when they let me work out in something like an exercise room. I guess it's for the guards. There is not much in it. Some weights, a treadmill, a punching bag, and some mats for calisthenics. Here I have a television and some books, but that's it. Oh, and by the way, this room is bugged. They are monitoring everything we say, and there are several cameras that watch our every move."

"Do you know what Dad is doing?"

"Not specifically. He's mixing prescription drugs with just enough poison to make people sick without killing them.

That's all I know. I'm basically held hostage to force him to keep working for them. Now they have you, too. What are you doing here, anyway? How'd you get here?"

"We came here to find you and Dad. When Mom couldn't reach you on the cell phone, we got worried. I went to Winnipeg to join Jack, Mr. Donavan, to try and find you. We went to the cabin and discovered a bunch of phony bear tracks, so we knew you'd been kidnapped. Then we found a wallet with a receipt in it that led us to a building supply in Carlsbad, New Mexico that gave us clues that finally led us here."

"Wow, you found my wallet?"

"What do you mean, 'your wallet'?"

"I lifted it off one off one of the kidnappers. I picked his pocket."

"I didn't know you could do that."

"Something I learned in college."

"So that's what you learned in college!"

"Yeah, that's what Dad said. But it turned out to be helpful, I think. Anyway, I didn't know what to do with the wallet so I dropped it in the water by the dock. I figured somebody would drag the lake sooner or later."

"Well, good job, Michael. That wallet led us here."

"How did you find us? I don't even know how we got here or where we are, until now. We're near Carlsbad, huh? We were drugged and we just woke up here. I knew it was a remote place because I heard them talking about bringing in supplies on horses and flying things in with a chopper. It doesn't sound like you could drive in here."

"Jack, Mr. Donavan, rented a small ultralight-type airplane, and we flew in looking for you, but they shot us down."

"Then they hit you on the head?"

"Yeah, well, not before we had a huge gunfight. You couldn't hear that in here?"

"Not really, I thought I heard some... A gunfight! You were in a gunfight?"

"Actually, I killed two of them."

"WHAT! You killed somebody?"

"Two somebodies, actually."

"Oh, no. We're dead."

Chapter 48

Friday, May 27
Near Carlsbad Caverns, New Mexico

Jack was secured with zip ties and wrestled into a small but well-furnished office. Then he was tie-wrapped to a chair. A guard stayed in the room while a stocky man with no neck came in and seated himself behind the desk. He opened a wallet, which had been taken off of Jack, and began to sift through the various cards.

"Your name appears to be Jack Donavan. Is that right?"

"Uh huh."

"And you are a pilot, and you have several credit cards, and well, this is interesting, you have a concealed pistol carry permit. I wonder. Why would a pilot need to carry a concealed weapon? Here's the thing, Mr. Donavan. You and your woman are going to die. I'm sure you are aware of that. The only question is how you will die. What I need is information. I need to know why you killed two of my men and wounded two others. I need to know who you work for, how you found this place, and why you are here. I need to know who knows about us. And you are going to tell us."

"We came for the professor and his son. We don't care what you are doing here. We just wanted to find William and Michael McMurray. But you shot us out of the sky. Your guys started shooting at us. All we did is defend ourselves."

"What you did is not the issue here, Mr. Donavan. I'm not here to judge you. I'm going to get information from you, then exterminate you."

"I'll tell you everything I know. We don't work for anybody. The girl you knocked out is the daughter of the professor. I'm here to help her find her father. That's all there is to it."

"No, Mr. Donavan. That's not all there is to it. And you will tell me what I want to know. As you can imagine, we are really good at extracting information. I suspect you have more than a casual relationship with the daughter. So I will deal with her and let you watch until you decide to cooperate."

"Don't touch her! I already told you I'd tell you everything I know."

"Oh, we won't touch her, Mr. Donavan. I don't let my men get involved with rape or molesting women. It's not good for them. They know, if they touch her, I'll take them out and shoot them myself. I have far better ways than that."

"What are you going to do?"

"Do you have any experience with fire ants, Mr. Donavan? They are really nasty creatures, especially here in this parched land. Their bite can give a person pain beyond belief. We also have scorpions and spiders that do similar damage. And the little suckers love honey. What I am going to do is stake the pretty lady to the ground. Actually, I know of a fire ant hill nearby. Then we will cover your lady with honey. The ants will crawl into every orifice of her body and drive her insane with burning stings. She will die from it, of course, but she will suffer hours of excruciating pain, maybe even a day of it, before she dies. And whenever you decide to tell me what I want to know, I will shoot her in the head and put her out of her misery. Do we understand each other, Mr. Donavan?"

"Yeah, I got it."

"Good. Now I'm going to put you in the same room with her and her brother and let you think about it for an hour. Talk it over if you like. Then, in exactly one hour, I'll come and get you and see if you are interested in cooperating."

From the moment he was captured and tied, Jack had been looking for some weapon, something, anything, he could use as a means of escape. The only thing he could see was a coffee mug filled with sharpened pencils on Mr. No-Neck's desk. As he was being released from his chair, he leaned over the desk, stumbled, falling to the floor, knocking over the mug of pencils. As he was pulled back to his feet, the no-necked man came over and looked at him, shaking his head. "Now that is one of the oldest tricks I know, Mr. Donavan. I'm disappointed that you thought I would fall for that." Then he turned Jack around and searched his hands, then his shirt, until he found the pencil Jack slid up his sleeve. "But I suppose I can't fault you for trying. See you in an hour, Mr. Donavan."

Chapter 49

Friday, May 27
Near Carlsbad Caverns, New Mexico

Jack was taken to the prison cell room where Michael and Cassy McMurray were being held. His zip ties were cut off. He was pushed into the room, and the door was locked behind him. Cassy ran to him and threw her arms around his neck. They held each other for a few minutes. Then Jack put his hand on her head. "You've got a quite a goose egg growing there. Are you all right?"

"Just an annoying headache. I'll be fine. But Jack, I killed two men. I've never even imagined killing somebody, and I shot two men to death."

"And that's two less that we'll have to kill to get out of here. You did the right thing, Cassandra. You shot in self-defense. We'd both be dead if you hadn't."

"What about your arm?" Then she looked down at it. "Oh my! Your sleeve is full of blood. Come over by the sink. We need to clean and bandage that. They didn't even bandage it. Didn't they realize this would become infected?"

"I don't think they believe I will live long enough to get an infection."

"Well, I do. Let me clean and bandage that. Oh, Michael, you remember Jack?"

"Yes. Hello, Mr. Donavan. I'm sorry we had to meet again under such difficult circumstances. I really appreciate you coming to find us. But I'm afraid our position is quite hopeless."

Cassy instructed her brother to tear a strip of cloth off one of the bed sheets. Then she began cleaning and wrapping Jack's arm. While she worked, Jacked talked, with occasional winces of pain. "The three of us have just become a three-person army, with the single purpose of getting out of here."

"Mr. Donavan, you should know this room is bugged and visually monitored. They can hear and see everything we do."

"Okay, thanks, Michael. Come close. We'll speak softly. I will whisper to you. That will probably make them nervous enough to come get us real soon. Both of you need to understand this very clearly. They will kill us, and your father. Kill or be killed is the absolutely only options we have. Is that clear?" They both nodded. "Mr. No-Neck... "

"Max. His name is Max," Michael interrupted. "They call him Mr. Max."

"Well, Mr. Max plans to torture Cassandra to get me to tell him who I am working for and who else knows about this place."

"But we aren't working for anybody. Nobody even knows we are here."

"You know that, and I know that, but Max will never believe that. He plans to inflict pain on Cassandra until I talk. When I talk, he will stop the torture and simply shoot her in the head. Then he will execute the rest of us, probably the same way. So we have no options but to fight, to kill or be killed. Just make sure that is very clear in your minds. Now, Michael, tell us everything you know about the layout of this place."

"It's pretty simple, really. The whole place is a square. There is a square hallway around a laboratory in the middle where they tamper with the drugs. Father is in there now with two other guys. One they call Rabbi. I never heard the name of the other guy, he looks like a geek from the fifties, but I don't think they have guns. Around the outside of the square hallway there are various rooms—Max's office, living quarters for the guards, and the workout room. There is a small kitchen room, too, but I think they bring in food pretty much all prepared. They must have found a cave with a water source because the guards' rooms all seem to have running water, like this one."

"Talk to us about the rooms outside the square hallway. Tell us what's behind every door."

"I don't know all of them. We are at the far back end of the square and the entrance is opposite us in the center front of the square."

"Take us around the square from our position."

"Okay. To our left is the kitchen, then around the corner are the quarters for the guards. I think there are two to a room. To our right is a storage area, then the workout room, and when you turn the corner, to the left there is another room I've never seen opened, then Max's office. When you turn the last corner, by the cave entrance, there is an area for equipment. They have some sort of tractor or backhoe in there. And then, in front, there is an entrance with both a small door and a large door."

"I knocked over a mug filled with pencils in Max's office hoping to get a weapon, but he found the pencil I stuck up my sleeve."

"Too bad." Cassy seemed deflated.

Then Jack put his lips right in her ear and whispered, "I expected him to look for that one, but he didn't find the one I stuck in my pants." Then, still whispering, he addressed both of them. "This whispering we are doing will probably incite the guards to come any minute. When we hear the latch turn, all three of us need to run toward the door. I will stab the first guy in the eye. That should allow Cassandra to grab his gun. Michael, you grab the second guy and wrap your arms around him until I can get one of their guns and shoot both of them. Hopefully, there will only be two, and we need to kill both of them fast. Then we need to shoot our way out of here."

Chapter 50

Friday, May 27
Near Carlsbad Caverns, New Mexico

The plan seemed to work, at first. Michael looked scared to death, because he was. And this made the guard monitoring the room nervous. So he called Max and reported all the whispering. Max told him to take someone with him, go in now, and bring Donavan and the girl to his office.

When the three prisoners heard the latch turn, they rushed the door. In one continuous move, Jack jerked the door open, dragging the first guard into the room and stabbing him in the eye with the long sharpened pencil. As he was screaming, Cassy grabbed the semi-automatic handgun he was holding and wrestled it away from him. Meanwhile, Jack, still holding the bloody pencil, stabbed the second man in the neck. Michel was on him like a sprung trap. He wrapped his arms around him, trapping his rifle close to his body. Seeing Cassy already had the first guard's gun in hand, Jack unsheathed the handgun from the holster of the second guard and shot him in the head. Michael watched the side of the man's head disappear right in front of his face. Shocked, Michael immediately let go and the guard fell to the floor. As the second guard was falling, Jack turned and shot the first one three times in the chest. Jack picked up the rifle, made sure there was a bullet in the chamber with the safety off. Then he handed it to Michael and said, "Shoot anybody you see that isn't one of us or your father."

"But the men in the lab are unarmed," Cassy reminded him.

"Okay, don't shoot the lab guys, but if there is any doubt, shoot. If you hesitate to shoot somebody with a gun, you'll be dead."

Then they rushed into the hall. Jack told Michael to turn to the left and shoot anything that moved. He turned to the right and put Cassy, armed with the first guard's handgun, in between them. He instructed her to back up whoever encountered gunfire first. But the hall was quiet. There was no gunfire or doors opening or people talking. No sound at all. "Where are they?" Cassy wondered.

138

"Waiting for us to turn the corner, I suspect," Jack said, then added, "let's find out." He walked back into the room and pulled out one of the dead guards. He dragged the body down the hall to the turn, then pushed it out around the corner into the adjoining hall. Immediately, a hail of bullets riddled the body as Jack let it fall to the floor. "Yup, that's where they are. I suspect we'd find the same thing around the other corner."

"So we're trapped here," Michael concluded.

"Let's review our situation," Jack suggested. "We know there are four dead guards. Michael, how many do you think there were altogether?"

"I think there were eight, plus Max, plus the two guys in the lab."

"Yes, that's what I counted, too. And now four of them are dead and two are wounded, although we don't know how severe their wounds are. So, for sure there are two healthy guards, plus Max. That makes it three against three, if the guys in the lab don't have guns."

"Which explains why they haven't rushed us," Cassy added.

"But they still have the advantage in that we are trapped here," Michael repeated. "We are actually sitting ducks. They could force us out with smoke, or tear gas, or chemicals."

"Michael, stop being so negative."

"No, he's right, except, if they had tear gas, they would have used it by now. But Max isn't the patient type. They'll rush us. Michael, stop looking at us. I told you to keep your gun trained on that corner and shoot anything that moves." But it was too late. A hand with a gun came around the corner Michael was supposed to be covering and began shooting. Michael was too slow with the rifle to respond. Hearing no response, the guard stepped into the open and began firing. One bullet hit Michael's rifle and knocked it to the floor. Jack turned on the guard and shot him in the shoulder then again in the chest two times. The guard fell backwards to the floor.

Jack wondered why Cassy didn't fire. She was standing in front of Jack, beside Michael, facing the guard with her gun in her hand, aimed at the guard. But she didn't shoot. She just stood there.

Then she dropped to her knees. Then she fell backwards to the floor with a stream of blood running out of her belly.

Chapter 51

Friday, May 27
Near Carlsbad Caverns, New Mexico

Jack grabbed Michael by the arm and dragged him down over his sister, who lay bleeding profusely on the floor. Then he ripped the sleeve off his own shirt, wadded it up and pushed it into the wound. "Hold pressure on that wound," he yelled in Michael's face. "Do NOT let that bleed. Keep that pressure on tight. Got it?" Michael only nodded, but he pushed the cloth hard into the wound. Then Jack looked at Cassy and said, "I'll be right back."

Jack knew Cassy's only hope was to secure the cave and get an Aero-Med helicopter on the way immediately. The first thing he did was to check the hall behind them where the guard's riddled body lay on the floor. That hall was abandoned. Next, he took the handgun off the dead guard who shot Cassy. He checked the clip. It still had 5 rounds in it. Then he put a full one in the gun he had already lifted off the guard who they'd killed in the room. With a semi-automatic .45-caliber gun in each hand, he headed down the hall. He kicked in the doors of each guard's room. Behind one he found an unconscious man wrapped in bandages, behind another he found a guard who was awake with only bandages around his shoulder. "Get up, hands in the air," Jack commanded. Then he patted him down, finding two guns and a knife, which Jack relieved him of, then marched him out in front of him and down the hall.

Seeing no one, Jack went directly to Max's office, put two bullets in the lock, and kicked the door open. Pushing the guard into the office in front of him, Jack went in shooting. Bullets riddled the body of the lead guard, but before he hit the ground, Jack had emptied both clips into Max and the only other sniper. As he fired, Jack felt one bullet graze his leg, another one hit his arm, and one tear through the flesh in his side. But he kept on firing. Within 20 seconds, Max and his last guard lay on the floor, oozing blood from various places. Jack gathered up the guns and threw them in the wastebasket. Then he located his cell phone in Max's desk and dialed 911. He carried the basket full of guns with him outside, where he hoped for a good signal.

"911. What's the nature of your emergency?"

"Listen closely. There has been a shooting and one girl is bleeding badly from the abdomen. Several others are dead and wounded. I need the Aero-Med helicopter immediately. Do not call the police, or anybody else, until you get that chopper on the way. I am an FBI agent, and all is secure here. But we need that medical helicopter STAT."

"Sir, what is your loca...?"

"Just listen. I don't have our exact coordinates, but we are approximately ten miles directly west of Carlsbad, New Mexico and about five miles north of the Caverns' National Park. We are in an artificially enclosed cave in a remote area, but I will make a fire in front of the cave with all the smoke I can muster. Tell the pilot to look for the smoke. I will also leave this phone on so you can trace it. Remember, medical first, police second. Got it!"

"Yes sir. I will inform them immediately."

"Thank you." Jack left his phone outside, then ran back into the cave facility and directly to Cassy. She was bleeding badly. Michael was still holding the blood-soaked rag on the wound, but she was barely conscious. "Cassandra, can you hear me?"

"I can hear you. Jack, I have to tell you something."

"Save your strength, baby. Just rest. We have a chopper on the way."

"No, Jack. It's no use. I'm not going to make it."

"No, no. Don't say that. You're going to be all right, Cassandra. Just hang with me. You're going to make it."

"I thought you were the realist, Jack. I'm dying. You know it, and I know it. The bullet tore through my belly, and I'm bleeding to death. That's okay with me, Jack. I'm going to be with Jesus, and I'm not afraid."

"No, no, no."

"Jack, I hope you find Jesus Christ as your personal Savior because I want to see you in heaven some day. But right now, I need to tell you something."

"No, Cassandra, honey, stop that."

142

"Shut up and listen. I love you, Jack Donavan. I have fallen completely in love with you."

"I love you, too, Cassandra. Just don't…" But she was already unconscious.

Chapter 52

Friday, May 27
Near Carlsbad Caverns, New Mexico

Jack grabbed his gun and went around the side of the square hallway to the door of the lab. The door was locked with a slide bolt from the outside. He slid the bolt open and stood to the side of the door just in case someone in there had a gun. Then he pushed the door open and entered the room gun first. He pointed his .45 at the three men he saw, all of whom had their hands in the air, and looked really scared. "There are no guns in here," the taller one said. "We are unarmed." Then Jack addressed the older man.

"I take it you are professor McMurray?"

"Yes, sir."

"Do they have any guns in here?"

"Not that I've seen."

"You come with me. The other two of you, stay put." Then Jack led the elder McMurray out into the hall and bolted the laboratory door shut again. "Now listen closely." Jack stuck his face down very close to the professor's. "Your daughter has been shot. She is unconscious and bleeding badly."

"Cassy is here?"

"And shot and unconscious and bleeding badly."

"Where is she? I want to see her."

"Can you help her medically?"

"No, I am not a medical doctor. I'm a chemist."

"Then seeing her is not the priority right now. There is an Aero-Med helicopter on the way. But we are in an isolated location. I told them to look for a fire and lots of smoke outside this cave. I need you to go outside and build a smoky fire, burn whatever you can find, but make sure the pilot of that chopper can see the fire. There are probably some matches or a lighter or something in Max's office."

"I have a lighter here in my pocket, we use them regularly in the lab."

"Good, then get at it. A big fire, got it?"

"Yes, I understand."

Jack went back to Cassy. Michael was still holding pressure on the wound. Jack could still feel a pulse in her neck, but she was barely breathing. He gently did CPR on her. He kept blowing puffs of air in her mouth and pumped lightly on her chest, just to remind her heart to keep beating.

The professor built a fire, then came in and found them gathered around Cassy. He held his daughter's hand, and her brother held pressure on the wound while Jack continued CPR. But she never regained consciousness. After a few minutes, Jack chased Professor McMurray back outside to wait for the helicopter and direct them to Cassy when they came.

It took the Aero-Med helicopter 15 minutes to get there. The paramedics strapped Cassy to a gurney. Jack helped them carry her out and into the chopper. They put her on a respirator, started an IV and secured the gurney. The head of the paramedic team said she would be flown to the Carlsbad Medical Center. Then he started back toward the cave.

"Hey," Jack stood in his way, "where do you think you are going?"

"There are other injured people in there and you are also bleeding. We need to assess everyone's condition and put the injured on the helicopter."

"No, you don't. Those are thugs, kidnappers, and terrorists. They are either dead or they'll wait for the next chopper. Now get that girl to the hospital right now!"

"I'm sorry, sir, but I need to assess their condition."

Jack pulled out the .45 he had stuffed in his belt. He put the end of the barrel on the forehead of the paramedic. "I said get that girl to the hospital RIGHT NOW!"

The man froze. Jack cocked the gun. He looked at Jack's eyes and saw this was no idle threat. "All right," he said, "but I'm reporting this."

"Fine. That will give me an opportunity to report how you tried to let the girl who saved this country from tampered drugs bleed to death while you wanted to make sure the terrorists were okay. NOW GET GOING."

He looked at Jack a few more seconds, them said to the pilot, "All right, let's go."

145

As soon as the helicopter disappeared over the hill, Jack grabbed his cell phone and called his FBI agent friend Billy Montgomery. Recognizing Jack's number, Billy pushed *Answer*. "Hey, Jack. How's it going? Get any more clues about the location of the kidnappers?"

"Billy, I need your help, like right now. We used an ultralight aircraft and found the terrorists. They shot us down and a complex gunfight ensued. Most of them are dead, two are okay, and several injured."

"Holy crap, Jack, how'd you…"

"Just listen. Cassandra was shot in the belly. She's being airlifted to the Carlsbad Medical Center. The police will arrest or detain everybody until they get it all sorted out. I don't have time for that. I need to get to that hospital ASAP. So I need you to call the police or the sheriff or whoever-the-heck is in charge here and tell them I'm a part-time FBI agent on special assignment or something. I don't care what you tell them, but I need the cops off my back for a while, and get the McMurrays released to my custody. I'll answer all the questions later, but I need to get to that hospital right away. Can you do that, like now? Actually, I hear a chopper. I'm sure that's the cops."

"I'll get on it, Jack. You have done special assignment flying for us on drug runs, so it should work."

"Work it out with your department or whatever later, Billy. I need the credibility now. The police helicopter is coming over the hill as we speak."

"I'll get right on it, Jack. But just as soon as you can, call me back with a full report, okay?"

"You got it Billy, thanks."

A helicopter with *SHERIFF PATROL* written on the sides descended into the valley in front of the drug lab cave. An overweight officer in uniform with a shirt that stretched tight over his belly climbed out of the back and drew his gun as he approached the cave. He was followed by a skinny man wearing glasses, also in uniform. A third officer, a female with short blond hair, stayed in the helicopter with the pilot. Jack was standing unarmed with his hands up, facing the officers. "My name is Jack Donavan, I am on special assignment with the

FBI. This facility has been secured, but there are a lot of bad guys in there. Some are dead and some are injured."

"We'll be the judge of who's the good guys and bad guys," the heavy officer answered. "Meanwhile, everyone is to be secured and kept in custody." Then turning to the thin officer, he said, "Cuff 'em."

Chapter 53

Friday, May 27
Near Carlsbad Caverns, New Mexico

For 20 minutes, the sheriff's officers kept everyone secured in handcuffs—Jack, the McMurrays, the guys in the lab, and the terrorists who were still alive. Jack and the McMurrays were cuffed to a bar inside the *SHERRIF PATROL* helicopter. The pilot and the female officer, a slender woman about 30, remained in the aircraft with them. She inquired about the various blotches of blood on Jack's clothing, but he assured her they were not serious injuries. She opened a first aid kit and began cleaning and dressing Jack's wounds.

When the heavy officer finally came from the cave, he had Jack's wallet in his hand. "I retrieved your wallet from the desk in what appears to have been their office," he said slowly. "It confirms your name is Jack Donavan, all right. I see you are a pilot, and you have a handgun CCW permit. But I don't see any ID that says you're FBI."

"No, I'm on special assignment. I'm not a regular fulltime FBI agent."

"Uh huh. Well, Mr. Donavan, I'm going to have to keep you in custody until we can confirm..." About that time, the officer's phone rang. He hit *Answer* and walked far enough away so those in the helicopter could not hear the conversation. As he talked, he occasionally looked back toward the aircraft. Finally, he tapped it off and came back. "So...it seems your story checks out, Mr. Donavan. At least you seem to have some friends at the FBI who insist we let you go and treat you well. You and the McMurrays are free to go. Can we give you a lift somewhere?"

"Actually, it would be really great if you could just give us a lift over these hills to the little airport south of Whites City. I have a vehicle there."

The overweight officer uncuffed Jack and the McMurrays, then he instructed the pilot to take them wherever they wanted to go. "There's a lot of carnage in there, Mr. Donavan. Some dead and some pretty shot up. I'd appreciate a full report from you before you leave town."

"Be glad to, sheriff. I'm not going anywhere. The professor's daughter is in critical condition at the Carlsbad Medical Center. That's where we'll be if you want us."

"Yeah, we had a complaint from the paramedics that you forced them at gun point to leave the others behind. There is another Aero-Med on the way to get them."

"They are kidnappers, terrorists, murderers, and the muscle behind the national drug scam. That girl is a hero. There is no way I'd let them risk her life so they could check on those scumbags in the cave."

"Oh, I understand. I'm just saying we had a complaint that will have to be checked out. But you're free to go. I hope the girl makes it."

The helicopter pilot, with the female officer accompanying them, gave the three men a quick five-minute ride over the rugged terrain and let them out at the small Carlsbad Caverns' Airport, located off the southeast corner of Whites City. The three men thanked the pilot, then ran to Jack's rented Expedition. Jack put Carlsbad Medical Center in the GPS and began exceeding the speed limit as he followed the arrow on the screen.

The McMurrays were more talkative now. They talked about the kidnapping, the drug scam, and the rescue. But mostly they talked about Cassy and her condition. At one point, the professor asked Jack, "Wouldn't it have been quicker to have the helicopter fly us directly to the hospital?"

"I thought about that. For sure, the helicopter would get us there quicker, but I figure she'll be in surgery for several hours before we can see her anyway. And if they move her, we want to be able to move with her. So I thought we better have wheels."

"Um…Mr. Donavan…?" Michael offered a tentative question from the back seat.

"Jack. Call me Jack."

"Well, Jack, I watched you with my sister. It seems that the two of you have become, shall I say, close, like romantically close."

149

"You could say that."

"Really?" The professor said looking directly at Jack now from the front passenger seat. "Just how would you describe your relationship?"

Jack looked over at him for a moment, then he looked back at the road and said, "I'm in love with your daughter."

Chapter 54

Friday, May 27
Carlsbad Medical Center
Carlsbad, New Mexico

They located her in the Surgical Center. But they could only sit in the waiting area. During that time, William called his wife and brought her up-to-date on the situation. Jack could, of course, only hear one side of the conversation, but it was obviously emotional and difficult. Arrangements were made for Cassy's mother to fly to Carlsbad, arriving the next day.

The phone call made Jack think of Abby. She should know. He asked the McMurrays if they knew her number but neither did. Then he coaxed the professor to ask the hospital for Cassy's personal belongings. When they were delivered, Jack pawed through them until he found Cassy's cell phone. He scrolled to "Recents" and pushed on Abby's name.

"Hi there, kid. How's it going?"

"Abby, this is Jack Donavan."

"Oh. Hi, how's it going, handsome?"

` "I'm sorry, Abby, I have bad news. Cassandra has been shot."

"Oh no! How is she, will she be all right?"

"Abby, you need to know that it doesn't look good. We found her father and the drug lab. There was a gunfight, and she was shot in the belly. She is in surgery now."

"So she's still alive? So there is still hope. I need to pray. I'm not so good at prayer. Oh dear God, not Cassy, no, no, no, not Cassy. I need her. She's the only friend I've ever had. Don't leave me alone. Oh, dear God, no. Please! Please keep her alive. Jack, I'm coming there right now. Where are you?"

"We are at the Carlsbad Medical Center, in Carlsbad, New Mexico. If you want to fly in, I'll meet you at the airport. But, Abby, she...she's real bad. Maybe you should wait unit we know..."

"No. I'm coming right now. I have to be there. Now."

"All right. I'll keep you posted on her condition. Call me when you know your arrival time. I'll text you my number."

Cassy was in surgery for nearly three hours. Finally, the doctor came out and called out, "William and Michael McMurray." As they approached the doctor, Jack stood behind them. The doctor was sullen and reserved. "I'm Dr. Anderson. We have removed the bullet and repaired the damage, but she is bleeding internally, and we can't do anything more to stop it. I'm sorry, but her chances are not good."

"Can we see her?" the professor asked.

"Yes, I think that's a good idea. She is not conscious, but it may be your last chance to say goodbye. I'm very sorry. We did everything we could. Just walk through those doors, and the ladies at the desk can tell you where she is."

William and Michael disappeared through the double doors under the sign "Surgery." But Jack turned and followed the doctor down the hall. "Dr. Anderson." The doctor stopped and turned. "I'm Jack Donavan. I was with her when she was shot. I…I'm…We were very close. I'd like to know your frank and honest opinion. Well, I'm not suggesting you would be dishonest, what I mean is, just exactly what do you think will happen? How long does she have?"

"I'm sorry, Mr. Donavan. She will die within the hour."

"Thank you."

The doctor turned and walked away.

Jack did not go to Cassy's room. He left the waiting area, went through the lobby, and outside. He walked a while until he found a park bench surrounded by bushes and trees. He sat down and did something he had never done before in his life. Jack Donavan prayed.

*Dear God, I'm not sure how to do this. As you know, this is a first for me. You sent me an angel, a beautiful angel, and through her, You revealed to me that You really are there. Oh, I know she wasn't a real angel, she is more beautiful than any angel I could imagine. But she said she wanted to be, hoped to be, a messenger from You. So, in that sense, she was an angel. And now she'll never know that she was used by You. She is the only person I ever met who would not accept me for what I was. But then I guess, neither do You. She called me a filthy rotten sinner. And that's what brought me to my knees. That's why I'm here now. She was right. I **am** a filthy rotten sinner.*

I've been reading Your gospels again, and I understand that I am a sinner but Jesus the Christ Your Son paid for my sins on the cross. So right now, I want to receive Him as my God and Savior. Come into my life and save me. Thank you, Jesus ... Thank you for forgiving me. I'm no saint, but I'm going to do my best to spend the rest of my life serving You, dear Jesus. Umm...There is one other thing. I realize I don't deserve Cassandra. And I am not, like, trying to make a deal with You or anything. I'll serve You, no matter what. And it seems like You are taking her away. But...well...oh never mind. I just don't deserve her. No deals God, no deals. Just...thank You for using her to open my eyes to the truth. I guess I'm supposed to say, "Amen."

Jack got up and walked back to the hospital. This time, he went through the surgery doors and asked the girl behind a large desk where Cassandra was. She gave him the room number. As Jack was approaching the room, a nurse was coming out. "Is this the room of Cassandra McMurray?" Jack asked. The nurse nodded. "How is she?"

"I'm sorry, sir," the nurse said with a somber face. "She didn't make it. I'm terribly sorry."

Jack walked into the room and saw William and Michael standing on either side of the bed. The heart monitor showed a flat line on the screen. When the McMurrays saw Jack, they looked up. Their eyes were filled with tears. The professor was unable to speak. Michael said, "She never regained consciousness. She died about ten minutes ago." Jack figured that was the exact time of his prayer. She entered heaven at the same time he received Christ. He hoped she would know. "Come on, Dad, we should go now," Michael said. He walked around the bed, took his father by the arm, and led him out of the room.

"If you don't mind, I'd like a few minutes alone with her," Jack said.

"Sure," Michael responded quietly, "take all the time you want. We'll be in the waiting area."

Jack approached the bed slowly. He bent over and kissed her for the last time. But her lips were colorless and still. Jack began to weep. He could no longer hold it back. The only woman he ever truly loved was gone. Finally, he gained his composure. He put his hand alongside her face, kissed her one last time, and backed away.

But as he lifted his arm from the sheet, his hand became tangled in a cord. He absentmindedly shook his hand to free it, but the cord did not leave. So he reached over with his other hand to unwind it. As he did, he noticed that it was not plugged into anything. He found himself holding the round male end of a silver-looking plug. Looking around, he could see nowhere it should be. But just before he let it drop to the floor, he noticed a female type receptacle in the heart monitor. Jack never was sure why he did it, maybe just by habit from plugging headphones back in that had vibrated loose on airplane panels, but he plugged the silver end into the hole on the heart monitor. All of a sudden, the monitor came to life, displaying a regular heartbeat.

Chapter 55

Jack jerked the sheet back off Cassy's head and felt for a pulse. His hand was shaking so bad, he couldn't feel anything at first. But then, finally, he felt it. "Suffering succotash, she's alive." Jack stuck the oxygen hose back in her nose and ran out of the room and up to the desk. "Where is Dr. Anderson?"

"He is with a patient right now."

"What room?"

"Right across the hall, but he can't…"

Jack was in the room before she could finish. "I need you right now!"

"I'm with a patient, Mr. Donavan. I'll be…"

"Is he dying?"

"Well, no. I'm checking his…"

"Then I need you now, like right now!"

Jack grabbed the doctor by the arm and dragged him out of the room and down the hall into Cassy's room. "I'm sorry, Mr. Donavan, there is nothing more I can do for…"

"Look." Jack pointed to the heart monitor. "She's alive."

"What the heck. She was flat line, I saw it myself."

"Somebody disconnected the cord. Probably one of the McMurrays pulled it out accidentally when they were leaning over her."

The doctor unwound the stethoscope from around his neck and listened to her heart, then to her lungs. "Well, she's alive and breathing. It's very shallow, but she is definitely breathing on her own." Then he looked at the catheter coming out from under the blanket. "Would you look at that?"

"What? Look at what?"

"The last time I was in here, that line was full of blood. Now, it's clear. So is the one draining the wound. It appears that the internal bleeding has stopped. That's amazing. I can't say it never happens, but I wouldn't have given her a 1% chance of making it."

"And now?"

"Better than 50% anyway. The IV is still in. We'll know shortly. If she's going to make it, she'll regain consciousness soon. I'll go tell her family."

"Could I have a few minutes with her first?"

"Sure. Actually, I'm really busy right now. You tell them."

Jack pulled up a chair next to the bed and waited. He stroked her hair, and held her hand, coaxing her to wake up. Finally, he just put his head down on the bed. *No deal, God, no deals, but please, please, please.* Then he heard the most wonderful sound of his entire life.

"Jack? Jack?" His head shot up and his eyes, though full of tears, were looking into the most beautiful brown ones he'd ever seen."

"Oh, baby, you're alive, you're alive."

"Why? Was I dead?"

"Yes. Well, no. But we thought you were. How do you feel?"

"I don't feel too bad. My belly is sore, but I don't seem to be in any severe pain."

"That's probably because of the meds. You have a bad hole in your belly. You were bleeding internally, but it stopped, so don't move anything, we don't want it to start bleeding again."

"Okay. How long have you been here? What happened?"

"You were shot at the cave, do you remember?"

"Um…yes, we were shot down, we were in a gunfight. I killed some guys. Then I got shot. Yes, I remember now. I remember you leaning over me. I thought for sure I was dying."

"Do you remember what you said to me?"

"Yes, I said, 'I love you.'"

"Do you remember what I said?"

"No, I must have passed out."

"I said that I love you, too."

"Oh, Jack. What a wonderful thing to wake up to."

"Cassandra, listen to me. I have to go get your father and brother. They are out in the lobby, and they think you are dead."

"Oh, dear."

"But first I have to ask you something."

156

"Okay."

"Cassandra McMurray, I love you with all my heart, and I want you to be my wife. You know, for richer or poorer, sickness and health, until death do us part—that kind of wife. Will you marry me, Cassandra?"

Cassy put her hand on the scruffy beard that had grown on his face. "Jack, I'm totally, hopelessly in love with you. I'd marry you in a heartbeat. But you know I can't marry somebody who has not received Jesus Christ as their personal God and Savior."

"Yes." Jack took her hand in his. He sat back with a big toothy grin that spread from ear-to-ear and said, "Yes, I know."

THE END OF PART I

PART II
THE PHILANTHROPIST

*The following events take place
between July 4 and August 8
[about six weeks after Part I]*

Chapter 1

The banquet hall on the top floor of the Fitzgerald Building in downtown Chicago was filled with employees of the Fitzgerald Family Trust Company for the company's annual Fourth of July party. There was dancing, eating, drinking, talking, joking, flirting, gossiping, and laughing, but no complaining. A live band played music fit for dancing, but most people seemed to just prefer the socializing. Salads, cheese, fruit, and entrées, beef, veal, chicken, fish, mutton, and duck, plus desserts to die for, crowded the entire west wall of the hall. On the north wall there was a bar where drinks were available for the asking. One could get most common varieties of wine and champagne, along with soft drinks, espresso, and various specialty coffees, but there was no beer or hard liquor.

A band played from the east wall where there was also a podium set up. The south wall was lined with a bank of windows that displayed a spectacular view of the traffic on the Chicago Loop. The center of the room, although crowded by some small round tables, permitted sufficient room for dancing, or just socializing.

At 8:00, a young man wearing a black tuxedo stood on the podium and tapped annoyingly on a microphone until he had everybody's attention. He thanked them for coming, told a few silly jokes, which got more groans than laughs, then he introduced the president of the company, Mr. J.D. Fitzgerald, II.

After an enthusiastic applause, J.D. took the stand. An unimpressive looking man, who had just turned 64, J.D. Fitzgerald, II was, physically speaking, medium everything. He was medium height, medium weight, medium build, with medium brown hair mixed with gray. But in every other way, he was no medium. The Fitzgerald family was one of the 20 wealthiest in America. His father, J.D. Fitzgerald, started the business with one small trust company in Chicago, 71 years ago.

Unlike his son, J.D. Fitzgerald was tall, thin, and physically impressive. With very little education, he began helping his friends make money by following the biblical book of Proverbs, and especially without going into debt. Friends told friends, and soon people were paying to learn what J.D. considered common sense. Then he began to train others and wrote his plan down in a book entitled "Wealth With Wisdom." The book became a best seller, and J.D.'s team was soon pursued for financial and estate planning, as well as dealing with the IRS, while navigating the tax laws, legally.

J.D. was intelligent, witty, honest, energetic, entrepreneurial, generous, God fearing, and still alive. At 90 years of age, with the help of a cane, he walked by himself, drove a car to work three days a week, and was sitting at one of the little round tables at the Independence Day party, watching his son take the stand.

Unlike J.D., J.D., II graduated from Harvard Law School before joining the family business. At that time, they had 15 offices in 7 major cities. Working alongside his father, and finally heading up the business, J.D., II was the leader his father had hoped he would be. But he was not a man of God, like his father was. He also lived far too "high-on-the-hog" to suit J.D., who repeatedly, and verbally, frowned upon his son's expensive clothes, jewelry, cars, airplanes, boats, and his seven multi-million dollar homes scattered all over the world.

J.D. Fitzgerald, II wasn't very good at giving speeches, but then he didn't have to be. He raised his hand in acceptance of the applause. "Thank you, ladies and gentlemen. Thank you... Thank you... My good friends, it is a privilege to be with you this evening. I will not take much of your time. I see that you are enjoying socializing with each other, and it seems a shame for me to interrupt it. So I will be brief. As most of you know, we have done very well the first half of this year in spite of the financial recession, or maybe because of it. (A few chuckles rippled through the audience.) At any rate, even though the national unemployment rate went higher, we were able to add many employees nationwide, while still increasing our profit margin for the year. Our family would like to thank each of you for this. We realize many companies have worked hard without this result. So we are thankful to each of you for your energetic service that made this happen. As you know, we are not a public company, nor are we a union company. So we wish to share our profits with you. Each of you, and all of the employees in our 57 offices throughout the country, will receive a mid-year bonus equal to two weeks of your regular salary."

The room erupted in cheers and applause.

Chapter 2

Tuesday—Wednesday, July 5-13
Chicago, Illinois

He saw her through the window. It was not by accident. He had been told to look for her. So he decided to look in from the outside. He had walked this way and passed this restaurant many times before. He remembered seeing the sign "The Corner Grill" being there for years. It was, after all, the only establishment on that corner. He had never gone inside, but on this hot July day, he looked in the window and could not look away.

Hers was not the exquisite beauty of a movie star, or a model adorning the cover of *Redbook* or *Cosmopolitan*. She was too innocent looking to be a movie star, and too thin to be a cover girl. But she had the sweetest face he'd ever seen. It was more narrow than round, with a light complexion and a few freckles across her cheeks and nose. She had big blue eyes, and strawberry blond hair in a ponytail that nearly reached her waist. He felt silly, stupid, like some infatuated teenager. He was 30 years old, for heaven's sake. This was absurd.

Nonetheless, he found himself walking back and forth, up and down the street just to pass by The Corner Grill. He felt like a stalker. And he repeated it, during his lunch hour, every day for a week.

The second week, on Monday, he dredged up enough courage to go inside. From his "stalking" the week before, he learned that if he waited until nearly 1:00 P.M., the crowd thinned out enough that he could get a booth by himself on the right side, as one entered the door of the diner. She always worked the left side. That way he could sneak a peek at her while picking at his food. He was careful, discrete, and watchful. He repeated this process on Tuesday and Wednesday. He was sure she didn't notice him at all.

She noticed.

On Thursday, he came in and followed his routine. He took off what appeared to be a uniform jacket with the name "John" written on the left front. He removed his cap, raked his hand through his thick crop of neatly trimmed brown hair, and slid into a booth to the right of the door. Being six-foot-one, he had to slide the table ahead a bit to get in.

"He's here again," Sally whispered to Abby, peeking out from the kitchen. "You go wait on him."

"No. I'm…He's…on your side."

"But he keeps looking at you."

"But he doesn't want to talk to me or he'd sit on my side. He knows I always work this side."

"Abby, he's gorgeous, and he is not wearing a wedding ring. You can't just let him sneak peeks at you. He's probably just shy. He looks like a construction worker or a security guard or something. He probably just isn't confident in his social skills. Don't let him get away without at least meeting him. He doesn't know how to break the ice. He needs you to prod him along. Go, go, go."

"But…"

"But nothing! Get going, he'll leave if we don't wait on him pretty soon."

"But I'm…"

"You're what?"

"Scared."

"You're kidding. You wait on construction workers all the time. You flirt with them, get them talking and joking around. You're an expert at it."

"Yeah, but none of them look at me like that, and he's…"

"Gorgeous?"

"Well, yeah."

"All the more reason to get over there. Like **now** would be a good time."

"Okay, okay, okay, I'm going to do this." So Abby, armed with her order pad and pencil, approached his table. Normally, she would have boisterously asked something like, "What can I get you, handsome?" Or "How-yado'n, big guy?" but she could only manage, "Can I take your order…sir?"

He panicked. What was she doing over here? This wasn't her side. This was the safe side. "Oh, ummm, yes, I usually have the soup of the day and a chef salad, and umm coffee, yes, some coffee."

"Okay, I'll be…bring…that will be right up, that is, I'll get that right away…for you… sir." Then she hurriedly retreated into the kitchen, walking past two other customers waiting to order.

"Well?" Sally wanted to know.

"I froze. I couldn't say anything. I just took his order and ran like a coward."

"You, the magpie of the restaurant business, just took his order and ran? Get out there and talk to him, girl! Look, when you take out his order, ask him if you can sit and have lunch with him. If you don't, I swear I'll drag you out there myself."

Since his order was a regular on the lunch menu, it was ready in just a few minutes. Abby, more nervous than if she were serving the Prince of Wales, approached his table with food in hand. She set the food down and smiled. Then he smiled. Then she turned and ran back to the kitchen.

"Well?" Sally inquired, this time with both hands on her hips.

"He just smiled and, and, and, he is sooo cute. I just, I couldn't say anything."

"Abby, you…! Okay that's it. Come on."

Sally grabbed her arm and pulled her from the kitchen into the dining room, awkwardly bumping into several chairs and customers. Abby protested, "NO. Sally. Stop it. Don't pull… Oh, excuse me. Pardon me. I'm sorry. Sally! I'll just… Oh… Hi," as they came to a stop at his booth.

"Now look," Sally began, "this is getting ridiculous." But she was addressing the mysterious man in the booth. "Abby here thinks you are very handsome and…"

"SALLY!"

"AND she is on her lunch break now, and she would like to sit here and eat it with you, but she's too shy to ask. And apparently, you are too shy to ask her. So, since there is nobody else to introduce you two, this is Abby. Her name is Abigail Edna Davidson. And I just happen to think she's the prettiest girl in the whole world."

"Sally, stop saying…"

"So do I," the man in the booth interrupted.

"Sally, don't say things like……….. You do?"

164

"Absolutely!"

"And you should see her with that beautiful hair out of that stupid pony tail," Sally added.

"I'd like that," he said. And, as Abby's face was turning even redder, he added, "I'm sorry, Abby, she's right. I have been too shy to talk to you. I have been looking at you for days. I was beginning to feel like a stalker, so I came in to meet you, but then I was too scared to meet you. I would be honored if you would have lunch with me."

"Well, I, um… all right, okay, that…that would be nice." Abby slid into the booth across from him.

"There, see how easy that was?" Sally added, shaking her head as she walked away.

"Hi, I'm Abby."

"Hi, Abby, I'm John."

"Hi."

"Hi."

Chapter 3

Tuesday, July 5
The Royal Palace of the Arab King Abdul-Ahad Mahmood

King Abdul-Ahad, known in his own country by the title "Emir al Mumenin" [*Commander (or King) of the Faithful*], sat at his desk in the office of his royal palace overlooking the Arabian Sea. He was speaking on the phone with his wife, who was who-knows-where, buying who-knows-what for their daughter's wedding. The king was a thin man, with the distinct olive-toned skin and prominent nose of the descendants of Ishmael. He was, nonetheless, a handsome man, five-foot-ten inches tall, 46 years of age, with a neatly trimmed beard and a thick crop of dark hair, usually covered, as it was today, with the Bedouin style headdress that his countrymen preferred.

The conversation with his wife was, as it usually was since their daughter announced her engagement to an American banker from Chicago, about the wedding. Unlike the more conservative Arab world, which was offended at the mere idea of marriage to a westerner, Abdul's wife, Queen Daniyah saw it as socially advantageous, and an opportunity to display her wealth—in America.

"I know, you and Fawzah will organize the wedding party," the king agreed, "but...yes, we have the location settled. The wedding will be in the Grand Ball Room of the Trump International Hotel... Of course, it is a luxury hotel, it's actually a tower on the north side of downtown Chicago... All of us will stay there... Yes, Dani, the plan is for all the crown jewels to be there... Well, we are working on that now... No, we will figure a way to transport the real jewels. Bakr is handling all of that, and he will be here momentarily to go over all of that with me, so I will know more by this evening... Yes, of course, dear, good-bye."

Not three minutes after his wife's call, the male secretary of King Mahmood sent him a text to tell him Bakr Hasan was waiting in the parlor. The king replied, "Send him to my office." Two minutes later, his old friend was at his door.

First, the two men repeated the standard praises to Allah, hugged, and exchanged kisses on the cheek. Bakr Hasan had been the servant of King Abdul for 12 years, and of his father 34 years before that. At the age of 66, Bakr had a wife, six children, and 18 grandchildren. He was balding, round-faced, and quite a few kilos overweight, but still healthy and eager to serve king and country. After 10 more minutes discussing the welfare of their families, they got down to the business of going over the upcoming royal wedding.

"I would like to say, emir, that in all my days of serving you, and your father before you, I have not found anything quite so complex as the plans for this wedding. Not that I mind, you understand, it is an interesting challenge."

"Let me guess," the king suggested, "most of the complications come from my women."

"Well, of course, I would suspect the complexities of most weddings are generated by the bride and her mother."

"Actually, most of the complexities of life are generated by women, wouldn't you agree?" Both men laughed briefly.

"Possibly," Baka continued, "but what makes this complex is that it will be in the American city of Chicago, and that the crown jewels will be transported there. My staff has a plan to suggest to our emir, but first I must ask an obvious, and probably ridiculous, question, but…has consideration been given to copying the crown jewels and leaving the original gems safe here in the National Archives?"

"Were it up to me, my friend, we would for sure leave them here. But my wife is quite clear on the matter. She wants the actual jewels to be displayed at the wedding. They will be on display in various secured cases around the Grand Ball Room. And some of them will be worn by the members of the wedding party. She wants Fawzah to wear the royal crown which my wife has never been able to wear because she is not of royal blood."

"For the purposes of insurance, can you give me an estimate of their worth?"

"No one can place a value on crown jewels, but if each diamond, ruby, sapphire, and emerald were detached and sold on the open market, they would bring something in the neighbor-hood of 100 million."

"Oh, my, 100 million U.S. dollars?"

"No, 100 million euros."

"So that's nearly 130 million U.S. dollars?"

"Actually, 127 million at today's exchange rate," the king corrected, glancing down to look at his computer.

"It is just that, well, many jewelers can make cheap coun-terfeits, but there are also very good ones. It would be so much safer to have them copied by an expert and..."

Raising his hand, the king interrupted with, "I know, I know, but believe me, that will not happen. My wife has actu-ally become an expert on the subject of precious gems. Since our marriage, she has traveled the world changing much of our wealth into precious stones. She tells me these gemstones are a better place to invest our wealth than oil and natural gas. As you know, many of the crown jewels were originally collected by my great-grandmother. My grandmother and my mother added to the collection. But my wife has multiplied it four times over. And she has actually studied the subject. I'm telling you, my friend, I have been in the most formal of parties in Moscow, Paris, Rome, and New York, and before we leave, my wife will tell me the value of the stones each woman is wearing and who has on authentic gems and who is wearing copies. She is as good as any professional gemologist at recog-nizing a copy. So I'm afraid, Bakr, the only question is, 'Can you protect them on their journey to America and back?' With the emphasis on 'AND BACK.'"

"Yes, my emir, that is the objective. And here is what my staff proposes. The wedding is on Tuesday, August 9. This steers clear of our Friday holy day and the Christians' Sunday holy day. We suggest that on Saturday, August 6, the crown jewels be removed from the National Archives and flown by your 747, Royal One, to the Midway Airport in Chicago, arriv-ing that evening. I feel quite confident about that since we can provide all the security we would provide for yourself, or the president of the United States, for that matter. The displays at the wedding can be protected the same way. The wedding hall, which is the Grand Ball Room of the Trump International Hotel, can be completely secured. The most vulnerable time is between our landing at Midway Airport and the wedding itself. The American authorities will not allow the jewels to remain on Royal One overnight, and the hotel will only allow them to be displayed two days before the wedding. So they must be stored somewhere in Chicago overnight, Saturday, August 6, so they can be moved to the hotel Sunday, August 7, to be on display the day before the wedding, August 8, and during the wedding on the 9th."

"Have you found a secure location for them on Saturday night?"

"Yes, we believe so, emir. After many meetings and much searching, we have determined the most secure vault in the city is in the Fitzgerald Building. It is located four blocks south of the Trump International Hotel, and they have the most technologically advanced safe in the city. It is reinforced with so much iron and concrete, they claim that if the whole building were bombed into rubble, the safe would remain intact and unaffected. I have seen it myself, and it is quite impressive. The hinges on the door alone are as big around as my waist. They have secured many valuable items for domestic and foreign dignitaries in the past. So it is my suggestion we entrust our crown jewels to the Fitzgeralds."

Chapter 4

Wednesday, July 13
Chicago, Illinois

"So is that what you usually have for lunch?" John gestured with his head, referring to the plate Sally brought out and set in front of Abby.

"Um-huh."

"Two hamburgers, a large pile of onion rings and fries, with mayo and ketchup to dip your fries in. You can stay that thin eating like that every day?"

"And a bowl of soup and apple pie ala mode. Sally and Anita, that's the other two girls who work here, they hate me. They can't stand it that I can pretty much eat whatever I want and not gain weight."

"Do you have some sort of super metabolism or something?"

"Maybe, but I don't eat much in the evening, mainly because we can't afford much. I eat my big meal at lunch because Joe, that's Joe Gorki the guy who owns this restaurant, he lets me eat lunch free."

"That's really nice of him."

"Yeah, Joe's cool. Alice, that's Joe's wife, she's nice, too. She does most of the cooking now. Sometimes she gives me some food to take home to Grandma Edna."

"So you live with your grandmother?"

"That's right."

"Do you have any other family?"

"No." At that she looked down at her half-eaten burger and said nothing. There was silence for maybe a whole minute.

"I'm sorry, I didn't mean to pry. You don't have to talk about it. We don't have to talk about anything you don't want to."

"No, it's okay, it's…it's just that I've never had a family, except Grandma Edna. My mother died in a filthy hotel room in Detroit when I was born. I never knew her and I have no idea who my father was. I don't think my mother knew either."

170

"Oh, I'm sorry, I didn't mean to bring up something that hurts you."

"No. Well, actually, if you plan to hang around, you should know what kind of a girl I am. My mother was a prostitute, a drunk, and an addict. She died of an overdose. I was placed in an orphanage and with three different sets of foster parents. None of them liked me very much, although I can't say I blame them. I just had one friend, named Cassy, and if it wasn't for her, I'd probably be like my mother. Cassy saved me in more ways than one. She was my only family until Grandma Edna found me at my high school graduation. I've lived with her for the last six years. I've had two years at the community college, but now I just work here fulltime."

"I see."

"The point is, I'm not a college girl. I'm not a career woman. I'm not anything. I just work as a waitress. We live in a small row house. We have no money, no expensive clothes, no expensive jewelry or expensive anything. We don't even own a car. We live on grandma's small pension check and my salary here. This job is not a stepping-stone for me, John. This is all I have and all I will reasonably ever have. I'm 26 years old and dirt poor. So if you want to hang around, that's what I am. I think you are real cute. Actually, I think you are the nicest looking guy I've ever seen. I mean not like just handsome but nice, you got real nice eyes and you seem 'real' and sincere and all. At least I hope so. Anyway, I'm not trying to run you off. I really want to get to know you. But you need to know, that's what I am."

"Abby, I don't care if you are rich or poor. I just want to get to know who lives inside that beautiful body. I just want…"

"Okay, well, see there is something else you need to know right up front. I don't have guys climbing all over me asking me out all the time. You know why?"

"That, I can't imagine."

"Well, it's because I'm a Christian, and I won't go to bed with anybody until I'm married. As soon as guys find that out, they're out of here. Well, the word has gotten around so they don't try any more. You need to know that, too. So, well, there you have it. If you want to come around, well, that's who I am."

John smiled one of those smiles that transformed him into the cutest thing she'd ever seen. She jumped a little when he put his hand on top of hers. Then he said, "I received Christ as my God and Savior when I was 16 years old. I'm no saint, but I've tried to live for God. And I won't have sex outside of marriage either. Now Abby, I need to tell you something, and you need to believe me because I try real hard never to lie, okay?"

"Okay." Her heart was pounding and her eyes were fixed on his like a deer in the headlights.

"I need to go. It's because of my work. It's not because you are poor, or who your mother was, or anything. I just simply have to go to work. You need to know that it's not that you ran me off. Okay?"

"Okay. So will you be back?"

"Of course, I'll be back. Not today. And sometimes I can't come because of work, but don't go thinking you ran me off."

She just nodded and kept her eyes fixed on his as he stood up. He put his hand alongside her face, smiled, and walked out.

John went back to work. But at the end of the day, he got in his car and began to drive west out of Chicago. He took the Eisenhower Freeway, then the Tri-State Tollway north to Elmhurst and made his way to the Fitzgerald mansion.

The Fitzgerald family mansion is surrounded by twelve wooded acres closed in by a ten-foot high concrete wall with an iron barred gate that opened only by a code, which, if you had the appropriate credentials, was entered by a guard stationed in front of it. After being approved, John drove up the long driveway bordered by neatly trimmed Colorado blue spruce trees on both sides until he reached a large circular fountain directly in front of the house. Then he had to choose whether to drive around the circle to the left or the right. Most visitors turned right, circling the huge fountain in a counter clockwise direction so they could let their guests out at the door from the passenger side. The staff would often drive the circle clockwise so they could park the limos in the seven-stall garage, which sat perpendicular and to the right as you faced the mansion. The garage also had a second story above it where some of the staffed lived.

The mansion itself was three stories high, made of huge stones with pillars separating curved arches across the entire front side. The main entrance was covered with a cathedral style dome, which was extended over the drive so that visitors could let their guests out in a covered area if the weather was unfavorable. Alongside and behind the perpendicular garage, was a large parking area for guest vehicles.

John parked his car in the guest area and approached the mansion's main entrance. Here, he received the approval of another security guard before entering the house. Once inside the door, he took the elevator to the third floor. Then he turned left and walked to the end of the hall and knocked on the door. J.D. Fitzgerald struggled to his feet, came over and opened the door. "Do you have a few minutes?" John asked.

Wrapping his arms around John, the elder Fitzgerald said, "I always have time for my favorite grandson. What can I do this fine day, for J.D. Fitzgerald, III?"

Chapter 5

Wednesday, July 13
Elmhurst, Illinois

"Your favorite grandson? Grandpa, you have two grandsons, and I'm the only one that will put up with you."

"Well, there you go. Proof positive." As he chuckled, the 90-year-old patriarch led J.D., III to a comfortable chair and repositioned himself behind his MacBook Pro. Then he picked up his pipe. He tapped out the old tobacco and opened a large box to resupply the bowl.

"How come you have such a huge box of tobacco, Grandpa?"

"It's a blend of three kinds. I have it sent here from three different places in South America and mix it myself."

"Why do you buy it in bulk? Are you trying to save money?"

After looking at him out of the top of his eyes, J.D. ignored the financial dig and said, "I buy it in bulk so I don't have to mix it so often. This box has its own humidor, so it will keep in there a long time. But you know what? I'll just bet you did not come to talk about my pipe tobacco, or make a social visit, for that matter. I'm assuming you have a situation."

"Wise as usual, Grandpa. Actually, I have two situations I'd like to discuss with you."

"I doubt that."

"What do you mean, you doubt that? How could you possibly know what I want to talk about?"

"I don't. But you wouldn't drive all the way up here during rush hour with two situations. I'd say there is a # 1 issue and a #2 issue. And #2 can wait, while #1 is crucial. So give me the Cliff Notes on #2, then we'll talk about #1."

"How do you always do that? It's down right scary how you can figure me out. Yes, well, you're right. But #2 is important, even if it's not 'crucial.' It's about Dad's deal to handle the crown jewels of King Mahmood. I wouldn't have taken the deal in the first place, and now he wants me to be in charge of it. This is by far the most risky thing we've taken on. He

174

built this huge vault, and now he wants to put expensive stuff in it. There's a lot of money in this Arab deal, but I don't think it's worth the risk. We are talking about protecting over a hundred million in jewels. And the thing is, they are not just gemstones. They are the crown jewels of one of the most wealthy Arab kings in the world."

"It's not just the money. Your father is making a statement to the world that he can play at this level. And he wants you to handle it because he is grooming you to handle everything. You are 30 years old, you've been out of law school for four years now. And you have done an excellent job. Your father wants to retire soon and go live in those darn mansions he's built all over the world, and play with the toys he's accumulated. If you pull this off, it will tell the world you are a global player."

"You know, Grandpa, I like the work of the trust company you set up. Helping people with their financial needs by applying the book of Proverbs, that's really cool. But I don't care about our family fortune. And I can't stand all the opulence Mom and Dad live in. I agree with you about their houses, cars, airplanes, and boats—no, make that palaces, limos, luxury jets and yachts."

"They aren't Christians, Johnnie. That's all they have. With no eternal hope, they have to get it all here and now."

"They think they are Christians. They go to church and give a lot of money."

"But you and I know they have never received Christ as their God and Savior."

"Yeah, I know, Grandpa. Ever since you led me to Christ, you've been my mentor, discipler, and teacher. I wouldn't know squat about the Bible if it weren't for you. My parents are lost, and they seem to be determined to stay that way."

"I thank God every day for you, Johnnie, but it's not because of me that you're saved, it's because the Holy Spirit of God plucked you from the fire. I gave the same gospel message to your father, too, when he was young, but he never saw the sense of it. When your father married his first wife, I tried to witness to her, too, but she wasn't interested. When your father divorced her and married your mother Lois, I talked with her

175

about Jesus many times. But her heart was hard toward the gospel message. Your parents are nice people, good to the staff and generous. But their bottom line is money, money, and more money. You are the joy of my life. God graciously saved you and turned your heart to delight in His Word. I thank Him every day for that."

"To get back to item #2. I have an idea I want to talk to you about concerning these crown jewels."

"But it can wait, right? What's item #1?"

"Oh, um, item #1. Yes, well, I want to know… I need… I…aaa…met a girl."

Chapter 6

Wednesday, July 13

"Hello"

"Hey, kid, how's it going?"

"CASSY, I haven't talked to you in ages. Are you married with children and grandchildren?"

"Abby, we talked last Sunday. That's what, three days?"

"Whatever. So how's the wedding plans coming along? No wait. First I have to tell you something. I met someone."

"Like a male someone?"

"Like a prince out of a cartoon come to life someone, except he's poor. But he does have a job."

"Wow, who is he?"

"I don't know."

"What do you mean, 'you don't know'? If you met him, you must know something, besides the 'prince' description."

"Actually, not much."

"What's his name?"

"I don't know."

"How can you not know his name?"

"Because he didn't tell me. Well, his first name is John."

"So, like, what does 'John' do for a living? Let me guess. You don't know."

"No, but I think he's an ex-con out on parole who got a job working on construction or as a security guard."

"They wouldn't give an ex-con a job as a security guard."

"Okay, so he probably drives a bulldozer or he's a janitor or something. He had on a Cubs baseball cap and an old windbreaker jacket. He came into The Corner Grill and said he'd been stalking me."

"WHAT! He's a STALKER?"

"Oh, it was just an expression. He just saw me and was too shy to meet me. But he also said he was a Christian."

"Did you first tell him you were a Christian?"

"Well, yeah."

"So maybe he told you that just to con you into going out with him."

"Okay, okay, so I'll find out more about him. Change of subject. What about the wedding?"

"We have a definite date. Saturday, August 6."

"Wow, that's just, like, what? Three and a half weeks?"

"Yeah, sorry about the short notice. As I told you Sunday, it was a matter of lining up the church and the minister. You need to fly in Thursday, August 4, if you can. We got you an electronic ticket with Delta. Just go to the Delta kiosk at O'Hare and stick in some I.D. The machine will issue you a boarding pass. The rehearsal and the dinner are on Friday evening, and the wedding is on Saturday at one o'clock."

"You've had lots of delays in putting this wedding together."

"Well, first I had to heal up enough to walk down the aisle."

"And ACTIVELY PARTICIPATE in a honeymoon."

"ABBY! Well, yeah, that, too. Anyway, now it's all set up, except we don't know all the groomsmen yet. But I will have three bridesmaids. You, of course, are the maid of honor. But don't worry about the dress. Jack is paying for all of the wedding party clothes. Actually, he is covering everything except the rehearsal dinner, which my father insisted on paying for."

"Who are the other bridesmaids?"

"Next to you will be Audrey Moses."

"Yes, I remember you telling me about her—the 19 year-old black girl who works for Jack. Her mother was a prostitute and Jack got her off the streets. Kind of like you saving me from a life on the streets."

"I never thought of that comparison."

" I can't wait to meet her."

"She's cute as she can be, with a bubbly personality—you'll love her."

"Who's the third bridesmaid?"

"Okay, now don't say anything nasty. It's my cousin Mary Ann."

"Oh, really! The stuck-up, snobby, obnoxious, fat girl?"

"Abby, now don't start…"

"Do they actually make a formal dress that size?"

"ABBY!!!"

178

"Seriously, you should check that out."

"Just stop!"

"How'd that happen? You hate that chick."

"Never mind. It's family politics."

"And the wedding is in your Assembly of God Church in Ann Arbor?"

"Yes. It will be like coming home for you. There are lots of people who will love to see you again."

"And others, not so much—including the pastor."

"Well, it didn't help that you constantly criticized his sermons."

"But he said some really dumb stuff."

"Well, you could have just talked to him about it, instead of muffling a crude description of horse manure into a sneeze during his sermons."

Chapter 7

Wednesday, July 13
Cicero, Illinois

"I don't know what he does, Grandma Edna. I think he's like a bulldozer driver or a construction worker or something. He had a Chicago Cubs baseball cap, and he wore a windbreaker jacket with his name on it."

"So, all you know about him is that he's, and I quote, 'the most handsome guy I've ever seen...etc. etc.' Is that right?"

"No. Well, almost, yeah."

Abby and Grandma Edna lived in Cicero, Illinois. Cicero is the eighth stop on the blue line of the "L" train heading west out of downtown Chicago. Their home was a small narrow row house with two floors. There was approximately six feet between their house and the one on either side of them, which included a fence. All the houses in the neighborhood were poorly kept, most in need of repair. Their house sat at street level, with no basement. It had tan wood shingles and a black-tarred roof, both of which should have been replaced years ago. When they could afford Grandma Edna's arthritis medication, she could walk with a cane, but when they had to pay heating or electric bills, they were forced to let her prescription lapse for a while, and she had to stay in her wheelchair. So Edna lived on the first floor of the tiny house, while Abby occupied the upstairs.

Everything inside the house was poor, shabby, and old, but clean. As one entered, there was a kitchen on the left with a small square wood table and two wooden chairs which served as a dining area. To the right was the living room. On the far right wall was an old stuffed couch with threadbare arms and cushions. There was a homemade afghan draped over the back, which adequately covered several holes. On either side of the couch were two round tables, each holding a small lamp. Perpendicular to the couch were mismatched stuffed chairs in roughly the same condition. Behind the living room, and between the living room and kitchen, was a small hallway that led to Edna's bedroom on the right and a bathroom on the left. At the back of the hall was a narrow steep stairway that led to the second floor. There, Abby had a bedroom and a study room.

Grandma Edna was still 5 foot eight, thin, and at 81, quite wrinkled about her cheeks and eyes. Given that, she was actually quite attractive. Looking at her fine features and green eyes, one was tempted to think, *My, I'll bet you were really pretty, several few years ago.* Actually, she was an 81-year-old version of Abby. Her hair was gray and cut just below her ears. But it used to be strawberry blond, like Abby's.

They were both sitting at the small kitchen/dining room table. Edna in her wheelchair and Abby on one of the hard wooden chairs, eating the salisbury steak dinner Joe Gorki's wife Alice had given Abby to take home.

"But you do know he had been stalking you for days."

"No, that was, like, just a joking way to put it. He noticed me and was too shy to come in and introduce himself. And when he did come in, well, I noticed him right away. Then I noticed he was stealing looks at me, but he was too shy to say anything. And then Sally forced me to talk to him, but I froze because he is… "

"So cute, when he smiled, you went bonkers. Yeah, yeah, yeah, I got that part."

"Well, he is."

"Abby, honey, you don't know anything about him. He could be a criminal, a member of the mob, a drug pusher, part of a street gang, or an ex-con. He might want to kidnap you."

"Grandma, he is, like, 30 years old. He's not in a street gang. He doesn't dress, look, or act like a criminal. And what would he kidnap me for? My money? I DON'T THINK SO. And I'm too old to be a white slave candidate."

"Money isn't the only thing guys want. Have you looked in the mirror lately? You are the one who is gorgeous. Maybe he just wants sex, and he's too cheap to pay a prostitute."

"Oh, for Pete's sake, that's ridiculous. I told him I was a Christian and didn't go to bed with men, and he said he'd received Christ at age 16 and wouldn't have sex outside of marriage either."

"Really!"

Chapter 8

Wednesday, July 13
Elmhurst, Illinois

"You met a girl? Now, that's interesting. I'm thinking, my grandson is 30 years old. The tabloids call him the number one most eligible bachelor in Chicago. His mother keeps throwing beautiful, wealthy, socially significant women his way. He dumps every girl he goes out with. And he drives all the way over here through rush hour traffic on a Wednesday to tell me he 'met a girl'. Now that's what I call a #1 item. So, Johnnie, when did you meet this girl?"

He looked at his watch. Then J.D., III said, "Five hours and twenty minutes ago. But actually, Grandpa, that's not actually the best question. I only actually met her once, actually."

"Okay, so what is the right question, 'actually'?"

Then J.D., III began. While looking at the floor, he spoke quickly, almost babbling and running his sentences together. "For example, a different question would be 'How many times have I seen her?' and the answer to that would be about 12 times because last week I saw her through the window in The Corner Grill. You remember The Corner Grill? It's four blocks up town from our building? Anyway, later I found out that she's been a waitress there for years. I've never been in there before, but I saw her so I walked back and forth in front of the place just to get another look at her, and I did that at lunch time for a week until I finally got the courage to go inside, and that was on Monday, and it wasn't until today that I met her, and I wouldn't have met her then except she noticed me noticing her, but she was too shy, too, but then the other waitress, she introduced us, and we talked a few minutes and then I had to go because I was late for an appointment with one of King Mahmood's guys. But I want to marry her."

The old man began to laugh. "A waitress, huh? This is going to get your mother a few extra sessions with her therapist."

"She is also dirt poor and her mother was a prostitute who died of a drug overdose when she was born, and she was placed in an orphanage, then in foster care."

"This just keeps getting better and better."

"But then her grandmother, who didn't know she existed, found her at her high school graduation, and she's been living with her grandmother ever since."

"And better and better."

"And she said she was a Christian, so if I was going to keep coming around, I should know she won't have sex before marriage."

"And even better."

"I need your advice, Grandpa."

"What for? You seem to be doing just fine."

"No, I'm not. I didn't give her my last name. Abby, that's her name, is Abigail Edna Davidson, anyway she has no idea who I am. And I'm afraid to tell her."

"Why?"

"Because of the Fitzgerald fortune, of course."

"Are you afraid she'll want you for your money or social status, like all those girls your mother sets you up with?"

"No! Just the opposite. I'm afraid she will reject me because of all that. The social gap between us is bigger than the Grand Canyon. I didn't tell her because I don't want to scare her off. Besides, if I just came out and dated her openly, the tabloids would drive her crazy and plaster strange pictures of her all over town. She'd run from me like a scalded cat. I want to spend some time with her first. I figure if we spend some time together, maybe she'll come to like me, and that will soften the blow. But I'm right in the middle of this deal with those darn crown jewels, and my father wants me to take over your multi-million dollar corporation, and my mother wants to marry me off to the wealthiest socialite she can find. I need your help, Grandpa."

"Well, let's think it through and come up with a plan."

"Grandpa, first let me ask you...this sounds like I'm in junior high or something...do you believe in love at first sight? Is this love or just physical lust or something? Am I just following my gonads or could this be real love?"

"I know a guy who fell in love the first time he saw a girl, and they were happily married for 57 years."

"Really?"

"Yup."

"Who?"

"Me. Your grandmother was the only woman in my life from the moment I saw her until she died 14 years ago. When I first saw her, she was 19 years old and the most beautiful girl on the planet."

"Was she poor?"

"Poor as a rag doll, but then so was I."

"Oh, yeah, I forgot. It seems hard thinking of you as being poor. So love can happen all at once?"

"Love is the slipperiest word in the language, Johnnie. Romantic love is self-oriented. It has to be turned into giving love if it's going to last. But if I read the Song of Solomon correctly, romance is designed to get us married. So it does play a significant role. Just realize you need to be a giver if you want to be a lover. Romance is about getting. Marriage is about giving. You need to have someone you want to give to for the rest of your life. As soon as your marriage focuses on getting, you're in trouble."

"So can you help me with a plan?"

Just then John's mother knocked on the door, and immediately opened it. "Johnnie! I thought I saw your car drive up." J.D., III rose to give his mother a hug. "Will you be staying for supper? Oh please do, we see so little of you these days, since you insist on living in that tiny cave of an apartment."

"Well, I just came to talk over a few things with Grandpa, but I haven't eaten, so sure, I'd be glad to stay for supper."

"Oh, excellent. I'll have a place set for you. It will be so much fun. Bill and Janice Collingsworth will be joining us. You remember them. He's the president of the First National Bank. Their very attractive, available, single, 24-year-old daughter, Martha, will be here, too." She smiled and walked out. As she closed the door behind her, she said, "Dinner is in 30 minutes."

J.D., III sank back to his chair, put his head down, and covered it with his hands. After a few minutes, he looked up at his grandfather. The two looked at each other a few seconds. Then the old man burst into laughter.

Chapter 9

Thursday, July 14
Madrid, Spain

Klaus Becker did not like dealing with Arab Muslims. They could not be trusted, especially if you were not another Arab Muslim. They would also lean toward religious fervor rather than logic and reason. But their value was in their determination, and their determination usually came from their religious fervor. That also brought money and force to the table, which was always helpful.

Klaus Becker worked incognito. Even his own people did not know what he looked like. He hired them, placed them, and paid them, all by a means which could not be traced. Sometimes communication was electronic, sometimes through regular mail, sometimes a young boy or a homeless person would drop off a message or a payment. But his agents were never deceived, and they were paid well, and promptly. So they were loyal to a man they had never seen. Klaus thought long and hard about sending an agent to today's meeting. He almost canceled it several times. But in the end, it looked like it would work, and work out well for both parties. He knew the Arab's goals were religious and political, but his were only financial.

Klaus Becker was a thief.

Ghazi was the #1 servant of the leader of his country's Muslim conservatives. He cared nothing about money or luxurious living. He also despised the Americans and the Europeans who lived that way. He did not like meeting with a German. He hated their atheism, their secularism, and their total disregard for the will of Allah and sharia law. He had disagreed with his own leader about using them. But in the end, he acquiesced because this would help bring about the change of government his country required, the embarrassment of America (The Great Satan), and restoration of the true worship of Allah.

Ghazi was a terrorist.

Madrid was chosen only because it was a neutral site. Even the outdoor restaurant was chosen at random and at the last minute—so that neither could station their people on the site. The time was set for noon when it would be busy. Both Ghazi and Becker's agent, a man named Hans Reinhardt, carried a red cloth in their left hand for positive identification. Both were prompt. Both wore traditional business suits. They greeted one another with a handshake and were seated at an outdoor table. There was no small talk or casual conversation. They spoke in English.

"May I just call you Ghazi, or do you prefer another name or title?"

"'Ghazi' is fine, and you?"

"Just 'Hans' is sufficient."

"Very good."

"Well then, Ghazi, let me review the arrangement as we understand it. Basically, you would like our team to steal the crown jewels of king Abdul-Ahad Mahmood, while they are being kept at the Fitzgerald Building in Chicago, and turn them over to you for a percentage of their street value."

"Specifically, for 10% of their street value."

"We will need more than that, as I am sure you know."

"I am not authorized to approve more than that."

"Sure you are."

"But your job is brief. Your team must simply get the gems from the Fitzgerald vault and hand them over to us. We are providing protection, getting the jewels out of the country, and selling them. Selling these jewels is not easy nor do they retain their street value. They must be re-cut and sold separately so that they cannot be identified. This reduces their value and takes the work of gemologists. You are thieves, very good ones, possibly the best. But I do not believe you are prepared to introduce the stones on the market without suspicion."

"Oh, we could also have them cut and sold, but it is true, Ghazi, that is not what we do. And that's why our leader is interested in this deal. But if you could do this yourself, you wouldn't be here."

"Your expertise is appreciated, but we also need these jewels to be stolen by white-skinned westerners."

"Explain."

"The true, sincere, Koran-following Muslims in my country believe King Mahmood has sold out our faith and our people to

186

western godless ways. He has ignored the clear teaching of the Koran and compromised with the Americans to bring the evils of the west into our land. The purpose of this theft is twofold. First, it will show our people that Abdul-Ahad Mahmood is a fool and a traitor for bringing to America the Crown Jewels purchased by our oil and natural gas money. We will tie the theft to a deal with the American government, but they must be stolen by white-skinned Americans. I know you are German, but you must use Americans or at least convince the surveillance cameras that you are Americans."

"And the second reason you want the jewels?"

"To finance our revolution, of course."

"Of course."

"And may I ask how you plan to get the jewels from the vault? I understand it is one or the most secure in the world."

"And probably the newest one of that size. It cannot be forcefully opened, so it must be opened with the key."

"The key? The safe has a key?"

"Just a metaphor, Ghazi. The safe can only be opened electronically, by a computer off-site, with a password kept only by the Fitzgerald family. That family is the key."

"How do you know all this and how will you get a family member to use such a password?"

"That's what we get paid for, Ghazi. Your assurance is to know we have a man on the inside who has been working for the Fitzgerald Trust Company for six months now. He has been patiently gathering the information we need."

"But the wedding of Fawzah Mahmood to the American infidel was only announced a week ago. How could you have a man on it for six months?"

"That's why you came to us, Ghazi. We are prepared. We have people working in five different companies globally. We pick the places where the largest financial deposits are made and infiltrate that operation. Our leader placed a man there six months ago because they built the most up-to-date vault in the world and started housing expensive merchandise. We have been waiting for an item worthy of our talents. This is such an item."

187

Chapter 10

Thursday July 14
Chicago, Illinois

When John did not show up during the lunch hour on Thursday, Abby worried. She was sure she had run him off, in spite of what he'd said. Sally tried to reassure her, but she was not reassured. He said he could not always be there, so she took some comfort in that. But he had been there every day for a week and a half, even if she had only known it for three days. It was just too coincidental that he would be missing the day after she told him how poor she was and her background and that she wouldn't have sex outside marriage. At 3:15, Joe called her back to the kitchen.

"You wanted me, Joe?"

"You have a phone call." Joe Gorki pointed with his thumb to a phone on the wall.

"Thank you... Hello?"

"Hi, Abby, it's John."

"Oh, hi." She tried not to sound relieved.

"I'm sorry we couldn't have lunch today. I had to work. I got an assignment at the last minute. I don't have a cell number for you, so I called The Corner Grill. I hope that's all right."

"Yes, of course. But I should not talk too long on this phone. Actually, I don't have a cell phone. We have just one, and we leave it with Grandma Edna in case she needs help during the day. I really should go now. But thank you for calling."

"Abby, wait. Can I see you after work? Maybe we could take the bus to the shoreline, have a walk near Lake Michigan and find something to eat."

"That would be nice. I get off at 4:30 today, but Grandma Edna is expecting me."

"Could you call her and see if it would be all right if you come home a few hours later?"

"Yes, I can do that."

"Great. Then I will come by The Corner Grill for you at 4:30."

He was on time, actually a few minutes early. Abby was a few minutes late. She had no time to change, or any different clothes to change into. So she just made a quick trip to the restroom behind the kitchen. She took off her apron, touched up her make-up, released her hair from its ponytail and brushed it out.

When she came into the dining room, he was sitting at his usual booth, sipping coffee. He just stared at her with his mouth half open while she said good-bye to Joe and his staff. When she walked over to his table, all he could manage was, "Wow, you look amazing."

He did not have on the jacket or the baseball cap. He wore black slacks with a tan shirt open at the collar. The clothes seemed a little more dressy and revealed a body that looked like it received a regular workout.

"You look good yourself."

" Shall we go?" They walked out into the warm afternoon and to the bus stop in the middle of the next block. John suggested they go to the Navy Pier and ride the ferris wheel, then eat at Billy Goat's Tavern and Grill in the Crystal Court building. She said she had not been there for years. So they waited for 12 minutes for the bus that would take them east, toward the Lake Michigan shoreline. As they were waiting, he looked at her and said, "I never realized that you were shorter than I was. I mean, I knew you were, but I mostly saw you when I was sitting down. I'm saying, five-foot-eight."

"You guessed it. And I'd say you were, um, oh, about six-foot- two."

"Close. Six one."

They got on a crowded bus, which did not give them a seat for ten stops. After they finally sat down, Abby said, "John?"

"Yes?"

"John what?"

"What?"

"I mean, who?"

"What, who?"

"John who?"

"This is beginning to sound like an Abbot and Costello routine, like 'Who's on first?'"

189

Abby laughed but then continued, "I mean, what is your last name? You know, most people have at least two parts to their name, called a first name and a last name. Some even have three. For example, my name is Abigail Edna Davidson. And your name is John...... ?"

J.D. Fitzgerald, III looked at her, then he looked down at the floor. Then he looked at her again. Then he looked out the window. Then she said, "This is not a difficult question, John. Those of us without Alzheimer's or amnesia don't usually have a problem with this one. We can make this an open book test if you like, you can take time to look in your wallet and check your driver's license or something."

John smiled, looked at her and said, "Abby, we have to talk."

"Our first date, and it sounds like you are breaking up with me."

John chuckled a little. "No, no...it's...I...I have been thinking about this ever since I saw you and, well, I know it sounds crazy, and it's not a reasonable thing to ask, especially since we've just met and all. But...I have a proposal I'd like you to consider."

"Wow, all the way from breaking up to proposing in less than a minute. That could be a record."

After another brief laugh, John took her hand and said, "I'm not going to get down on one knee on this bus, but... would you see me for two weeks before I tell you my last name or my job?"

"Now there's a proposal a girl doesn't get every day. I'm going to bet no girl has ever had a proposal like that. Let me see if I understand. You want me to go out with you, and we talk, and you get to know me, but I can't get to know you. Is that right?"

"No, no, no. You can ask anything you want and I'll either answer honestly, or tell you I don't want to answer that for two weeks. The point is, I don't want to lie to you. I want you to know I will never lie to you. I just want to intentionally with-hold that information. Now, I know you could easily find out if you started digging. But I'm asking you not to do that—for two weeks. But I want to give you control of the discussion."

"How's that?"

"If at any time during the next two weeks you tell me you will not continue to see me unless I tell you, then I will tell you. So you have the control, but I'm asking you to wait. Okay?"

"But I can ask whatever I want?"

"Yes, but..."

"I know, I know, you can refuse to answer, but only for 14 days, right?"

"Right."

"All right, John."

"Actually, my family calls me Johnnie."

"Well, now, that's progress. You have a family, and they call you Johnnie. Okay, Johnnie Q. Whoever, I accept your proposal. First question. Are you an escaped convict?"

Chapter 11

Friday – Tuesday, July 15-26
Various Places in the Chicago Area

For 12 days they dated. From about 4 until about 8 P.M. they were together, every day including Saturday and Sunday. Abby talked about her childhood experiences without a real mother or father and cried a few times. Then she recounted some of the adventures she had with Cassy, and they both laughed a lot. John told her he had a mother and father, a half-brother from his father's first wife, and a grandfather. But he only talked about his grandfather. He said that he worked at the Fitzgerald Building, but not what he did there. He spoke of a few isolated incidences of his childhood, but he was careful to not include any clues about the wealth that surrounded it. They spoke some about social issues and even a little about politics.

But a big part of their discussion was about God and the Bible. Abby never could get the hang of going to church, but to please Edna, she attended her grandmother's Baptist church. John went to an independent Bible church, which was theologically very similar to the Baptists.

They disagreed about a few things. She believed all the spiritual gifts were operable today, like the Assembly of God Church in Michigan that she attended with Cassy. Although she did not participate in tongue speaking, prophesying or healing, she believed some of it was real. John didn't. John believed men should not, and women should, wear something on their heads while praying. Abby didn't. John believed every Christian should go to church on Sunday. Abby didn't. And they found it interesting debating those things.

But for the most part, they agreed. They both believed that the Bible was the inspired inerrant Word of God. They believed it should be understood literally, determining the author's intended meaning through the context. They both believed that humans are all sinners and therefore unacceptable to a holy God, but that God sent His Son, who was born as Jesus of Nazareth, to die on the cross to pay for man's sin. Both believed that Jesus had to be received by a prayer-like decision.

They agreed that since there was no other provision for man's sin, all other religions were manmade ideas. Neither were universalists, nor did they believe God tolerated sin or other religions.

They agreed that the Bible forbids divorce and remarriage, fornication, and therefore cohabitation. They believed that this age of grace would end with the Rapture of the church, followed by a terrible time of Tribulation on earth, followed by the Second Coming of Christ, followed by a thousand-year reign of Christ on earth, followed by the judgment of all unbelievers, and the eternal state of everyone either in the New Jerusalem or the lake of fire. They talked for a whole "date" about the apparent conflict between man's free will and God's sovereignty. In the end, they decided that somehow both were true.

They walked and talked, and somewhere during the third "date," they began holding hands. Sometimes John would put his arm around her waist. And sometimes Abby would rest her head on his shoulder. But he never kissed her. First, she was uneasy about it, wondering if he would. Then she was uneasy about it, wondering why he didn't. Their noses touched a couple of times and twice his lips brushed against hers. But no real kiss.

On the 12th day, they discussed meeting each other's families. Abby wanted John to meet her grandmother. John did not want Abby to meet his parents, for reasons he said he would explain after two more days, but he did want her to meet his grandfather. So they called both grandparents and arranged a meeting where John and his grandfather would come to Abby's and Grandma Edna's house for supper. John suggested they bring along take-out, but Grandma Edna insisted on making the whole meal.

Chapter 12

Wednesday, July 27
Cicero, Illinois

J.D. Fitzgerald and J.D. Fitzgerald, III arrived in front of Abby's and Edna Davidson's tiny row house in the six-year-old Ford Explorer owned by J.D. Fitzgerald, III. It took a few minutes for the senior Fitzgerald to exit the vehicle and make his way to the door. John walked slowly alongside his grandfather, but the old man walked steadily on his own. Abby opened the door and introduced herself. She was nervous, but mostly about how it would go introducing Grandma Edna. When J.D. spotted Edna sitting in the living room in her wheelchair, he walked directly to her and extended his hand. When she took it, he kissed her fingers. "I am so happy to meet you, Mrs. Davidson."

"Edna, please call me Edna."

"May I call you Miss Edna? The southerners do that, you know, and I rather like it."

"Yes, of course, if you like. I've never been called that before."

"Well, all the better, then. No one told me you were such an attractive woman, Miss Edna. And what a wonderful home you have here."

"It's small and old, but we like it."

"It's perfect. I love it. It's cozy, warm, and surrounded by paintings. Where ever did you get all these paintings? They are magnificent."

"Well, actually, I painted them."

"Really! They are very good. Do you sell them?"

"Oh, no, I can't imagine anyone paying money for them."

"I suspect you are wrong, Miss Edna. I'm no art critic, but I've bought my share of paintings, and these are quite professional."

"You flatter me, sir."

"Oh, no, Miss Edna, I never flatter. And I am so sorry I did not introduce myself. My name is John."

J.D., III and Abby were a bit surprised at being sidelined. Both had anticipated an awkward period of introductions, followed by a stilted time of meaningless small talk, while hoping the grandparents would eventually speak freely. Instead, they warmed up to each other so quickly, the young people had to catch up.

"Grandma," Abby broke in, taking J.D., III by the hand and leading him into the living room, "This is John, or I guess, this is also John."

"It is good to finally meet you, ma'am." J.D., III also took Edna's hand but did not kiss it. "Abby has told me so much about you, I'm glad to finally make your acquaintance. And just for clarification, Grandpa and I are both named John. My family calls him Grandpa and me Johnnie. And I might just say, Grandpa is a bit odd, but he never flatters. I've never known him to say something he did not truly believe."

"This painting here," J.D. interrupted with his back to everyone, having made his way to the far wall where he had put on glasses to examine the picture. "This painting of the lovely girl next to the straight-tail Cessna 172, is that Abby?"

Edna scooted her wheelchair closer to the wall before answering. "No, actually, that's me. I painted it from an old photo. It's the day I soloed."

"You fly? You're a pilot?"

"Oh, that was years ago. Yes, I earned my private pilot license when I was 19 years old. My father had an airplane back then. Cessna stopped making the straight-tail 172s years ago. That was a brand new airplane back then. I loved to fly. My son was a pilot, too, but he was killed in a car accident."

"Oh, I'm so sorry to hear that," J.D. said, turning back to look at her. "When is the last time you have flown?"

"Oh dear, it has been over 30 years. Do you fly, John?"

John looked over at Johnnie as if to ask permission to answer the question. Johnnie shrugged his shoulders and nodded. "Yes, actually, Johnnie and I both fly. I don't fly by myself any more, but Johnnie stays current. He has his private, commercial, and instrument ratings."

Abby looked at Johnnie with a shocked expression on her face. He looked back at her and grimaced a bit. "Well, you didn't ask," was all he could manage.

From then on, the conversation went to airplanes and flying, mostly, comparing flying in the 50s to flying today. Abby found herself left almost completely out of the conversation. But she didn't mind. Actually, she was a little relieved. She envisioned an evening where she would have to carry the discussion. Now she could barely get a word in. As they ate, Johnnie tried to bring her in by explaining things from time to time, but the bulk of it was John and Edna sharing stories from the 1950s and 60s. The stories continued over a delicious blueberry cobbler Edna had fixed for desert.

As they were putting on their coats to leave, John surprised everyone. He walked up to Edna, took her hand, and said, "Miss Edna, I would like to ask you out on a date. Would you have dinner with me at my favorite restaurant tomorrow evening?"

"What!"

"What!"

"Why, yes, John. I would love that."

"What!"

"What!"

"We could ask the kids to join us for a double date, they seem to be getting nervous."

"Well, yes, I guess we probably should do that," Edna chuckled. "We wouldn't want to be rude."

"Although they will probably spoil the fun, my grandson is such a conservative."

"Well, nobody ever accused Abby of being a conservative."

"I don't believe this," Johnnie said looking at Abby. "They're talking about us like we're not here."

John continued with his back to the young people, "Hmmm…a liberal and a conservative. That might be interesting. Anyway, I suspect we should probably invite them or else they'll make a fuss. What do you think, Miss Edna?"

"Oh, I suppose." Now both of the grandparents began to chuckle.

"It's a date, then. A double-date. We will pick you up a bit early, about 4:00, if you don't mind. And my favorite restaurant is a bit formal. You just need to wear a dress of some sort."

The men said their good-byes and left. As soon as they were in the car, Johnnie turned to his grandfather and just stared at him a few minutes.

"What?"

"A date?"

"I like her. I like both of them. It will be fun. I haven't been on a date since your grandmother died."

"To your favorite restaurant?"

"Yeah, so?"

"Grandpa, your favorite restaurant is in New York City!"

Chapter 13

Wednesday, July 27
Vienna, Austria

Klaus Becker arranged a final meeting between Hans and Ghazi in a coffee shop near St. Stephensplatz, in the center of Vienna. After a brief handshake, it was down to business. Hans began with a review of their situation. "The robbery of the Mahmood dynasty Crown Jewels is scheduled to take place on Saturday evening, August 6. Let me review the objective generally, to be sure we agree. Then we shall discuss details. The goal is for my team to obtain the jewels from the safe at the Fitzgerald Building in downtown Chicago. Then we shall hand the Crown Jewels over to you, and you shall wire our fee to a Swiss bank account. You will then take them out of the country, launder them, and use the proceeds for whatever you like. My understanding is you intend to finance a Muslim Jihad against the government of your own country. But that is no concern of ours. The point is, there will no longer be any need for you to contact us. We will get our fee on the front end. We will essentially sell the jewels to you immediately after the robbery. It that your understanding?"

"That is correct."

"Then there only remains the matter of our fee. We need 25% of their street value."

"I have been authorized to offer you a flat 20 million U.S. dollars. We will put it in any account you like upon reception of all the Crown Jewels. If you insist on more, we walk now."

Hans thought about that for a while without speaking. Realizing this was all he would get, and it was within the limits Klaus Becker had approved, he agreed. "All right, Ghazi, but we get the money before you get the gems."

"We will make the exchange at the same time."

"Good."

"Now my superior would like to know exactly how you plan to take the jewels and escape."

"Getting the jewels out of the vault is not difficult," Hans continued. "As I mentioned when we met previously, we have a man on the inside. The third generation Fitzgerald, a man named J.D. Fitzgerald, III is in charge of housing the jewels. Since he is a family member, either he will have the code for opening the safe or he will know who does. After the jewels have been obtained, the younger Fitzgerald will be handed over to you as a hostage to insure your escape."

"And the escape plan?"

"Before the robbery, we will hijack one of the family helicopters and force their pilot to fly us to the heliport on the roof of the Fitzgerald Building. That will not raise suspicion since their executives use it regularly. We will enter the building from the heliport. We expect to arrive at 7 P.M. This is before the gems are deposited and the royal entourage has left. We will wait until they leave. After that, there should be only a crew of guards, a few janitors, and the younger Fitzgerald in the building."

"How many men will you have, and where exactly do you want our people?"

"Altogether, our team has seven men. We will be armed with automatic weapons, grenades, and plastic explosives. You will station sharp shooters with rifles and grenade launchers on the roof of the surrounding buildings. Their job is to blow up anything that comes down the streets surrounding the Fitzgerald Building after the robbery begins. We will gather everyone in the first-floor lobby. We may have to shoot a few of them just to prove we are serious. Then I will call 911 myself and give instructions for the police to stay at least one block away. They won't listen, of course, and that's where you come in. Your snipers will destroy any police vehicle that enters any street surrounding that building. After obtaining the jewels, I will instruct the helicopter pilot to fly due north until he is forced to land by a police or military aircraft."

"How will you get out of the helicopter before it's forced down?"

"We will never be in it. Our inside man has learned that there is a passageway that the Fitzgeralds discovered under the building when they bought it back in the 70s. That will lead us out to the subway tunnel, which will take us to the subway station, which will lead us out beyond the police barricade. While the police are focused on the helicopter and the hostages still in the Fitzgerald Building, we will simply emerge from the subway station. We shall then walk to North LaSalle Street, where you will pick us up, and we will exchange the gems."

"So all you need from us is fire power on the adjacent roofs, is that correct?"

"Yes, but there is one other item. Trust. I don't want you to just shoot us and take the jewels, nor do you want us to shoot you."

"Well, of course. Do you have something in mind?"

"Yes, Ghazi, I do. I have recorded both today's meeting and the one in Madrid."

"WHAT!" Ghazi stood up suddenly.

"Take it easy. Relax. Sit back down. You will have a disk, and I will have a disk containing both discussions. If both of us come out alive and the deal goes as planned, then we each simply destroy our disks. But if one of us does not survive, then he can have the disk made public by some associates. For example, I will have mine in the hands of a friend who I will pay to not send the disk to the press, the FBI, and Interpol. I will pay him every day until I return. If I stop paying him, he sends the disk. You can do the same. That assures each of us that both of us will come out alive and well. Who says there is no honor among thieves?"

Chapter 14

Thursday, July 28
Chicago

Abby and Grandma Edna were ready by 3:30. They each wore the new dress they bought for the wedding of a friend at church a year ago. Edna's was light blue with lace about the neck and sleeves. Abby's dress was navy with a high cut neckline, covered shoulders, and short sleeves. Edna had her hair done, and Abby wore hers down and loose, curled slightly under at the ends.

After 3:45, they both began to peek out the window on a regular basis. At 4:06, a long black vehicle pulled up in front of their house. From a chair across the room, Edna, who could only see out part of the window said, "Looks like there's a hearse out there."

Abby ran to the window. "No, that's a limo."

"What's it doing here?"

"Looks like the mafia."

"Probably some drug lords. We know the people across the street do drugs."

"I wish they wouldn't park there. The guys won't be able to pull up to our..." Then Abby let out a gasp that sounded like she'd seen a ghost.

"What's the matter, dear? Are you all right?"

"I'm not sure. Johnnie just got out of the back door of that limo."

When Abby answered the door, he presented her with a white rose and a "Wow, you look terrific." Then he also gave one to Grandma Edna and offered her his arm. "Shall we go? I persuaded Grandpa to wait in the car." The limo driver was holding the door open, and as Edna ducked down to get in, John extended his hand to help her. Then he greeted everyone and introduced their driver, an elderly man named Gerald Evans. Edna sat next to John, facing backwards, while Abby sat next to Johnnie, facing forward. As they started, Abby looked at Johnnie and said, "I can't believe you guys rented a limo."

"We didn't," Johnnie answered.

"What did you do, steal it?"

Then Johnnie pointed to his grandfather and said, "It's his. But if you don't like it, he has five more of them you can choose from. Ladies let me introduce you to J.D. Fitzgerald, one of the wealthiest men in America. If I recall correctly, Forbes had him #18 last week."

"And," his grandfather added, "Let me introduce you to J.D. Fitzgerald, III."

They sat in silence for almost a minute. Abby's mouth was open, but no sound came out. Finally, she managed to say, "The Fitzgerald Building." Still sitting on the front edge of the seat, she faced Johnnie nose-to-nose. "You said you work at the Fitzgerald Building. But you own the building?"

"Yes, well, I also work there."

Speechless, she collapsed back into the soft leather. After a few minutes, she looked at Johnnie again. "Are you... Is this... for real? Is this, like, some sort of elaborate joke you guys are pulling?" With that, Johnnie reached into his pocket, pulled out his wallet, and handed her a stack of cards. She looked at a driver's license, a private pilot's license, a social security card, and several credit cards. The driver's license had his picture on it, and all of them said *John David Fitzgerald, III.* She handed back the cards, put her head back on the seat and closed her eyes. Then she opened them and looked at Johnnie again. "I thought you were, like, wanted by the law, or out on parole, or in the mafia or something."

"Interesting," John injected, "and yet you continued to see him for two weeks."

"Are you disappointed?" Johnnie asked Abby.

She laughed nervously a little before she said, "I don't know what I am."

"Well, I know what I am," John said. "I'm hungry. And it will be a few hours before we get to the restaurant. There are usually some pretty good snacks in this fridge. But there is better food on the plane."

"THE PLANE?!?" both Abby and Edna said at the same time.

202

"Yeah, Grandpa neglected to tell you his favorite restaurant is in New York City. We'll be flying there on one of his private jets." At this point, neither of the women could speak.

But John could. "By the way, I neglected to say how beautiful you girls look tonight. Don't they look beautiful tonight, Johnnie?"

"Stunning."

"But, Miss Edna, I have a question," John continued. "When we were here yesterday, you seemed bound to your wheelchair. Today I saw you walk to the car with ease."

"Oh, that's because I took my arthritis medicine today. When I take it, I can walk quite well."

"So why don't you take it every day?"

"Oh, we can't afford that. The medication is very expensive, and our only income is Abby's job and a small pension. Sometimes we have to pay bills with the money."

"What pharmacy do you use?"

"Walgreens on South Laramie. Why?"

John pulled out his cell phone and punched a button. "Hi, Alice. I need you to call the Walgreens drugstore on South Laramie and give them the name Edna Davidson, 12876 West 26th Street. Whatever she gets there is on my card…. That's correct….nope, no limitations or expiration….. Yes, uh huh. Thank you, dear. You're a jewel. Bye."

"John, what are you doing?"

"Calling my secretary. She's terrific. Gets every detail. When you're my age, you need someone like her."

"No, I mean, are you paying for all of my medications?"

"I am paying for anything you buy at that drugstore. My guess is Medicare pays for surgery and doctor visits but your insurance will not cover your prescriptions or incidental medical needs. Well, now they are covered."

"But I…what…why would you do that?"

"Because I can."

Chapter 15

"What kind of plane is this?" Abby stared at the aircraft, still in disbelief.

"It's called a Cessna Citation CJ-3. It's grandpa's smallest airplane. He also has a Gulfstream 250 and 450. But this is my favorite. It's sleek as an arrow and cruises at over 470 miles per hour. It's like a rocket with a cabin inside."

They were introduced to the pilot, a thin dark-haired man named Bob Randolph. Bob helped them get on board and settled in their seats. As she was being helped up the steps, Edna asked, "Is there a copilot?"

"Yup," John answered. "There is. You're the copilot, Miss Edna."

"Oh, no, John. I haven't flown in over 30 years. I couldn't possibly fly this airplane."

"Not to worry, Bob is single-pilot-certified in this airplane. He flies it by himself all the time. We often have customers sit in the copilot seat. Please sit up there. It's the best seat in the house. Bob will coach you along and let you fly it as much as you like. Just do what you are comfortable with. But I'd suggest you get your hands on those controls. She's smooth as silk, and Bob won't let you make any mistakes."

"Oh my, well, if you say so. It would be a thrill just to sit up there."

"I'll help you get buckled in. When we get to our cruise altitude, I'll come up and see how you're doing."

John helped Edna negotiate the entrance to the cockpit and get settled in the right seat with her headphone, seatbelt, and shoulder harness on. Then he settled himself in the front part of the main cabin. This particular Citation was arranged with a divider in the main cabin. Johnnie told his grandfather he would like to sit with Abby in the rear part so they could talk.

"Sure, sit wherever you like. There are some Cokes and sandwiches in the cooler and coffee in the thermos."

Johnnie and Abby sat next to each other, just in front of the wing. The seats were a light tan leather, large enough for Abby to sit beside herself. There was a table in front of them and large widows gave excellent visibility. "Do you think Grandma Edna will actually fly the plane some of the time?"

"Absolutely. My guess is she'll take it off, fly it all the way to New York, and land it."

"But, Johnnie, she hasn't flown for years. Is that possible?"

"Bob will talk her through it and help her when she needs it. But this thing is easier to fly than the Cessna 172 she soloed in. I'm not certified in this airplane, but I've made several takeoffs and landings with Bob. The hard part is all the backup systems, emergency procedures, and avionics. The radio work is a bit hectic, flying into New York. Also the throttles are different in a jet. But Bob will handle all of that. The basic yoke and rudder work is pretty simple. But sit back. This bird is not like an airliner. When it takes off, you will feel the acceleration. And it goes up at 4,000 feet a minute. We'll punch a hole in that cloud layer up there in no time."

Even with the warning, Abby gasped when the engines came to full power and she was thrust into the back of her seat. She watched in amazement as the aircraft lifted off and its nose pointed at the sky. In no time, they were through the clouds and beginning to level off.

"This thing is amazing!" She looked out the window a few minutes, then she turned toward Johnnie, who was only looking at her. "What?"

"I'm wondering how you are taking all this. What you are thinking about it all...and me?"

"I'm, like, so out of my world I don't even know...18th most wealthy person in the country. Just about how much is that?"

"A little over 12 billion dollars."

"B-B-B-Billion."

"Around 12 of them."

"My word. How did he make all that money?"

"He built the Trust Company on the idea of helping people follow the book of Proverbs, with an emphasis on staying completely away from debt. Then when Fanny May and Freddy Mac started making huge loans to unqualified homebuyers, Grandpa pulled out of the market. He had almost all his money in gold and other precious metals as well as oil and non-debt items before the market fell in 2008. When it hit 7,000, he started buying back in. He bought businesses, buildings, and land for a fraction of what it sold for before '08. Wherever there is debt, he gets out. When things operate without it, he gets in."

"Does he always live like this?"

"Actually, no. He's just doing this for us and your grandmother. I think Grandpa owns two suits that he bought at J.C. Penny's, and they are both old and cost less than $200. He wears no jewelry except a $29 watch he bought at WalMart. Until three yeas ago, he lived in a house about the size of yours and drove the SUV I'm driving now. Then he bought a car that was easier to get in and out of, but he got one that was five years old. Three years ago, it was decided that it was too risky for him to be living alone, so we moved him into my parents' mansion where he has a small bedroom and an office on the third floor."

"Yes, I've seen pictures of the Fitzgerald mansion. It's fabulous."

"Yeah, my dad agrees with Grandpa about making money, but not about spending it. Mom and Dad live the high life— mansions, boats, airplanes three times the size of this one, Rolex watches, gold jewelry. I don't think he's ever owned a suit that cost less than a thousand dollars, and he has a closet full of them. And he dresses like a pauper compared to my mother. Abby, I want you to know I'm not like that. I'm like Grandpa. I hate all that opulence. But he and I are Christians. My parents are not. Grandpa led me to Christ when I was 16, and he has discipled me ever since. My parents go to church and play the Christian game, but they have never received Christ as their God and Savior, and they could care less about following the Bible. We keep praying for them, of course, but they are stuck in this world."

"But you have to live there, too, if you work for your father."

"Yes, and I don't want to deceive you about that. If you stay with me, you will have to do some of that, too—making trips like this one, and sometimes to London, or Paris or the Mideast, or who knows where. And from time to time, you will be asked to dress up in one of those ridiculously expensive dresses and go to some stuffy party full of rich people."

"I'd be totally out of place at one of those parties."

"Abby, let me tell you something. If you walked into one of those parties wearing a burlap bag, the next day all the women would be wearing burlap. If you looked like you look right now, every man in the room would fall in love with you. And every woman in the room would hate you, because no matter what they wore or how long they spent at the beauty parlor, they'd look like hags next to you."

"Johnnie, you are being silly."

"I am not. Just look around when we walk into that restaurant tonight. All kinds of rich people will say 'Hi' to Grandpa, but they will all be looking at you—the men for one reason, the women for another."

"No, they won't."

"Wanna bet?"

"Would you stop that!?!"

"Well, they will."

"I have a serious question."

"What?"

"Could you leave all this?"

"In a heart beat. I have a law degree, and I've passed the bar in Illinois. I could set up shop as a small-time lawyer and live in my apartment and be happy."

"Then why don't you?"

"It's about calling. This is where God put me, and I think I can use Grandpa's idea and help people understand that it comes from God's Word. I can also help steer the money toward missions, evangelism, and the teaching of the Word of God. But mostly it's about being a witness for Christ through the work itself.... Abby, I also have a serious question. A request, actually."

207

"Okay."

"Please don't run away. Give me a chance. Give it some time."

"I'm not running away, Johnnie. I want to be with you. You're...I'm...but...we are so far apart."

"Not spiritually. Spiritually, you are more wealthy than I am. And that's what counts. This money is just worldly stuff. It's ultimately worthless. We will leave it all behind, and it will all burn up."

"I'd really like to hear your grandfather's views on the whole money thing. But, truthfully, I'm a little intimidated by him."

"Oh, he's easy to talk to. Besides, you might be stuck with him."

"What do you mean?"

"Have you noticed how our grandparents look at each other? What if they fall in love and get married? I've not seen Grandpa that interested in a woman since Grandma died. Actually, I've never seen him interested in a woman at all since Grandma died."

Abby began to laugh. She laughed and laughed. In the midst of laughing, she said, "They would never do that." Gradually, she stopped laughing and her smile began to fade. Then her eyes widened and she suddenly turned and looked at Johnnie. "They wouldn't, would they? Johnnie tell me they wouldn't... Oh no. Oh my, oh my, my, my, my. Ooooh, my."

Chapter 16

Thursday, July 28
New York City

Sure enough! As the waiter led them to their seats in the restaurant, many people stopped J.D. Fitzgerald to say "Hello" and tell him how they'd missed seeing him. Then he would introduce them to his guests. But all eyes were on Abby—the men for one reason, the women for another.

When they finally got seated, Abby commented, "I must admit, I have never been in a restaurant where it took me 20 minutes to get seated while being led to my seat."

"Sorry about that. I used to come here often, and there are a lot of old friends."

"Oh, no, I didn't mean to complain. I think it's wonderful that you know so many people who all seem to be so friendly and interested in you."

Three waiters took drink orders then brought out fresh fruit, hot nuts, and a tray of various pates and spreads with hot bread and whipped butter. J.D. offered a prayer for the food.

"What do I do with all this silverware?" Edna wanted to know.

"The rule of thumb is to start from the outside and work in," Johnnie informed.

"Or you can do what I do," J.D. interrupted. "I just pick the fork I like and use it for everything." This was followed by laughs all around.

"Grandpa, Abby would like to know your philosophy of money, but she is too shy to ask."

"Johnnie!"

"What would you like to know, dear?" Abby was sitting to his right, so J.D. put his wrinkled hand on top of her smooth one and continued, "Would you like to ask a specific question or should I just babble on? I'm used to babbling, but I'd rather hear what's on your mind."

"Um, well, what about all the warnings in the Bible about wealth?"

"Yes, let's write down some passages about money, so we can talk about them one at a time." The elder Fitzgerald put on some reading glasses, took a pen from his shirt pocket and asked the waiter hovering behind him for a piece of paper. A whole pad of paper was delivered 30 seconds later. Then looking to the elderly lady on his left, he said, "My handwriting is a bit shaky. Miss Edna, you're the artist, will you be our stenographer?"

"Sure. Glad to."

"Whoever thinks of a verse, Johnnie can read it on his iPhone, and Miss Edna can jot down our comments. Let's start with Psalms 24:1."

"Let's see, give me a minute to get the app working. Here it is, Psalm 24:1 *The earth is the LORD'S, and all it contains, The world, and those who dwell in it.*"

"That tells us all wealth belongs to God. Actually, there is also a verse in Haggai 2 where God says, *the silver is Mine and the gold is Mine.* Now, look up 1 Samuel 2:7."

"Ummm...just a minute. It says: *The LORD makes poor and rich; He brings low, He also exalts.*"

"So we know, for reasons all His own, God puts His wealth wherever He wants it. In the Old Testament, it is more of a blessing, and in the New Testament it is more of a stewardship, but the reason I have more wealth than most is only because God decided to put some of His wealth with me. He puts it in the hands of good people, bad people, hard workers, lazy people, honest people, and thieves. But make no mistake about it, the money is God's. It's His and He decides where it will be placed. It does not belong to me. I'm just a caretaker who will stand before the Judgment Seat of Christ and give an account for what I did with it."

"But you made your money helping people make money," Abby added.

"Yes, there is another significant biblical principle. It is also true that if you follow the wisdom of the book of Proverbs, most people, most of the time, will have sufficient wealth. A disease or disaster can wipe out anybody, and a few will be in the right place at an opportune time to get rich. But the reason I have financial wealth is not because I was somehow smarter or better or wiser. Actually, moderation is ideal. Years ago, I memorized Proverbs 30:8-9. It says: *Give me neither poverty nor riches; feed me with the food that is my portion, that I not be full and deny You and say, "Who is the LORD?" Or that I not be in want and steal, and profane the name of my God."*

"But Mr. Fitzgerald, sir," Abby interrupted, "as I recall, there is also a verse in Proverbs which says: *Do not weary yourself to gain wealth, cease from your consideration of it."*

"Yes, that's Proverbs 23:4," Johnnie added after searching for it on his phone.

"And," Abby continued, "look up 1 Timothy 6:9-10. I remember studying that with Cassy. She's the friend who led me to Christ and tried her best to disciple me. I can't quote it, but I remember it's a warning about being wealthy."

"Just a minute. Yeah, here it is. It says: *But those who want to get rich fall into temptation and a snare and many foolish and harmful desires which plunge men into ruin and destruction. For the love of money is a root of all sorts of evil, and some by longing for it have wandered away from the faith and pierced themselves with many griefs."*

J.D. answered, "The Bible tells us to work hard, not go into debt, take care of our families and those around us in need. But we are not to try to get rich. Paul warned Timothy, and all of us, not to be someone who wants to get rich, someone who loves money, or someone who longs for it. Our work may or may not make us wealthy, but we are never to work for wealth. As soon as we do that, we are serving money instead of God. And that is the core difference between the Fitzgerald Trust Company and all others I know of. We are not trying to help people get wealthy. Our planners make that clear right from the start. We are trying to help people have stable finances through stable lives, not use biblical principles to get rich. If we set a goal of being wealthy, we will tend to justify sin when it aids in our pursuit of wealth."

Grandma Edna leaned back, took a sip of coffee and added, "And Jesus gave us a heavenly perspective not found in Proverbs, didn't He?"

"Yes, that's important to recognize. Proverbs is just about living in this world. When Christ and the apostles came along, they added a whole new element, a focus on the eternal. And the eternal always trumps the temporal. So we suggest a person follow the financial wisdom of Proverbs as sort of an earthly, temporal foundation, but trump it with a heavenly perspective."

"Do most of your clients do that?" Abby asked. "I mean, trump the earthly with the heavenly?"

"No. Probably not."

The discussion went on during their soup and salad. Before the entrées came, Johnnie excused himself to use the restroom. Edna followed suit. This left Abby alone at the table with the elder Fitzgerald. "I hope you aren't offended by my questions, Mr. Fitzgerald. This is not just a theoretical issue for me."

"Oh, I know. My grandson is not pursuing you because he needs a date to the prom. I know both of you are thinking about the future. So, of course, you need to think about our way of life." He put his hand on her arm and squeezed a little. "You ask all the questions you want, dear. I would love to have you in the family. You and Johnnie will have to figure out your future personally. But if I can help give perspective, or help with anything else at all, you just let me know."

She reached over and kissed him on the cheek. "You are a sweetheart." Just then the younger Fitzgerald returned. Abby looked up at him before he sat down and said, "You need to know that I think I have fallen in love with your grandfather."

"Oh great, just great! I take her on a double date, and she falls for the other guy."

Chapter 17

"This sirloin is terrific," Abby announced about halfway through her steak. Then she set down her fork, the one she used for everything, and looked at J.D. "I have a question. Jesus told the rich young ruler, *go and sell your possessions and give to the poor, and you will have treasure in heaven; and come, follow Me.* I understand your perspective, Mr. Fitzgerald, but how do you really know that you aren't justifying keeping the money? I realize the rich young ruler was asked to give up his money because it was keeping him from God, or maybe it was his god. But how can anyone with money know whether or not that's true of them?"

"Excellent question, Abby. And I suspect in the end there is no way to be completely sure. Unlike my son and daughter-in-law, Johnnie and I are committed to the idea that we could walk away at any time. But there is probably no way to know that unless we chose to, or were forced to, do that. And we don't feel convicted of the Holy Spirit to do that. Of course, it could be we have become insensitive to the Spirit's conviction."

"But Abby," Edna answered her granddaughter between bites of roast duck, "the Bible does not condemn being wealthy. Abraham was godly and wealthy, so were Job, Joseph, David, Daniel, Boaz, Joseph of Arimathea, the Lydia of Acts 16, and the wife of Herod's steward in Luke 8, who supported the apostles. Jesus' friends Mary, Martha, and Lazarus seemed to be wealthy, at least wealthy enough for Mary to anoint Jesus with expensive perfume. Jesus didn't tell them to give it all to the poor. Actually, in that case, it was Judas who suggested they do that."

"Grandpa and I see the biggest problem as one of living in luxury," Johnnie added. "In Luke 16, Jesus told the story about the rich man and the poor beggar named Lazarus. I'll look it up... Yes, here it is. Let me read it.

Now there was a rich man, and he habitually dressed in purple and fine linen, joyously living in splendor every day. And a poor man named Lazarus was laid at his gate, cov-

ered with sores, and longing to be fed with the crumbs which were falling from the rich man's table. besides, even the dogs were coming and licking his sores. Now the poor man died and was carried away by the angels to Abraham's bosom; and the rich man also died and was buried. In Hades he lifted up his eyes, being in torment, and saw Abraham far away and Lazarus in his bosom. And he cried out and said, "Father Abraham, have mercy on me, and send Lazarus so that he may dip the tip of his finger in water and cool off my tongue, for I am in agony in this flame." But Abraham said, "Child, remember that during your life you received your good things, and likewise Lazarus bad things; but now he is being comforted here, and you are in agony."

What is interesting to me is that it seems Abraham, who lived 2,000 years before this rich man, was far more wealthy in his day than the rich man in this story. He probably could have bought out this rich guy ten times over. So why was Abraham in paradise lecturing this guy about wealth? Well, it seems to me, the difference is, this rich man was *habitually dressed in purple and fine linen, joyously living in splendor every day,* whereas Abraham lived in a tent. Plus, this rich guy ignored the needs of the poor man named Lazarus. Abraham used his wealth to take care of others. He even rescued Lot with 318 young men born into his household. Abraham could have lived in a palace somewhere, but he chose to live in a tent."

"Now that I think about it," Edna broke in, "Jesus is actually the perfect example here, as in everything else. He was able to live as wealthy as He wanted. Anybody who can feed over 5,000 with a few loaves of bread and couple of fish, get a coin from the mouth of a fish, command a huge catch of fish, and raise people from the dead, does not need money to be wealthy. A Creator has ultimate wealth. He could live however He wanted, but He seemed to live with nothing but His daily bread and the clothes on His back. He said: *The foxes have holes and the birds of the air have nests, but the Son of Man has nowhere to lay His head."*

"Actually," Abby half agreed, "Jesus saw everything as belonging to God the Father, and He used it for eternal purposes."

"Exactly," J.D. summarized. "And that's the point of Luke 16. The parable at the beginning of the chapter is about an unjust steward who was praised by his master for being shrewd. And his shrewdness was that he prepared for his future by helping others who would welcome him into their dwellings. Jesus applied this by saying, *make friends for yourselves by means of the wealth of unrighteousness, so that when it fails, they will receive you into the **eternal** dwellings*. The point is to take earthly wealth, which actually isn't ours anyway because it belongs to God, and turn it into heavenly rewards, which is our true wealth."

Abby pointed with her fork at Johnnie, and said, "Look up James 5 on that app of yours. Read verses 1 and 5."

"Okay, just a minute. Verse 1 says, *Come now, you rich, weep and howl for your miseries which are coming upon you.* Verse 5 says, *You have lived luxuriously on the earth and led a life of wanton pleasure; you have fattened your hearts in a day of slaughter.*"

"If the problem is living in luxury," Abby continued but turned and looked at J.D., "then aren't we doing that right now?"

Chapter 18

J.D. took a sip of coffee before he said, "I believe that whatever luxury we reward ourselves with will detract from our eternal rewards."

"Really, wow! Why do you think that?" Edna wanted to know.

"Because in the sermon on the level place in Luke 6, Jesus said, *woe to you who are rich, for you are receiving your comfort in full.* So it seems to me, we really have to be careful about giving ourselves rewards here on earth. The point seems to be to leave this world with the scales balanced against you."

"I don't understand," Edna looked puzzled.

"Life isn't fair or just. We receive things and we give things. The goal is to exit this life having given more than we have received."

"How can you give more than you receive?" Edna asked.

"Because we creatively develop what God has given us, like the servants who were given different talents to invest in the parable of Matthew 25. The good and faithful servants took what the master gave them and made more, but it was more for the master, not more for the servant to spend on himself."

"Let me see if I got this right," Abby broke in. "You think we should take what God has given us and make money or develop our talents or whatever God has given us, use it for the Kingdom of God, and then God will owe us something to balance out the scales, since we gave more than we received."

"God doesn't owe us anything," J.D. clarified, "because a creator has no obligation to His creation. But life might. Life is not fair or just, it does not balance out the scale of justice. We leave life with those scales tipped either for us or against us. But God **is** just. So you want to leave this life with the scales balanced against you, so God will balance the scales the other side of the grave. Of course, you understand, none of this is about salvation because we can't get rid of our sins by doing good. Balancing the scales will do nothing to get rid of our sin. Salvation is by grace through faith in Christ's payment for our sins on the cross. Salvation is always by faith, but judgment is always based on works. So you want to leave this world having given more than you have received, having forgiven more than you need to be forgiven by others, having been wronged more than you wronged others, having given your shirt when they asked for your coat. In other words, having the scales balanced against you."

"Then should we be having this dinner?" Edna continued her inquiry.

"Well," J.D. now spoke, looking at Edna, "there are other reasons for the occasional posh event. Not every use of wealth is to gratify ourselves, or reward ourselves on earth. Jesus went to a banquet put on by Levi, and He had lunch with a Pharisee who was at least well-to-do. He allowed His feet to be anointed with expensive perfume, and dined with Mary, Martha, and Lazarus. Those upscale events were not for the purpose of luxurious living. Jesus had another agenda. And so do we. We're here because these young people need to figure all this out. Well, that and the fact that I just wanted to go out with you," J.D. said, winked at Edna, and watched her blush a bit. Then he continued. "It seems to me that the problem with the rich man in Luke 16 is not that he occasionally spent some money on a certain activity, but that he *habitually dressed in purple and fine linen, joyously living in splendor every day.*"

"But we all do that, don't we?" Edna added. "I mean, in America, the poorest of us lives in splendor every day."

"True," J.D. agreed. "What bothers me is how we all live, and actually almost have to live, in the west. Statistically, we all live on top of the world. And what's even more scary is, we live on top of the world historically. The average American or European puts his pants on the same way I do. There is not much difference between them and me. But there is a huge difference between how we all live compared to the whole ancient world. The poorest in America have it better than the Pharaohs of Egypt and the Caesars of Rome. Caesar did not have antibiotics, ibuprofen, packaged food, a microwave oven, flush toilets, a flat screen TV, a computer, Kindle, iPod or cell phone. And he had to ride to work bouncing along standing on a platform behind the back end of a horse. And we don't have to go back to ancient times to make the comparison. Just a hundred years ago in America the average life expectancy was 47 years, 95% of all births were in homes, the leading causes of death were pneumonia and the flu, only 14% of homes had a bathtub, and most women washed their hair once a month with Borax or egg yoke shampoo."

At that, both women grimaced. Then Abby said, "Okay, Mr. Fitzgerald, maybe we are all guilty of living in luxury, but we can't ignore Jesus' statement that *it is easier for a camel to go through the eye of a needle, than for a rich man to enter the kingdom of God.*"

"Remember, Jesus said that about the rich young ruler who walked away from Jesus because he could not walk away from his wealth. And without question, that is the danger of wealth. We are all in the position of this rich man. So it seems to me we all have a burden and a stewardship we will be accountable for at the Judgment Seat of Christ. For example, my financial accountability is greater than yours. I will be held accountable for this dinner, whether it is for myself or the Kingdom of God."

"Isn't that always the danger with wealth?" Abby insisted. "How can you know if you are using it for the Kingdom of God or just enjoying it for yourself?"

"That's true, my dear. And I don't deny I enjoy certain aspects of the wealth God has given me. For example, I enjoy the opportunity to give you this little trip and our evening together."

"And I really appreciate it," Edna inserted. I have enjoyed it immensely, especially flying the Citation. And I will also use your generous gift for purchases at the drugstore."

"And, you see, I would be insulted if you didn't. It would rob me of the opportunity to give if you didn't accept it. Actually, that's why I didn't tell you where we were going this evening because I was afraid you'd turn it down."

Now Edna put her hand on his. "Really, John, I can't tell you how much I appreciate this. This evening is something I will remember the rest of my life."

"Me, too, Miss Edna. Now, how about dessert?"

Chapter 19

Thursday, July 28
Between New York and Chicago

For some reason, it is not socially inappropriate to radically and suddenly change the subject and direction of a meal conversation. And so it was with the rest of this meal. Topics included the pastor of Edna's Baptist Church, Johnnie's reluctance to deal with the Arab Crown Jewels, Abby's relationships with the other waitresses at The Corner Grill, and John's pipe smoking.

On the way back to the airport, J.D. took them past the building where he started the second office of The Fitzgerald Trust Company over 50 years ago. Some of the people they had met that evening were among his first clients there.

Edna was once again encouraged to fly copilot, which she once again accepted, with no hesitation this time. J.D. said he wanted to take a nap, so he sat where he did on the way over, but he slept the whole trip home. Abby and Johnnie also sat in the same seats. They both gazed out the window after the take off, which in a C-J3 is more like a blast off. The cloud layer was gone. The night air was clear. They watched the lights of Manhattan until they disappeared in the distance. Then Abby sat back in her seat and closed her eyes. "What a wonderful evening."

"I think Edna liked it."

"Are you kidding? She'll be talking about this for weeks, months, probably the rest of her life. She went nuts over the opportunity to fly this airplane. You didn't hear her, but when we landed, she told me she was in love. Scared me to death. Then she said she was in love with this airplane. I think I gave an audible sigh of relief."

"But you fell in love with grandpa."

"I sure did. He's adorable. If only he were just a little bit younger." She put her hand over her heart and swooned. Then she giggled. Then she

219

stopped giggling. Her expression turned serious as her eyes met Johnnie's. Their gaze expressed feelings neither of them had spoken. Then it intensified. Their eyes were making love in a way their bodies had avoided. Then his mouth covered hers. The kiss that had been waiting in the wings took center stage. She managed to untangle her arms from his grasp and wrap them around his neck. It lasted until somewhere over Ohio. When they finally pulled away, there were tears in her eyes.

"Are you okay?" he asked. She sniffed a bit and nodded. "Abby," he continued, "something happened inside of me the moment I saw you through the window of The Corner Grill. Most would say that it was lust. But it wasn't. Well, it was. But that's not all it was. I don't need the money, Abby. I need you."

This time, she initiated the kiss. And it lasted until the engines began powering back for their descent into the Chicago area. She snuggled her head up under his chin. He put his hand over the hair that was alongside her face. She was not sure their sudden, strange, unlikely, relationship could last. She was not sure what to think about the money. But she was sure of one thing—she was head-over-heels in love with John David Fitzgerald, III.

But she didn't say so. What she said was, "I feel like I'm in a fairy tale. Every girl dreams of a prince, who will come along and sweep her away in his golden carriage. But I feel like it's really happening."

"Yeah, well, the golden carriage is about to hit a significant pot hole."

She sat up straight, eyes wide with a worried frown between them. "Why? What?"

"You're going to have to meet my parents."

Chapter 20

Friday to Monday, July 29–August 1
Chicago, Illinois

Johnnie was a busy man. It wasn't just the arrival of the Arab Crown Jewels, although that added to the workload, it was the burden of running the company. His father was currently traveling back and forth to London on a weekly basis, setting up the first overseas branch of The Fitzgerald Trust Company. This left Johnnie in charge of the whole American operation.

When he started the company, J.D. only hired Bible-believing Christians as his financial counselors. Then he put them through a rigorous six-week course, after which they were on probation for a year as they assisted a trained counselor. His son had relaxed that standard. J.D. II was a responsible businessman, but he didn't appreciate the significance of hiring Bible-believing Christians because he wasn't one himself.

Johnnie was returning the company to his grandfather's standards. Although the restrictions did not apply to the secretaries, the custodial staff, or security personnel, the financial counselors were to all be Christians who were grounded in the Bible, had taken his grandfather's original course, and put in a year assisting a trained counselor. Since his father had hired some counselors who were giving more secular advice, Johnnie had to undo that, being careful to not get sued by personnel who would claim they were being discriminated against because they were not Christians. Being a lawyer helped, but sorting all that out with the managers of their offices all over the country led to multiple meetings and many hours on the phone.

On Friday and Saturday, he worked late. Since he had no other time to see Abby these days, he asked her to bring dinner over from The Corner Grill, which they ate together in his office. On Sunday, he went with Abby and Grandma Edna to their Baptist church. Then he took them out to dinner. In the afternoon, he and Abby went for a walk at a park near Glenn Ellen. Then Monday, it was back to the meetings and phone calls, and a Corner Grill take-out dinner with Abby in his office.

But Tuesday would be different. That was the frightful day she would join him for dinner with his parents. It had to be Tuesday or Wednesday because Abby had to go to Ann Arbor on Thursday for Cassy's Friday rehearsal and Saturday wedding. Wednesday, Johnnie and his father had a dinner meeting in L.A. with the director of their California operation. So that left Tuesday.

Tuesday evening, August 2

Johnnie asked Abby to arrive at the Fitzgerald Building by 7:30. Because of the late arrival of J.D. II from London, their dinner was not scheduled until 8:00. The security people knew Abby now, so she was simply greeted by each one as she made her way to Johnnie's office. She was dressed the same as she was for their double date. This was the best dress and purse and shoes she had. Her hair was the same, too, down and loose and parted on the side so it curved across her eye and down her back, the ends curling slightly below her elbows. Even though they all knew who she was, the head of every person in the building still turned to follow her—the men for one reason, the women for another.

When she arrived at his office on the 35th floor, there was no one in the greeting and waiting area except a middle-aged janitor named Bobby Andrews, who was emptying the wastebaskets. She had met him last Friday. He greeted her warmly. They exchanged comments about the weather and the recent Cubs victory over the Yankees. Then Bobby left, pushing a large trash container.

Last Friday, Abby had also met Johnnie's executive assistant. An efficient looking woman in her mid-50s named Bernice Dykstra. Bernice often stayed late when Johnnie was there. But not tonight. Her desk was spotless and her chair empty. The door to Johnnie's office was cracked open, his back was to Abby, and he was talking on the phone. She knocked on

222

the door anyway. He waved her in without turning around. His office occupied the corner of the 35th floor, with one row of large windows viewing the Chicago skyline south toward the Sears Tower and another row looking east toward Lake Michigan. He had a large mahogany desk with four leather chairs facing it. To Abby's left, there was also a bar and a conference area with a glass-top table and high-back chairs. The office was actually bigger than his apartment. It had been his father's, and now it was his. And so were the responsibilities that went with it.

Abby was shocked when she first saw it last Friday. But now she just admired the view, while he finished his conversation. "No, of course. You can't let him go just because he's not a believer. But if he is violating our planning criteria… well, that's what I mean. Be sure you don't…" Then turned to look at Abby. He stopped mid-sentence, stared, then said, "I gotta go, Pete. I'll call you tomorrow." He dropped the phone on his desk and managed to stammer, "You're… you look…. breathtaking."

As he moved toward her, she said, "What are you talking about? I'm wearing the same thing I did for our double date. I don't have anything el… Johnnie, don't you… now don't mess me up. Don't… you'll ruin my… Johnnie, stop that. I'll…" But the kiss was inevitable. She first put both hands on his chest in protest but soon they had slipped to the back of his shoulders, pulling him toward her, deepening the kiss. When he finally pulled back, she said, "What am I going to do to keep you under control?"

"Nothing will work, if you show up looking like that."

"Yeah, well, now we're late. It's 7:40, and you said dinner was as 8:00. How are we going to drive all the way across town in 20 minutes?"

"We aren't. The helicopter is waiting for us on the heliport."

"Oh….. my….. word!"

Chapter 21

Same evening, Tuesday, August 2
The Fitzgerald Mansion

Abby had never been inside of a helicopter. So, at first, she was fascinated by the liftoff from the heliport and the ride over the Chicago skyline. But as they turned west and began to descend into the back yard of the Fitzgerald Mansion, she clung to Johnnie's arm. When they landed, she was holding his hand so tight that her knuckles were turning white. "Don't worry," he encouraged, "it'll be fine."

"Johnnie, I'm not worried—I'm terrified!"

"Of what?"

"Your mother."

"She's more afraid of you than you are of her."

"That's not possible."

"Sure it is. You threaten her female domination of the family."

"I don't know what that means, but I know I'm scared to death."

The blades of the chopper finally stopped, and they made the short walk from the back lawn to the back porch of the mansion. Johnnie started to open the door and was met by Lucy, the 67-year-old maid he'd known all of his life. She greeted him and Abby warmly, then said that the meal was on the table, and the family would be down shortly. "Meanwhile, I'll give you a little tour," Johnnie suggested. Then he whispered in Abby's ear, "Mother is being stylishly late. She's trying to intimidate you."

"It's working."

Johnnie showed her the library, the den, the kitchen, the living room and the dining room before his mother and father appeared at the bottom of a large winding stairway. "Hello, Mother, hi, Dad."

"How are you, Dear?" His mother spoke to Johnnie but she was looking at Abby.

"This is Abby, Abigail Davidson. Abby, this is my mother Lois Fitzgerald and my father John David Fitzgerald, II."

"Oh, yes, the waitress," his mother said. But it was J.D. II who shook Abby's hand and welcomed her to their home.

"Good to meet you, Mr. Fitzgerald, Mrs. Fitzgerald."

"I'm sorry we couldn't meet you sooner," Lois Fitzgerald began with a pseudo-apology. "I was organizing the remodeling of our home in the Bahamas. Then a friend asked me to scoot over to Aruba for a few rounds of golf. She is such a dear, I just couldn't turn her down. They have quite a nice course at the Divi Villa. My, don't you look nice. I like that dress."

"Thank you."

"And those shoes. Very unique. Wherever did you get those shoes?"

"At Goodwill."

Mrs. Fitzgerald laughed and said, "I don't reveal all my shopping sources either, Dear. There are some things we ladies just need to keep to ourselves."

"No, I really did get them at Goodwill. There is a Goodwill store just two blocks from our house. I get most of my clothes there."

"Oh."

Then the elevator door next to the stairway opened and J.D. shuffled out. "Well, would you look at that? How is the prettiest girl in Chicago?"

"Oh, Mr. Fitzgerald," Abby went to him as a port in the midst of a social storm. She had her hand out, but instead of shaking it, he gave her a big hug. "You know, Lois," the old man had his arm around Abby while he looked at Johnnie's mother, "Abby and I are madly in love. We would be getting married, except she doesn't like pipe smoke." Everybody laughed, except Lois. But the social ice had been broken, and instead of sinking, Abby felt like she had her foot on a more solid rock.

Chapter 22

Tuesday, August 2
Chicago,
A Downtown Restaurant

Thinking he might actually get a chance to meet his boss for the first time face-to-face, Hans Reinhardt went to an assigned restaurant just off the Chicago Loop at 8:00 P.M. But, after escorting him to a seat, a waiter handed him a cell phone and walked away. Hans looked at it wearily, then picked it up.

"Hello."

"Good work, Hans, everything seems to be in place."

"Thank you, Mr. Becker."

"There is something else that may be an asset."

"Yes, sir?"

"The young Fitzgerald has a girlfriend. Now, I know he's like the most eligible bachelor in Chicago, but this one is different. Our undercover man in the building tells me she is something else—looks like Sleeping Beauty in the old Disney cartoon. Fitzgerald III is nuts about her. If we had her, he'd cooperate for sure."

"Excellent. I'll have someone locate her, nab her Saturday evening, and bring her to the party. We'll keep her around long enough to make sure Fitzgerald is cooperative in opening the safe. Then we can hand both of them off to the Arabs as part of the exchange for the money. But what do you think the Arabs will do with them?"

"I don't know. I suspect they will keep them until they are safely away, then dispose of them."

"So what's our timing?"

"The Crown Jewels come in next Saturday evening, August 6. We'll let the entourage that brings them from the airport secure them in the safe at the Fitzgerald Building."

"I'm not doubting you, boss, but wouldn't it be easier to acquire them before they get locked in the safe?"

"There are two problems with that. First, we want to make sure they are real, that somebody didn't pull a switch and bring in some fake ones. And Mahmood's wife is a gemologist.

226

She's determined to make sure the real gems are on display. We want to wait for her to confirm that they are the real thing. And the newspapers say she will do that right then, on the spot, when they enter the Fitzgerald vault. Bringing in our own gemologist would be really bulky, but with her, we don't need one. The other reason is simple. The security around those gems will be huge until they are locked in that vault. Then everybody will just assume they are safe. Also, we want to wait until evening. Rush hour will be over and all the regular workers in the building will have gone home. And you just gave me another reason. It gives us time to bring in the girlfriend."

"How many people will remain in the building?"

"After the gems are in the safe and the royal entourage leaves, there should be about a dozen, maybe as many as 20. There will be some armed guards at the entrance and by the vault. Fitzgerald's secretary will probably be there as long as he is, and there will be a few night janitors working. You'll have to take out the police guards, but that should be about it. The building is not all that secure. It was never designed to be a bank or to house security boxes. There is no cash or valuables in it except what's in those lock boxes. It's basically just an office building."

"When will the Arab snipers be in place?"

"The Arabs will get into position Friday night, August 5th. They will stay on the roofs of the adjacent buildings all day Saturday."

"And our team?"

"You, plus six of our guys, will hijack the Fitzgerald helicopter called "Chopper 2." All the Fitzgerald aircraft are kept in their own hangar at Midway Airport. Chopper 1 is always available for Fitzgerald II, but Chopper 2 is for any company executive who needs it. So they always have a pilot that stays on call at the Midway hangar. We are tracking Chopper 2 pretty close. Right now it's at the mansion. One of their VPs has it scheduled Wednesday to Friday, but we don't see it being scheduled next Saturday. You will kidnap the pilot at 6:30 Saturday evening. Then the seven of you will take him from there and force him to fly to the Fitzgerald Building, arriving at 7:00. You will cuff the pilot to his seat. Wearing ski masks, the seven of you will leave the chopper. The masks are just for the rooftop security cameras. Once inside, you can take them off."

"How do we get in? Won't the entrance from the heliport be locked?"

"Yes, it took our inside guy quite awhile to get the code. You'd better record it somewhere. It's 538*58-37#345. Usually, that door is not guarded, but you should be ready, just in case. Then enter and secure the building floor-by-floor from top to bottom. The jewels will be in the vault on the ground floor. So if you start from the top, you will have all the hostages on the ground floor when the safe is opened."

"When do the gems arrive?"

"It's hard to be specific. They should get there between 7:00 and 8:00. My guess is 7:30. Once they are secured in the safe, your team will lock down the building, *persuade* the young Fitzgerald to get the gems out of the safe and secure a group of hostages in the lobby with the C-4 explosives already hidden in the building. Our undercover man knows where they are. Remember, you must never reveal the identity of our undercover man because his escape will be to simply walk out of the building as one of the hostages. After you have obtained the jewels, you will put your ski masks on seven of the hostages and make them board the helicopter so the authorities will assume you re-boarded it to escape. Then you will instruct the pilot to fly north under the threat that the Arabs on the adjacent buildings will blow him away if he doesn't. While the cops are chasing him, and trying to free the hostages from the bomb threat, the seven of you will get out through the tunnel along with the younger Fitzgerald and his girlfriend. Then we sell the jewels to the Muslims for 20 million, and we're out of there."

"How will the Arab snipers get out of Chicago?"

"I have no idea."

Chapter 23

Tuesday, August 2
The Fitzgerald Mansion

Grandpa prayed for the food and dinner was served. There was small talk and a little business talk. J.D. II asked his son about the security for the Crown Jewels. Johnnie asked his father about the progress in setting up the London branch office. They discussed some of the differences in the British financial culture, the pound sterling versus the Euro, the impact of the Euro zone debt crisis and the inflation of the dollar. Failing to find a place to jump in, Lois finally just interrupted with: "So, Ms. Davidson, tell us something about yourself. I've only heard that you are a waitress."

"Please, call me Abby. Yes, I am a waitress at The Corner Grill downtown. That's where I met Johnnie."

"Yes, so I understand. It seems a bit strange. Johnnie has met so many *elegant* ladies in so many lovely places. Why, just the other day he had dinner with the daughter of the president of our First National Bank."

Abby looked over at Johnnie. "Just the other day?"

He shook his head. "Mother you trapped me with that girl, like you usually do. You didn't tell me she would be here until after I agreed to stay for dinner. And," he looked over at Abby, "it was a couple of weeks ago. And," he looked back at his mother, "I don't think I said five words to her the whole meal. And," he looked back at Abby, "I left right after supper."

"Yes, that was a bit rude of you. After all, she was a beautiful, well-educated, socially-stationed girl."

"Good grief."

"And could we hear something about you, Ms. Davidson, I mean, Abby?"

"What would you like to know ma'am?"

"Oh, something of your background, your parents, your home."

"Sure. My mother was a prostitute who ran away from home and died of a drug overdose when I was born. So I never knew her, and I've never known who my father was. I don't think she knew either. I was placed in an orphanage, then with several sets of foster parents, until my grandmother found me at my high school graduation. I have lived with her ever since."

"Oh, my. You poor child."

"Oh, I'm not poor. I have a friend named Cassy who led me to Christ and taught me the Bible. My grandmother is also a mature Christian, so we have a great time studying, talking, joking around, and just living together. We don't have any money, but I think I am quite wealthy."

Grandpa and Johnnie both smothered a grin, but Lois looked concerned. "I mean, you have not had any of the economic advantages which lead to the higher social graces."

"That's true, ma'am. I know very little about 'the higher social graces.' Cassy and my grandmother just taught me right and wrong from the Bible."

"Yes, well, that's fine, but what I meant was, you haven't had the opportunity to experience a higher standard of living."

"Why would I want to experience that?"

"Well, because it a blessing from God, and it advances the social standard. Society survives because it maintains certain standards. The lower classes have never advanced those standards. All through the history of western civilization, it was left to the wealthier classes to maintain proper social etiquette, without which society would plunge into ruin."

"Really? And all this time I thought it was sin that plunged society into ruin."

Grandpa and Johnnie were first thinking they would need to rescue Abby from a social onslaught. But now, realizing Abby could hold her own, they just sat back and enjoyed the show.

"Well, that's one way to put it," Lois continued. "But 'sin' is a very primitive concept. It tends to be intolerant, and it has very little discernment for the needs of people in a developing culture. We must move beyond such unevolved thinking if we are to advance society."

"So even though luxurious living is contrary to the Bible, you are saying it's good because it helps society evolve. Is that right?" Abby clarified.

"Of course, luxury advances society. It's just that simple, my dear. Without the royalty, aristocracy, and landlords of Europe, there would be no western development. For example, we have six mansions besides this one. They are all over the world. Each of them are built and furnished with the best, often most expensive, material available. This gives the cultures where they are built a high standard of excellence. Most people cannot achieve that, of course, but it gives them a standard to strive for. As they reach toward that standard, or try to imitate that standard as best they can, the whole society moves forward. For example, your clothes are nice because they imitate the more costly ones worn by Johnnie's other girlfriends."

"Mother, I don't have other..."

"Whenever the royalty of the developing western world maintained an expensive or extravagant lifestyle, it allowed the middle classes and the poor people to have a standard to aim for. It was also an encouragement for the poor to know their royalty or aristocracy could present such a standard. Why do you think so many people study the Tsars of Russia or the Hapsburgs of Austria and visit the Hermitage in Saint Petersburg or the Winter Palace in Vienna? The same is true of valuable jewelry and expensive clothes....and shoes."

Chapter 24

Wednesday, August 3
Chicago, The Corner Grill

It was Abby's last day of work before a long weekend. Tomorrow, she would fly to Ann Arbor for Cassy's rehearsal on Friday and the wedding on Saturday. She would miss Johnnie, but it would be great seeing Cassy and some old friends. Johnnie was with his father in a meeting in L.A. today, so she would not see him for four or five days. But she was relaxed, joking with customers, and teasing Joe about his cooking. Then, about 2:30 in the afternoon, she was in the back, picking up a soup and sandwich special for a customer, when Alice came in and said, "Abby, there is someone out front who would like to speak with you. A lady—a well-dressed fancy-looking lady. Doubt she's ever seen the inside of a grill before. She asked if you could have some time off to talk with her and handed me this $100 bill for your time. I said that was up to you."

"Thanks, Alice." Abby felt fear creeping up her body like she was sinking in quicksand. Cautiously, she emerged from the kitchen into the seating area of the restaurant and faced Lois Fitzgerald.

"Hello, Abby."

"Mrs. Fitzgerald."

"I'm sorry to interrupt your day, but I thought we should talk a little bit face-to-face."

"All right." The two women took a booth toward the back of the restaurant.

"I have something to say, but I think I can make my point best if we continue our conversation from last night just a little. Would that be okay?"

"Okay."

"I just want to make sure we understand each other. It is clear to me that wealth and technological advances have improved the welfare of people tremendously since Jesus' day. Jesus and the apostles healed a few people, but today our post-modern western societies heal and feed thousands. Why, nearly every corner of every country is better off each year that goes by. We cure more diseases, live in a cleaner environment, travel globally, communicate instantaneously, and are less ignorant every day. And all this is possible because wealthy families like ours invested money into those endeavors. I want to make sure you understand that's what our family is all about."

"But the world is not better off morally," Abby added. "Every year the world gets worse morally."

"That's absurd." Lois was now getting impatient. "The ancient world had wars constantly, human sacrifice religions, hatred against blacks, women, and homosexuals. Christians had Crusades, the Inquisition, witch hunts, and were intolerant of anybody that was not like they were. Except where people like you are holding us back, we are improving on all of that."

"There is no evidence the modern world is better, just wealthier. The 20th century was the bloodiest century in all of history. And so far, the 21st century is worse. We also have pornography available at the push of key. Our divorce rate is around 50%, it's 80% for those who co-habitate before marriage, and children of divorced parents are four times more likely to get a divorce themselves. The divorce rate is destroying our families, our schools, and giving us high drug and crime rates. Let me read you something else." Abby opened her purse and took out a small piece of paper and read: "The worst ancient societies killed about 1000 people a year in human sacrifice. We kill 42 million babies a year globally through abortion, that's about 115,000 every day. In America alone, we kill 3,700 babies a day, that's 154 babies killed every hour. We have invented laws that have so far condemned to painful deaths without trial more than 56 million babies for the crime of being 'inconvenient.'" She put the paper back and looked at Lois before she continued. "And you seem to think this is moral progress. Somehow we are getting 'better' because we allow mothers to murder their unborn babies. The truth is, our societies are so sick that we actually need abortion to keep crime down since most of those babies would be born to the criminal and dependent parts of society. Eighteen years after Roe vs. Wade, the crime rate went down. Instead of trying to eliminate our sin, we have dealt with it by calling evil 'good.' Just scratch the surface anyplace in our society, and evil pours out.

233

Ya' know why kids can't read? Their parents are divorced, their mother is bedding some truck driver, their brother is on drugs and their sister is sleeping with her boyfriend, and they are not even teenagers yet. Most have family members or close friends involved in desperate sin."

"Much of that is simply because you define social changes as sinful, and refuse to help them live their own lifestyles."

"You've got to be kidding me."

"Yes, well, there is no reason for me to take any more of your time," Lois concluded. "It's just that I wanted you to see very clearly that you will never fit into our family. I think this discussion proved that conclusively. I realize that Johnnie is attracted to you, but he never stays very long with any girl, so I don't want you to think that just because he is infatuated with your good looks, that there is a future for you with him."

"Thank you for being straightforward and honest with me. Johnnie and I will have to see how we fit together. But, Mrs. Fitzgerald, I have no intention of trying to fit into your family. My only intention is to see how I can best serve God."

Chapter 25

Friday, August 5
Downtown Chicago

Jamal Qasim was a naturalized American citizen of Arab descent. After receiving his citizenship, he decided he wanted to be a police officer. Three years ago, at the age of 27, he graduated from the police academy and joined the Chicago Police Department. Two years ago, at the age of 28, he met and married a 24-year-old Arab immigrant named Basima. One year ago, they had their first child, a girl they named Hannah. Three months later, Basima became pregnant with their second child.

At 7:45 P.M., Friday, August 5, Jamal kissed his pregnant wife and baby girl, and left for work. Extra work. Because the crown jewels were coming in tomorrow, many of the officers were called upon for special duty. Jamal drove to the station, checked in, picked up his squad car, and began his patrol at 8:30. The evening was pretty much routine—prostitutes on the street corners, kids selling drugs, a few traffic violations. But Jamal saw nothing suspicious that would pertain to the arrival of the jewels. Then, as the sun began to disappear behind the Chicago skyline, a white panel van drove up behind Jamal's squad car. The driver honked the horn. Jamal pulled over, turned on the red, white, and blue flashers, loosened the strap on his 9mm Glock, and walked back to check out the honker.

As he approached the van, Jamal noticed it had no side windows, and there was a magnetic sign attached to the side of the van with black letters spelling out "Randolph Delivery Service." The driver leaned his head out the window and showed Jamal both his hands. "Sorry to bother you, officer, but I have been trying to locate the Hatfield Security Company. I have a delivery for them at this street address, but no one seems to know where they are. I have been looking for a half hour with no success. I thought maybe you might know where they are located."

"Please step out of the van, sir. And keep your hands where I can see them."

"Yes, of course, but I just need a location for…"

"Open the back doors of the van, please."

"What is this? I am just asking for help and I get searched?"

"I have never heard of your delivery service, sir, and most people do not stop a squad car to ask directions," Jamal explained, "so I am going to ask you one more time to open the rear doors."

"Okay, okay, no problem." The driver walked around to the back of the van and opened the van's rear doors. This revealed a few packing blankets, several empty plastic bags, and one box covered with brown paper wrapped with twine.

"This is your only delivery?"

"It's my last one for today. If I can find this Hatfield Security Company, I can go home."

"Those plastic bags do not look like they are for shipping material. The only place I have seen bags like that is body bags at the morgue."

"We use those for perishable items, like…, Oh, excuse me, my cell phone is vibrating, it is probably my partner, he has been walking this block to find the address. May I answer him? He will wonder where I am."

"All right, but make it quick."

"Yes, of course. Thank you…. Hello,… yes, well, I asked a police officer, and he is now searching the van. …Yes, you should. Okay…Yeah, see you." The man clicked off his phone and began to climb into the back of the van. "I will show you what's in those bags." He brought the bags to the back door. As Jamal leaned in to look at the bags, he felt a sharp pain, like a bee sting, in his neck. Before he could get his hand on his gun, he was being pushed into the van from behind, and before a minute passed, his world turned black. The two men pulled Jamal's body into the van, closed the doors, and wrestled his uniform off of him.

The van driver said, "Sorry, I had to change the plan."

"Yes, I was already in position in the back of the squad car."

"Who would guess he would be so curious about what's in the van."

"I figured something was up. It was taking way too long for him to return to his car."

"I had to fake a call from you in order to make a call to you. Allah be praised that you figured out the problem, and we are back on schedule."

The second man, the one who had approached Jamal from behind and injected his neck, looked down at the unconscious Jamal. "It's amazing how much he looks like me."

"Well, that's the idea. Ghazi studied photos of each officer of the Chicago PD to find a man with an olive complexion. Fortunately, he actually found an Arab immigrant. Then it was just a matter of matching him with the one of us that was the closest in appearance. That just happened to be you."

The Arab in the white panel van drove west out of Chicago into the farming country of western Illinois. There, he pulled Jamal's unconscious body out of the van and into a nearby woods, shot him two times in the head, and drove back to Chicago.

Chapter 26

Tuesday, August 5
Downtown Chicago

The Arab who put on Jamal's uniform also took his wallet, which had all Jamal's information: his badge, his driver's license, police identification card, and three credit cards. He also took his radio and cell phone. Then he got into Jamal's squad car, turned off the flashing lights, and drove away.

After driving around for about ten minutes to be sure he was not being followed by another police car, he parked in front of the Cameron Bank Building, which sat directly across from the Fitzgerald Building. The sun was now gone and man-made lights defined the city. The phony officer entered the bank building and walked up to the night watchman sitting behind a booth, manning several surveillance cameras. "Evening, officer. What can I do for the Chicago PD this fine evening?"

"I hope you mean it's a fine evening because the White Sox just took the Yankees three games in a row."

"That is absolutely what I mean. I have been waiting all year for this."

"Me, too," the phony officer replied, now with one elbow leaning on the security desk. "I'm so darn sick of those Yankees pulling in the top players all the time. But in answer to your question, I would like to check your building."

"Sure, what for?"

"Big honk'n load of jewels coming into the Fitzgerald Building across the street tomorrow. Just want to be sure there is no chance of snipers being positioned in the surrounding buildings."

"No problem. What do you need?"

"Just need to have a look around. How much can you see with those monitors?"

"Not everything. But we can see the stairwells and the elevator entrance areas on all the floors. It would be pretty hard to go from one floor to another without us seeing it."

"Any on the roof?"

"No, just the 36 floors."

"Any outside?"

"Just by the main entrance at the ground level."

"All right, well I'm going to check out the roof and just have a look around. I should be back in, oh, say, a half hour."

"Sounds good."

"Here is my badge and ID. You should probably check it out with the station."

"Oh, I don't think that's necessary."

"No, please, call it in. Give my badge number and description. At least that way they'll know I didn't just sit in the squad car and listen to the ball game all night."

With a brief laugh, the security guard agreed. As he phoned the Chicago PD, the phony officer took the elevator to the 36th floor, then walked up one flight of stairs and opened the door to the roof. Once there, he walked to the back of the building and turned his flashlight on and off five times. Soon a wire with a grappling hook came sailing over the edge and landed on the roof. The officer grabbed it before it could slip back and began pulling on the wire. It took him seven minutes to pull up the entire wire and the cabled ladder fastened to the end. Next, he secured the ladder cables to two different structures protruding above the roof. Then he flashed his light five more times. Seventeen minutes later, three more Arabs, dressed in black with firearms strapped to their backs, climbed the 36 floors, pulled the ladder up behind them, and stationed themselves on top of the building. The phony officer only greeted them briefly, then returned to the lobby of the Cameron Bank Building.

"Satisfied?" The security guard asked, leaning back on his chair with his hands behind his head.

"Yup. Looks good up there, but be sure you keep a close eye on those cameras tonight. We don't want any bad guys in this building."

"Will do."

"Did you check me out with the dispatcher?"

"Yes, sir. He described you to a tee. He said he was glad you were working hard for a change."

With a chuckle, the phony officer waved as he walked out the door. Then he drove to a Quick Mart and bought some beer, some coffee, a dozen donuts, and a half-gallon of milk and paid for them with Jamal's Master Card. He exited the store, threw the purchases in a dumpster, drove the squad car back to the police station, parked it out front, and walked away.

Chapter 27

Saturday, August 6
The Mahmood Royal Family National Archives, 5:00 A.M.
[9:00 P.M., August 5, Chicago time]

The schedule for loading the Mahmood royal family jewels had changed. They were scheduled to be picked up from the Archives at 8:00 A.M. and secured in Royal One for transport to Chicago at 8:40. With the knowledge of no one except the royal family, Bkar decided to change the schedule. The most vulnerable time for the jewels was in transport, first between the Archives building and the airplane, then in Chicago between the airplane and the vault at the Fitzgerald Building. So, just in the odd case there was a plot to steal them in route, Bkar moved up the time three hours. Even his own security team did not know it until they were roused out of bed early and sent to guard the transfer. At 5:15, they were taken from their display cases and put into three shoebox sized metal containers and taken under armed guard in a security truck to the aircraft.

King Abdul-Ahad would not travel to Chicago until the day before the wedding. But his wife Daniyah would accompany the crown jewels and join her daughter Fawzah to display the jewels, prepare the wedding hall, and outfit the wedding party. She boarded the 747 at 5:40, just 5 minutes before the gems arrived. She took a half an hour to personally examine each one. Then, satisfied they were all there and all authentic, she took out her cell phone and called Mr. J.D. Fitzgerald, III.

Chapter 28

Tuesday, August 5
Downtown Chicago

At 10:40, the phone rang on Captain Broadmoor's desk. He gave it a puzzled look. It had to be from inside the station. Even then, most used their cell phones. "Broadmoor."

"Captain, this is Sargent Winfield at dispatch. I'm not sure if this is a false alarm, but I'm getting antsy about it."

"Talk to me."

"Well, sir, it's about Jamal, that is, officer Qasim. I can't locate him. He was checking the Cameron Bank Building, which makes sense, it being directly across from the Fitzgerald Building. But he didn't report in, so I called him, but I couldn't raise him on his radio or his cell. I figured the signal was probably blocked in the building, so I let it go a while. Then a few minutes ago, I called the night watchman at the bank and he said Jamal left there a half an hour ago. And I still can't reach him."

"Okay, have whoever is covering that area stop in and have a talk with the security people at the bank. Then put out an APB on his car. We should also run his credit cards. Let's see if he bought anything where somebody can ID him."

"I'm on it, captain."

"Winfield?"

"Yes, sir."

"Did you say the last time you spoke with him was at the Cameron Bank Building?"

"Well, not exactly, sir."

"Not exactly?"

"Well, no. Actually, I spoke with the night watchman who called in to confirm his badge number and his ID before he inspected the building."

"So how long has it been since you actually talked to officer Qasim?

"Um, well, I guess, it's been, let's see, yes, he called in that he was checking on a white panel van at 9:35."

"So we haven't actually had contact with him in two hours, is that correct?"

"Yes, sir, but I figured the building was…"

"I understand. Let's just get on this right away."

Chapter 29

Saturday, August 6
Ann Arbor, Michigan

Cassy's wedding rehearsal, and the dinner which followed, was enjoyable for Abby. The best man wasn't there yet, but Jack said he'd get him caught up on the formalities. Abby didn't know the other two groomsmen either, but one was a guy who flew with Jack, who looked like Santa Claus.

It was a great time of getting reacquainted with old friends. At the dinner, Abby sat with Cassy's parents and reviewed some of the hilarious (and some not so hilarious, and some downright dangerous) situations she and Cassy got into as kids. They also talked about Professor McMurray's abduction and what it was like to be kidnapped and forced to work on the drugs. Although Abby had heard all about it from Cassy, it was interesting getting the story from her father's perspective.

But now it was Saturday. Now it was 1:00 P.M. on Saturday. Now the church was full, Jack's mother and Cassy's parents had been seated, the groomsmen, the groom, and the minister were already on the platform waiting for the bridesmaids. Jack's daughter Jenny had just finished spreading rose peddles on the runner that stretched from the back of the church to the platform. Now Abby would lead the bridesmaids down the aisle. The organ was playing some Bach piece that Abby couldn't name. The girls were lined up in the foyer just outside the sanctuary. One of the ushers, Cassy's cousin on her father's side, peeked inside to be sure they were ready. He turned to Abby, and said, "It's your turn. Knock 'um dead."

Abby's hair was twisted and gathered behind her head. She carried a bouquet of flowers. Her dress swished and crinkled as she walked down the aisle in uncomfortable yellow high-heeled shoes that matched the color of her dress. She smiled and nodded at a few people she knew from six years ago, and a few she had just met at the rehearsal. In front and to her left, she could see Cassy's mother turned sideways, smiling at her. Abby was nervous, but things were going fine. No need to worry. Everything was proceeding as rehearsed.

Until.

Abby looked to her right. She was about halfway down when she noticed an old man sitting next to the aisle in the third pew from the front. From the back, he looked amazingly like J.D. Fitzgerald. But that was silly. Impossible. She would be sure and tell him he has a look-alike double in Michigan. But she couldn't stop staring at him. The resemblance was uncanny. When she got even with him, she stopped dead in her tracks. It **was** him. And beside him sat J.D. Fitzgerald, II and Lois Fitzgerald. The two men smiled at her and nodded. Mrs. Fitzgerald glanced at her flatly, then looked forward. But Abby just stood there with her mouth open. She almost dropped her flowers. Finally, puzzled and confused, she proceeded down the short distance toward the front of the church.

Then her whole world stopped.

Abby looked forward and saw the minister, who was glaring at her. His plastic smile had gone all the way through neutral into a frown. Then she looked at the groom, and then glanced over at the best man. For a second she stared in unbelief. Then she gave an audible gasp and stopped. This time she did drop her flowers. She stood with her mouth wide open staring at Johnnie.

The other bridesmaids had already started down the aisle. Not knowing what to do, Audrey stood still. Mary Ann, not knowing Abby had stopped, almost ran into Audrey. Abby stared and stared, not able to move. Johnnie smiled at her, raised his hand and waved with his fingers. Abby considered running, but she was trapped. They had set her up. Tricked her. *But how did Johnnie get...? Why...? Who...?* Finally, she looked down and realized she was standing on her flowers. She slowly bent down and picked them up and proceeded to her place on the minister's right.

Then the wedding party proceeded normally. When Cassy was given away by her father and took her place in front of the minister, it was Abby's job, as the maid-of-honor, to straighten the train of Cassy's dress. As she did so, Abby leaned over, put her mouth next to Cassy's ear and said, "Next, book the church for a funeral, you are sooooo dead."

Chapter 30

Saturday, August 6
On the street, downtown Chicago

"Hello."

"Hans Reinhardt?"

"Who is this?"

"Klaus Becker asked me to call." The voice was clear, with a strong southern accent. "We have not met personally, but we will be working together on the job tonight. I am his inside man at the Fitzgerald Building. My identity will remain anonymous, but I assure you I will be assisting you at every step with any information you need. I will call you at 6:10 to be sure you have the pilot and helicopter secured. I will meet you inside the door at the heliport on the building. There I will let you know the situation, the exact location of the vault, whether the gems have arrived yet, and the people on each floor. The youngest Fitzgerald should be there and Klaus has some men picking up his girlfriend."

"My understanding is the safe is electronically locked, and it can only be opened from an off-site location. But the young Fitzgerald either knows how to open it or he knows who does."

"That's correct. And if he hesitates, put a bullet in the girl's leg and he'll roll over like a puppy."

There was a brief silence, then Hans asked, "Are the security people armed?"

"No, only the police, and you can easily neutralize them. You'll need very little firepower. Chicago does not allow guns in the city, so we will be the only ones with guns. Of course, the siege that will take place outside the building is another matter. But that's up to the Arabs."

"Becker said that's under control. Ghazi is positioning snipers with some pretty sophisticated firepower on the roof of the Fitzgerald Building and the one across the street. They'll keep the building clear until we're long gone. The police will be focused on the chopper and the hostages. And my understanding is you have the information on the escape tunnel."

"The escape route is straight forward. I was actually able to get into the tunnel entrance once. I wasn't able to walk the whole route. It's quite a long walk, but I know it leads to the subway tunnel. From there, it is only a short distance to the station where your team will simply walk away while the cops are chasing the helicopter."

"Looks like you have done your homework. Your infiltration into their organization is about to become very lucrative."

Chapter 31

Saturday, August 6
Ann Arbor, Michigan

The wedding continued as planned, except every time Johnnie looked over at Abby, she glared back, her eyes closed to narrow slits. The minister finally pronounced Jack and Cassy, Mr. and Mrs. Jack Donavan, and the wedding party returned down the aisle to the church foyer where they would form a line to greet the guests. Abby refused to look at Johnnie during the recessional as they walked arm-in-arm. But when they reached the foyer and the sanctuary doors were closed, all of them burst out in laughter, except Abby. "Soooo dead," Abby repeated, looking at Cassy. "You are soooo dead. And YOU," she pointed at Johnnie, "You'd better call 911 on that iPhone of yours. You are about to need serious medical attention."

Still laughing, Cassy wrapped her arms around Abby's neck and kissed her on the cheek. "We finally got you. After all the stunts you have pulled over the years, we finally got you. I would have given anything to see the expression on your face when you saw Johnnie."

"I wish I had a picture of it," Johnnie said, still laughing. Then, as Abby glared at him through those narrow slits, he put on a somber face and stood at attention, then started snickering, and they all broke out laughing again, except Abby.

"And you," Abby said to the groom. "I thought you were an honorable man. How could you participate is such debauchery?"

"Actually, there is a little more debauchery. Let me introduce you to this gentleman," Jack said taking Johnnie by the arm.

"*Him*, I know. Unfortunately!"

"I don't think you do. Abby, this is John David Fitzgerald, III, my brother."

"Your, …. your, …. your…."

"Brother."

"But how could…?"

"J D Fitzgerald, II is also **my** father. I was born in Chicago, where my mother met him when she was going to Northwestern University. They married, had me, and divorced a year after I was born. After the divorce, my mother and I moved to Canada, where she married Carl Donavan, who adopted me and gave me his last name."

Abby stood speechless for a few seconds, then she said, primarily to herself, "Then J.D. is also your grandfather?"

"True. At first, we didn't see much of the Fitzgeralds. My mother received a generous divorce settlement, and I received an additional gift when I reached the age of 21. We were pretty much on our own. But after my stepfather died, and I had my daughter Jenny, we got reacquainted with the Fitzgeralds. I rediscovered my brother and we've become good friends—we talk regularly, we even do some flying together. I also see grandpa about once a month. Jenny is his only great-grandchild."

"Yeah, wow, how about that? And Johnnie saw me in The Corner Grill because…"

"Because I told him about you," Cassy interrupted. "I asked Jack if there were any more like him at home, y'know, like, jokingly? But he said, 'Well, yeah, I have a half-brother in Chicago whose mother drives him nuts with high society chicks he can't stand.' So Jack introduced me to Johnnie over the phone, and I asked him to introduce himself to you. But when he saw you, he got all shy about meeting you and, well, you know the rest."

"You deceived me," Abby said turning toward Johnnie.

"Yeah, but not permanently. I just withheld a few things."

"I'd say!"

"He really wanted to tell you, honey," Cassy inserted. "But we talked him out of it and into this surprise. Come on, girl, admit it. We finally got you."

The reception that followed had lots of food but no alcohol or dancing. It was, after all, in a very conservative Assembly of God church. It was also an afternoon affair. It began right after

249

the wedding and lasted until Jack and Cassy left for their honeymoon at 3:30. Even though she still pretended to be angry, well, anyway, miffed, Abby was forced to sit next to Johnnie with the rest of the wedding party.

"You deceived me," she repeated.

"No. Well, yeah, but it wasn't a lie. It was more like a surprise birthday party. It was just a funny surprising way to tell you."

"I wasn't laughing."

"But when you looked up and saw me and dropped your flowers and stepped on them, the expression on your face was ha, ha, ha... ahumm, cough, cough, cough."

More narrow slits.

"Oh, come on, Abby. As I understand it, you were on the delivery end of jokes like this all your life. You were just on the receiving end this time."

"And don't forget who is the queen of practical jokes around here. I'd go into witness protection, if I were you."

"Hey, I was just a pawn in all of this. Cassy did it. She, like, kind of introduced us, in a way, sort of. Anyway, when she found out I went bonkers over you, she wanted me to keep the family connections quiet until she thought of a sneaky but surprising way to tell you. Then she thought of the wedding."

"I heard that." Cassy, hearing her name mentioned, leaned over and spoke past Jack, who was seated between her and Abby. Then she added, "I love you, Abby."

Jack then put his arm around Abby and said, "We all love you, Abby."

"Gosh, you people are hard to be mad at."

"Attagirl," Johnnie added. Being seated on her left, he put his arm around her over top of Jack's.

"YOU are not off the hook."

"I am if you want a ride back to Chicago. Cassy only got you a one-way ticket with Delta. But there is a Citation sitting at the airport with a big soft leather seat that has your name on it."

"You flew in with the...? Of course you did."

"Or you could try to book a flight, fly standby, pay through the nose for a last minute ticket, wait at the airport all night for a flight with an available seat, and sit next to some fat guy smelling of beer and BO. Orrrrrr…"

"That's blackmail."

"Orrrrrr… a nice large comfy leather seat in one of the world's sleekest airplanes that will get you to Chicago in about 20 minutes."

More narrow slits.

Chapter 32

Saturday, August 6
In the air
Between Ann Arbor and Chicago

"Now, isn't this better than sitting next to the fat guy?"

"Yes, and thank you."

"So can we be friends?" Johnnie added, putting out his hand for a handshake.

She looked at him for a few seconds. Then she took his face in her hands and kissed him briefly on his lips. Then she kissed him a bit longer on the lips. "I'll think about it."

It was a clear afternoon. Abby turned and watched the traffic, a mile and a half below them on I-94, begin to back up as it approached Gary, Indiana. But while Abby was watching the traffic, Johnnie was watching Abby. "You still don't like the money, do you?"

While still looking out the window, she said, "Your grandfather has a great perspective, but it does bother me. Like, why are we up here flying back to Chicago in a luxury jet and all those people down there are driving, taking the train, or flying back seated next to that fat guy?"

"Abby, I'd rather ride back to Chicago on the tailgate of a pick-up truck seated next to you, than fly in this Citation without you. I'm here because it would be hard to do my job without it. I had a meeting in Chicago this morning, and I have to be back to Chicago by 7:00 to meet the queen of the Mahmood family and receive the Crown Jewels. And it's not that this job is more important, it's just that this is the way it's done. Remember, I'll leave this job if you want me to. I don't need it."

"But you feel called to it. I'd never let you do that."

"It's not that I've had some vision from God or something, it's just that I was born here, and there is a great opportunity to steer some people in an eternal direction. But it's like grandpa says, 'God doesn't need us to take care of His money. He'll put it wherever He wants.' It's just that I feel a kind of responsibility."

She turned and faced him before she said, "And I'd never get in the way of that. It's just that Jesus said *it is easier for a camel to go through the eye of a needle, than for a rich man to enter the kingdom of God.* I'm afraid the money might make it harder on me before the Judgment Seat of Christ. And then there is the fact that your mother hates me."

"Well, yeah, there is that."

"You admit she hates me?"

"Of course, she does. She's been steering the family in the direction of spend, spend, spend on earthly pleasures. She's limited as long as grandpa is alive. She's just waiting for him to die so she can go crazy spending money on stuff. And now you threaten all that."

"I don't see how I'm a threat. I would never control anything."

"Yes, you would. I'd insist on it. Besides, you'll have influence. I think my father liked some of what you had to say. At least he listened, he didn't just blow you off. My mother will push the money in completely secular directions."

"But that won't happen if you are running the business."

"I can't do much about the spending. I can deal with how the company makes money, but I don't have a veto about how the family spends it. My mother is the major influence there. Of course, that's why she wants me to marry one of those materialistic high society girls who will join her in *gaily living in splendor every day.* My mother sees you as a major 'Delete' button to her plans."

"She hates me."

"Abby, my mother and her friends are self-centered, materialistic, liberal snobs. You are a beautiful, God-fearing, Bible-loving believer, with a rather odd personality that I am totally in love with. As I told you, you challenge my mother's domination of the feminine side of the family. She's been…"

"Wait a minute, time out."

"What?"

"My 'rather odd personality' that you… what?"

"Well, you are a bit odd, I mean you…"

"Never mind my personality, what did you say about how you felt about it?"

"The same way I feel about all of you, all the time. I'm in love with you—completely, incurably, irrevocably in love with you. I have been ever since the first time I saw you in The Corner Grill."

She stared at him for nearly a whole minute, neither of them saying anything. Finally, she said, "Well, then, Mr. J.D. Fitzgerald, III, we have a significant problem. Because I am also hopelessly in love with you." The kiss that followed lasted until the wheels squeaked out a landing at Chicago's Midway Airport.

Chapter 33

Saturday, August 6,
Midway Airport, Chicago

During the kiss, Johnnie had taken out the pins that were hold-ing Abby's hair. It now flowed down over her shoulders, ex-cept what was tangled in Johnnie's fingers. Her arms had locked themselves tightly around his neck again. She had lost awareness of everything but him. Only the sound of the wheels on the runway broke the spell. Well, the kiss anyway. They continued to hold each other during the rollout. As the Citation turned off the runway and proceeded toward the Fitzgerald hangar, Abby managed to say, "I don't want to leave you."

"Don't leave me. Stay with me all evening. You can watch the gems delivered and put in the safe. Then I'll have to make sure the security is in place and we can leave. I'll take you home about 10:00."

"Oh, my, I forgot about the gems being delivered. I shouldn't be a part of all that. I'll just see you tomorrow."

"No. Please. I want you with me. I'll be busy with various arrangements, but I really want you there. It will help me just knowing you are there."

"This is really not my thing, Johnnie. I'll just take the train and..."

"Okay, well, there is another reason. I didn't want to say it, but you will be safer with me."

"What do you mean, 'safer'?"

"If someone wanted to steal the gems, the easiest way is to kidnap you and use you to force me to open the safe. So I'd like to have you with me so I know you are all right."

"Johnnie, you don't really think someone would do that... Do you?"

"No, but it's possible. So stay with me. All right? Please?"

"Well, if...you...think...Johnnie, what's all that?"

As they approached the ramp, Abby could see flashing lights everywhere. Red lights, blue lights, white lights, rotating beacons, and flashing strobes. They were on fire trucks, police cars, limos, and a huge 747 jumbo jet with *Royal One* written on the side in English and in Arabic. All of them sat just outside the Fitzgerald hangar. Their Citation slowly inched forward and parked close, nearly under the right wing of the huge jumbo jet. Abby could see five police cars and three limos, but she lost count of the Chicago police and the Arab security guards standing on the tarmac. She found herself holding tightly to Johnnie's arm again.

"That's the queen and her royal gems. They're waiting for us, but actually we're not late," Johnnie added looking at his watch. Then he kissed her quickly on her lips. "I have to go greet the queen in her aircraft, then escort her and the gems into one of the limos. After that, I will come and get you. I'd like you to wait here. It should only take about 15 minutes."

"Johnnie, are you sure it's all right for me to be part of this? I can just take the train home."

"No. Please, Abby, don't do that. It will be fine. Just wait here for me. I'll come and get you. Promise me you won't run off. Just wait here. Okay?"

"Well, all right."

"Are you okay with being here alone? The pilot is up front, but he needs to stay by the radio. You can sit up there with him if you like."

"No, I'm fine. I'll just brush my hair and re-do my makeup."

"I'll see you in a few minutes, like 15, or maybe 20."

"Yes. Go. I'll be fine."

She watched him cross the ramp, walk up the high stairway that led to an open door near the front of the 747, and disappear inside.

She began brushing her hair and looking around at all the lights and vehicles and security personnel. Then she stopped and wondered why she was here. How on earth did a poor girl with no parents, no money, no social graces, wearing the only decent dress she owned, end up here, sitting in an airplane worth over 6 million dollars? She was in love with a millionaire. No, a billionaire. She didn't even know what a billion dollars was. Well, she knew it was a thousand million but what did that actually mean? Her only financial thoughts were about balancing a budget with her waitress salary and Grandma

Edna's pension check. Now she was loved by a man who was heir to billions of dollars, mansions all over the world, planes, helicopters, limos, and several huge buildings like the Fitzgerald Building downtown. And he'd told her he loved her. What if he asked her to marry him? Oh, how she wanted to be his wife! Wow, that would make her and Cassy sort of like sisters. But, she was getting way ahead of things. WAY ahead. Johnnie had said nothing about marriage. But he had talked about a future together. Anyway, they were in love. That she knew. And he knew. And that changed everything. The flight back from Ann Arbor had changed things. They were now tied together in a way not easily broken.

She began brushing again. The thoughts about the vast economic canyon between them began to trouble her again. But somehow they were on a level playing field. What leveled the field? It wasn't just their love. That would not be enough to bridge the gap. It would seem like it at first, but there is no way it could survive his mother's onslaughts and the demands of the business and the fortune. That only happened in fairy tales and movies.

Then she stopped brushing again and sat up straight in the seat. It was God. It was their belief in the God of the Bible and their faith in Jesus Christ that leveled the playing field. It was as grandpa said, 'God puts His money wherever He wants. Some of it is here because, for reasons all His own, He has decided to put it here.' Grandpa was right. And by the way, wasn't it interesting she was already thinking of him as *grandpa*. But that meant she was also where she was because of what God was doing—whatever that was.

Abby began to pray. She just praised God because of who He is, worshipped Him because He is worthy, told Him she feared Him and loved Him because He is sovereign, and because He is a God of justice and truth and holiness. And He is good—all the time. She thanked Him for her life, for Cassy, for Johnnie, and for this situation. The only thing she asked for was wisdom to deal with what was around her, and in front of her, in such a way that God would get the glory. When she finished, she felt a strange sense of peace and calm and confidence she had not felt since she learned of Johnnie's wealth. She began brushing again and thought of Philippians 4:6-7.

Be anxious for nothing, but in everything by prayer and supplication with thanksgiving let your requests be made known to God. And the peace of God, which surpasses all comprehension, will guard your hearts and your minds in Christ Jesus.

Chapter 34

Saturday, August 6
Chicago

It was all of 20 minutes before Johnnie emerged from the open door of the jumbo jet. He descended the stairs with Queen Daniyah Mahmood on his arm, followed by security guards carrying three golden shoe-box-sized containers. The queen and the containers, plus two of the guards, entered the center limo. The other guards then got into the limos in front and behind. Johnnie stooped over to help the queen get in. Then he walked over to the Citation to get Abby.

They crossed the tarmac amid an exhibition of flashing lights and entered the queen's limo. Johnnie introduced Abby to the queen. He thought Abby would be shy and intimidated but instead she was forthcoming and inquisitive. She asked the queen about their upcoming royal wedding and told about the one she was just in, leaving out the embarrassing parts. The queen seemed fascinated with the difference between the marriage ceremonies. The discussion more than filled the time between Midway Airport and the Fitzgerald Building.

Upon arrival, Johnnie led the queen into the lobby while holding Abby's hand and being followed by three Arabs carrying one container each and four others who stationed themselves around the boxes. The lobby was filled with people—reporters, news crews, many of the Fitzgerald Trust Company staff, and visitors who had just come to see the jewels, and the queen.

The Mahmood family had previously agreed to allow one camera inside the vault to view the inspection of the gems. The police parted the crowd as the entourage crossed the lobby and approached the large iron door of the vault. Johnnie then dialed a number on his phone, spoke a few words into it, and the large slide-bolts began to move. Once the bolts were retracted, the hung door slowly swung open. Then the queen, the gems, and Johnnie entered the vault. As they went in, Abby tried to free her hand from Johnnie's. When he looked up, she silently mouthed the words, *I'll just wait here.* Johnnie shook his head and held tight to her hand, leading her into the vault with the others. A designated cameraman followed and recorded the event. Each box was opened individually. Then the queen took out a small thick magnifying glass and looked at each piece. When the first box was inspected, it was closed and the second was opened, and the same for the third. Abby checked her watch and noted that the whole inspection took 13 minutes.

"Well, that should do it," the queen declared. "They are all here and all authentic." Then she turned to Johnnie, stretched out her hand, and said, "Thank you for your accommodations, Mr. Fitzgerald. I am sure the jewels will be quite safe. We shall return to collect them tomorrow at 10:00 A.M."

Johnnie took the queen's outstretched hand and kissed the back of it lightly. "Glad we could be of service, your majesty."

When they left the vault, Johnnie dialed a number on his phone and talked to someone a moment. Then the door slowly closed as it had opened. The lobby was still filled with people. It seems the people were more interested in seeing the queen than the jewels. Once she reentered the limo and left, the crowd thinned out quickly. Within 20 minutes, the lobby was empty of all but the building's night staff, the reporter and cameraman, plus three armed police, stationed two inside the main entrance and one in front of the vault.

Abby and Johnnie stayed in the lobby until the security was in place. Then they got on the elevator to go up to Johnnie's office. As he hit the button for his 35th floor, Johnnie's finger accidentally brushed over the button next to it for the 33rd floor. "Oops, I guess we'll be making a stop on the way." Then he turned to Abby. "You were fantastic."

"Why, what did I do?"

"You made the queen feel comfortable, got her engaged in conversation, talked about real issues in her life without her feeling threatened. She loved you." He put his arm around her. She put her head on his shoulder. Then the door opened to the 33rd floor. There was no one there. Johnnie thought that was a bit strange. The staff would all have gone home, but usually the janitors would still be working. Then the door closed and they ascended two more floors to the 35th.

When they entered the outer office, Bernice Dykstra was still at her desk and Bobby Andrews was just leaving, wheeling out his trash container. Johnnie was relieved to see someone was still working. "Hi, Bobby. You see the show downstairs?"

"Naw, I saw the queen of England once. I figure, you seen one queen, you seen 'em all. I'll catch it on the news. Good night, Mr. Fitzgerald."

"Good night, Bobby. And what about you, Bernice? Did you see the queen?"

"Yes, I stayed just long enough to see the queen come in. Then I came back here to make all the computer entries and no-tify the Mahmood family that the jewels were in the vault. I'll be leaving in about 10 minutes."

"That's about how long it will take me to wrap this up. I'll be in my office. Why don't you wait for me, and we'll all go down together?"

As Johnnie entered his office, the two women began to talk about Cassy's wedding. Bernice admitted she was in on the plot against Abby but was sworn to secrecy. She couldn't wait to hear Abby's side of what happened. As she unfolded the events of the day, Abby found herself laughing along with Bernice.

The women hardly noticed that it was nearly 20 minutes before Johnnie finished up and came out of his office. "I'm done here for today. You girls ready?"

"Actually, we were just discussing your treacherous plot against me," Abby returned.

"And, yes, I am finished here," Bernice added.

"There is one more thing." It was a male voice with a Ger-man accent. Looking up, they saw a middle-aged man standing in the doorway.

"Can we help you with something?" Johnnie asked.

"Yes, indeed." The man pulled a 45-caliper semi-automatic handgun out of his pocket and pointed it at them. "You can lay face down on the floor with your hands behind your backs."

261

Chapter 35

Saturday, August 6
The Fitzgerald Building, Chicago

"Come on, come on, we don't have all night. On the floor. Hands behind your back. You, too, Ms. Secretary, get out from behind that desk and on the floor."

As Bernice slid her chair back, she let her foot move forward enough to step on and trigger a silent alarm switch that registered an emergency with the Chicago Police Department. Then she joined Abby and Johnnie on the floor. Once they were secured with zip-type tie wraps, Hans Reinhardt searched them for weapons. He didn't find any, but he took cell phones from Bernice and Johnnie. Abby didn't have one. Then he helped them to their feet. He threw Bernice's phone on the desk, but he kept Johnnie's. Then the four of them took the elevator to the first-floor lobby.

When the door opened, they could see a group of people seated on the floor with their hands tie-wrapped behind them. They were sitting in a circle with their backs toward one another. Johnnie noticed Bobby seated among them, looking really scared. The formerly-armed policemen were there, too.

As soon as Johnnie and Abby had left the lobby for his office, guns were simultaneously pressed against the temples of all three armed officers. They were relieved of their weapons, zip-tied, and placed on the floor. Then all the others were forced to join them, all back-to-back in a circle. Next, a block of C-4 explosives was placed in the center of the circle and wired to a detonator that responded to a phone signal. That was the scene as the four of them walked out of the elevator into the lobby.

About then, they could all hear the sound of police sirens in the distance, gradually getting louder. "Sounds like they are playing your song," Johnnie said to his captor.

"That's just the CPD. They are coming because your secretary hit the alarm button before she left her desk. She saved me the trouble of calling 911. Then Hans took out a cell phone and dialed a number. "Hello, sergeant. This is the leader of the team that is stealing the Crown Jewels from the Fitzgerald Building. Actually, I will need to speak to your captain, but first you should stop your squad cars just short of the street in front of the main entrance to the Fitzgerald Building. If they enter that street, they will be blown away. Sure, I'll hold, but keep those cars off my street." A minute later, there was a loud explosion outside, near the building. "Hello, captain. Your sergeant needs to pay more attention. My men just disintegrated one of your squad cars and I'd guess a couple of good officers. If you want them to keep doing that, just keep ignoring me and send cars down that street. Those boys love the target practice…. What do I want? The jewels, of course. And if you try to enter the building before I leave, I have 23 people here who will die. And if you don't let my team escape in that helicopter on the roof, I will ignite the C-4 they are sitting on, and there will be an awful mess here in the lobby. Do we understand each other? …Good." He tapped off the phone, and looking at one of the other thieves, said, "Tie the secretary up with the others." Then Hans gave the phone back to Johnnie. "Open the vault."

"Okay, but it will take about 15 minutes."

"No, it won't. I saw you open it a half hour ago, and it took less than five. Then he walked over to Abby, pulled her down to a chair, and said, "In five minutes, I start putting bullets in the pretty lady. First, in her legs, then her arms, then I blow off her shoulders, one at a time. Get the picture? She will be full of very unsightly holes, if that vault is not open in five minutes. If it doesn't open at all, I put one right between her eyes. Got it?"

"You don't understand. I will be glad to open the vault, but it will take 15 minutes. It was that quick before because we were all set up to open it. Now, I have to call my contact and set it up again. Seriously, it will only take a few more minutes. I'm being as cooperative as I can. Don't shoot her."

"All right, Mr. J.D., III. I'll give you a few more minutes, but if I sense a delay or any tricks, the beauty, here, gets it. Got it?"

"Yes, I understand." Johnnie began dialing. Then he spoke into the phone. "I need the vault opened immediately... Yes, I know, just hurry….Right." Then he looked over at Hans. "He's getting the code into the system. It will just be a few minutes."

"Why do you want the jewels?" Abby asked the thief.

"What? Shut up, lady."

"Why do you want the jewels?"

"If you don't shut up, I'll put one between your eyes right now."

"No, you won't. You need me alive to keep forcing him to open the vault, remember? So why do you want the jewels?"

"To put on my Christmas tree next year. Why do you think I want them, you dumb broad? Haven't you heard? It's all about the money."

"Why do you want money?"

"Stuff a sock in it!"

"Why do you want money?"

"Are all blonds this stupid?"

"Actually, it's strawberry blond. Notice the reddish tint? Yours is blond, actually."

Noticing the robber was about to explode with fury, Johnnie stepped in with, "Um, Abby, maybe we should just let this go for now."

"Why? He's going to shoot us anyway. We can ID him, so he can't let us live. Actually," Abby looked up from her chair at the robber, "What's your name? Come on, you can tell me. I won't tell anybody. I'll be dead after you get the jewels, right?"

"How do you shut this chick up?" Hans said, but he was more irritated by the fact that she was calm and unafraid than he was by her questions.

"So why do you want the money?"

"Son–of–a …"

"You mean you don't know?"

"To make me happy, okay!?! Now will you shut the heck up?"

"That won't work."

"AAAAAAAAA!!!"

"Solomon tried that. He was one of the wealthiest men who ever lived. He had more money than you will get out of those jewels, and he tried to use it to be happy and concluded it was all *vanity, striving after wind.* And he was smart, too, a lot smarter than you are. You don't even know how you will turn the money into happiness. Did you know there is no correlation whatsoever between wealth and happiness? And let's say you get, like, a beach house in the Bahamas or something, with a big boat and lots of booze and drugs and women. When you are old, and that's not too far off for you, you'll get sick and be in pain and you won't remember any of that pleasure. The funny thing about pleasure is, when it's over, it's over. When you are old and in pain, your past pleasure can't help you anymore."

"Does nothing shut her up?"

"And Jesus said, *But woe to you who are rich, for you are receiving your comfort in full. Woe to you who are well-fed now, for you shall be hungry. Woe to you who laugh now, for you shall mourn and weep.* He also said, *Blessed are you who are poor… Blessed are you who hunger now… Blessed are you who weep now… Be glad in that day and leap for joy, for behold, your reward is great **in heaven***. Oh, and by the way, Jesus was never ever wrong about anything. How about you German-thief-man? Have you ever been wrong? I'd say you have. You are wrong about this. Because some day, and soon, you will have to leave whatever pleasure you get from these jewels, and you probably won't get any, but you will have to leave it all behind and face God with nothing, squat, natta, zero, zilch."

"Open that vault now, or I will shoot her just for the fun of it."

Chapter 36

Saturday, August 6
Chicago Police Department

"Hello. This is Captain Broadmoor... Listen, you already killed two of my officers and destroyed a squad car, why should I... A bus! What for? ... All right, all right, but it will take some time... Yes, okay, I'll get it for you, just don't hurt anyone." Then he clicked off the phone. He immediately pressed an intercom button. "Sergeant Winfield."

"Yes, sir."

"Send an empty city bus to the Fitzgerald Building. Then come up to my office and bring Officer Cummings with you."

"Yes, sir."

Two minutes later, both officers, one male and one female, were seated at a table across from the captain in his office. Captain Broadmoor was a tall, imposing man in his late 50s. He had completely gray hair, thick as wool on a sheep. He stood ramrod straight. And when he sat in a chair, it was the same way, almost like he was still standing. Sergeant Winfield was 45, overweight, balding, with a round face that displayed a small mustache. He was unimpressive looking, almost sloppy, but he had been on the force for 23 years and knew everybody in the police department and most of the fire department and many of the paramedics. Very little happened on the streets of Chicago Sergeant Winfield didn't know about. Officer Janice Cummings was 35, tall, thin, with straight dark hair that curled up slightly just above her shoulders. She was not what you would call a beauty, but attractive enough to draw mild flirting from most of her male counterparts. She was also the best in the department at researching the Internet. The captain often jokingly called her their 'Chloe,' after Chloe O'Brian, the computer expert on the old '24' TV series. Which is why she now sat here at the captain's table.

"Those guys are **not** getting those gems out of that building. Cummings, I want you to find out every possible way in or out of the Fitzgerald Building."

"Yes, sir. Can I use your computer?"

"Yes, of course, and Winfield, I want to know what's going on inside and outside of that building."

"I have men as close as we dare go. They report on regular intervals, but there is almost no way to know what's going on inside, sir. We had three officers on guard, but they have all been taken as hostages. This is a well-organized, professionally-orchestrated operation."

"Let's review what we know."

"Well, the Fitzgerald helicopter landed on the roof heliport at 7:05 P.M. Seven men with ski masks on got out and entered the building, but we believe the pilot is still in the aircraft. We think the leader is the one with the German accent with whom you talked on the phone."

"So the pilot has been in the helicopter over an hour, by himself?"

"Yes, sir. We expect he is tied up or cuffed to the seat. For some reason, he is unable to use the radios. They may have destroyed them or just taken out all the headphones. There would be a back-up hand microphone and possibly a handheld radio, but if there is, the pilot can't reach them or he would have used them by now."

"It seems that they want us to believe that's their way of escape, but they are making it very obvious. And why the bus, if they plan to use the chopper? What happened after the helicopter arrived?"

"The limos arrived with the queen and the jewels at 7:47 and left at 8:23."

"And our men were in the building at that time?"

"Yes, sir. Three of them."

"Did they report anything we could use?"

"Not that I can tell. You can listen to the tape of their report, if you like."

"No, but it does tell us something."

"What's that, sir?"

"The thieves had no intention of stealing the jewels before they were locked in the vault. That means they were confident they could open the vault and also confident they could exit the building after obtaining the gems. What happened after the queen left?"

"The Fitzgerald's office triggered a distress signal at 9:05 P.M. Our squad car was destroyed at 9:12, while you were on the phone with the German. At 9:25, seven people, wearing ski masks, entered the helicopter. Then nothing until this last call, demanding a city bus at 9:42. So it seems that either the chopper or the bus is a decoy."

"Cummings, how long does it take to open a vault like that, if you have the people who can authorize it under your control?"

"I'm checking here. Well, that safe is pretty new technology, but it looks like the best guess is about 15 minutes."

"Fifteen minutes? If he originally called me at 9:12 and was getting the vault opened at that time, that's 9:27 before he gets it open. So the six people entered the helicopter just before the vault was open. At least some of our thieves were still in the building. Then he called for a bus at 9:42. That's 30 minutes after he began opening the vault. If it took 15 minutes to open the vault, what has he been doing for the last 15 minutes?"

"I don't know, sir."

"He was leaving, that's what. The bus is just to divert our attention. So where is he?"

Sergeant Winfield's cell phone buzzed. He answered, listened for a minute, then said, "Sir, the chopper on the roof has started its engine."

"Follow them with the police helicopter, and scramble the Coast Guard, too."

"Yes, sir."

"It's been over 30 minutes now since they opened the vault. Even if we assume it took them half that time to board the chopper, why just sit there for 15 minutes before starting the engine?"

"Captain, I think I have something."

"What is it, Cummings?" The captain got up and walked to his desk, and looked over her shoulder as she studied a complex diagram on the captain's computer.

"This is a schematic of the old tunnel system which runs all over the place under Chicago. Most of it has been abandoned for years. But see this small passage here? It looks to me like it

leads off this subway tunnel right to the basement of the Fitzgerald Building."

Chapter 37

Saturday, August 6
Chicago Police Department

Captain Broadmoor straightened, cursed twice, followed by, "That's it. That's how they are getting out. Excellent work, Cummings. How long would it take them to get out that passage, to the subway tunnel, and to the subway station?"

"Well, it's a pretty long passage, and it's old. It probably has significant water in spots. I'd say it would take 45 minutes, maybe an hour, to reach the main subway tunnel. From there, it's just a few minutes through the subway tunnel to the station."

"He called me while they were on the move, so he was already in that passage when he called asking for the bus. Which means they are still in that passageway."

"Yes, sir, they would have to be, if that is their escape route."

"Oh, that's their route, all right. Sergeant, how many officers can you put at that subway station right now?"

"One is there now, two more are within a block of it, another, two blocks. I can have four of them assembled in about five minutes."

"Do it. Have your man on site watch that tunnel to see if anyone is walking on the track. When the others come, start down the subway tunnel, then proceed up that passage and walk it back all the way to the Fitzgerald Building. We'll nab 'em in that passageway. Get the trains on that line stopped. And close down that station."

The sergeant's phone was buzzing almost constantly now. "Captain, the Fitzgerald helicopter was just forced to land. Everyone on board was a hostage. No thieves." Another call. "Our men have cleared the roof of the bank building across the street. The snipers were gone. There was a cable ladder on the side. I guess they just climbed down. Should we enter the Fitzgerald Building, sir?"

"Yes, go get the hostages out."

"What about the C-4?"

"There is no C-4."

"You sure?"

"Yes, occupy the building now. Then start down that passage. We'll trap them in there."

Another call. "The four officers are gathered at the subway station, sir. Do you want them to wait or start down the tunnel?"

"Start down the tunnel, like I told you before, and hurry up about it."

The sergeant's phone buzzed again. He listened briefly then reported, "We have entered the lobby of the Fitzgerald Building, sir. You're right. The C-4 was a fake. And there are no thieves. The hostages are fine, except they say the thieves took young Fitzgerald and his girlfriend with them."

"Send some officers into that tunnel after them, six if you can. With the six coming up from the other end, there is no way out. We got 'em."

Chapter 38

Saturday, August 6
Chicago

Soon after the group of nine, seven thieves plus Abby and Johnnie, left the building and headed down the basement passageway, Hans Reinhardt's phone rang. He said some things in German, then apparently acknowledged the instructions given to him over the phone. Neither Johnnie nor Abby knew enough German to tell what it was, but something was definitely wrong. They picked up the pace until they reached a dugout area to their right. It looked like an old passage that had caved in, with broken pieces of wood laying on the sides and floor. The thieves turned in there and began throwing the wood aside until a small hole appeared about five feet in. Then one guy squeezed through the hole and grunted out a command. Johnnie and Abby were pushed through the hole from the outside and pulled through from the inside. Then the rest of them came in. The backpack they had put the jewels in was also shoved through, along with another sack about the same size. Then the last thief pulled the boards back over the hole. All of them had small flashlights, which revealed a damp dirty room full of cobwebs, old boards, and a wet floor. Hans Reinhardt then looked at the two hostages and spoke in English. "Our informer tells us the police are searching the passageway looking for us, probably from both ends. The group from the subway station should pass here first. When they do, we will proceed on our way. If they decide to search this side room, we'll kill them. If you two make the slightest sound, we'll kill you and them."

So, they waited.

About 10 minutes later, they could hear the CPD team coming up the passageway from the direction of the subway station. They didn't even slow down in front of the entry to the old room. They just passed on quickly as if it wasn't there. About two minutes later, one of the thieves opened the second backpack and began passing out some baseball-type caps and vests which said "POLICE" on them with the CPD logo. The German leader looked at Johnnie and Abby again, and said,

"Get these on. And, you, strawberry blonde, get that hair stuffed up under that cap." Then they all crawled back out the hole and proceeded down the passageway.

As they stumbled along in the dark, their only light being the flashlights carried by the thieves, Johnnie could easily see why the police did not stop to investigate their hole in the wall. The place was full of half-collapsed side rooms and passages just like theirs, heading off in both directions. None of the side passages appeared to be a place that thieves on the run were likely to crawl into. Finally, they reached the main subway tunnel. Then Hans Reinhardt ungracefully pulled the duct tape off the mouths of his prisoners. "There will be a crowd and maybe even some cops at the station. We have to look like police assigned to patrol this tunnel, so don't get stupid. We will proceed out of the subway station down a block and get into a panel van. The slightest signal from either of you, and I shoot the other one. Got it?"

"Yes."

"How about you, strawberry blonde, you got it?"

"Yeah, yeah, I got it."

Chapter 39

Saturday, August 6
Chicago, and West

The group of nine, wearing police vests and caps, walked out of the passageway into the subway tunnel. Then they made the short walk down the tunnel to the station, crossed over the tracks and climbed up to the boarding platform. They saw no uniformed police but suspected some to be officers in plain clothes. After reaching the street, they turned right, but after walking a half a block, four of the Germans did an about-face and started walking the other way. When the Americans also stopped, Hans said, "Never mind them, just keep walking straight ahead." They walked several blocks until they reached North LaSalle Street. Then they turned right. They were on North LaSalle only a few minutes before a white panel van pulled up alongside of them. There was a magnetic sign attached to the side of the van with black letters spelling out, "Randolph Delivery Service." The side door slid open and they all got in. The van began to move while Johnnie and Abby were pushed to the back seat. Their hands were zip-tied together and to each other's. Then their legs were fastened to the bottom bar of the seat in front of them.

Obviously, the Germans did not speak Arabic, and the Arabs did not speak German because they spoke to each other in English. There were only two Arabs in the van. The driver and a man sitting behind him. Both carried side arms, and the one who wasn't driving had a semi-automatic rifle, with a large clip attached, laying across his lap. He and Hans were the only ones who talked.

"Who are these people?"

"Hostages. Very valuable. He is J.D. Fitzgerald, III. His family owns the building and the safe that housed the jewels. The woman is his girlfriend. We used them as insurance against any potential problem exiting the building. You can do the same, if you have trouble getting out of the country. When you are clear, dispose of them however you like."

"Are the Crown Jewels in that rucksack?" The Arab with the rifle pointed with his head without moving his hands from the gun. Hans nodded and handed over the sack. The Arab looked inside for a long time, then said, "I will call to have your money wired." The Arab made a call. The conversation took longer than Hans expected. Then he realized the Arab was also asking about what to do with the hostages. Finally, he closed the phone and said, "Okay, it is done. Where can we drop you?"

"Anywhere, as soon as I confirm the transfer." Then Hans made a call and spoke for a time in German. There was a delay—then more conversation. Finally, he tapped off his phone and said, "Enjoy your jewels." The van stopped, and he got out without saying another word or looking back at the hostages.

The van traveled northwest out of Chicago in the direction of Rockford, Illinois, but then turned left onto a smaller road. About 10 minutes later, Abby fell asleep with her head on Johnnie's shoulder. They rode for a while. It was hard for Johnnie to tell what direction they were going in the dark, but they seemed to have driven into a farming area. After what must have been an hour of driving in rural northwest Illinois, the van made a right turn into a small airport. Johnnie could see a lighted sign that said De Kalb Taylor Municipal Airport. But the van did not drive to the terminal building. Instead, it circled the airport and entered an area where there were several rows of T-hangars. Johnnie glanced down at his watch. It was 1:23 in the morning.

The van stopped in front of a hangar in the middle of the second row. The driver got out and rolled out a twin-engine aircraft. The two men loaded the gems and some other gear into the aircraft. Then they relocated Johnnie and Abby in the back seats of the plane.

Johnnie recognized it as a piper Seneca V. It had six seats, counting the pilot and co-pilot. The four back seats were arranged so that two faced forward and two faced backward. The Americans were tied in the same manner as in the van and placed in the two forward-facing back seats. The two Arabs sat in front. The van driver was also the pilot of the Seneca. The aircraft taxied out and took off on runway zero-two. The air-

275

port had no control tower. They simply took off and circled to the north. Soon, they penetrated the cloud cover. The aircraft made several turns while in the clouds. Then, a few minutes later, it broke through on top. With no visibility below and only stars above, they ascended into the night sky.

Chapter 40

Sunday, August 7
Entering Canada

Abby fell asleep again. Johnnie dozed but not for very long at a time. At 4:05, the plane landed and refueled at a small airport Johnnie couldn't identify. There was a tiny administration building, but no one else around. When the aircraft landed, Abby woke up.

"I gotta' pee."

"Me, too."

When the engines shut down, Johnnie said, "Hey, up there. We need the toilet." The Arab in charge looked back without responding. "Toilet, we need the toilet," Johnnie repeated. The Arabs ignored them and went about buying fuel from a self-serve pump on the poorly lit ramp. Then one of them disappeared for a time. Then the other. Then they cut the ties of the hostages and escorted them into a small but clean building with one toilet off the far end. First Abby, then Johnnie, used the toilet, with their hands still tied and the door partly open. There was only one small window near the ceiling. Escape with their hands zip-tied was impossible, even if they weren't being watched. They were once again secured to the back seats of the Seneca. At least they were more comfortable now. Before starting the engines, the pilot tossed two candy bars back into their laps. Then they took off and reentered the night sky.

The Americans were wide-awake now. Since the two Arabs up front were wearing headsets and the Americans were not, they could talk without being overheard. While munching on her candy bar, Abby said, "Where do you think we are?"

"About to cross the border into Canada, I suspect. I figure they originally filed an IFR flight plan to clear the Chicago airspace without suspicion. I could see a squawk code on the transponder up front. The refueling stop must have been in the States because they did not have to clear customs. Now they are just squawking 1200."

"What's a squawk code?"

277

"It's a four-digit number assigned by air traffic control which the pilot dials into the aircraft transponder. It reflects a radar signal from the ground that allows the controller to monitor the altitude, direction, and speed of the aircraft. But when flying VFR, according to visual flight rules, they just squawk the universal VFR code of 1200, and they are on their own. The air is constantly full of airplanes squawking 1200, especially over the sparsely populated areas in the central U.S. and Canada. They will simply cross over to Canada and blend in with most of the other aircraft squawking 1200 and flying by visual flight rules."

"How do you know we are over Canada?"

"All night the big dipper has been out the right widow and slightly in front of us. The end of the dipper points to the north star which is right there, see it?"

"Oh, yes, so that's north, so we have been flying sort of west northwest?"

"I figure about 300 degrees on the compass. That would put us near the Canadian border, probably over Manitoba by now."

"Look, Johnnie, the North Star is moving up in front of us. We are heading north."

"You're right, we are."

"Johnnie." Abby laced her fingers together with his.

"What, honey."

"They are going to kill us, aren't they?"

"I suspect that's the plan. But we aren't dead yet. And that means these guys don't have orders to kill us, or we would be. It doesn't mean they won't, if we try to escape, it just means someone higher up on their food chain wants us held hostage until they check us out, or until they get the gems."

"So as soon as they get the gems, they will have no reason to keep us alive."

"True. But if they don't have them, they will need to keep us alive to get them."

"Yes, but as soon they all meet up, they'll have them and we're dead."

"I do have one more card to play."

"You do? What?"

"They don't have them."

278

"They don't have what?"

"They don't have the royal jewels."

"What are you talking about? Of course, they do. They're in that backpack right there."

"No, they're not."

"But I saw them take them out of the boxes in the vault and put them in there."

"They were never **in** the vault."

"How can that be? I saw them put in there, I mean, we all did. There was a camera there. It was on TV."

"They are fakes. Expensive imitations, but imitations nonetheless."

"But the queen verified them as being real."

"She was in on it. When I went up to visit her in the 747 while you were waiting in the Citation, I convinced her to allow us to move them to a different location, and put the imitations I had prepared in their place. We made the switch on her airplane. Then the fake ones were taken off and escorted downtown. After we left, the real ones were taken away."

"Where are the real ones?"

"Somewhere no one will decide to look."

"You going to tell me?"

"Are you sure you want to know?"

"Yes."

"Grandpa's pipe tobacco box. They are laying in the bottom covered with pipe tobacco."

Chapter 41

Sunday, August 7
Manitoba, Canada

They appeared to be making an approach on a small airport near a village. But when they were over the runway, just about to touch down, the plane went to full power, and they were back in the air. The aircraft changed course slightly but remained just over the treetops.

"What was that all about?" Abby wanted to know.

"Avoiding the radar. If anyone was tracking them, it would appear they made an approach and landed at this airport. Since they never went back to altitude, the radar can't tell they took off again. Now nobody can see them or track them."

They flew on at treetop level for nearly two more hours. The sun was up now, so they could get no indication of their direction of flight from the stars. They could only see mile after mile of Canadian wilderness.

"Abby." He took her face in his tied-up hands. "Listen, I've been thinking about this. Informing them that the jewels are fake is not only my last card, it's a dangerous one to play. We cannot predict a response to it. We need to try and escape. We will land soon because we are almost out of fuel. Just keep your eyes open for an opportunity. Abby, we have to be willing to kill these guys to escape. Are you up for that?"

"Oh, my! Are you sure?"

"I'm sure. It may not come to that, but we can't hesitate if it does. And it probably will. Remember, they for sure plan to kill us. There is no way they can let us live."

Within 10 minutes, their twin-engine Seneca landed on a very narrow gravel strip with trees close in on each side. The runway was in a shallow small valley. One would need to be right on top of the runway to see it was there. At the far end and to their left was a small cabin. It sat in a grassy area about halfway up a hill. A stone path led from the runway to the cabin. Alongside the cabin, sitting about three feet off the ground, was a tank with a hose running down to the runway. Johnnie figured this was a gasoline tank placed up by the cabin so aircraft could be refueled by gravity flow, without a fuel pump.

The Americans were taken to the cabin, their legs left untied but their hands zip-tied in front of them. They were allowed to stretch their legs and walk around inside the cabin and each given a sandwich and a bottle of water. There was only one room. There were cots along the wall to the right as you entered and a table and chairs on the left. A hand pump over a sink supplied the only water. But there was no indoor toilet. The pilot went out to refuel the aircraft and remove their bags. The other Arab was left to guard the Americans and the jewels.

"So why do you want the jewels?" Abby asked the Arab.

"Oh, no." Johnnie groaned under his breath.

The Arab just stared at Abby. So she tried again. "You speak English?"

"Yes, I do."

"So, why do you want the jewels?"

"They will be used to restore our country to the submission of Allah."

"So, Allah needs the money, and you are stealing it for him?"

"Um, Abby…"

"You infidels have no understanding of the Islamic faith," the Arab spat back.

"You're right about that. Maybe you could explain it to me. How long have you been a Muslim?"

"My father was Muslim and his father before him."

"I see, so if your father was a Buddhist or a Hindu, or a Christian or a Jew, you'd be following those religions. Is that right?"

"We are born according to the will of Allah."

"Oh, so Allah is sovereign over where you are born, but not over his wealth? He's out of money, so you have to steal those jewels for him? That seems a little contradictory, don't you think? How do you know the Islamic religion is right?"

"It has been the belief of millions of people for hundreds of years."

"The world is flat. That was the belief of millions of people for thousands of years. Millions of people believe in worshiping pieces of rock and carved images and horrid idols. And they have done it for thousands of years. Millions of kids believe Santa Claus will come down their chimney on Christmas. Do you believe in Santa Claus?"

"Umm, Abby, maybe you shouldn't..." Johnnie tried to interrupt, but the Arab answered Abby.

"Our belief comes from the Glorious Quran."

"Where did the Quran come from?"

"It was recited to the prophet Muhammad by the angel Gabriel."

"How do you know Mohammed was a prophet?"

"You infidels have no faith. Mohammed ascended into heaven from Jerusalem. Allah told him the truth about many things the Jewish and Christian infidels have perverted."

"How many people witnessed that?"

"I don't understand your foolish questions."

"Well, for example, the miracles of the Bible were witnessed by lots of people. The flood of Noah is recorded in ancient records all over the world. Millions of people saw God use Moses to part the Red Sea. Lots of people saw the walls of Jericho fall down flat. Lots of people saw Jesus' miracles. Lots of people saw Jesus alive from the dead. Even Josephus recorded that. Lots of people saw Jesus ascend into heaven. These were publicly verified events. So how many people saw the angel Gabriel dictate the Quran to Mohammed, or how many saw Mohammed supposedly ascend into heaven from Jerusalem? How many people can verify that?"

"Those things are a matter of faith."

"Yeah, just like Santa Claus, right? You are telling me there is the same evidence for the heavenly origin of the Quran and Mohammed's being a prophet, as for Santa Claus coming down the chimney? Both have lots of believers and the same evidence. Right?"

The Arab began to curse and swear using the name of God and Jesus Christ. Abby, who had been pacing the floor of the small cabin, swung around and grabbed the Arab by the throat, shoved him against a wall, put her face against his and said, "Don't you EVER blaspheme the name of my God!" The Arab, totally surprised by this, pushed her back so hard she stumbled and fell backwards to the floor. Johnnie ran to her and helped her to her feet. Then she walked right back up to the Arab, put her face in his and said quietly, "Some day you will be on your knees before Jesus Christ, begging Him not to throw you into the lake of fire."

The Arab pushed her away again. This time she stumbled back into Johnnie's zip-tied hands. The Arab pulled his gun and pointed it at her. "You wretched infidel, I would shoot you right now if I were not instructed to keep you alive. When the others arrive, I will make sure I am the one to shoot you through the head."

Chapter 42

Sunday, August 7
Somewhere in the Canadian Wilderness

They sat on the chairs for a while, no one saying anything. Johnnie searched his mind, and the room, for an idea of escape. He could think of no plan where they would survive. They needed some sort of weapon, but they had none. If they could get something to cut the hard plastic ties, it might give them a fighting chance. But there was nothing. They sat in a one-room cabin where their every move was monitored. Attempting to physically overcome two Arab jihadists with semi-automatic weapons, while Johnnie and Abby's hands were tie-wrapped, was suicide. And soon there would be more jihadists. Johnnie decided he could not wait for that. So when the pilot returned from refueling the airplane, Johnnie played his only card. "Gentleman, I have some information you might want to know before you bring those jewels to your superiors."

"Be quiet, infidel."

"What information?" the pilot wanted to know.

"They are fakes."

"Who are fakes?"

"Not who, those jewels there in that backpack. They are just copies of the originals. They are not real."

The other Arab gave a mocking chuckle, "Likely story. You have no way of escape, so you tell lies. Very typical."

"I don't lie."

"How do you know they are not real?"

"Because I had them made. They are quite expensive forgeries, but definitely not real. They are made of glass, quartz, rose quartz, amethyst, smoked topaz, and a few other real, but inexpensive stones. The whole thing is worth, oh, maybe a couple of thousand U.S. dollars. Although it cost me a lot more than that to have them made."

The Arab, who had pushed Abby, opened the sack and poured out the gems on the table. "They look real to me."

"Are you a gemologist? Because that's what it would take to tell the difference. I paid good money to have those made."

"He's lying."

"How can you prove your claim? If these are not real, where are the real ones?"

"Well, let's see. It's 10:05 Sunday morning. I'd say they are about to be loaded in an armored car to be taken to the Trump Hotel. They will be put in display cases this afternoon for the wedding tomorrow."

"I tell you, he is lying," the more belligerent Arab said in Arabic.

The other responded in Arabic. "But we should be sure. It would be embarrassing to deliver copies to our leaders. We have authorized 20 million U.S. dollars to the German. If it was for worthless stones, we will lose our heads."

"He just wants us to think that so they can trick us."

The pilot Arab then turned to Johnnie and spoke in English. "How can you prove these are not real?"

"I'm sure you have someone in Chicago you can call. Ask them if the real jewels are on display. Or just call a local Chicago news station. They will all be covering it."

"There is no cell phone coverage here."

"All right, here is what you do. Take one of the phony diamonds and put it on the table and hit it with a hammer. If it is real, it will just sink into the wood on the table. If it's glass, it will shatter."

After some more arguing in Arabic, the jihadists decided to conduct the experiment. They laid a large clear-looking crystal on the table, supposedly one of the world's largest diamonds. Then they struck it with a hammer. The fake diamond shattered in a million pieces.

"Go ahead, try it on some of the other ones. Some won't break easily because they are real stones, but they are not emeralds, rubies, or diamonds."

The pilot, now also furious, said, "You tricked us."

"I never said they were real."

"We should kill you right now."

"I get to shoot that female infidel."

"Now just hold on there," Johnnie raised his zip-tied hands. "All is not lost."

"Explain."

285

"You don't need jewels, you just need money. You gave the Germans 20 million and you need about a hundred million. Right?"

"And?"

"And I have it. I can have it wired anywhere in the world."

The Arabs looked at each other and spoke in Arabic. "Is that possible?"

"I suppose. He is the grandson of a billionaire."

Looking back at Johnnie, the pilot said, "Then that is what you shall do."

"First, you need to get that lady safely back to Chicago," Johnnie insisted. "When I get positive verification that she is back in Chicago, in police protection and unharmed, I will call my accountant, and he'll wire the money anywhere you like."

Abby ran up to him. "Johnnie, no. I'm not leaving you. Don't make me go back without you."

The pilot nodded, but a furious argument broke out between the two Arabs in Arabic. Then the one who hated Abby said, in English, "No. That infidel woman dies now."

Johnnie had his back to the Arab who spoke. But what made him turn was the sound of a cartridge being chambered into the barrel of a semi-automatic handgun. As Johnnie turned, he lunged forward, grabbed the gun, and pushed it aside as it fired. He could feel the bullet enter his chest.

Chapter 43

Sunday, August 7
Somewhere in the Canadian Wilderness

Johnnie figured the bullet had entered his chest, traveled upward, and lodged in his right shoulder, but he held onto the gun. The Arab, caught off guard, fumbled the gun, then tried to regain his grip on it. Both men held the gun, neither of them securely, but Johnnie was stronger. He forced the gun barrel back until it pointed at the Arab. Then he pulled the trigger, twice. The first shot caught the Arab in the ear, but the second went up through his chin, blowing off the top of his head. Johnnie immediately grabbed the Arab's shirt and swung his body around facing the second Arab who fired three times, sinking bullets into the dead body.

The Arab's body had offered protection, but now it was sinking in Johnnie's arms and getting clumsy to handle, especially since Johnnie's hands were still tied together. The other Arab, seeing the advantage was now his, took the time to aim at Johnnie's head. But the time was not well spent. Before he could pull the trigger, a chair came crashing down on his head, stripping the gun and knocking him to the floor. He spun around on the floor, grabbed the gun, and pointed it at Johnnie. But now, free of his dead-human-body shield, Johnnie had the time to aim and fire. Two shots buried themselves into the Arab's chest, one hit just below his neck, the other tore through his heart. He was dead within a minute.

Abby stared at the man she had just disabled with a chair, now laying on the floor in a rapidly forming puddle of blood. Then she looked up and screamed when she saw Johnnie, also lying on the floor in a pool of blood. She had no idea that he had been shot. "Oh, no, no. Johnnie, how can I help? I don't know what to do. Tell me what to do."

"Are they both dead?"

"Yes, for sure. But you're bleeding real bad."

"I know. If they are dead, the next thing is to stop this bleeding. Get a piece of cloth from somewhere and hold in on the wound." Abby ripped off part of the dead pilot's shirt and held it against the wound. "Is there a hole in my back?"

"I don't think so. You are soaked in blood, but I don't see a hole, just this one in your chest."

"That means the bullet is still in there. That's not good, but at least there is only one place that I'm bleeding."

"Can you tell how bad it is?"

"Well, I'm not coughing up blood, so apparently, it missed my lungs. That's good. The blood is oozing out, not spurting, so it missed a major artery. That's also good. The bullet seems to be lodged in my shoulder some place. That's not good, but the immediate danger is blood loss. We need to keep this wound closed as much as possible. There should be a first-aid kit in the airplane. I can hold this for a bit. You go out and see what you can find. Some alcohol and some bandages and tape would be helpful. But hurry, I don't want to pass out bleeding like this."

Abby got up and ran out the door and down the small hill toward the plane. The baseball cap she had been wearing since the robbery escape, blew off in the wind, releasing her hair to a stream of reddish gold flowing behind her. She climbed into the plane and began to look frantically through every pocket and space she could find. Finally, behind the last seats, she saw a white plastic box with a red cross on it. She opened it quickly. She didn't bother to identify what was in it, but it was full of stuff she figured must be useful. Seeing no other first-aid boxes, she closed it, climbed out of the plane, and ran to the cabin in an all-out sprint.

Together they cleaned the wound, poured alcohol in it and bandaged it up as tight as they could. There was adhesive tape that they wound around Johnnie's shoulder and neck. But even with all this, the blood oozed through.

"We've got to get out of here," Johnnie insisted.

"But you're still bleeding. You shouldn't move until the blood clots. Besides we have no idea where we are or where to go or how to get out. We are trapped here by the forest."

"There is one way out of here. The way we came in. That Piper Seneca out there. They were even good enough to fuel it up for us."

"You can fly that thing?"

"As long as I can stay conscious, I can. It's dangerous, but I see no other options. We don't want to be here when the friends of these dead guys arrive. Once in the air, the GPS will tell us where we are, and the shortest route to the nearest airport, where we can get some help. I'll need you to help me up."

With his good arm wrapped around Abby's shoulder, Johnnie stumbled down the path toward the aircraft. He was amazed how weak and dizzy he was. He was certainly in no condition to fly an airplane, but they had no choice. When they reached the Seneca, he slowly and painfully crawled into the left front seat.

"They have a bag with food and water in it. Go back and grab that a second, while I start the engines and get this thing turned around." Abby just nodded and ran back to the cabin.

Once they were primed with fuel, both engines started easily. Johnnie needed a lot of power to turn the aircraft around in the loose gravel, but finally it was in position, nose pointed down the runway. As he looked out the right side, he could see Abby running back down the hill, her hair flying out behind her, with a satchel in her hand. When she climbed into the seat next to him, she said, half out of breath, "I figured, what the heck, I might as well take the fake jewels. Then I thought, Well, if their friends find them there with the jewels, they will think they shot each other fighting over them. After all, the guns are theirs and the other Arabs probably don't even know about us. Of course, they'll wonder what happened to the airplane, but they'll probably just take the phony jewels and leave. So I just grabbed the food bag and I put that first-aid kit in here."

Chapter 44

Sunday August 7
Chicago

At 10:00 Sunday morning, elderly J.D. Fitzgerald got out of a taxi in front of the Fitzgerald Building in downtown Chicago. With the help of the cane he had been using the last two years, he walked into the lobby. The police barricades, which had been in front of the building all night, were now removed. The building had been thoroughly searched, and the police captain was finally convinced that the thieves were not in the building or the tunnel system underneath it. So the building was once again open. Normally, there would only be a few people in the building on Sunday, the security guards, plus a few who came in to catch up on their work or prepare for a Monday morning meeting. But today, there were also reporters and visitors, just curious to have a look at the crime scene. As the elderly Fitzgerald walked through the lobby, some nodded a greeting, others elbowed those next to them and pointed out who he was. He walked up to the reception desk where Freddie Monroe, the head of the building's security, almost knocked over his chair getting to his feet to greet him. "Mr. Fitzgerald, good to see you, sir. So sorry about the robbery and the kidnapping."

J.D. shook Freddie's hand, then hooked his arm up around Freddie's big shoulder and said, "Thanks for meeting me on short notice, Freddie. Let's go up to Johnnie's office where we can avoid those reporters over there." Freddie Monroe was an African American man who stood six foot tall and weighed 210 pounds, without an inch of extra fat. He was 55 years old and had been the head of the building's security for the last 12 years. They rode the elevator in silence to the 35th floor. Then J.D. slid a card through a slot on Bernice's outer office door, which responded with a click, and the door eased open. They went through the reception area and repeated the procedure on the door leading to Johnnie's office. "Have a seat, Freddie, I'll make us some coffee. No not there, let's sit over there on those big chairs in front of the desk."

"Thank you, sir, but you don't have to make coffee for me."

"Oh, it's no problem. Johnnie has the same coffeemaker I have. I like to make it. He's gotten me into this espresso coffee. I think I'm addicted."

As J.D. made coffee, he asked Freddie about his wife and daughters and his new baby grandson. Then J.D. hooked his cane over his arm and brought over two large mugs of coffee and sat them on a small table which separated the large chairs in front of Johnnie's desk. "I think you take it with just cream, is that right?"

"Yes, sir, thank you, sir."

"Freddie, how long have you worked for us?"

"I came here as a janitor when I was 17 years old. That was 38 years ago, sir."

"Freddie, I have a problem, and I believe you are the one who can help."

"I'm so sorry to hear about the jewels and the kidnapping. If there is anything I can do, you just let me know, and I'm on it right now."

"Oh, the jewels are no problem. They'll be delivered to Queen Daniyah Mochmood right on schedule this morning at the Grand Ball Room of the Trump Hotel."

"But how can that be? They were stolen last night. The police never caught the thieves. I thought they got away with the jewels."

"Oh, we are a little tricky ourselves, Freddie. Trust me, the jewels are safe. Check the local news about noon, and they will record the delivery. No, the only concern is Johnnie and Abby. And all we can do right now is pray for them. Until they can give us some signal as to where they are, we can only wait and pray. The police finally figured out that they were out of the building and began checking roads, buses, trains, and air travel. My son is over at the station now waiting for any information that we can act on. But they are long gone from the city. It's up to our kids to make a move we can identify."

"So how can I help, sir?"

"After I heard about the kidnapping, I began to pray. Then I began to think. Then I called the police and began asking questions. There is something here that just doesn't add up."

"What's that, sir?"

"The thieves knew the combination to that heliport door over there. That's apparently how they entered the building. Very few people know that combination. I don't know it. I'll bet you don't know it either, do you, Freddie?"

"No, sir, I have to get Johnnie's executive assistant, Miss Bernice, to open it if I need to go up on the heliport."

"The thieves also knew exactly how the vault had to be opened. They knew Johnnie had to phone an off-site location where a code could be entered into a computer program to open it. They also knew about the underground passage that led to the subway tunnel. Very few people knew about that."

"That's true, sir. I am head of security, and I didn't know how the vault could be opened. I know where the door is that leads to the tunnels, but I didn't have the combination to open it."

"Freddie, we have a mole. Someone who works in this building is one of the thieves."

Chapter 45

Sunday, August 7
Somewhere in the Canadian Wilderness

Johnnie had never flown a Seneca before, but he had flown similar twin-engine aircraft. The gravel runway was short and narrow, and the aircraft was heavy, being full of fuel. The take-off run used the whole runway, but when he pulled back on the yoke at the end, it lifted off, climbed over the trees and across the Canadian wilderness. Not knowing where they were, Johnnie pointed the airplane south until they got a signal on the GPS.

"There seems to be a village here called Paint Lake," Johnnie tapped the screen. "There is no airport listed on the GPS, but they have a road called highway 6, and we can probably land on that."

"How long will that take?"

"At 220 knots, let's see, the GPS says 43 minutes. But Abby, I'm...not...feeling...so...." The blood loss had taken its toll, and even though he struggled to stay awake, Johnnie's world went black, and he slumped forward against his shoulder harness.

"Oh, my. Oh, no. Johnnie, wake up! Johnnie, I can't fly this thing. Crap, crap, crap, oh crap. What do I do? What does this thing do? Ooookay, that tilts the wings and this must lift the nose. Oh my word, that came up fast! Which ones are the throttles, and where is that landing gear thing? What do these pedals do? Oooo. Don't do that again. I can't land this thing. I'll kill us both. JOHNNIE, YOU HAVE TO WAKE UP. Where is that water, there were water bottles in that bag. Here, okay, maybe some water splashed on his face. JOHNNIE."

He groaned and began to regain consciousness. "Johnnie, you passed out, and I can't fly this thing. There are no roads anywhere, but you've got to land this thing before you pass out again."

"Okay, um, see if you can find um...some place flat...or a river or a... a good-sized creek with sandbars on it."

"Well, there is a ridge in front of us, that may mean there is a river on the other side."

"I'll get us down low, just in case."

"Yes, there is a small river, and it has sand bars all along its banks. Can you land on one of those?"

"I'm going to give it a try. Flaps down, nose trimmed, gear down."

"Johnnie, I just saw a cabin, we flew over a cabin. There may be somebody there who can help us."

"I'll circle back. We'll try to land as close to it as we can."

He gave the Seneca power. It climbed up over the ridge and circled around to make a downwind leg. When he got parallel with the river, Johnnie could see the cabin. He flew downwind a ways, that way he could lower the Seneca over the river a considerable distance before landing. Just before the sandbar, he intentionally lowered the wheels into the water to quickly slow the aircraft down, keeping it just above stall speed with the throttles until they reached the sandbar. Then he pulled both throttles to full off and hit the brakes. The airplane skidded through the sand, hit a log that caved in the nose wheel, then skidded sideways and came to a stop at the edge of the water on the far side of the bank.

"Wow, good job. Are you okay? Johnnie, you don't look so good. I'm going to run over to that cabin and see if I can get some help."

He only nodded and closed his eyes.

Abby ran across the sand bar, which fortunately was on the same side of the river as the cabin, splashed through some puddles and climbed a small path that led to the door. As she approached the small log-built house, she began calling out for help. But when she knocked on the door, it just swung lazily open to reveal an empty one-room shack.

She looked around and called out again, but there was no response. It was little more than a shanty with a cot, a wood stove, and an old wooden table and two chairs. There were some old musty looking blankets folded on the cot and a large coat hanging on the wall. There was a lantern and some candles on the table, but no sign of recent life, no water supply, no electricity, and no food. Abby returned to the airplane, finding

Johnnie lying still with his eyes closed. "I'm sorry, Johnnie, there's no one there. It's just an empty shack. It doesn't look like it's been used in months."

Johnnie forced himself to wake up. "Help me out of here. Does it have some place I can lay down?"

"Yes, there is a cot and some blankets."

"I need to lay down, stay immobile, and hope the blood clots on this wound."

So Abby wrestled him out of the airplane, helped him limp across the sandbar, and climb up the path to the cabin. Johnnie lay on the cot and Abby covered him with the blankets. "I think I'm getting a fever. And the blood is still leaking out of the bandage. I can't leave here. I'm sorry, but you are going to have to go for help on your own. I saw a canoe pulled up alongside the path. You will have to take that down river until you fine someone with a phone."

"Johnnie, I don't think I can..."

"As soon as you get to a phone. Call grandpa. Do you know his private cell number?"

"I do, actually. He gave it to me and told me to call him if I needed anything. I memorized it. But Johnnie, I don't want to leave you here. What if you get worse, or you need something, or animals find you?"

"There are some snacks and a few bottles of water in that bag in the plane. Just give me a candy bar and a bottle of water, then take the rest with you. You have to do this, Abby. If you stay, we'll both die. We can't survive here very long."

Abby returned to the plane and retrieved the food bag. She took a candy bar and a bottle of water. She left the rest near the cot where Johnnie could reach them. They focused on each other's eyes. Then Abby knelt down next to the couch and put her arms around his neck. They just held each other for a few minutes. Then she kissed him lightly on the lips and said, "I love you, J.D. Fitzgerald, III. Now, don't you die on me."

"Abby, I need to ask you something, and I want an answer now, before you go." Wincing in pain, he dug his hand in his pocket. Then he pulled out a beautiful diamond ring. "Abigail Edna Davidson, will you marry me?"

Abby was speechless. She just knelt there beside the cot staring at the ring with her mouth open. Then she pushed her hair behind her shoulder and looked at him, wondering if she had heard him right. "Um…Abby, this question requires a response."

"Oh, my word, yes, yes, yes, yes, yes…. Yes. Oh, my love." She wrapped her arms around his neck again. He took her face in his good hand and kissed it, then struggled free of her neck-hold, took her hand and slipped the ring on her finger. With tears in her eyes, she managed, "Where did you get the ring?"

"I took it out of the backpack of royal jewels while you were going to the plane for the first-aid kit. It's a fake diamond. I'll replace it with a real one when we get back."

"You most certainly will not! I am never taking this ring off. And you are not replacing the stone with anything. You had this made, you chose it for me from all the royal jewels. This is the ring I'm wearing the rest of my life."

"But Abby, it's just silicon dioxide. It worth like maybe $20. I can get…."

"No! I'm keeping this ring!" She hugged the ring to her chest. Then she kissed him again, very briefly on the lips, got up and went to the door. As she opened it, she turned back and pointed her finger at him and said, "Do NOT die on me, you got that!" Then she was gone.

Chapter 46

Sunday, August 7
Chicago

"A mole? You think someone who works here was feeding information to the thieves?"

"And I think we can narrow it down to one of 20 people."

"How's that, sir?"

"Because, Freddie, when the thieves entered the passageway, the police entered the building. As soon as the captain learned they were in the passage, he immediately put a team of officers together to enter the subway tunnel and then come up the old passage toward this building. There is no way the thieves could get out that subway station before the police team entered the tunnels. The police tell me there was one officer at that station from the get go, before the other officers joined him for the search, even before the robbery took place."

"So how did they get away?"

"It is actually quite easy, if they knew they were being pursued. Underground Chicago is honeycombed with those old passages. Some date back before the great Chicago fire. If they knew they were being pursued, all they had to do is divert into a side tunnel or an old boiler room or storage area. There are hundreds of places to hide under there. Since the police thought they were going to surprise them, they didn't think to look in all the side tunnels, rooms, and spaces. At least not until it was too late. Once the police team passed the hiding thieves, all the thieves had to do was walk out the tunnel and down the street, with Johnnie and Abby as prisoners."

"But that would mean someone informed the thieves that the police were coming, after they entered the building and freed the hostages."

"Exactly. And there were 21 hostages, right?"

"Right."

"And you were one of them, right?"

"Right."

"So we have 20 suspects to investigate. Tell me who those 20 hostages were, because one of them is our mole. First of all,

did you notice anyone making a phone call right after the police released them?"

"Almost all of them. They were calling family and friends
to tell them about the robbery and that they were all right."

"So that won't help us. Now who were the 20?"

"Let's see. There were only two women. That pretty new
receptionist, Miss Gloria, and Johnnie's assistant, Miss Bernice. The others were all men. There were three police officers.
Oh, yes, I forgot, there was one other woman, a reporter and
her cameraman who photographed the jewels. Then there was
my security guards and a few of the janitors."

"How many security people?"

"Let's see, let me think and count... seven, there were sev-
en of my guys held hostage."

"How well do you know them?"

"Five of them have been with me for over 10 years. The
other two are new. Young guys, kinda silly, always joking
around. I can't see them being informants, or knowing much of
anything, actually."

"Two women, three policemen, two reporters, and seven
security people. That leaves seven janitors. Is that right?"

"Yes, sir."

"What do you know about them?"

"Not much, really. I know their names, but that's about it."

"Do they always clean the same floors?"

"Well, yes, I think so. There is a janitor for every two
floors, I think."

"So, Freddie, you are telling me the janitor for this floor,
the one we are on, the one who cleans Johnnie's office, would
be the same guy all the time?"

"Sure, Bobby Andrews. I know him pretty well. We talk
some. He's a big Cub's fan, like me."

"So he has a key to this office?"

"Actually, no. Only Johnnie and Bernice have that. But he
has one for Bernice's outer office."

"Would all the information we just discussed be kept somewhere in her office?"

"I suspect so."

The elder Fitzgerald got up and opened the computer on Johnnie's desk. He brought up the list of their janitorial staff, located a photo of Bobby Andrews. The note under it said he came here as an immigrant from Germany on a green card, and they hired him as a janitor, two weeks after the new vault was installed. J.D. emailed his photo to the Chicago Police Department. Then tapped his cell phone once, then tapped it again. "Hi, son. This is pop. You still at the station?... Good. I just sent them a picture. Name he is going by is Bobby Andrews, but I'm sure that's an alias. Have them put out an APB on him. And get the Feds and Interpol involved. This guy worked for us, and I believe he is the leadership behind the whole thing."

Chapter 47

Sunday, August 7
North of Paint Lake, Manitoba

Abby still had on the dress she wore home from Cassy's wedding. Fortunately, she had changed into some soft shoes she had purchased at the Good Will store near her house two years ago. The dress was now dirty and torn, with streaks of Johnnie's blood smeared on it, but it was all she had. So she wrapped her hair into a knotted ponytail, put her water bottle and candy bar on the floor of the canoe, and pushed it into the water. Whoever left the canoe also left a paddle under it, so she was able to paddle and maneuver as she drifted downstream. She paddled until she was too tired. Then she drifted a while. Then she repeated the process. Paddled. Drifted. Paddled. Drifted. She had been descending the river for nearly two hours when she heard the sound of rushing water. She sat up as tall as she could and looked ahead. But when she saw the falls, it was too late to get to the bank. The canoe was already sucked into the current. All Abby could do was keep it straight and ride it out. The water boiled between huge rocks and sucked the canoe down a 5-foot drop into a deep pool of water. The nose of the canoe plunged into the pool like a submerging submarine. In seconds, it was under water, and so was Abby. When she surfaced, all she could think was *hold onto the canoe, don't lose the canoe.* Somehow, she did. But everything else, her water bottle, her candy bar and her paddle were washed away in the current.

Abby was now drifting downstream, completely under water except for her head and an arm clutching to the back end of a submerged canoe. Her legs dangled beneath her in the water, touching nothing. After a few minutes, she realized she had no idea what was under her and she was drifting at a tremendous rate of speed. She could come upon a rock or a submerged log that could cut her or break her leg in a second. She needed to somehow get the canoe toward land. Slowly, she began to use her body as a rudder and inch the submerged canoe closer toward shore. Things seemed to be progressing well until she got close. Then the front of the canoe caught a small tree and swerved sideways. The current filled the inside with a great force and buckled the canoe, wrapping it around the tree like closing a jackknife.

Abby made her way to shore by pushing herself along the side of the collapsed canoe. When she got there, she just stood and looked at it a few minutes, wondering if it was possible to free it from the current. Then she looked at the forest all around her. It was thick with dense undergrowth, briars, and thistle bushes. It seemed impossible for her to negotiate a way to civilization through that forest. The canoe was her only hope. For a few minutes, she stopped and prayed. She spoke out loud, praising God for who He was. Then she thanked Him for her life, for her salvation, for Cassy, for Johnnie, and now a hope of marriage, and a whole new challenge. Somehow, standing in the middle of this wilderness, her only ride out of there wrapped around a tree, she felt calm, even confident. For the first time, she felt she could even handle Johnnie's mother and the Fitzgerald fortune, with the right perspective. Then she begged God to preserve Johnnie's life until she could get back to him. Then she said, "In Jesus' name, amen," and began looking for a stick she could use to pry the canoe off of the tree.

That, however, required her to re-enter the freezing water, push and shove and pry. Finally, when she felt she could not endure the cold water a second longer, it came loose and immediately started down stream. She jumped in after it. It took another half hour of work before she could drag it to shore. Once there, she braced it against a tree and began tugging and pulling until it was more-or-less straightened out. But the aluminum had cracks in the bottom. So it would leak. She found a suitable push-pole, got back in the canoe, and reentered the river. Now all she could do was poke and prod away from rocks and logs, but she was also moving much faster. Every 15 minutes or so, she had to make her way to shore and empty out the water that had leaked in. But the sun was still warm, so within the hour, she was completely dry. Her dress was torn to shreds. The hair that had escaped the ponytail stuck to her face, which was streaked with mud. Her arms and legs had multiple scratches, some of which were bleeding, and her side ached from being bruised by the rocks. But she was now warm and dry. And she was thankful for that.

As she drifted along, she continually scanned the shoreline for houses or cabins or a road, or any sign of human life. Nothing. And now she was facing a new problem. Darkness. The shadows were getting long and the air was getting cool. Soon it would not be safe on the water. It got darker and darker. Finally, after she nearly hit a rock because she didn't see it until the last minute, she decided she had no choice but to get out of the water. She pulled the canoe up on the shore. She found a flat spot, gathered together a bed of leaves, turned the canoe over on top of it, and crawled underneath. It was pitch dark now and getting cold. She gathered her legs up under herself in a fetal position and fell asleep.

It was still dark when something bumped the canoe. She woke with a start, but lay perfectly still. The bump came again, moving the canoe slightly. There was enough moonlight that she could see some of the forest floor under the edge. Then her fear went to sheer panic. About six inches from her nose she could see the hairy leg of a brown bear.

Chapter 48

Monday, August 8
North of Paint Lake, Manitoba

The black toenails of the bear were shining in the rays of moonlight that had made their way to the forest floor. Abby froze. And prayed. The bear bumped the canoe again. She could now see a black nose not 18 inches from her own. A large snort of hot air and steam came from the black nose. Then, convinced there was no easy food available, the bear began to walk away. It was nearly an hour before Abby moved anything. She was shivering from the cold night air and ached all over but she did not move, nor did she sleep. After an hour, she began to see slivers of light in the forest. The sun was coming up. It was time to get the canoe back on the water. She was shaking so bad she could hardly get her badly damaged vessel back on the river. But she had no time to think about it, because as soon as it hit the river the canoe began to move and she was engaged fulltime in using her pry-pole to avoid rocks and logs. After another hour, she was beginning to warm up again. She was working hard and the sun was warming her body enough to ward off the shivers. But no houses. No roads. No sign of human life. The good thing was she was now in a larger river and moving right along. There were less rocks and logs sticking up. So wherever she was going, she was getting there faster. The GPS in the plane had indicated that this river eventually emptied into Paint Lake, and once in the lake, there was a row of houses on the right side.

Abby lost track of the number of moose and deer she saw in or near the edge of the river. Two times she saw bears fishing on the river's edge. It would have been beautiful, if she had not been in a half-panic to find the lake—and the houses. She was not sure Johnnie would last another night in that cabin, or that she could endure another cold night under the canoe on the riverbank. What if this river only led to a secluded lake with no way out? Eventually, maybe even the next night, she would be nothing but wolf food. Every turn in the river revealed only more river. When she was about to panic, the river straightened out. Finally, she could see it ended in a large lake. She maneuvered her canoe to the right and poked and prodded her way down the shoreline. Then she saw it. She hoped it was not a mirage or a trick her mind was playing on her, but she saw what looked like a dock sticking out into the lake. Then she saw another, and another. Then she began to see the houses. She started to cry as she pushed her way to shore. When she was still in about 3 feet of water she jumped out of the canoe and ran toward the house in soaking wet tennis shoes. She wondered how she must look—a torn bloody dress, scratches everywhere, hair tangled and plastered to her face. But she ran to the first house and pounded on the door. A man in his late 60s came to the door.

"Oh, my goodness, dearie. What happened to you?"

"There has been a plane crash. I've been on the river two days. My boyfr.., um, fiancé is injured, bleeding badly in a cabin up the river. Do you have a phone I can use?"

"Yes, of course, come in. ALICE, COME DOWN HERE. Come in, come in, you need rest and some warm clothes and food and those scratches…"

"Thank you, but first I need a phone."

"Right there on the kitchen counter."

She punched in the number and waited. "Grandpa! I mean Mr. Fitzgerald, oh, thank God I got you… Yes, yes I'm fine, but Johnnie is hurt, oh grandpa, he got shot saving my life… I think so…. Yes, here's how to find him."

Chapter 49

Monday, August 8
Chicago and
North of Paint Lake, Manitoba

Three hours after the first call from Abby, Grandpa Fitzgerald's cell phone, which had been in almost constant use ever since, rang again.

"Hello…. ABBY, thank goodness you called back. You told us where Johnnie was but not where you were. My phone didn't record the number, it just said 'unknown' so I couldn't get back to you… Yes, he's going to be all right, the Canadian Red Cross picked him up 20 minutes ago. They said he'd lost a lot of blood and had a developing infection. They also said he probably wouldn't have lasted another day. But he's going to be fine. They airlifted him out with a helicopter, and they're taking him to a hospital in Winnipeg…. Yes, but Jack and Cassy are still on their honeymoon…. Well, my son called Jack yesterday. Last I heard they were coming here, but you should call Cassy and tell them Johnnie will be in Winnipeg. Actually, so will you… Well, because I have our jet helicopter heading your way. He has been in the air for about two hours. He will refuel, then pick you up, probably by this evening. Then he'll fly you over to join Johnnie in Winnipeg… Oh, you are welcome, dear, but you have to let me know exactly where you are, so I can pass it along to the pilot. What's the address there?…. Uh, huh… uh, huh… got it. The last house in the row, just before the river. I got it. By the way, we talked the police into releasing your purse and Johnnie's wallet. There is enough identification in there to get both of you through Canadian customs. We have also notified the officials about your kidnapping. They sounded cooperative. Anyway, I put the wallet and your purse in a carryon type bag. Then I got you a few changes of clothes. I had to guess about your size. I also put in a new iPhone for each of you, activated and ready to use. I threw in some cash because you may be there a few days or a week before Johnnie is released… Oh, you are very welcome … I don't know, dear. I couldn't possibly 'Guess what?' Tell me.... Engaged! That's fantastic! When did you have time to.... Really, just before you left? ... He did? With one of those fake rings? I'm sure he will replace that with a real one as soon as you get back to.... Oh.... Oh.... Oh...well, alrightiethen. If you really want... Yes, I see. You are one special girl, you know that? So how did you get out of there and to where you are now on Paint Lake?... A canoe?... A waterfalls... How high?... under the canoe?... Almost eaten by a bear!?!...

THE END OF PART II

Epilogue

It was the day before the wedding rehearsal, two days before Johnnie and Abby would be married in Grandma Edna's Baptist Church. Abby wanted them to get together before the formal festivities began. *Them* meant six of them—she and Johnnie, Jack and Cassy, Grandpa Fitzgerald, and Grandma Edna. They decided to go out for dinner, and Cassy said she knew the perfect restaurant. The conversation was fast flowing, sometimes serious, usually humorous, a bit informative, often silly. They joked about the past and discussed the future. They also ribbed Abby about her stories, especially about her adventure down the river—the waterfall was now 20 feet high and the bear was over 8 feet tall. After the main course, they ordered dessert and coffee. The conversation, as it so often does at meals, bounced easily from one topic to another.

"Mr. Fitzgerald, what's the deal with the thief that was informing as a mole in your company?" Cassy asked.

"We knew him as Bobby Andrews. His real name was Klaus Becker. He was the head of a very sophisticated operation. They had stolen some big time artifacts and gem stones all over the world. He was running this op from inside our building and scavenging information from Bernice's office. He probably went through her desk, her wastebasket, her cabinets, anything she didn't lock up. He most likely even accessed her computer when she stepped out for a break. Anyway, Interpol picked him up when he got off a plane in Berlin."

"Did the Arabs ever get their money back?"

"I doubt it. Last I heard, the EU had located the bank account and froze the assets."

"That brings up a question I had, Jack," Abby asked. "Did they ever catch the people behind that phony drug operation— where Cassy's dad and brother were kidnapped to get the formula right?"

"I'm afraid not. We got all those making the drugs, of course, but not those pulling the strings. We know Senator

Benedict is involved, because he took the wallet out of security."

"So why don't you tell the authorities?"

"Because we can't prove it. My friend at the FBI knows about it, and we are all keeping our eyes on him. But we have no proof he took it. There is also nothing to trace him to the guys making the drugs. There were phone calls made to a number traced to a cell phone registered to a guy who died last year. I'm sure it went to the Senator. He probably just pitched it in the river or something when we found the drug cave. But he doesn't know we're watching him, so we'll get him eventually."

Then Jack changed subjects, again. "So, Abby are you going to use your wedding to get even with us for the trick we played on you at ours?"

"Oh, no, that will come when you least expect it. Keep looking over your shoulder. Your day will come. You should be living in constant ongoing fear, anxiety, horror, things like that."

"Edna, what do you think about the fact that Johnnie and Abby will be living upstairs in your house?" Cassy asked.

"Great. They have practically rebuilt the place. They fixed the roof and the shingles, remodeled the whole upstairs and put in a toilet and kitchen up there. But I am hoping they will need more space in about 9 months." This was followed by some Ooos and Aaas and more laughter. Abby's face turned a bit red.

"So what do you think, Johnnie. Is Abby going to be able to handle your mother?" Jack asked his half-brother.

"Are you kidding?!? I saw her take on a German thief, a Muslim jihadist, and the Canadian wilderness. I can't wait to see her with those materialistic airheads in my mother's world."

"What do you think about your wedding plans?" Cassy asked Abby. "Has it come together the way you wanted?"

"It's fine, but I never realized marrying a Fitzgerald would be so complicated. You know how small Grandma Edna's church is. I have no idea how many people we offended by not inviting them because we couldn't get them in the church. And

308

we had to let at least two TV cameras in. Of course, the reception in the ballroom atop the Fitzgerald Building will hold a bunch more, but even there, we had to cut out tons of people Johnnie's mother thought should be there. I'm just glad all of you will be there. And grandpa, I am so thankful that you agreed to give me away."

"Can't think of anything I would rather do. It's the only item on my bucket list. Of course, I may be a little slow getting down the aisle, but we'll make it."

"It's just that I never had a father or a grandfather."

"Well, you do now."

"Oh, I just have to do this," Abby said with tears in her eyes. She got up from her place at the table and walked around to the opposite side where the senior Fitzgerald was sitting. She wrapped her arms tightly around his neck while standing behind him. Then she kissed him on the cheek.

As she was returning to her seat, Jack said, "You'd better be careful, this is a pretty fancy restaurant. They may have rules against public displays of affection."

"Well, they may just have to just get used to it," grandpa said. "I'm beginning to really like this place. This may become my new favorite restaurant. The food's great, the service is good, the atmosphere is superb. It even has an appropriate name." Grandpa held up a menu and pointed to the name on the front – *The Corner Grill.*

THE END